KAMIN-TOLAGH

a novel

Edwin Ahearn

Book V
Book VI

Kamin-Tolagh

The tug of history, often very ancient history, is felt throughout these works. A large amount of information about the past is disclosed in the narrative, but for the purposes of these extracts a reader needs to know that long before the land was Arbhal it was Owan, and the Owanil, a gifted, energetic, but often arrogant people conquered and then lost a vast empire on both sides of Arnan, the inland sea.

After some centuries of obscurity, during which their island-based priesthood, the Atarlum, was essential to the preservation of the Owani culture and language, the Owanil, through a series of opportune events, were able to regain control of their old realm, imposing themselves as an aristocracy on a numerically superior mixed population of Other Races (their own slighting term for all those without a pure Owani pedigree). Their old speech, however (the Owanilú), has become a scholar's language, surviving mainly for ceremonial and religious purposes, and in titles and proper names. Kargul has been the strongest ally for the Atarlum, Preference, and the restoration of exclusive Owani privilege and power. Kamin Tolagh is the heir of one of the oldest and most powerful of all the Great Families.

Books I and II begin shortly after the end of the Jinzal War and the investiture of the Rodlakh as Rabsahi. Kamin-Tolagh has won honor and recognition. He is now the trusted Captain of the Household. Yet, there are important confidences that are kept from him. He grows restless and yearns for adventure. The military expedition headed by Shumat, Captain of the Armies, and Kamin Tolagh set out to the Farther West on a mission to destroy the last of the jinzal. What he discovers changes the course of history.

Book III and VI resume the tale when roughly three years have passed. Kamin-Tolagh has founded an empire amid the wild tribal lands of the Farther West. His rule restores the old ways of Preference. Though he is condemned as an outlaw, many families leave the Heartland to join with him and take up new estates. The old legends and tales of riches spur Kamin-Tolagh to explore and conquer unknown lands.

Book V and VI show the gradual changes taking place now that the empire of Kargusai is seven years old. In search of conquest, Kamin-Tolagh acquires rich lands of the Hrin. Here he learns the source of their gold. A campaign immediately follows which has unexpected consequences and will almost certainly lead to war with Arbhal.

Kamin-Tolagh

V.

32.

Banakit was heart of the Colony and its granary; its green vale produced two-thirds of the food grown, while the town itself, beside the Navu, was near enough halfway between Kamsilat and the frontier fortress of Drin Navuna.

Upon first arriving in the Colony, Dolvid had found that a new magistrate at Banakit had been among many appointments neglected by Saidhan in his final, failing year. The functionary, normally from the Army of the West, was traditionally also military commander for the region, and enjoyed a pleasant official residence, standing on a fir-clad hillock in the midst of town. When Aëlu made clear active administration of the Colony was entirely in his hands, one of his earliest decisions was to abolish the post at Banakit, or rather to absorb it into functions of the *Nim'* — in this instance, acting *Nim'*. His point had been, seat of the Colony's government should be there, rather than Kamsilat, which was too distant from the Frontier. Later someone recalled Saidhan himself had long ago advocated the same move, and might have implemented it, but for the opposition of Doleni, who resisted being a fingerspan farther from Arnan, from the Mainland she never stopped longing for.

Like Âna, Rodlakh had admitted the obvious advantages of Banakit for serving the Colony, but neither had been pleased with the idea of Dolvid removing himself a very full dayride more distant from Kadon Dinul. That day, however, was won back when the Patriarch, with surprisingly brief negotiation, agreed to reopening of the so-called Forbidden Road, direct route across the Island from east to west, with its well-equipped ports on each coast, formerly, and now again, a normal part of the straightest route between Colony and capital.

Official residence and home for Dolvid and his family remained the Great House at Kamsilat, but it was at Banakit he had sat and was still sitting as magistrate in large numbers of legal cases left over from Saidhan's tenure, and there, in conference with officers from the Army of the West, he worried over the Colony's defenses. From fir-clad eminence he could look southward across the Navu, up to high, domed hills, threaded by passes called collectively the Lunu Tezh' Gate. Across those hills, six years ago, *jinzal* armies had poured down into the vale, nearly trapping the Army of the West in its retreat from the Frontier. Elsewhere, the Navu was a greater torrent, roaring in rocky gorges, but here, nearer source than outlet, quiet and unruffled between level banks, no impassable barrier, and there was no reason why other enemies could not use the same way; Kamin-Tolagh, if he came, was intelligent enough and daring enough to choose the trackless wild of the undefended Lunu Tezh', rather than battering against the hard strength of Drin Navuna; as the Mainland realm was open in the south to seaborne invasion, it was vulnerable here by land.

Dolvid began by ordering restoration and garrisoning of the ancient watchtowers up in the Gate. The Protectorate beyond had been made less mysterious by events of the Jinzai War, but defense of its long, ill-defined border and scattered population became no more practicable; regular long-range patrols were most that could be managed.

If he had wanted to man those borders, he could not have found the troops. The cavalry of the West was reaching its lowest ebb, short, above all, of experienced officers at squadron and half-squadron level.

Partly for that reason, partly from a conviction as to their effectiveness, he raised and saw to training of infantry companies, armed principally with pikes. Century after century, with a sort of hereditary disbelief, cavalry commanders commenting on tactics had written that even in the open, level field, foot that stood together could withstand the most determined charge by heavy cavalry; only after their ranks broke did they become easy game for horsemen. Nearly five hundred years ago, the brilliant Pir Kallikuk had speculated thoroughly trained foot, well-armed with long weapons, could always defeat equal numbers of first-class cavalry simply by standing still, but while isolated episodes in battle had tended to confirm that supposition, the traditional view of infantry as ill-equipped and shuffling rabble, too poor to afford mounts, had continued to prevail.

Dolvid's companies, equipped and paid for out of his own pocket, would be mounted infantry — riding to battle, that was, on horses unsuitable for cavalry, of which there was always an ample supply. Their fighting would be on foot, in tightly ordered formations, with heavy pikes as their main weapon. Soon, pikes of three different lengths evolved, shortest still longer than a man's height; in receiving a cavalry charge the front rank, with these pikes, would drop to one knee, bracing their weapons against the ground, and resting on their shoulders the longer pikes of the second rank, who in turn helped support the longest in the third rank, forming a dense hedge of heavy points. The men, mainly part-time soldiers who rode in from farms all over the Vale of Banakit, underwent endless drilling to adopt this basic formation swiftly, and maintain it in changing circumstances, and fresh tactics were developed as their skills increased; they learned to advance or retire steadily, maintaining an unbroken front of menacing points, and to form a tight, bristling square, soon named *the hedgehog*. The effect of a single, huge, many-legged beast was added to by adoption of a curved oblong board shield of beech-wood, shoulder-high when grounded, much reducing the dense-packed formation's obvious vulnerability to bows; strapped securely to left forearm but also with a handle to grip, it was provided with a rounded cutout for pike high on the right side, and the men drilled in using their shields either as an additional barrier against charging cavalry, or as a practically continuous roof to protect against missiles.

For officers, he had gone to the Army of the West, somewhat shyly asking that thoroughgoing cavalryman, Bradhinal of Ân, to find him volunteers. He was astonished but not displeased when Shudarr, son of Shumat, expressed a keen interest; his father, after all, was not without a reputation as a leader of horse, but perhaps despair at matching Shumat's eminence in that branch was what induced the son to try something different, or else he was just tired of hearing about cavalry tactics; whatever his motives, the young man became a leading advocate and valued officer of the new infantry, and could often be found in off-duty hours making complicated diagrams of ingenious formation-movements. At his urgent plea, these new duties were concealed from his father, and Shudarr was officially a member of Dolvid's personal staff.

A hardworking, not unhappy first year; he had been back to Kadon Dinul four times, not pleased by Elamirr's reborn ascendancy, but finding the realm could endure without his own daily attendance on the *rabhsai*. Now, as the early Colony summer was beginning, he rode down from Banakit to Kamsilat, where, for the first time since Banak's reign, the Pledging would be held this year. Before that midsummer observance, Dolvid was looking forward to time with his children, and to prying open, at last, the packing cases that held the intimate documents bequeathed to him by Laluvoi, Rodlakh's almost-legendary grandmother, an historical treasure he had not dared as much as glance at while there was such a backlog of Colony business. At this distance from Kadon Dinul, where the daily crisis, a thunderclap at the New Residence, diminished to a faint rumble, he had hopes of regaining the balance needed for the writing of history.

After reunion with Aëlu, dependably tender, he was informed a parcel of books had arrived. Most were copies he had requested, but among them was the expected stranger, and without a glance at the text Dolvid went to the back cover, and found Âna's letter.

It warned him to expect an official dispatch from Rodlakh, informing him of the arrival, by way of Hrin trading vessels, of a communication from Kamin-Tolagh, described by Âna as `extremely conciliatory' in tone; evidently his conquest of part of the Hrinani (word of which had trickled back to the realm some weeks ago) had made him confident he must now be accepted by the *rabhsai* as a fellow-ruler of consequence. His letter, a copy of which Dolvid would see, proposed `talks aimed at furthering of commerce based on restoration of friendly relations between our domains.'

As you have warned, Âna wrote, *Kamin-Tolagh's access to ships and apparent control of fine navigators makes it more dangerous than ever to pretend he does not exist. My fear is Rodlakh's response, without consulting you, will be unyielding; I have already seen the draft of a harsh reply prepared by E., whose opinions you are aware of.* Rodlakh, it seemed, meant to bring Dolvid up to date only when he came to Kamsilat for the Pledging.

Concerning Elamirr, there were two other major points, both extremely sensitive, which she hoped she could discuss with him in the near future.

As a distress signal, it could hardly be plainer. Next day, after the regular weekly official package arrived from Kadon Dinul, with the promised copy of Kamin-Tolagh's friendly but autocratic letter, Dolvid told Aëlu he must, after all, go to the Mainland.

Choosing fabrics for refurnishing in preparation for their invasion by titled midsummer guests, for once she let disappointment show: "This is not fair. You have given the realm its share of you, and it's taking mine as well."

"You must cure the habit," ruefully, "of marrying men of whom that can be said. It is Kamin-Tolagh."

"War?"

"No, peace." He gave substance of the letter the *rabhsai* had received.

"And you believe, have reason to believe, Rodlakh is going to stand firm." She shook her head with her wry smile. "No one is going to call our *rabhsai* devious, whatever else they say of him. A craftier statesman would offer unacceptable terms, all the while parading his deep desire for peace. Then, if war came, Kamin-Tolagh could not tell the world how every attempt at friendship had been rebuffed."

Arvat came in while Dolvid was assembling documents to take with him. "Master, they say you are going to the Mainland." The man's self-importance had inflated when asked to return here, a request made with gritted teeth, and only because his years of service as Saidhan's recorder might make Arvat useful in untangling carelessly-kept accounts at the Great House.

"You may have to find a bed with friends, or at a hostelry," cheerfully. "They say half the New Residence is closed, except to cats; they have had a plague of mice."

"So I have heard." Âna had noted it in passing in her letter, but Dolvid wondered how Arvat got his news — and then guessed he must have heard from Tellis, his sister, whose husband Rhunilat would be, as it were, captaining the cats. Having to use such unbiddable servants would offend his strong sense of order and propriety.

Arvat, by the work-table, had picked up the volume that had concealed Âna's letter. "I see you have my sister's amusement."

It was indeed the book written by Tellis, the not-exactly-a-romance Rhunilat had mentioncd. Taking it from Arvat, Dolvid stuffed it in with his documents; he would glance at it on the journey.

Still it was very strange to be welcomed ashore at the once-hostile Island port of Doniftu, stranger to have his small escort reinforced by a friendly detachment of *Adanum Plakh'*, and to set out in such company on what had been the Forbidden Road. At Pavani, on the eastward shore, he was permitted to make use of the hostelry long available only to those making or returning from their pilgrimage to Lunu Midhi; arriving there well after dark, he decided a few hours of rest might serve his mission better than haste, but was robbed of sleep by Tellis. Having begun her book on the crossing from Kamsilat to Doniftu, he now resumed it, and at dawn, time to embark for Owan Sai, reached the end.

As the author's husband had bewilderedly said, it was like, and then again, not like, a romance. Tellis had made a new thing.

With most romances, it had a basis in history, its times in fact derived from Dolvid's celebrated reconstruction of the *Song of Tales*. The period was that chaotic time shortly before the Return, late in the Wars of Cleansing, when Owani and Gabhani, allies against the common enemies, warlords and lawless scavenger-bands, were rivals for leadership in the new realm that was to emerge. Glorious, bloody, bitter, noble and treacherous years, but Tellis, while her clear sympathies, like Dolvid's, were with the cheated Gabhanil, kept her cool gaze on people rather than great events. The romances, without exception, let stylized attitudes stand for men and women; heroes were invariably brave, heroines completely virtuous, villains monstrously evil, the common folk vulgar and the grand, grand; all made stilted gestures in a language predictable as a proverb.

Tellis did otherwise; no one in her book was entirely bad or indisputably good, and incident, of which there was no shortage, served to make her characters more, not less, individual; conversation, quarrel, courtship were important as deeds of battle, and much more entertaining. Though dressed in the clothes, armed with the weapons and caught up in the conflicts of five centuries in the past, these, drawn from her own observation, spoke and felt like living men and women. At times she dared to guess at their private thoughts.

Dared was the operative word: Tellis had made astute alterations, but for a knowing eye had failed, half intentionally, to disguise her actors beyond all recognition. Dolvid took special interest in a learned, well-meaning but disastrously indecisive Owani leader, who stupidly missed his chance to wed with the tale's most winning woman (just as he had once, twice missed his chance with Tellis), joining instead with the ruthlessly selfish daughter of an Island noble, a calculating beauty whose ambitions were to bring about his death.

Most readers, including Rhunilat, would lack knowledge to make that identification, and other portraits were shrewdly camouflaged — Rodlakh's father, Lambarr, for example, only barely detectable in the affable, inept sea-captain, blithely garrulous as his vessel drifted aground on a mudbank, and some of Laluvoi's mannerisms almost parodied in an old farm-woman treated by many as a seer, though she herself, while pleased with her little empire of abject followers, made no such claim. What was certain was this book, *Tales of Harbor Gate*, would be widely read. And extensively imitated, by anyone who could hold a pen; the easy, natural style would delude many writing such a tale was as simple as yarning with friends.

He arrived red-eyed at Owan Sai in the middle of a dull day, and rode numbly up Harbor Way, thinking he could steal a nap at his house before going to the New Residence. But word of his arrival preceded him, and his escort was met and replaced at Harbor Gate by glittering Household men commanded by Rodlakh's brother. Orbanak, after a warm greeting, assured Dolvid the mouse incursion had been greatly over-reported; cats had the upper paw, and a scuttle-free suite was available at the

Residence. The *rabhsai* was hearing a hard case at law, and would see him in the hour before dinner, unless there was business that could not wait.

Official duties discharged, Orbanak asked after his friend Shudarr, and the attractive smile dawned: "Is it true he is mudding about with companies of foot?"

"*Asai*, he is on special duty with my staff at Banakit."

Grin broadened. "Captain Shumat won't hear otherwise from me."

Renewed hopes of brief rest were again ill-founded; he had scarcely washed himself free of salt and grime when one of the discreet Residence servants arrived, bringing cool *raminat* and light food, closely followed by Âna in a blue day-gown. Dolvid took and kissed her proffered hands.

"I thank you," she said, then explained, "for coming." She glanced over her shoulder to be sure the servant had gone; oddly, his status as a visitor made his being alone with the *rabhsayu* less open to comment.

"Rodlakh is being magistrate."

"Orbanak told me."

"Orbanak." She made a peevish face. "He is in love."

"He is eighteen. He should be." Deprived of his lofty rank, Orbanak would still be sought-after as a handsome young Household officer.

"He should not," dogmatically. "Not with Morulis."

"In earnest? Or just as everyone else is?" Sighing after the desirable wife of Elamirr with a kind of agreeable hopelessness was a popular Residence Quarter game.

"In mortal earnest; not all his doing; at his birthday feast last year Morulis was speaking to him with her eyes; our soldier-prince has enough admirers to understand that language. Poor Morulis! A message from the *Mankh'* has more fun than Elamirr can manage; she is a stopped-up spring. Orbanak must make her feel reborn."

"Are they bedding together?" Dolvid knew she had not developed a sudden taste for gossip; this must be one of her two sensitive points concerning Elamirr. If Morulis's husband were an Owani, he would be at worst mildly irked, or, considering Orbanak's nearness to *rabhsayum*, obscurely flattered. But as a married man he kept the outlook of Burantal, and his smouldering vigilance over Morulis, quaint by Heartland standards, could also become dangerous.

"If not, they are wasting a lot of effort to make it seem so. By this time, exactly two men in all Kadon Dinul have not noticed, and one of them, happily, is Elamirr."

The other, then, must be Rodlakh, who would be affronted if he knew, and annoyed with his brother. Elamirr, on the other hand, would be murderous. "Nothing good can come from this. Something will have to be done."

"Can you?"

"I think so. What else about Elamirr? You said two things."

"His influence is growing again. Is he honest?"

"So far as I can tell. Why?"

With a deep breath, Âna recounted a recent case, in which a Heartland cattle-breeder had been accused of bribing a tax-assessor, since deceased. Elamirr, contrary to his normal attitude towards the Families, had urged that beyond a reassessment of the taxes in question, no action should be taken against the man. Bribery had not been proven, and a prosecution, Elamirr argued, would be seen as revenge on the man, who had been outspoken in opposition to many of Rodlakh's reforms.

"Not characteristic Elamirr, on past performance. Perhaps he is starting to learn moderation, or would want that to be seen."

"Or can be bought," briskly. "I do not see much moderation in his draft for a reply to Kamin-Tolagh. Oh, how could anyone think we can say to a man who, after success in a war, is talking peace, we do not want his friendship, but would accept his surrender?"

"Is that our message?"

"In effect, unless we can get it modified."

Annoyance that had been swelling inside throughout the journey sprang suddenly into leaf and blossom. "I can't understand the *rabhsai*, that he can so much as contemplate dispatching the most important message of his reign, without consulting his *Bôdhrai*. What do I hold the appointment for?"

"He hates quarrels." simply. Tellis's book having put it in his head, Dolvid was bleakly reminded of Rodlakh's father, who would do anything to avoid controversy.

Later, Âna reluctantly gone, Rhunilat, who came to say the *rabhsai* was free to see him, beamed with the pride of a new father when Dolvid gave him a note for his wife. He would no doubt see her, but wanted to lose no time conveying his admiration for her book.

"You thought it, um, well-written, *Bôdhrai*?" — obviously still baffled as to what the book was.

"Better than well — I would give all my histories to have written it."

Rhunilat emitted a stopped sound, the fragment of a tentative chuckle. He was right, Dolvid was exaggerating, but not by much; he had always admired Tellis, but foresaw when he next met her he would be suddenly shy, as in the presence of genuine talent.

As they came to the steps up to the Personal Suite, Rhunilat remarked the book had been very well-received by the Families, and passing hand-to-hand around the Residence Quarter copies were becoming shabby.

Ten, he answered, when asked how many had been made. "With the author's consent," on impulse, "I shall set the five best scribes at the Bronze Residence to producing a new edition of twenty-five. Tellis deserves more readers." Quite soon, with a book so popular, home-made copies would begin to appear, not only with the inevitable errors and inadvertent omissions, but with additions and alterations according to the taste or whim of the amateur copyist; a large authentic edition would help ensure survival of the author's own text.

Rhunilat, not celebrated for his munificence, started to mumble about the cost, but brightened when Dolvid said it would be his gift, including supplying of materials. "For me, it is an opportunity to make the excellence of our new Colony paper better-known." As acting *Nim'*, he had been able to command what, four years ago, he could only recommend; the Colony now imported flax and waste linen for its papermaking. Over its own grumbling resistance the paper industry had revived, and even collectors of wood were better off; the scrap they gleaned was bundled, and sold to the Mainland for fuel and kindling.

"Arvat, I should tell you," cutting off thanks. "Is well, and we keep him busy."

"Tellis will be glad to hear it — " Rhunilat could not keep distaste for his brother-in-law out of his face.

Rodlakh was more cheerful than Dolvid could remember him since the day of his investing and marriage. "I can guess why you have come," warmly grasping his hand. "You might have saved the journey, though I am always glad to see you. Was your crossing calm? Aëlu is not with you? She is well, though? Your children? Lambakh is beyond belief; I swear he has grown a span since Halving-Day. Have we fed you? Are you hungry?"

The cold shadow came again, Lambarr to the life — though Lambarr had never deliberately used his cordial manner to fend off unwanted debate, as his son was doing. The father would have permitted discussion, and let Laluvoi do the listening.

Âna came in quietly while Dolvid was still trying to get through the spate of lightweight questions with the irreducible minimum of delay mandated by courtesy. She had changed to a formal gown of deep red, and was arrestingly lovely, her dark hair simply brushed out. Gravely, they met again.

"At risk of your displeasure, *Rabhsai*," Dolvid began, when they were seated. "Kamin-Tolagh's letter has to be discussed."

The smile did not waver. "My displeasure does not come into it, but there is nothing to discuss. Does Shumat know you're over? He has been wanting to talk to you about recruitment in the West."

"I have not been in touch with anyone," near rudeness. "This latest overture cannot simply be — "

"A nothing," with a gesture of airy dismissal. "An outlaw has no voice."

"Twenty years ago, the military commander at Yuvakh Din said exactly the same. Narn, the entire farther Northeast, are part of your realm, *Rabhsai*, because Shumat had other ideas. That outlaw became a loyal subject — and grandfather to Shumat's children."

"Ott, you mean?" Rodlakh remained good-tempered. "But I do not think he had held and betrayed high positions of trust, before becoming an outlaw. We really have nothing to discuss."

Âna leaned forward, wrists on knees. "Dolvid has come from Kamsilat," she protested.

"Well, and we are glad to see him." Another careless wave. "I have made my decision."

With some sleep, Dolvid's temper might have worn longer. He got to his feet. "If that is so, *Deghi*, I must request leave to resign all titles and posts I hold in your *rabhsayum*, effective at once."

Today, Rodlakh was unshakable. After showing mild astonishment, he made a comical face, as if at a joke between friends. "I do not give my leave. Come, be reasonable."

"Without leave, then, I have to quit my duties." At a glance, Dolvid could not tell whether shock or approval predominated in Âna's tense face. He was trembling, but not dismayed to discover he really meant it. Rodlakh's former anger on this point made it conceivable his official service was actually over, but that would have its consolations; in consideration of their past friendship, surely, Rodlakh would let him return to making histories: his admiration of Tellis's extraordinary book had been shot through with envy of the time she had to write it.

At last, Rodlakh's expression changed. "You would? You would leave us, abandon all your rank and accomplishments, just because you cannot have your way?"

"My way, *Deghi* — " becoming angrier, "is not the question. I am supposed to be *Bôdhrai* to the realm, but I am no use to anyone if I am forbidden to bring up matters of the gravest importance, if I am to hear about decisions affecting fundamental policy only when they are already settled."

"But you are not actually resigning, here and now."

"Dolvid is known as a man of his word." Âna's voice was quietly factual, but in her eyes anxiety showed.

Rodlakh stood. "Well," soothingly. "Let us not come to irrevocable decisions so early in your visit." He disliked being hemmed in, and was close to being flustered, hands clenching and unclenching at his sides; failure of his attempt to ward off this clash with inconsequential geniality had left him with no plan in reserve. "How long," he asked, "will you be at Kadon Dinul?"

"If I am still your *Bôdhrai*, at your pleasure, *Deghi*. If not, there is no reason for me to be here a day."

After silence: "You will have dinner with us, at least. That I insist on." He gave his father's uncertain nod, and, astonishingly, abruptly, left.

"You have won," Âna murmured.

"Not yet; tactics are only the beginning of battle." Also, if he had gained a point, at what cost? Rodlakh would not forget being forced to retreat for lack of reinforcements.

"I meant, he will discuss Kamin-Tolagh with you. Let him be next to bring it up."

"Good."

Âna was in two minds whether to go or stay; her body was half-turned as, like an afterthought, she asked, "Is he sincere in his desire for friendship? Kamin-Tolagh."

"Great Hrafi, what harm can it do us to act as if we believed so? One way or another, I am certain we are not done with Kamin-Tolagh, nor Kamin-Tolagh with the realm."

Shumat's views were remarkably similar. He sought Dolvid out very early next morning, in preparation for a meeting Rodlakh had decided on, true to Âna's forecast, at the end of a very long dinner where talk of everything else in the realm had included not a mention of Kamin-Tolagh.

"What can he do to us? Send raiders dressed as traders to hamstring our *pefral*? Sell us poisoned fruit? Not that we won't keep a watchful eye on his ragtag regiments, but I would rather be trading with him than beggaring the realm to raise armies against him, and the provincial lords will agree, those who have things to sell."

This was half a joke, but had a grim sound. Seeing his perplexity, Shumat turned the talk to defense; natural for him, when it came to the West, to ask about his son. "I hear he's left the Frontier, and is with you at Banakit?"

"Special duty. He is a good officer."

"He will be, when he discovers he doesn't know it all, and learns to listen. You should not coddle the boy — I was hoping he'd see kiln-bread service out there; long days, short nights on hard beds, are what he needs. Send him back to the Frontier."

"He is too valuable where he is. He has plenty of hard work, don't worry. I know a friend of his in the Household, though, who needs to spend less time in a soft bed."

Shumat grunted and grimaced together. "Real cavalry service for that one would lance a boil we have all been watching swell."

"Bradhinal, as you have heard, is desperately short of squadron-officers."

The grin prevailed. "Lovely. Dorrmas will let him go, if I speak to him. But will the *rabhsai* agree to it?"

"If the suggestion comes from the right quarter. The *rabhsayu* has been especially concerned; Morulis when she came here was under her personal protection."

"Then how in Zhôl's name — " Shumat bit off the unfinished thought, but plainly it was not only Owanil of the Residence Quarter who deplored Morulis's taste in husbands.

That husband, with his always slightly overwrought expression, was already waiting outside the Private Audience Chamber. After greetings, Dolvid, to forestall the looming subject of Morulis, told Elamirr, "Your Burantal uncles have been with us in the Colony." The Marionette Guild had arrived early for the Pledging, and were taking a reduced version of their show all the way to the Frontier.

"Yes, I have heard, Master," Elamirr said, and explained, "Arvat keeps me informed about happenings at Kamsilat."

And Elamirr Arvat, about Kadon Dinul, Dolvid deduced, no longer wondering how Arvat had heard about the mice.

As if part of his thoughts, a large-framed but wraith-slender cat went across the width of the Oak-Wall Chamber, with a steady, purposeful step.

"Look at this, Master, is this a royal residence? And we have strict orders from Rhunilat, be good to puss, she is our friend. There must be a dozen of them — I would rather have the mice running around."

Yes, of course, even beyond Rhunilat's passion for things in their proper place, Elamirr would dislike a creature beloved for its beauty, impossible ever to master, or completely own.

Aside from long friendship, Shumat was good to have at this meeting for faintly shabby racial reasons; his general agreement with Dolvid's opinion about Kamin-Tolagh would make it difficult to characterize as Owani softness towards one of his own — although Âna, too, with her comment on Dolvid's threat to resign, had left small doubt she too was of his opinion. And there was perhaps no need to play those tiles, with Elamirr eager to display his new moderation. After informing the *rabhsai* news of Kamin-Tolagh's latest success had caused a fresh handful of Heartlanders to set out to join him, Elamirr, instead of reviling them, shrugged. "The realm has not much use for loyalty so easily seduced."

Âna said, "This communication of Kamin-Tolagh's — "

"A trick, *Asayu*," Elamirr was swift to assert. "As I have held from the first."

"Perhaps not," Shumat said.

"Oh, but it is, of course it is," Dolvid unexpectedly conceded, not willing to follow this debate through back-alleys where *sincerity* and *true intentions* could be wrangled over for endless unprofitable hours. "In large part, such an overture must be a trick to gain the advantage, just as a friendly response would be a trick for the same purpose. Powers are on good terms with one another because each perceives a benefit; they are not sentimental bed-friends, each needing reassurance the other's love is real. Let us put aside any judgment except what is best for the realm; a ruler — " this full in the face of the silent Rodlakh — "acts for the general good, not out of his personal feelings."

"True," Rodlakh said. "But personal knowledge can shed light on general good — if considering a treaty, he needs to ask, is it likely to be kept? And when the other party is a known oathbreaker — "

"Nor is it to the general good, *Deghi*," Elamirr interjected. "If it is seen oathbreaking and betrayal of trust are rewarded rather than punished. Beyond the right, the *rabhsai* has has a duty to punish unfaith."

Dolvid, having waited in vain for the *rabhsai*'s objection to being instructed in his duty by a junior advisor, said, "In the real world, this particular guilt could not be punished without slaughtering the innocent. Clearly, Kamin-Tolagh's men are not going to surrender him to the *rabhsai*'s justice; to carry out this duty we would have to fight a war where thousands would be killed and maimed, ours as well as his."

"No one, *Bôdhrai*, is advocating war," Elamirr said.

"That is so," Âna, tartly. "It is no great secret we lack any plan to reach out and show Kamin-Tolagh our wrath." The irony did not please Rodlakh, but she was not daunted. "If we do not mean to make war, why not make peace with him?"

Unanimity among his three most trusted intimates was starting to have an effect on Rodlakh, whose face was thoughtful. Then Elamirr, as if modestly seeking information, asked, "To make friends with Kamin-Tolagh, wouldn't we have to rescind his outlawry?"

"Almost by definition," Dolvid said. "I do not see how the acknowledged ruler of another realm could be an outlaw in this."

"Then is it not probable some of the *rabhsai*'s subjects who would hesitate to approve of a declared outlaw would feel free to admire a friendly neighbor?"

"Who cares what young fools admire?" Shumat demanded.

"Exactly," Dolvid relieved him by saying. "The *rabhsayum* of Rodlakh is just, prosperous and holds high hopes for the future: we cannot refuse to do what is right and sensible because of a few idiots who parade their disaffection as a distinction."

"Among the Families, is it only a few?" Elamirr, with his obsession.

Dolvid was sole unmixed Owani present. "If we doubt the loyalty of the great majority of one of our several peoples, we do an injustice, not only to that people, but to the moderation and skill with which Rodlakh *Rabhsai* has governed. Some of our wealthy will resent becoming a little less so, so no one has to starve, but the large part of any race is fairminded and recognizes fairness." He hoped Rodlakh knew he had not abruptly become a flatterer. "I do not believe Kamin-Tolagh can outbid that."

Âna was approving, but Elamirr's face was that of a *zhabhu* player who had drawn a good tile; he had taken out and was holding a folded page. "Nevertheless, Master, while Kamin-Tolagh asks openly for our friendship, his man is secretly telling our Heartlanders what that means." He handed Dolvid the page, a letter, much like those of Lavsila's intercepted in the past, like them written in a cultured hand with neither address nor signature, apparently intended for some landowner. Neither Rodlakh nor Kamin-Tolagh was named in a message mainly hints and allusions, but *their lord* and *the exile* were easily identifiable in context.

"Apparently," informing the others as he scanned it. "A letter written to reassure one of Kamin-Tolagh's Heartland admirers about the very overtures we have been discussing; he is not to suppose talk of a reconciliation indicates a change of heart; on the contrary *the exile* will be in a better position to aid and inspire the *rightful aspirations of our race*. Stuff about *other powers to champion us*, which I take as a reference to the reactionary party at the *Mankh'* — where does this come from?" he asked, as he passed the page over to Rodlakh.

"It fell into my hands," complacently.

"I see that. From where? From the sky?" The letter could hardly have provided Elamirr with a more timely or telling argument if he had manufactured it himself.

"Surely," Rodlakh chided, making a face over the letter, and passing it on to Âna. "The point is not where it comes from, but what it is."

"But one may bear on the other," maintaining his quiet composure, though absolutely convinced the letter was a forgery; in his ear its tone clanged like a cracked bell. He hoped fervently it had duped Elamirr; the alternative was unthinkable. "I know it was not written by Lavsila."

"How can you *know*?" Rodlakh demanded.

"Style," simply.

"*Style*?" Elamirr echoed dubiously.

"How do you recognize a man's face?" — continuing to address the *rabhsai*. "You do not say, yes, that is his nose, his mouth, the width between his eyes — you *know* it. I have spent my life with the written word, and this was not penned by Lavsila, or any Owani of his class." There were none of Lavsila's irritating but elegant sarcasms, and the allusions to race — `*half-ape advisors to a mongrel lord*,' and `*the untainted purity of our ancient blood*' — were too heavyhanded: Owani disdain was difficult to mimic without exaggeration.

Yet the tide, which had been running in direction of the moderate view, had turned. Elamirr explained he had bought the letter at Market Gate hostelry, from a man of the Arbhu Hills, who half-admitted he had filched it from a minor landowner, understanding it to be the copy of an original in the possession of Ghuradh Khelaghati. In other circumstances, Rodlakh might have been first to challenge such a rickety provenance, but his assent to this debate had been grudging at best, and he seized on the Market Gate Letter (as the document came to be called) as the excuse he wanted for closing down discussion. He added the affair of the letter must be gone into `from all sides,' meaning, presumably, there must be an investigation both of its origin and of the disaffection it appeared to exploit; the vagueness of this instruction had Dolvid wondering for a vertiginous half-minute whether Elamirr had cooked up the document at Rodlakh's behest, to produce its chilling effect on this gathering.

No, not possible; trapped in his implacable attitude, Rodlakh was Rodlakh, without the guile needed to tease a puppy. Elamirr was another question, but whatever truth might be, conciliation was at present a dead issue; the most combined influence of Âna, Shumat and Dolvid could achieve was to persuade the *rabhsai* not to go any farther with the draft reply submitted by Elamirr, for the moment changing unfriendly response to no response at all. Dolvid sailed for Kamsilat next morning, not before another private meeting with Âna, who was angrily promising to ferret out the truth about the Market Gate Letter.

33.

Fretasi, enthralled by columns of figures, reached for a piece of ripe, golden fruit, glanced at it, and returned it to the dish, wiping her fingers absently on the breast of her dressing-gown. "*Asai*," she began heavily. "Your pardon, Lord, I mean to say — "

"It doesn't matter."

"Expenditures, Lord, have climbed terribly. The war, and after — "

"Much of that is finished now." Largest additional cost had been the hiring of ships to transport troops and mounts.

"But outlay here at Hyolenstr — " despondently. To modify and reorder largest of the houses a regiment of workmen had been employed, many still on the strength. For emblematic reasons, Kambanal was installed in Iolfrant's vast residence, and Kamin-Tolagh's occupation of what had been Huolafidn's house had meant a double retinue of guards, of servants and of Hrin cooks, excellent, but making hiring of tasters also advisable; with Kamin-Tarú joining him here for the summer there were dressmakers and hairdressers, a large number of musicians and dancers, all sorts of hirelings for his and his sister's pleasure and comfort. Additionally, with the end of fighting, there had been a distribution of gold to the troops, while wholesale promotions in rank had been conferred. All this, according to the principle put forward long ago by Iruvakh, by spreading wealth to many hands, contributed to general prosperity, and signs of that could be seen at Hyolenstr, where trade was flourishing, but Fretasi's cheerless job was to warn that the imperial treasury could not beggar itself to create affluence.

"We have money coming in, now."

She did not brighten. "Revenues, Lord, everywhere, are well below our anticipation. From most of the Heartlanders, we have not much above a token payment with a signed promise."

"Harvest will be in soon," and before she could sigh again, he swiftly added, "As Iruvakh says, it takes more than a season or two to make idle lands productive. Next year will be better."

A shuffling of pages. "Most disappointing are receipts from Zelu Bablakhi. More gold was coming to us when you had only a half-share. Are your men there skilled enough for trading with those naked ones?"

"That is not the question," impatiently.

It connected, so he believed, with the ending to the war, flat and unsatisfying as stale beer. The siege of Guodvestr reached a standstill, stones hurled by newly-constructed *zhin'pefral* seldom worse than a nuisance to defenders, who did little but watch and wait. Reluctantly, he had conceded he would have to storm the bridges over the moat, and accept the losses that entailed. Casualties would all be men of the tribes, endlessly replaceable, but he begrudged waste of the investment in time for their teaching and drilling; in the north there were barely enough trained men left for minimal security, far fewer than were needed for peace of mind.

Several of the strong, straight *buoth* trees, good-sized but well short of full growth, were cut down and trimmed, each fitted with short cross-beams and a solid bronze beak, massive rams for two dozen men to handle. But before this work was completed, course of the war was determined by a month-old event, countless sea-miles away, in Rodlakh's realm.

On quayside at Thenimala, as was later told, mariners from the followings of Iolfrant and Nestos began abusing each other's *hrithust*, as forger and traitor, respectively, and in the resultant brawl, two of Nestos's men were killed.

Though Kamin-Tolagh was not informed, this incident brought Nestos, with his coalition of fellow-*hrithuod*, actively into the war; a dull winter morning came when the besiegers found the port hemmed in by sea as well as land, a dense fleet of vessels, bristling with bowmen, in the broad mouth of the estuary.

Gratifying as assistance was, Kamin-Tolagh could not confer with a completely elusive Nestos, and decided to proceed with his own plan. But on the eve of the assault, his presumed allies, against irresolute opposition, landed over a thousand men on Stink Spit, bows, pikes and a small number of horse. From this position, they negotiated, still without any consultation, *negotiated* the surrender of Guodvestr, the city opening its gates to Kamin-Tolagh's entry only after a committee of leading *hrithuod* had decided their rival and colleague, Iolfrant, together with what remained of his chief supporters, should be allowed to sail away unmolested in the two dozen or so largest of their ships. There was not so much as a search to see what treasure or treasures they took with them.

They had sailed, according to much-delayed report, to a cluster of islands well south and west from the tip of the Froghushei, where Iolfrant had traded for years. There, he seized the island with best harborage from its ill-armed inhabitants: "Desperation," Kambanal aptly said, "and a feeble enemy, can turn pigeons into eagles." Iolfrant was installed there plotting ways, it could not be doubted, to return to his *onhritha* in triumph. In the meantime, Kamin-Tolagh strongly suspected, if it had not already been accomplished long before, Iolfrant had made a new landfall on the coast where Zelu Bablakhi was, and had by some means induced many of the savages to bring their gold to him. While Kamin-Tolagh's inscrutable alliance with the other *hrithuod* had survived his initial anger over the settlement they had made, he was not going to persuade them to give up a large part of their trading revenues for an indefinite time, using their ships either to blockade Iolfrant's island retreat, or to patrol the great south-and-east-facing curve of coast on the far side of Flamûrai.

This inconclusive state mirrored, on larger scale, failure to exterminate the Sranadatta clan when he deposed them, and just as Iolfrant, for his own purposes, had given aid to that remnant, there was now the deferred but genuine worry he in his turn would find a powerful patron with an eye for eventual spoils. With all the miles of land-border, little guarded by natural barriers, uncomfortable to think that ally might well be among the Hrin. Not Iolfrant's old friend Svedion; he, awed or impelled by cynical self-interest into an act at odds with his reputation for deep religious convictions, had come with permission to Hyolenstr, and publicly, ceremoniously acknowledged Kambanal as *hrithust*. The *dveyust-ranga-hrindan*, apparently, had not come up in their priestly conversation.

When, having pacified Fretasi with promises of economies, he went to see Kambanal, Oyestri was there in the smaller of two audience halls, bare by Owani standards, with a high, vaulted ceiling and the openness and ample light the mild climate made readily feasible.

They were discussing the *Hridveyuth*, whose popularity had expanded; not only in this *onhritha* but throughout the Hrinani he gave open-air addresses which drew large crowds of admirers, most of the poorest class.

"They go home happier, though I cannot tell why." Kambanal was holding half-a-dozen close-written pages, said to be a word for word translation from one of the man's lessons, transcribed by a skilled listener.

"Lords, he makes them promises," Oyestri creaked. "He tells churls, and their ignorant women they are as good as any goldsmith. Lords of your high standing are accustomed to flattery, which you rightly dismiss, but these people of the soil are easily taken in."

Kamin-Tolagh could not speak for his *sranim'* on this, but lords born to his rank were equally able to discount Oyestri's kind of back-door flattery. Kambanal, still reading here and there, said, "Hard to know what he is saying. Not treason, at any rate, and not sedition, unless there is something in the bird-talk I do not understand." He abandoned the attempt.

For once, Kamin-Tolagh wished he had Lavsila handy, whose taste for veiled ambiguities might permit insight into those of the *Hridveyuth*. A wish almost granted when Oyestri spoke again.

"Lords, this man goes everywhere unprotected, and has no guards when he speaks in the midst of great crowds."

"Why would he need guards?" Kambanal asked. "Who would want to harm him?"

"We Hrin are famously a people with passion in our opinions. He can at any time say words to offend and anger — someone." The bent, knowing smile came faintly.

Suggestion for removal of a latent nuisance, but Kamin-Tolagh disappointed him. "If this is so, and if we can find the *Hridveyuth*, perhaps he should be offered the protection of, what? a file of our cavalry, whenever he visits this *onhritha*."

To Kambanal as *hrithust*, he had adopted the convention of issuing orders in this advisory style, and Kambanal did not hunt for hidden meanings. "If he would accept them. He would need assuring there would be no interference with his travels or his gatherings."

Oyestri, peering from face to face, was deeply suspicious, but this was quite straightforward; though they had no shadow of an understanding with the holy man, Kamin-Tolagh found him, for now, potentially more useful alive. His habit of treating the Hrin as one people, ignoring political divisions, did not clash with a long-term aim of bringing the entire region into the Empire; in Lavsila's words, an idea of unity for the masses, and a renewal of dispute among their leaders, were the most promising conditions. Having seen a sample of their fighting men, Kamin-Tolagh knew he could defeat them piecemeal, but was far short of troops needed to hold such wide new conquests; some of the *hrithuod* might escape with their ships, and his coasts would be indefensible against their raids.

Once again, reduced yield from Zelu Bablakhi was discussed. "Over the years, Lords, amounts of gold brought down the river there have been now greater, now less. They are wild men, there, and not settled. They fight many wars."

The dark little men who brought their crude boats down the river, giving gold-dust for trinkets, knives, a measure of flour. Such scarecrows could hardly aspire to anything a warrior would call *war*, but when he said so, Oyestri dared to be impatient with the quibble.

"Bickering, then," testily. "Quarrels that keep them from the getting of gold."

"Quarrels among our northern peoples," Kamin-Tolagh said, "kept them from properly feeding themselves."

"Conquest?" Kambanal asked eagerly.

"There have been past attempts, Lords, to subdue those wild men."

"Hrin attempts, using Hrin warriors?"

"Ah. We have not, Lord, studied the crafts of war as you have. Maybe you can tame the gold-bringers."

Dubovai, who had been sitting silently by, thinking wistfully, it could be guessed, of his many unfinished maps, put in, "But they say the gold comes from miles inland, high in hills where the great river rises."

To this Oyestri did not object, but of the rumor Iolfrant had another site for trading with the river-people, he said, "Lords, I would have heard of such a place."

"Indeed," Kamin-Tolagh, bluntly. "Being his kinsman."

"This was being guessed, Lord," Dubovai put in, "three years ago, when I had the command there."

"But why would they trade with Iolfrant over us?" Kambanal wondered. "What has he to offer that we have not?"

"Lord, ask Oyestri about *sviranth*," Dubovai said to Kamin-Tolagh, exactly as if the old man could not hear him.

He did not wait to be asked. "The name of a poison," sulkily.

"In sufficient quantities, maybe," Dubovai agreed. "Or a slow poison, one embraced by its victim. Is it not also called `Dream-bringer' and `Mirror of *tvenanga*'?" He went on to tell what he knew. It was a grey or brownish intoxicating powder, derived from dried and cured parts of a plant not grown here, or anywhere within a long sea-journey, often pressed for convenience into small blocks. Though not pleasant to taste, it could be eaten as was, stirred into wine, or, most commonly in a small, closed room, sprinkled on the coals of a tiny, hot fire and the fumes inhaled.

"Like *dao*," Kambanal said.

"More powerful a hundredfold — " Oyestri abandoned his evasions. "If the *dao* can make your head float for an hour, *sviranth*, its adepts have said, could take away your body for a day or a week. Men praised the half-waking dreams it brought, with the joy of seeming truth in them, said it was like that best moment with a clever boy — or, if you say, with a skilled woman — but not so soon to ebb, lasting long."

Dubovai resumed. As for some was true of wine, this *sviranth*, eaten or breathed only once or twice, he had been told, made itself into a need, beyond food or drink, mating, sleep or shelter, a consuming appetite for which men would steal or kill, women give away their bodies. And its use wrecked health and shortened life, had been known to cause madness.

"Ah, long years ago, after only a short trial, Hrin of this *onhritha* were aware of its risks no less than its tempting delights. Since that time, *sviranth* has not been brought to the Hrin, nor to any people with homes and families and settled life. It is not part of our *ast-hryindao*."

The last, Kamin-Tolagh supposed, was why this intriguing substance had never been heard of in the realm of his birth, but Dubovai was disputing the claim. "I have seen a man here at Hyolenstr, Lord, who used to make ships' tackle. He is now said to be dying, but looks and smells a month dead. He has long been half-mad and unable to work, from excess of *sviranth*, and when the war came and he could no longer buy the powder, he fell deathly ill, and raving. This is only one; there must be others."

Oyestri was dismissive. "There will always be seamen who, for their price, will carry goods in secret, equally against law and belief. But, Lords, not the thousandth part of the *sviranth* our ships have carried can ever have come to the Hrin; its dangers, as I say, are too well-known, and its use is a blasphemy."

Kamin-Tolagh was marvelling at Dubovai's ability to inform himself, his quiet tenacity in doing so, and it was Kambanal who asked the obvious question of Oyestri: "Where, then, is the *sviranth* carried to by Iolfrant's ships?"

"Other parts," defensively. "We use it in trade."

"With the savages," not a hard guess, with most other possibilities eliminated.

"Many years have passed, Lord, since I set foot on a trading-ship."

Kambanal appeared ready to worry away at this, but Kamin-Tolagh gestured him to silence; Oyestri was often involuntarily useful, and with Dubovai's help the mystery seemed solved; the river-people brought their gold to Iolfrant because he had fostered a need for continued supplies of the *sviranth*. The rest of this would be discussed without Oyestri, who could be assumed to have ways for keeping Iolfrant informed.

Kamin-Tarú was glum. "I would wish to be here in the south all the time. What is at the Abu?"

This summer, yes, had come near the promise of culmination, the reward success was supposed to bring, till now denied. More time had been spent in idleness than in all past years together since before the Jinzai War, and then, he and his sister had been kept apart. The languid amusements of this place nurtured a mood for more; boats drifting lazily on the placid Hflen, and long feastings with unknown fish and shellfish, poached breasts of tiny wood-pigeons, tender cutlets of Hrin venison, which was eaten all year, being from tame herds of small, shaggy deer, an inexhaustible variety of strange and delicious vegetables and fruits. For the hottest weeks, he had discovered Iolfrant, besides the edifice occupied by Kambanal, and another on a coastal island, had possessed a mountain lodge to the north and west, in fragrant forests of fir and cedar, woods used in its graceful construction.

From there for a short time the Empire was ruled, till he became uneasy about the added days for news to reach him from Lavsila and Freighanai, sweating at Larghamit and the Abu. They had, true, not much of great urgency to report — or perhaps distance littled the importance of skirmishes west of Flamûrai, a brief clash between the Jai and the Laughing Owl over emaciated pasturage, Lavsila's proud, breathless recounting of minor events at Kadon Dinul.

Yet the nagging feeling northern empire would slip away without his personal presence was a shadow on the brightness of summer, like his irritation over continued existence of an Iolfrant still provided with ships and followers and a place of refuge; the danger of being waylaid by Iolfrant's fleet had kept him from going with Tú to the offshore island, where the house was said to perch like an eagle on rocky heights, and the clear waters teem with brilliant fish and wondrous growths of coral.

The third blemish, his disappointed wait for a reply from Rodlakh to the friendly letter he had taken such care with. So long as he could detect any suspicion of irony, he had kept asking for another draft from Lavsila, who had begun by regarding it as an exercise in strategy, to enhance Kamin-Tolagh's standing with the Owanil of the realm. That devious heart could never accept the letter for exactly what it tried to appear, a conciliatory overture: while Kamin-Tolagh aimed for sincerity, Lavsila strove to make the ulterior undetectable. Perhaps, in the end, he was right; between those who ruled over the diverse interests of populous and inevitably competing realms, there could never be entire and constant candor; if he could make peace, Kamin-Tolagh would still be trying to outdo Rodlakh, keeping watch for Rodlakh's attempts to discredit him — Lavsila warned, to depose him, absorb his domains.

That admitted, innocently eager to have his achievements acknowledged by the man he had helped make *rabhsai*, he had been genuinely convinced his new victories would oblige Rodlakh to take notice of the Empire; with midsummer past he was still unwilling to concede when Lavsila, visiting Hyolenstr, reported a usually-reliable informant at Kadon Dinul had heard the *rabhsai* intended no reply of any kind. "In the long run, your purposes may be served better by his intransigence; the whole realm will begin to see him as vindictive, and you as the man of peace." Yet strategic advantage was not always what he desired: in winning here at Hyolenstr, he felt nostalgia for a yet greater victory shared with Rodlakh and Shumat, not only the comradeship, but mutual regard of men made on the same scale.

"The Hrin," mind changed by having had them to serve her, "are better than any tribe you have conquered."

"Good craftsmen," he conceded, "fine cooks, they sing pleasant songs — "

"Servants," complacently, "who do not have to have some idea of manners and quiet beaten into them."

All true, and, as it happened, very much to his point. "Yes, but their gods took away their spines a thousand years ago, and to make fighters of them in going to take another century. While we need armies, we need the uncouth tribes."

"We are at peace," she reproached.

"For now," he half-agreed, and borrowed another thought from the surprising Dubovai. "The tribes are largely at peace, one with another, in part because we take away their hottest and most quarrelsome, and turn them into soldiers. But we have fighting for them to do, before we can take our ease like this."

"Shall we be long at the Abu?"

"You could stay here, if you wished."

After consideration, she shook her head. "I want to see Lavsila's house at Larghamit." A long way from finished, now slept in from time to time. "Besides, I should be with you, and here would be boring without you." Apparently, that led to a review of available amusements, because moments later, with no obvious connection, she said, "Kambanal should have a wife. We shall have to find a pretty girl of family for him." Kamin-Tolagh knew she thought the younger man charming, but a good part of that was Kambanal's uncritical admiration of her brother. She had not mentioned Chamya since hearing the news of the training-accident, and saying, with calm sincerity, it was a shame.

Unlike Kambanal, who, as newly-cultivated lands became productive, stood to become wealthy from his share in the revenues, Lavsila had to be given a stipend to make his portion of minor taxes into a reasonable income. If he had not found an undetected way to steal, he must still have access to family wealth; in the handsome main hall of his unfinished house he had been able to install twelve windows of Island glass. He proudly drew attention to them, and his tale of the expense and trouble was bragging not-very-well disguised as complaint: the Patriarch's representatives, uncertain the panes would be permitted to pass out from the Frontier at Drin Navuna, had sent them by ship to Nambalus in the Lower Paowan. From there they had gone by wagon, east and then the long road south to Thenimala, where for all anyone knew they were intended for some great house in the lands of the Hrin vessel to which they were transferred. After that and the immense sea-journey, it was a wonder, Lavsila said, a single pane had arrived unbroken at Larghamit.

With workmen still camped close by, the few habitable parts were islands of completion in the rough, bare and littered shell of a house, and if the food was no better than eatable after the riches of the south, Khalú contrived to make a virtue of plainness, saying that on her visit with Lavsila to Hyolenstr she had found the Hrin cooking, while delicious, quickly came to seem too fussy, nothing ever let be itself.

When, as it must here in the north, the subject of water came up, she spoke of her desire to have baths in the style of ancient Vrobhan, and Lavsila, over-hastily, declared any deficiency in water-supply could easily be made up with a high cistern kept filled by ten or a dozen water-carriers.

Kamin-Tolagh knew the story; Lavsila, having failed to find more than trickles of water in his probes of the ridge, had quietly brought in an old well-woman of the Gudi-la, who had smelt out two springs to provide barely adequate water for normal needs of the large house.

Kamin-Tarú was saying she had once stayed at a house of the Paowan where the baths, most luxurious she had seen, were made to resemble a natural pool, though far clearer.

Khalú smiled prettily. "At the eastward end of the Arbhu Hills? A house my father had built, and a great favorite of my mother's. As a girl, I spent whole mornings in the baths. Most agree they are the finest anywhere."

Kamin-Tolagh, knowing whose house that was, had thought his sister was elaborately teasing Khalú, but saw now she was annoyed not to have made the connection.

She was not put out for long, asking with eyes too wide, "Did Dolvid also enjoy the baths?"

A quick, wary glance to the present husband. "I do not recall we were ever at that house. I knew it mostly in my childhood."

Tú nodded tranquilly, and Kamin-Tolagh, having provisionally awarded one bout to Khalú, perceived his sister, for reasons that were obscure, was enjoying a private victory.

Later, when they were alone, she demanded irritably, "Why must Lavsila always lie, with his dozen water-carriers? He knows it would take a hundred at least to supply the baths Khalú wants. And where will the water come from?"

"Flamûrai?"

"The salt won't help Khalú's lovely skin."

These were diversions aside from serious discussion, which continued next day at the Abu, with Freighanai and Luzhan included. The subject was raising of forces sufficient to strike upriver from Zelu Bablakhi, and seize the source of its gold. If all he had been told about *sviranth* was true, it would be useless to do as they had when Zelu Bablakhi was first found, and as Freighanai diffidently counter-suggested, send a force along the coast, hoping to discover Iolfrant's new trading-place. Unless they happened to capture Iolfrant himself, he would find yet another spot for a landing, and no matter how often he was forced to move, the gold-bringers would follow him, drawn by their need for *sviranth*.

"The only lasting solution is to bring the country where gold is into the Empire."

"How large a country would that be, *Asai*?" Freighanai asked.

"How far upriver?" Luzhan added.

"Some days, I cannot get any exact information, but with a river to follow, it should be easier than when Nizhadh and I wandered over the Kufshei, looking for a way south. The people could not be as numerous, nor as well-armed as Iolfrant's, and those we overawed with fewer than two thousand men." Not long ago, he would simply have issued his orders, without need to make a case for the new campaign. The Empire was larger now, and complicated, with more points of danger, and those he had given rank had to understand their responsibilities.

Freighanai fidgeted. "Better, *Asai*, next year, the year after. In all, what with losses and the ones for garrison, we have sent near fifty squadrons to the Hrin lands — "

"We could find fifty times that many men."

"Oh, *men*, there's always men, *Asai*. But horses, weapons, hands schooled to hold them, those take time."

"If, as Oyestri says it is forest-country upriver, this will not be a campaign for *péfrapravádal*, and mounts can be chiefly ponies and small horses. At least half the force should be bows." Not all archery belonged to Tau-Suaka's men; to the west of Flamûrai, recent tribes to submit posessed good bows, not as fast or as deadly as the Hill Froghul', but a match for anything likely to be encountered beyond Zelu Bablakhi.

The hard sums were done; for the campaign he wanted one thousand to twelve hundred men. He could not imagine encountering an enemy that would not be overawed and easily defeated by half that, but would rather miscalculate on the side of excess; at worst the outing would be useful experience of field service for those not needed in battle. Luzhan would oversee rudimentary training of already-effective bowmen, to ride in companies and obey simple orders given in the *Hwanió*. At the same time, additional men would be prepared for routine duty in the south, so Kambanal could contribute battle-tested fighters to the expedition, though he would need to keep together a tough and experienced reserve, ready to move swiftly to any point of danger. Freighanai, meanwhile, had the difficult, potentially conflicting task of shuffling squadrons and reliable officers so as to maintain a reasonable security throughout the northern empire. Most supplies would come from the south, but the Abu would provide weapons and begin at once to produce large numbers of steel-tipped arrows. He wanted to begin the campaign near turn of the year, to take advantage of whatever cooler weather there was. Dubovai, who, for mapmaking purposes, had explored a short way inland when in command at Zelu Bablakhi, said that while the river flowed due east after being joined by its tributary coming down from Gronu Kizh'klaëdhiyu, it bent on a wide curve from the southward uplands, and not many days in that direction would be start of regions, also spoken of by Hrin seamen, where there was no season but everlasting summer.

Settling these questions, Kamin-Tolagh at last recognized the reason for the anxious forethought he was giving to details he would normally have dealt with as they arose; this would be much his best-prepared campaign, so as to keep open the possibility he would leave it to his subordinates. Months ago, when he began the expedition against Iolfrant, Kamin-Tarú had demanded why he as Emperor could not have others to do the fighting, as with building, or cooking, or the sewing of his outshirts. He did not fear the dangers and discomforts of the field, and it would never be beneath his dignity to take personal command of troops — and if those were his sister's beliefs, they were not her true reasons for speaking; she had not wanted him to leave her. Still, at some point he was going to have to trust his officers to fight battles, as they had, successfully, with unrest in the Kufshei, and at besieged Guodvestr during his absence. The prospective war, with reliable men of Kargul for leaders, should follow an established pattern, adversary's initial confidence shattered in a single pitched battle, followed by servile attempts at negotiation.

At this time of year he was seldom free of anxiety about an attack across Landegh, although in logic it should be less probable now Kadon Dinul was aware of his southern conquests; only his own death or capture, Rodlakh must see, could end the conflict, and for the realm to carry war into the Hrin lands was surely beyond even Shumat's capacities.

A nearer concern was Iruvakh, his bland intractability given new weight by Patriarchal approval, and clamorous needs of the Heartlanders, installed on their southern estates. Kamin-Tolagh, for the sake of his reputation as a friend of Owan, would be obliged to authorize *atarlal* of the *Edhrodilum* to consecrate those fields in *ga-Yalum*, but not before Iruvakh explained how this was to be done without offending the Hrin; typical of the change in the man that where once he had solicited respect for all belief, he now spoke slightingly of alien superstitions — typical, too, of Heartland arrogance that, planted with their small retinues, protected by a few hundred soldiers, in the midst of thousands whose religion was all of life, they saw no reason to tread warily. Oyestri, true, had said this new dedication of the fields would mean nothing to most Hrin, but the *Hridveyuth* wanted an explanation of exactly what it signified, and his influence with the masses was still an untested force. So far, though Kamin-Tolagh had permitted *edradhul* to go to the south, their activities were limited to giving purely practical advice. In his extended absence, and probably with the connivance of Lavsila, the restriction would soon be circumvented.

Iruvakh had just returned from Hyolenstr, when Kamin-Tolagh met with him at the Abu, a place which, with distressing rapidity, was taking on a forsaken air. With horse-breeding removed to the Man-mani valley, the western end was again a drill-ground. Growing-plots at the center were still tilled, but up on the mound departure of Heartlanders and some of the soldiers' families, with most of the many servants they employed, had made it like tales told of Tan Lughsai after the disastrous fire, with those who had gone there to serve and feed the *rabhsai*'s estate gradually drifting away. With the men of Kargul scattered, at Larghamit and Gronu Kizh'klaëdhiyu and Zelu Bablakhi, at Larghai's Notch and in Iolfrant's lands, it had less populace now than before the coming of the Heartlanders.

At the Residence, Iruvakh reopened an ongoing debate. "While His Enlightenment insists our *atarlal*, under the Second Treaty, do not require the *rabhsai*'s leave to journey through northern Lunu Tezh', He is aware that providing them escorts from His own retinue is of more doubtful legality."

"Whereas for men of mine to violate the realm's borders —" sardonically. "Why should I provide escorts for your *atarlal*?" In private talk, they omitted all honorifics.

"Not for *atarlal*. Shipments of *raminat*, of *ôdu*-globes, and of other Island goods in which you have expressed interest. These, I am instructed to say, the *Atarlum* is very willing to sell here, but cannot assume the risks inherent in their delivery — robbery, for instance." On an isolated stretch of coast, facing the Island, he explained, there was an ancient, secret landing, with a tiny cavalry-post, which the Patriarch would cede, without cost, to Kamin-Tolagh, if he would man it.

"Would I be guessing right if I predicted your *atarlal* will time their journeys, in either direction, to coincide with these men I send to guard our shipments?"

"Not an unusual practice. Lone travellers with the Ní-Tilagh to cross wait at Kir or the Fords farther south, to join with stronger companies."

This, though not specifically anticipated, could stand for the kind of extortion Kamin-Tolagh had feared from the first in admitting the *Atarlum*. Yet he needed the monopoly goods of the Patriarch; on his second visit the desiccated at-Sholidu had made him a present of a small amount of *raminat*, to remind him of its blessings when not staled by long storage — and the old stock was, in any case, almost exhausted. Shipments from the Island could be sent the far lengthier route travelled by Lavsila's celebrated window-panes, but export of both *raminat* and the light-giving *ôdul*, not forbidden, was closely regulated, and ga-Dozhusai, clearly, anxious to observe the Treaty, would not chance confrontation with Rodlakh on that issue.

While giving no conclusive reply, Kamin-Tolagh was grindingly aware Iruvakh knew he had won, but on the next issue he was going to have his way, and saw no reason to conceal his motives. Prosperity would be finished here if the Heartlanders altogether abandoned the Abu, depriving the northern tribes of income earned as servants, and from their crafts and small manufactures. If, however, Larghamit and the Abu remained places of pilgrimage and religious observations, new landowners of the south, as well as any who followed them from Rodlakh's realm, would be obliged to visit here several times each year, and so to maintain minimal households at the Abu.

Iruvakh was predictably ready to agree the only proper place for celebration of Zhôl's Day was and would remain the Kafai Zhaëli at Larghamit, but over *Shuda'sai*, the important midsummer observance, he shook his head dubiously. "At that time of year, under the sun here? They will invent good reasons not to make the journey, and *Shuda'sai* will become a mockery."

Conceding the point, Kamin-Tolagh went to the other end of the year, and had an inspiration. "We shall observe Fire Days at Larghai's Notch, with the watch-fire on the pinnacle there, a commemoration, at the same time, of the Great Fire, true beginning for the Empire."

"Very appropriate, Lord," doubly astonishing him, but there was an explanation for this ready concurrence: "We discussed, *g'Asalladh'* and I, the probability you would want to adapt some of the year's festivals to reflect a newer history. The very example I chose of how the old realm had done so was lighting of the watch-fire on the heights of Dramal, to link Fire Days with the Treaty of the Wind-Caves. His Enlightenment saw no objection, if no violence was done to the essential meaning and character of the observance."

"The long journey," with straightest of straight faces, "will give the holiday added meaning to those who attend. But it must be sole official observance of the Fire Days, anywhere in the Empire."

"Except for soldiers on active service, of course."

Kamin-Tolagh nodded, and got Iruvakh similarly to agree Spring Halving should be celebrated at Abu Ninusai, a name given on that day, it would be six years ago. He was confident most who came for Fire Days would then stay in their houses at the Abu rather than make the long double journey twice within ninety days. Autumn Halving, associated with harvest, was traditionally a rather dispersed celebration, with few great gatherings, and celebration of New Year of the Empire, a month later, was no business of the *Atarlum*'s.

Abruptly, Kamin-Tolagh said, "Let me have a written outline of escorts that would be needed." Concessions he had won had made him benificent, but it had also occurred to him providing troops to safeguard *atarlal* would make some of the dependency flow the other way.

No one was completely free of envy. Freighanai had attained rank beyond any possible ambition, sufficiently aware of his limitations not to covet or resent the title bestowed on Kambanal, once most junior file-leader in the squadron he commanded. Instead, he longed for the chance for field command such as Kambanal had in the war with Iolfrant, and as the time approached, never spoke with Kamin-Tolagh without an unsubtle intimation of his desire to have an active part in the new expedition. At last, with contingents of troops already leaving by the long overland route, others assembling at Larghamit, he went beyond hinting.

"You see, *Asai*," he ventured, one cool morning. "If I came so far as the trading-station, with the Hrin ships coming, I could keep in touch with the Abu, and you and the troops at the same time. See it's done right, if you send back for anything, *Asai* —" giving a vivid picture of the ever-increasing number of days that would stretch between him, at head of the army, and all other places where things could go wrong.

"What senior officer, then, would be left for Larghamit, or the Abu?" Dubovai, though not the best war-captain, would be in the field, making maps as well as leading troops, and so would the eager Niburai and steadier Namakhati, Luzhan for his special skill with half-trained tribal warriors.

Freighanai rubbed his chin with the back of a hand. "With leave, *Asai*, well, there's old Yaënsilat, without any duties."

"He is in retirement," mildly, though startled to hear the man mentioned. Four years now since the old squadron-leader had refused orders to burn the village, and won reprieve from the penalty for mutiny at the battle in the water-gap. No further action had been taken against him, and Kamin-Tolagh glimpsed his lean figure from time to time at the Abu, where he occupied a small house near the crossways, and tended a thriving vegetable-patch. Till Kambanal's wings began to spread, Yaënsilat might well have been best of all officers under Kamin-Tolagh, yet a pardon was unthinkable.

"But he wouldn't have forgotten his soldiering, would he?" This persistence was uncharacteristic; Kamin-Tolagh swallowed any annoyance for the sake of the man's candor.

"He is still admired by the younger men?"

"Admired, *Asai*? Well, I'd say, trusted. I know there are those who visit him, and he gives advice — not on army matters, or duties or so forth; they say he won't touch that."

For a young, single man of Kargul serving here, a subject aside from army matters where Yaënsilat's advice would be sought was hard to imagine; there might be point to keeping watch over who his frequent visitors were. "You cannot actually propose we give command at the Abu in my absence to a man who refused a direct order in the field."

"Is that what he did, *Asai*? If that's the case, no, out of the question. I had heard two or three different stories, but I was never told but that he'd taken his retirement."

"His age," to rebut the unasked question about leniency. "was taken into account; you may go on calling him retired."

"If it comes up, *Asai*."

He would send Freighanai, and stay behind himself, not here but at Larghamit, nearest to a center for the whole empire. Also a place where, if attackers were to overrun the Abu, there could be boats waiting to whisk him and his sister away, not simply to save them, but to allow war, and so the Empire, to continue. Less catastrophically, he could sail to take belated personal charge of the Zelu Bablakhi campaign, if that seemed advisable, though he must avoid arriving at the moment of success, not wishing to steal Freighanai's glory.

With this campaign, he had to endure a hardship of war new to him, which Tú pointed out was too familiar to her, the torment of waiting for word. Obvious but intolerable that news moved away from him at the speed of the advance; each hour of progress was an hour added to the carrying of dispatches. At first when Freighanai, preparations done, sent the columns forward, reports came regularly, and spoke of everything going according to plan. Carrying supplies and pack-animals, smaller ships of the *Hrithust* Nestos were able to navigate upriver till it broadened into marshy and reed-choked shallows where only the little boats of the river-people could make their way. This was where the river bent from the south, and beyond there were rapids, then a set of falls like a giant staircase, all unnavigable, but on the right bank was a network of well-marked trails, by which the river-people hauled their boats past the hazard. Just short of the marshlands, Freighanai set up his forward command and stockpiled reserve supplies; beyond there, he reported, as way mounted, forest thickened, and he cautioned the leaders, a forward section of three hundred led by Dubovai and Niburai, and the second column, twice as numerous, with Luzhan and Namakhati, to be on guard against ambush.

Some natives were glimpsed fleetingly among the thickets, but no word came of fighting; earliest scattered casualties were to the bites of wild animals and snakes, which were abundant.

Almost a month passed, and a new year in the *Mankh'* calendar approached; Heartlanders and others from the south began assembling for Fire Days; arrival of first Fretasi, then some of the new estate-holders with their wives, brought relief to the enforced pairing of Khalú and Kamin-Tarú, which had teetered on the edge of bickering for the past fortnight.

Full observance for the midwinter ritual was five days, with an absolute minimum of three, meaning the Heartlanders, coming straight from their cosseted life in the south, were obliged to camp, clustered about the cavalry-post at Larghai's Notch, at a time of year when mornings and evenings were cool and clammy, and when, on the central day, for the pious no flame could be lighted till the watchfire was kindled at sunset.

"A little discomfort," to an unamused Lavsila, "is proof of their devotion." Yet it was a poignant moment when the anticipatory hush of evening came, and yellow fire at last leapt up from the crown of the heights. Kambanal, with too many cares at Hyolenstr, had not made the journey, but the blaze was a sharp reminder of his awed whisper at sight of the burning hills, and Kamin-Tolagh's prophetic words, spoken near this place, were incorporated in the less-formal portion of Iruvakh's address: *With these flames...an empire is being forged.* Bloodless history to the Heartlanders, all that happened before they came, and of those remembered from the day of the Great Fire, most of the leaders were absent; Freighanai and Kambanal with their duties, Yaënsilat in disgrace. Niburai, whose chief part had been to lend Kamin-Tolagh his spare breeches, was somewhere upriver from Zelu Bablakhi, Nizhadh was dead, as was Chamya who had rapturously declared himself *péfrapravádai* that day.

Standing among Heartlanders and others released by completion of ritual to resume their inconsequential chatter, guarded by the uncommunicating Tau-Suaka, Kamin-Tolagh felt a state close to panic at the elusive impermanence even of comradeship, a brightness insubstantial as flame. He sought, found, and extravagantly hugged his sister. Bewildered by the gross violation of his own rule against open affection, she said, "What is it, Tam?" reaching a forefinger to his face. He realized in exasperation there must be a tear there.

"I was thinking about poor Chamya, how — young he was," a fatuous conclusion, but tremendously true on the day of the fire.

"I know," eager enquiry draining from her posture. "Such a pity," as before, shuttering herself with a conventionalism.

On the slow ride back to the Abu, a tribal rider met him with a message from Freighanai, sparsely commenting on the enclosed field dispatch written by Dubovai. It spoke of delays and difficulties in rough, overgrown terrain, where the river diverged into many small falls and boiling cataracts, and of a running archery duel with enemy hard to sight among the trees and dense undergrowth. It was growing warmer and stickier, with daily rains, but the vanguard hoped soon for a more open country.

He had a five-day wait for the next, penned in haste, rainstreaked and stained with mud. This time, chief author was Niburai, telling a confused tale of accumulated reverses, but chiefly angry with a numerous if largely invisible enemy which declined to stand and fight, preferring to sting and vanish. In his endorsement, Dubovai admitted he had briefly lost touch with the foremost units, but was now advancing to their assistance, despite enemies of his own to contend with. That report was two weeks old, and six days later Freighanai had appended his covering note, saying he would personally take some of the reserve up to the head of the main falls, to obtain a clearer picture.

Kamin-Tolagh lopped at least a day from the ensuing wait by returning to Larghamit. There, next news was from Freighanai alone, unable to enclose any dispatches from the field. He was out of touch with a reserve squadron, sent forward with a fresh supply of arrows requested by Dubovai, but hoped for definite word in a day or so.

"What can this mean? Freighanai has lost contact with a squadron between him and the forward reserve? And Niburai has men somewhere beyond those squadrons? This is not sense."

"It could be the weather — " unaccustomed to having military matters hurled at her. "Rain has made the roads difficult."

"In the Jinzai War, we brought an army intact through the Lunu Tezh', on roads scarcely better than a rumor."

"But knowing where you were going," a distinction keener than he expected, more disturbing than he liked.

But also he had been there, with his driving will, and he came near taking ship for Zelu Bablakhi now. But the difficulties described in Niburai's dispatch would be five weeks in the past before he could arrive, and he did not want to appear either foolishly over-anxious, or as lacking confidence in his chosen captains.

Further information, however, was nine long days in arriving, and his bad temper was becoming a byword with Lavsila's servants, who cringed as he passed. When it came, it was disaster, which all of Freighanai's native tact, his repeated refusal to give up hope, did nothing to mitigate.

He had written from a spot still more than two days upriver from the trading-station, for which he was marching with some one hundred and seventy men, most sick, wounded or both, all that was left of twelve squadrons. Others, he wrote, had been taken out by water, after he had bullied Hrin ship-owners into sailing their craft into the treacherous reedland shallows, and rumor persisted of a further sizable group, assembled from sections led by Niburai and Dubovai, still holding together, though Namakhati, with several other officers of Kargul, was confirmed dead, Dubovai gravely wounded. Freighanai, if with a disclaimer of wan hope, doubted that of all forces there could be four hundred left, and of those nearly half had hard fighting and a difficult journey between them and safety.

It could never be the same; a legend of invincibility was crushed, and no complete story of its destruction would ever be pieced together. Fullest account came when Freighanai arrived at Larghamit fifteen days later, having stayed at Zelu Bablakhi while survivors continued to trickle in by twos, threes, half-dozens. He had also been afraid the enemy that had mauled the squadrons, and followed them for days on the ragged retreat, might intend an assault on the trading-post itself, but it soon became apparent the head of the falls was, for now, as far as the wild men were going to venture. "Those forest apes weren't going to come where our long-weapons could be of use," bitterly.

Though he stumbled ashore dazed with weariness and long anxiety, Freighanai was unwounded, making him a rarity among those who had marched. Of twenty-six men of Kargul, seventeen were confirmed or presumed dead; Niburai had survived with slight wounds, but Dubovai, brought back on the same ship as Freighanai, was said by the *ramidu* who attended him to be on knife-edge between life and death.

After too many days to brood in, Kamin-Tolagh, convinced a failure of such magnitude must be the result of mismanagement and bad decisions, found first sight of Freighanai, even shattered Dubovai, moved him to fresh anger rather than compassion; such incompetence approached outright treason. But Freighanai had fed too long on horrors to care about the note of accusation, and his steely response had no hint of contrition.

"No one who was not there, *Asai*, could know what our enemies were."

Well before any human ones were seriously encountered, others had taken a toll; there were losses to snakes, to large, poisonous spiders; a straggler had been set upon by a prowling panther, while in shallow waters to be crossed there lurked a creature well-known in folk-tale and legend, described by Freighanai as a sort of huge, short-legged lizard, slow-moving on land, a powerful, wide-opening mouth set with dagger-like teeth. Half-submerged in water, it resembled a floating log, but a single swift snap of its jaws could take the leg off a man, and arrows had frequently rebounded from its tough, knurled hide.

Deeper into the forest, always warmer with frequent heavy rain, stinging and biting insects were everywhere, and the soldiers acquired special horror of a rust-hued centipede long as a man's forearm, its bite usually fatal. Food here putrefied with dismaying swiftness, and pracically all the men suffered from fevers and loose bowels; to add to that misery, clothing, too long drying in the steamy air, could not be washed on the march.

These daily troubles continucd amid a series of miniature ambushes, inflicting steady losses of a man or two, the enemy, shooting small arrows from deep cover, able to move in silence through densest growth, practically invisible. Nevertheless, in hopes of emerging into open country, the vanguard had pressed on, Dubovai keeping pace a half-day behind.

With the army weakened by losses, illness, bad food, hard marches made harder by lack of sleep and airless trails, the enemy, or a coalition of enemies, closed in, and now many of their arrows were poisoned. Dubovai, having to turn frequently to engage wild men who assailed the rear of his column, threatening communication with the reserve, lost touch instead with the forward companies.

They named it the forest war, but there was never anything to call a battle, nothing but brutal skirmishes along practically the entire line-of-march, fierce and determined attackers coming now from one side, now the other. Most Kargul' officers dead or disabled, Niburai, with what remained of the vanguard, decided on retreat, but Dubovai, himself hard-pressed, was unable to fight his way forward to assist. His own rear was no longer secure, and of reinforcements sent by Freighanai, only mauled remnants of two squadrons reached him. Hearing nothing from the forward companies, he determined on withdrawal, while he had sufficient strength to save some men.

For days, they fought and died, sickened and died. Freighanai, moving up from head of the falls with too few reinforcements, constantly hampered by enemy bows, fought his way to meet the wounded Dubovai, and helped conduct dazed and dispirited survivors back to where boats were waiting, nervous and unwilling. Judging any further advance could achieve nothing but loss of further lives, he then held his position, as yet unable to believe these ragged scraps were all that remained of his hundreds. His count at that time had reached three hundred and forty, with many unlikely to live long. He had no later news of the men under Niburai.

This tale was told at the house of Lavsila, with backtracks and repetitions, but no change in his manner, neither apologetic nor defiant, but with the deep underlying anger and agony of a man who, in failure, can think of nothing else he might have done to change it.

The remainder, supplied to Freighanai by Niburai, was not much different. The young officer had found himself sole fit Karguli in charge of a body of rather less than three hundred, all that remained, though he did not then know it, of the leading formations. For nearly two days they were trapped on a steep hillside, retreat prevented by a mountain-torrent in sudden spate. There were enemy on three sides, inaccessible above, from where they maintained a constant downpour of their small arrows, but nowhere daring to close in while Niburai's men could still hold weapons. Yet those men were dying steadily, and at last Niburai had whole and least-wounded rope themselves together, and led them through the torrent, with some of the injured and what little supplies there were carried on pack animals, hauled at with ropes, jabbed with knives in their hindquarters to make the beasts brave the stream. Some time later, Niburai was told that without leave or any discussion, most tribal troops had quietly killed those of their comrades too ill or badly wounded to be moved. There had been shuddering tales the wild men, given live captives, took pleasure in using them in games revolting to describe.

Escape from that trap gave temporary respite from enemy bows, and Freighanai now believed the wild men, having seen off the first and last of their invaders, had been content merely to harry, but for Niburai men and animals continued to die of sickness and wounds, and his pace was a crawl. Six days after Freighanai, despairing of more survivors, had turned back, Niburai beyond hope came warily from the forest, leading one hundred and thirty-four exhausted, famished, failing, and in some cases, dying men.

That was the tally, and must by now be considered final, except for continuing subtractions from those who had come out alive, which might yet include Dubovai.

"This wasn't a war, *Asai*, it was dying, that's all," and Freighanai maintained that in the scattered places where it had come to real fighting, weapon to weapon, the squadrons, even at the end, outnumbered, weakened and wearied, had been too much for the enemy.

Kamin-Tolagh could imagine infinite possible questions — whether, for one, when the nature of the enemy had been ascertained, it would have been better to break formation, and send their newest archers, half-wild themselves, as skirmishers through the forest — but none to change the arithmetic of concluded events, or weigh what difference his presence could have made. All the history he recalled of past heroes, Larghai, Pir Perus, Pir Kallikuk, Great Banak, inveterate enemy of his house, told him, if there was greatness it was not in chewing at bitter husks of failure, but in the ability to ask, *what now?* In the past year, with battles in the south, scattered fighting elsewhere, and now this disaster, two thousand tribal troops had been consumed, and as many swallowed up by the minimal needs of security for his new domains. Four thousand men! more than could be found and adequately trained in a year — and the thought brought a new concern: "Luzhan? Is he alive?"

"I left him in command with Niburai at Bablakhi, *Asai*. Got a nasty arm from a poison arrow, but he says he'll mend, and he has that way of steadying men of the tribes, as you're aware. There's shaken men there, *Asai* — and some sick ones. A pair of what the Hrin call healers are giving a hand, but they could use a few real *ramidul*."

"Two are at the Abu, caring for the hangnails of the Heartland. They can — Iruvakh will certainly send them at once." Next to him, the unusually silent Lavsila, who had been making notes, reached for a new page to phrase the order as a request. With fresh levies in mind, it was a relief to hear of Luzhan's survival, though he had thought of the expanded effort to enlist and train new men in terms of continuing and completing his conquest of the Hrinani, not merely of replacing losses.

He could very nearly achieve a sour laugh at his own expense; the immediate aftermath of this failure was enormously beyond a question of altered priorities; the Empire was at a crisis. The men of Kargul were gone beyond replacing, and as critical was the heavy toll in animals, both saddle and pack; more than a thousand in all had been lost, and Freighanai, doubting the wild men had any other use for them, supposed they had been eaten by now. Also, he said grimly, they had come into a pretty windfall by way of weapons of all kinds, far too many of them blades of Dakbân steel, for which there was no match here in the West.

At this moment, as for months to come, no danger-point in the entire empire possessed a garrison Kamin-Tolagh would call adequate for security; all had been picked bare to provide men for Zelu Bablakhi, and reserves available to be hurried to any new danger consisted of a handful of squadrons, most half-trained.

"The magnitude of this reverse," Lavsila, without difficulty reading his face, "must not become known in the Hrin lands." Freighanai, ready to fall sideways from his chair with fatigue, had been sent to find warm water, food if he desired it, rest.

With Hrin ships in every phase of the expedition, that was clearly impossible. "At Kadon Dinul, rather." That meant it must be kept from the Heartlanders, who now had several means of communicating with friends and kin back home. The *atarlal* travelling back and forth were, relatively, a simpler question, since a single Patriarchal edict, requested by Iruvakh, could enforce their silence, and Dozhusai had reasons for humoring Kamin-Tolagh, none imaginable for informing Rodlakh of the abrupt vulnerability of the Empire.

Extent of tribal losses could be disguised indefinitely, assigning Kambanal the remnants of squadrons drawn from the northern Froghushei, and bringing back what was left of those borrowed from the south, giving them duties away from their home tribal lands. But while surviving men of Kargul could be ordered not to talk, the loss of seventeen, most with family, living close together at the Abu, could hardly be concealed.

"You need a shipwreck," Lavsila suggested, and expanded the idea. There would have to be some admission of a setback, but its gravity could be reduced if ten or a dozen of the men had been aboard a Hrin ship which foundered on its way to Zelu Bablakhi.

"A reconnaissance in force into unfamiliar country met with unexpectedly strong resistance, and other difficulties — "

"Spiders," bitterly. "Poison insects, poison arrows, bad weather, man-eating toothed lizards — "

"This Niburai — " mistaking the direction of Kamin-Tolagh's scorn. "He was unwounded, or practically so. Yet our

Freighanai makes him the hero, for coming back from a walk in the woods bringing one man in four."

"You are a fool. When you have been on such a walk in the woods — when you have come within a long bowshot of any battle, then you may speak about courage. Till then, teach me about water-gardens."

"Your pardon, *Lord*," stiffly. "All I meant was, it is not hard to find or make a hero when one is needed."

The principle became part of his story. "In battle, some officers and men were lost, Dubovai gravely wounded, but the main formations were brought out of difficulties, chiefly by the courage and leadership of Captain Niburai, who, with complete disregard for his own safety, and so forth."

"His rank is *kímukan*."

"He had better be at least an under-captain. All those who came back will need to be given promotions."

Kamin-Tolagh, part of whose mind had toyed with the opposite, saw the wisdom here, and nodded grimly. The disaster could not be indefinitely explained away or hidden, but time would lessen its stunning effect, and time would allow him to rebuild his armed strength.

"These losses put us in immediate danger?"

"We have never been anywhere else." But the financial implications had not occurred, till he glimpsed Fretasi, on the way to her newest gloomy calculations; now the small amounts of gold that had been brought for trading before the expedition would cease to appear.

A bizarre exercise, by words and forced smiles converting utter and costly failure into an incomplete success, with some regrettable attendant losses. When Niburai was brought back from Zelu Bablakhi, his straightforward account of a nightmare experience was in many ways admirable, but before he could begin to tell his tale again for dinners at the Abu, he had to be coached, principally by Lavsila, in a version of his deeds that belonged in the romances. Distressingly, Niburai, fed with gaudy and overblown revisions of his actions, soon came to believe every word, and his impersonation of the hero Lavsila had fabricated was instantly popular with the Heartlanders at the Abu, counting days to Halving and their return to the south. A good-looking, tall, well-made and unmarried man, Niburai passed on within a week to a third phase, modestly disclaiming worthiness of the renown his own adoption of Lavsila's tale-spinning had done most to establish.

When Lavsila, in tiresome Residence Quarter style, making gossip out of what was in fact breezily condoned, reported Pranúdhanai had been sleeping lonely as a result of Niburai's new eminence, Kamin-Tolagh vividly revisited the period of his own hero's welcome at Kadon Dinul, the lavish and demonstrative admiration of Pranúdhanai's wife, the same Ondhayu, then a foolish but precociously knowing girl. In the privacy of their bed, Kamin-Tarú commented affectionately, "Perhaps Niburai thinks he got back more than he gave, when you returned those breeches he lent you."

At another feast, Ondhayu fawning over tales she must by now have learnt as well as Niburai, Kamin-Tolagh made a brief comparison to the riverside trek through dense forest in the Jinzai War — a march, he could not add, that ended in smashing victory at the Lunu Tezh' Gate, not ignominious retreat from an enemy virtually unengaged. Ondhayu, silly still, sounded her throaty laugh, and with what passed for wit, quoted, slightly misquoted, a line from the Pir Perus cycle, "*New heroes come, and old deeds are forgotten.*"

A shocked and apprehensive silence among those near enough to have heard her, and then her husband launched nervously into a highly literary palliation, pointing out *in its context*, the line was ironic in intent, and the events of the tale demonstrated exactly the opposite. Kamin-Tolagh was struck with the thought he could have Ondhayu killed: Tau-Suaka was nearby, and if the pretty throat were to be cut, no one could prevent it, or would dare protest unduly. He was not only law but its abrogation, and no less than the Gudi-la or Man-mani, here the Heartlanders were his to dispose of.

The luxurious ferocity of the idea was enough by itself to repair his temper, and he said sweetly, "The ancient deeds of our long-departed youth teach us to judge the true worth of fresher accomplishments," raising his drinking-cup to a perplexed Niburai, who was quickly restored to his ostentatious modesty by the burst of applause that came. *As much in relief*, Kamin-Tolagh noted, *as admiration*.

They were at the house occupied by Tavrotosai, with its long, high main hall, and at the far end there was a mild disturbance in the doorway. Seeing Freighanai there, Kamin-Tolagh put aside thoughts of murder with his wine-cup, and went to him.

He was apologetic as well as agitated, and his breeches were all dust below the knees; if his ride was so recently finished, he must have had a lantern-bearer beside him.

"Your pardon, *Asai*, breaking in on your feasting. I thought you should have the news. Deserters, *Asai*, Laughing Owl men. Well, men — with their women and children, now." As a guard of honor for Niburai, some dozen troopers, actually all that were left unwounded of the best Laughing Owl squadron, had accompanied him from Zelu Bablakhi.

Left encamped by Larghamit, not on any duty roster, they had managed to slip away, striking south cross-country, and it was past three days before their departure was noted. Two more were spent in making sure they had not been summoned to the Abu, where also a message arrived from the officer at Larghai's Notch, asking for instructions. The Laughing Owl men had passed near there, telling his patrol they had been granted home leave at triumphant conclusion of the Zelu Bablakhi campaign. Mounted as they were on a motley assembly of pack and saddle horses, they were allowed to ride on, but the officer had become suspicious that these men alone had been singled out for favor, all men of one tribe, when no Jai, or Anga-jai, Chon'la or Ntara-golal had appeared.

Before receiving any reply to his query, the officer had taken a half-file down into nearby Laughing Owl country, and after dealing with evasions and much wide-eyed ignorance, ascertained the men had visited their huts only long enough to collect wives, children and other near kin, together with a few of their most prized possessions, and had struck out into rough, arid terrain to the north and west, carrying all the supplies and water they could quickly gather for a long journey. Someone recalled about half the men, connected with a leading family of their tribe, had relatives who years ago had migrated to the Lunu Tezh' Protectorate, living on the shores of En'tesh.

This, like the exasperating Niburai, but with grimmer potential, was a legacy of the Zelu Bablakhi misadventure. The men who had seen their squadron quartered around them were carrying news of that catastrophe, but the Lunu Tezh' was a backwater of the realm, and it might be months or years before the tale seeped into Kadon Dinul. More dangerous were the implications for the future of an empire's armies; with the added defection of entire families, for empire as a whole.

"They must be caught and brought back. The very thought of desertion must be crushed."

"They've got a long lead, *Asai*, four days by dawn."

"They are in bad country, with no trail for them to pick up before the fringe of Landegh. With wives and children, and the animals they have, their pace must be a crawl. They can be overtaken. This is a job for my Hill Froghul."

"If they reach the borders of the Protectorate, *Asai* — "

"That is wild and empty land, not guarded. We have an absolute right to pursue deserters from our armies."

Asked for his best man, Tau-Suaka regretted his kinsman Tando was still in the south, but on learning the nature of the hunt was proud to choose Hunghi-of-the-Whip. Surprising to learn the man had skills other than the one that brought him fearsome renown, but according to Tau-Suaka Hunghi had been, in the old, wild days, a tracker famed for his keen-eyed tenacity.

"He is to do all he can to catch and bring back the deserters, but avoid any encounter with soldiers of the realm, even at the cost of apparent cowardice."

"They are soldiers, Lord, the ones who run from us? When Hunghi catches them, they may be fools enough to fight. Twenty of our bowmen is enough."

"Fly or fight, they must be stopped, but some at least must be brought back alive. We shall then have another use for Hunghi." Exemplary demonstration for the tribes, Laughing Owl especially, that desertion brought punishment worse than simple death. A tale the fugitives had died in rumored distant parts was inadequate for the purpose.

"First light, Lord," delegating guarding of Kamin-Tolagh to an equally-ferocious subordinate, so as to give preparations his personal attention. "Hunghi rides at daybreak. If these wretches escape, Hunghi shall taste his very whip, till his ribs can be seen."

Good, Kamin-Tolagh decided. Thinking of how they were to pay for their treachery, these runaways, he felt uncoil the same dark excitement as when, at Hyolenstr, the nine naked sacrificial victims were bound together, but the sufferings he would inflict were not pleasure, but policy. Under the seductive influence, partly, of their sojourn by the gentle Hflen, among the flaccid Hrin, he had let a softness begin undetected to permeate many layers of the empire, a conjectured element in the Zelu Bablakhi fiasco, surely to be found in how the Laughing Owl had been allowed to decamp. Long before he had come here, the valley tribes had been chastened by the implacable Hill Froghul, and that hardness he must take as his own best model; not the flowers of Siv'loi, but the whip of Hunghi would be an emblem all would recognize.

34.

Shudarr's work with the companies of pikes, by this time simply regular drills to maintain the precision and flexibility of formation they had attained, did not exempt him from the roster of officers who in rotation led long-range squadron-strength patrols over the Lunu Tezh' Gate and deep into the Protectorate itself.

Nature of the country made these excursions largely improvisatory, their only standing order to visit the small cavalry post somewhat precariously maintained at headwaters of the Grânu, which was reached also by smaller patrols coming up the river valley from Entun' Tesh. Troops out of Banakit might be called upon to settle minor village disputes, occasionally to hunt down a lawbreaker or a wild beast that had been killing livestock, and were under instructions to investigate all rumors of unusual happenings. Duration of the patrols was set at two weeks, but that could only be a rough guideline, and Dolvid was not unduly anxious when Idmas, at a morning meeting, mentioned Shudarr's patrol had been out for nineteen days.

After going through the morning's yield of documents, a more immediate concern was wrestling with a letter for Kadon Dinul, dealing with the *rabhsai*'s abrupt decision not to renew certain long-term supply contracts, a complicated affair with many sides to it, none of which had been discussed with Dolvid. As so often nowadays, he was trying to find the right tone, where the maintaining of tact did not mute forceful expression of his views.

Since the Market Gate Letter ended debate over reconciliation with Kamin-Tolagh, Rodlakh had been tepidly distant, while Elamirr's power had continued to expand; almost offhandedly Dolvid had been informed his nominal assistant was to have the rank of *bôdh'loiki*, so as to be at no disadvantage in his daily dealings with others already of that standing, and word came from several sources that Elamirr's virtually independent establishment at the Old Bronze Residence, including not one Owani member, was progressively distancing itself from those loyal to Dolvid, of any race. Worse, it was apparent a number of decisions the *rabhsai* truly believed to be his own were strongly influenced if not originated by Elamirr. On his last brief visit to Kadon Dinul, Dolvid discovered to what an extent old factionalisms had been revived when landowners of the Families, who had once considered him their bitterest enemy, implored him to become their voice against taxes and other laws that, without stating their purpose, were increasingly framed so as to penalize the one group.

A symptomatic example was with measures adopted after Kamin-Tolagh's successes over the Hrin. It was quickly decided Iolfrant's expulsion abrogated his long-term agreement to purchase grain, and shipments would be halted, but when Dolvid joined Shumat in urging a ban, also, on export of Dakbân steel, and especially swords and other weapons which could someday be used against armies of Rodlakh's realm, Elamirr argued passionately against penalizing steelmakers by robbing them of income, although he was as strongly opposed to Dolvid's recommendation *rabhsayum* buy up surplus wheat to lessen the loss for those who had contracted with Iolfrant, sole perceptible difference being the race of those affected.

There were other instances of the same bias; beyond obtaining some amelioration by pointing out obvious injustices, Dolvid did nothing except maintain good relations with his own circle of well-placed friends, whose general view was that Elamirr, who displayed signs, not only of growing wealth but of increasing arrogance, was bound to overstep himself; meanwhile there was consolation — or self-deception — in believing the decency of men such as Shumat, Konir, Rhunilat, that, and the basic good sense of the *rabhsai*, were bound to triumph in the end.

Change was a long time coming. Âna, after months trying to prove the Market Gate Letter a forgery, felt Elamirr's interest in the supply contracts was for once nothing to do with race, and that he had taken gifts from those brokers who expected to profit from reassignments, as perhaps also from the Dakbân steelmakers.

Admittedly, under the old agreements, feed, for example, had occasionally been sold to the armies above market price, but there was something to be said for the growers' claim they were guaranteeing supplies also, in times of shortage, at the contract price, even if the market value of the goods were to double, and that they required in exchange some assurance of a return, compensation for keeping acreage in hay and other feed that could have been given to more profitable crops. The absolute nature of both arguments suggested existence of middle ground, which might have been found had there been any discussion of them before a decision was reached; so far as Dolvid was informed, there had not.

Breaking off his point-by-point commentary, he wrote irritably, *it seems,* Deghi, *I have become an historian of my own times, recording events I have no power to affect.* Signing his name, he folded and sealed the letter, and instantly wondered whether it should be sent. Without consultation, two admired women, Âna on the far side of Arnan, Aëlu on this, kept cautioning him to curb his anger, avoid the open break that would leave him without influence in the realm; he had continued to do so, over and again, troubled by the suspicion that in the name of peace he was yielding by inches territory he would surely have fought for as a whole; more might be accomplished by flat statement he could no longer be a part of the policies of this *rabhsayum.*

He had been working in his most private place, a small room at the top of the official residence, with a fine view south to the Navu and heights beyond; a spring day of silver and blue, and after some days of rain the Vale of Banakit, stippled with fresh green, had a new-laundered look, brilliant as stained glass with sunlight behind. Soon he would have to hear the day's quota of law cases, but decided to go first in search of *raminat.*

As he reached head of the stair, there came the clang of a bell, announcing arrival of message-riders, or other urgent business. When he came down to the oak-beamed entrance-hall, where shafts of sunlight striking through quaint coffer-pane windows softened shadows to glowing richness, Shudarr was standing, stiff-hipped and grimed from riding, helm in hand, all at once exactly his father, twenty years ago. Seeing Dolvid, he apologized for violating procedure by coming here direct instead of reporting first to the senior officers, apologized additionally for disturbing Dolvid, which he would not have done without good reason. "I have interesting prisoners, *Asai —* "

"Not *Asai,*" for the thousandth time since taking up his post in the Colony.

Shudarr, an habitual offender, suppressed a smile. "Master," he corrected. "Some, though, can't be prisoners, I think. They are here, however."

"From the Protectorate? What, lawbreakers?" Dolvid tried to be accessible, but did not want to examine every chicken-thief from the Lunu Tezh'.

He repeated a baffled gesture. "You had best see for yourself, Master."

Guarded by the slightly understrength squadron he had taken on patrol, his prisoners were eight soldiers and two officers, all with helms and military tunics similar to those of the realm, though insignia of rank were altogether unfamiliar.

Dolvid's attention went first to a pair of unhappy *atarlal*, one very tall and slender in robes of a *ramidu*. The other, somewhat shorter, somewhat older, was plainly in charge, and Dolvid had known him a very long time, though he had scarcely seen him in the recent past: at-Dhanurai. Little doubt Shudarr had intercepted a party bound for the Farther West, but a puzzle what use there would be in Kamin-Tolagh's domains for an effective but bookish teacher from the *Manadilum*.

"Dolvidh," at-Dhanurai said, not entirely astonished to see him. "Or, I should say, Dolvidh'*Asai* — "

"Not *Asai*." One thousand and one. As Faëdhal would say in twice as many words, to be spouse to the acting *nim'* did not entitle one to the style of hereditary overlordship.

"Well, but you are in charge?" He was unusually acerbic. "Then will you tell this young officer, as I have been trying for five days, *atarlal* on business of the *Atarlum* may not be detained. Under the Second Treaty, we are guaranteed — "

"A moment, *at'ai*," though courteously. To Shudarr, "You found these men where?"

A rapidly-sketched report: riding westward in convoy, the *atarlal* had been encountered together with five of the soldiers, the junior of the two officers, and a string of pack-animals, in tumbled country coastward from headwaters of the Grânu. Enveloped by nearly a full squadron, the soldiers had not attempted a fight, but the officer, who went by the name of Drusilakh, had refused to acknowledge he was one of Kamin-Tolagh's men, or say where his riding was bound. The *atarlal*, likewise declining to state their business or destination, both quite obvious to Shudarr, demanded, if their escort was to be made prisoner, to be returned to what they called "the landing."

On this hint, together with captives and non-captives, Shudarr rode back along their slight trail, and on a lonely stretch of coast where it faced the not-distant Island, he discovered a well-concealed cove, with moorings for middle-sized vessels, and a couple of new wooden structures, which, together with a large, dry cave, served as both warehouse and sleeping-space. There had been a brief scuffle with three additional soldiers, ended by a command from the senior officer, Antighal, as soon as he saw the numbers against him. Shudarr had then set out for Banakit without delay, bringing all the men and goods with him.

"You can see the squadron-leader acted properly," Dolvid told the offended at-Dhanurai, still determined to register his protest. "He was bound by law to arrest these foreign soldiers, and could hardly leave you and your companion unprotected in such a place."

"Just what I have been telling them, Master. That country — we have chased robbers and wild men there in the past, and the goods these men had with them — "

Dolvid hushed him. "You are in no sense prisoners," he told the *atarlal*. "I hope I can persuade you to stay and have dinner with me, but you are free to return to the Island when there is a ship from Kamsilat to take you, remain here in the Colony, or ride westward to the Frontier — to it, and beyond, if that is your wish. This the Treaty guarantees, but I cannot furnish you with an escort for your crossing of Landegh."

This was start of a game with many variations, to be played by the two officers as well; all stubbornly denied any connection with Kamin-Tolagh, declined to admit it as a reasonable assumption. Yet between the two pairs, soldiers and *atarlal*, there was no sensation of a firm alliance, rather the sidelong glances of men who fear some sort of betrayal.

Deciding to divide them, Dolvid quickly convinced the two *atarlal* they would be grateful for cool drink for their throats and warmed water to wash in. As a servant came to lead them away, at-Dhanurai said in the most confidential of voices, "I, we, the *Atarlum* and His Enlightenment, can accept no responsibility for any violation of your sovereignty. You are well aware we have no control over any foreign army."

"I have given my word. You will not be detained, or hampered in any way. But my master is Rodlakh *Rabhsai*, who may have questions to raise with yours."

Free now to concentrate on the soldiery, he decided the officers were file-leader or at best half-squadron material; the younger and more sullen, Drusilakh, spoke the few words he had with a strong rural accent of Western Kargul, while the other, Antighal, who would have been likable in different circumstances, lacked the stance of habitual senior command. Yet he had called the other *kímukan*, and if that was the rank indicated by Drusilakh's badge, a curve of four small stars, very like a segment of the device Kamin-Tolagh had put on the reverse of his coinage, then Antighal's near circle of five stars made him an under-captain. Perhaps theses men held one normal rank among themselves, and another inflated one when in charge of tribal soldiery.

Those with them now were easily placed, on the shabby side, with very poor boots, short men, faces a reminder of some Dolvid had ridden beside: these called themselves Jai and Ntara-golal, but were obviously a species of what, in the Army of the West, had always been collectively called Froghul, and when they spoke among themselves in tribal language, Dolvid could catch a Froghulú word he knew here and there. Their tunics were plain cloth of a coarse weave, but the officers, tall, with the broad-shouldered cavalry build, wore tunics very much the cut of ones worn in Kargul, rather longer than with other cavalries, less weatherworn areas showing where light-blue facings of the Karguli Provincial Cavalry had been removed.

When these indications of origin were noted, Antighal, who had evidently concluded lives, including his, were in no imminent danger, said nothing, but rolled his eyes expressively.

He was also first to chuckle when asked what customers the *atarlal* had expected to find in the sparsely-populated and impoverished northern Lunu Tezh' for *raminat* leaves or *ôdul* globes, the costly cargo of the pack-ponies.

This was play, but there was serious business to be done. "Tovakh baKargul," and the name had an instant alerting effect, "has vowed to treat as deserters any men formerly of his provincial cavalry now following his son. My proper course is to hold you here while enquiries are made. If his records were to show he was the lord to whom your first allegiance was sworn, it would be my duty, as agent of the acting *nim'*, and as *Bôdhrai* of the realm, to turn you over to his notions of justice, which are said to be rough-hewn."

Antighal cleared his throat. "Are you saying, sir, this might not be what you choose to do?"

"The Colony is famed for its hospitality, as the acting *nim'* for her forbearance — " a somewhat risky but potentially rewarding course beginning to germinate. "But you would have to be more forthcoming than so far."

Shudarr, permitted as a reward to remain when his four principal catches were reassembled for light food, was earnest about the violation of sovereignty this incursion represented, and puzzled by Dolvid's high spirits. But for Dolvid, who had maintained from the first the *Mankh'* could not be kept from communication with Kamin-Tolagh, the incident was hard to consider much more momentous than catching small boys making an unauthorized short-cut across a farmer's fields — though whether the *rabhsai*, prompted by Elamirr, would take it so lightly was another matter. A larger armed force, one strong enough to risk a fight, would be a serious violation; Kamin-Tolagh would have to be warned. He would probably deny all knowledge of the captive officers, who were going to have to pay with documentary evidence for being sheltered from Tovakh's wrath.

Delightful, too, when both *atarlal* vigorously denied *Mankh'* ownership of the valuables with the pack-train. He and the *ramidu* had merely been travelling, at-Dhanurai maintained, at the same time as a shipment of goods paid for, their delivery complete when landed at the little harborage Shudarr had found. These things, then, were the property of unauthorized intruders, legitimately forfeit, a windfall for the Colony. The generous shipment of *raminat* was particularly welcome.

"Unfair, really," to Shudarr a week later, "to sustain my reputation for clemency by making use of Tovakh's for the opposite."

Shudarr's face suggested he was indifferent to such niceties. "You achieved your purpose, Master."

He assented with a nod. It was just six days short of Halving, and they were riding to Kamsilat where they would embark for the Mainland to celebrate that most genial of holidays, New Year of the Fruitful Earth, as sometimes called.

In Dolvid's possession was a signed document where the two
military men admitted they were officers in the armies of
Kargusai, acting under orders when they led troops knowingly
within borders of the Lunu Tezh'. He was nervous about the
effect of this admission on the newly-unpredictable temper of
Rodlakh, who had to understand the promise by which their
signatures had been obtained, not to surrender them to Tovakh,
was binding and irrevocable. The younger officer, who was
married, wanted only to return to his wife and child, but
Antighal, a bachelor, was far from anxious to rejoin Kamin
Tolagh, and had innocently asked what rank he could hold if
enlisted in the Army of the West. Confirming Dolvid's
assessment, he admitted he had been no higher than a file-leader
before his squadron was broken up to provide officers over tribal
troops.

On the other side of Shudarr, Orbanak, who had brought part
of Dolvid's escort down from the Frontier, was puzzled. "I
cannot understand why Kamin-Tolagh would take such a risk.
There was no need." Rodlakh's brother was infinitely more
cheerful than last year when he had been wrenched away from
his Morulis to join the Army of the West; Dolvid, remembering
very well what it was to be eighteen and obsessed with a married
woman, had never belittled Orbanak's pain; if such agonies
became laughable in later life, memory was false, not those
consuming feelings.

With little spare time for brooding, Orbanak had quickly lost
his listless air, the defeated sag of his shoulders; patrols on
Landegh and the jocular, unpolished life of Drin Navuna tanned
and toughened him; he was said to have a regular bed-friend in
Kreshavu, and after three seasons it seemed safe to allow him a
return to the province of which he was nominal overlord.

"*Asai*, it must irk Kamin-Tolagh to deal with the *Mankh'* by
the roundabout route, using Hrin vessels out of Thenimala.
Then, too, he may have half wished to provoke some incident."

"Is he looking for war?" Shudarr, shoulders unconsciously
squaring.

Orbanak was subtler than his friend. "If I were *rabhsai*, I
would not force men to commit crimes so as to achieve
recognition."

Said with humor, but Shudarr punched hard at his shoulder.
"I've told you before," only half-joking. "'*If I were* rabhsai' is no

game for one in your position — not with the history of your House."

A well-taken point, if the manner made Dolvid wince, but the young men were completely at ease with each other; contrary to Shumat, who complained his son's foolishness was doubled in Orbanak's company, Dolvid did not think either a bad influence on the other.

When he had left Kamsilat, short weeks ago, the forest had been all shadow, brown of bare branches, with somber evergreens rising behind. Now the leafing was under way; the long, grassed hillside where Onebhal had ridden to a brave death in the Jinzai War again sprinkled with wild-flowers, white, blue, pink and butter-yellow, while in the Great House grounds buddings of maple, scarlet and rust, and cooler colors of crocus had all come at once with the chalky yellow traceries of willows bent over the Navu widening to its estuary, plum-blossom and the waxy cream of horse-chestnut not far behind.

Aëlu, alerted by the bell rung at the gateway, was on the Great House steps to greet them, and ever-hovering doubt as to whether Orbanak, as guest, was prince or merely squadron-leader, was unwittingly dispelled by Shudarr, who, flouting precedence, dismounted first, and grasped Aëlu's proffered hand.

After welcomes, Aëlu's first words were, "A parcel of books arrived for you. Oh, an official dispatch, also — " another inversion of precedence, and Dolvid realized she had guessed how he kept in touch with Âna's views.

He was obliged to read the *rabhsai*'s message first, while Orbanak and Shudarr were conducted to their guest-rooms and baths.

"Rodlakh has gone mad."   With Dolvid's thoughts on *rabhsayum* bordering on disaffection, if not outright treason, the *rabhsai* had written to be sure both he and Aëlu would be at Kadon Dinul for Halving, on which day Dolvid was to be publicly proclaimed and invested to mark his elevation to rank of hereditary *nimu*, making him the equal of provincial overlords of the Great Families.

"A peace-offering?" Aëlu ventured.

"A strange one, then. He knows quite well the only peace-offering I want; standing of a true *Bôdhrai*, opportunity to reconsider policies on which I was not consulted."

"But you are not going to refuse this?" — caution as much as query, and he thought admiringly there were few men who could be certain, as he was, such a question by a wife was free of concern for her own position.

He exhaled loudly. An almost unheard-of honor, a rank no one had been raised to since Saidhan, sixty years ago, and Saidhan had been born into the Great Families, not son to a book-minder, grandson to a chandler, as Dolvid was.

To forestall embarrassment, Rodlakh presumably had been prudent enough to sound out members of the Council, whose two-thirds approval this would require. Dolvid himself, of course, could not have voted, and Aëlu, who sat for the Colony, would also have been expected to disqualify herself; Orbanak had not yet taken his seat as *Nim'* of the Paowan, so it would have taken only the four votes of the remaining *nimul* to block the proposal, and that was assuming assent by the Patriarch. He did not think Tovakh, or his constant ally, Vinilat of Dramal, would easily have agreed, but Daënakh of Ân, who never forgot a mention of him in a gracious footnote in the *Song of Tales*, could have broken ranks, and carried with him his brother, Laënakh of Nîv: with no actual overlordship available, the change was purely titular, without effect on composition of the Council.

Mental thumb-twiddling, to distract himself from anger at the intended honor. The title he had no need for, and the money it brought with it — Rodlakh wrote about `grants and revenues to enable you to maintain state appropriate to this title — '* made the whole thing seem a monstrous bribe, or (more accurately) a ransom for the conscience of a *rabhsai*.

"Impossible for him to see it in that light. Your refusal would be a slap in the face; he would be hurt, disappointed, and then inconsolably angry, as anyone is at the rejection of what he thinks is a loving gift."

Independently but fervently, Âna agreed; Dolvid found her letter concealed in a dull and inaccurate book about boar-hunting, and she anticipated his thoughts. `You feel like declining this honor,' she wrote. `I can hear your huffiest voice:* Why should I be *Nim'* Dolvid when as *Bôdhrai* I am disregarded? *But our first thought, Rodlakh's and mine, was for your children. The half-brother in your household will be called* Asai; *they should not be of lesser rank.'*

In an aside, she added the information she was to bear another child late in summer. Always in the past she had used a degree of caution in this private correspondence, which was not ideally safe from unfriendly eyes, but here she was more than indiscreet: `*Refusal would be disastrous,*' she continued. `*He knows he has wronged you, but cannot find a way to say so — to himself, much less to you.*'

After apparently finishing the letter, Âna had reopened it to add fresh and fascinating news; a man of the city, Altorri, whose past reputation was a swampland of dubious, near-criminal and unprovably lawless activities, had at last been convicted in an elaborate conspiracy to defraud, in which he had very convincingly forged a deed and several old conveyances to falsify ownership of an Old Town house. With his confederates, Altorri would shortly be fulfilling his life's destiny, as an Island eel-salter, and the case would be only moderately interesting, except Âna, visiting the Bronze Residence to check on progress of the new, larger edition of the book by Tellis, had been informed quietly by one of the scribes Altorri had once or twice had dealings with Elamirr; the scribe had seen them together at Market Gate hostelry, and assumed Altorri worked as an informant.

`*Interestingly,*' she wrote, `*E. had meetings with a known forger, in the very place where he obtained the supposed letter of Lavsila's. Also, E. never once mentioned dealings with Altorri, although Rodlakh constantly discussed the case in his presence during the trial. The least hint Altorri had been of service to* rabhsayum *would conceivably have lessened the man's sentence; his defense, such as it was, contained nothing but idiotic denials. Your suspicion, dear Dolvid, that E. has been a* victim of fraud *may err on the side of generosity. But R. has become very impatient with my* bias *against E., and would not hear any of this from me.*'

Lastly, there came a restrained confession of her loneliness, and, moving beyond indiscretion in the direction of recklessness, some incautious endearments.

Dolvid sat back in his chair, fingers pressed to his eyes. At such a time he most missed being at Kadon Dinul, where there were questions to be asked that Âna's position made impossible for her, things to be done that might not occur to her. For a beginning, as soon as he arrived there, Dolvid would speak personally to the Patriarch, to ensure safety of the prisoner Altorri, whose testimony might yet be needed. Quite easy to imagine Altorri had been persuaded that to bring up his dealings with Elamirr would only worsen his case, but if Elamirr had been not merely gullible but deceptive with the Market Gate Letter, it changed everything; a man who influenced policy with forged documents could not remain in the *rabhsai*'s service. Moreover, the worst lie that could be imagined, one exploiting those ancient suspicions it had been first task of this reign to move beyond; Elamirr, if guilty, would be lucky to escape the Island himself.

He was a victim of the same dark spirit (*Hranakh* was its name at the *Mankh'*) that rode his hated Kamin-Tolagh, a greed for power that could justify any means. In a way, Kamin-Tolagh was easier to understand, bred in the slow-simmered rancors of Kargul, weaned on the frustrated ambitions of Tovakh, tortuous broodings of Petakoi. In Burantal, the youth of Elamirr had been surrounded by so much decency, it was almost necessary to believe there must be some error in Âna's careful account: Elamirr's two uncles of the Marionette Guild, who had wept at the death of Sebhal, and sheltered his companions at great risk to themselves, Dolvid's old friends, Untimarr and Morú, parents of Morulis.

For whom he spared a moment's sadness; after all, it may have been a mistake to bundle Orbanak off to the Colony; she might soon be in need of a well-placed friend. In marriage, with all the Heartland at her feet, she had chosen not her wealthiest admirer, nor highest in rank, nor handsomest and surely not the most polished, but what must have appeared to her the safest, a man of her native city, his family already interwoven with hers in past intermarriage, friendship and shared enterprises — though more intimate, roughly the same reasons as had influenced Dolvid in his choice of a trustworthy assistant.

Is something wrong, Master?" Arvat, bustling in to see if a scribe was needed, was alarmed to see him with tears on his face.

"Time. Time is wrong. It passes."

With that in mind, for one day Dolvid let business of the realm go to ruin in its own way, and enjoyed his family, startling the young officers with the wildness of his romping in the Great House grounds, becoming dishevelled, breathless and keenly happy. Shudarr, he noted, was comfortable instructing Sedukh in how to use a small bow, but otherwise rather shy of the children, whereas Orbanak met them with an unforced earnestness, and had an enviable gift for finding meaning in obscure prattle; Ayalis, now past four, followed him everywhere.

Nothing quite took away a feeling he would have to pay for this holiday, and as the evening meal was being served, dispatches from Banakit overtook him, bringing with them the doomed feeling he had tried to escape for a few hours. The news Idmas sent was terrible.

On the second day following Dolvid's departure, which was to say, yesterday, an exhausted messenger had arrived at the official residence, having travelled without rest all the way from a home on the western borderlands of Lunu Tezh'. Though agitated, the man gave a coherent report; his hamlet had been attacked from across the purely notional border by a company of fierce mounted bowmen.

A day or two earlier, the village had given temporary refuge to a band of about twenty-five to thirty fugitives, men, women and children, who had crossed the dry lands of south Landegh with wholly inadequate supplies of food and water. Their leaders, about ten or a dozen younger men, wore military tunics, from which, however, all badges of identification or rank had been removed. Though their language was recognizably related to that of their hosts, dialects were too dissimilar for much to be learned, except these strangers came from the south and west, where they had served a lord called Nôs-Ralaïn (Idmas apologized for his attempt at the spelling).

Living where they did, on the edge of wilderness, the villagers were not without weapons or some notion of defending themselves, but had no answer for the ferocity of the attack that came, after they had ignored a demand, made, though heavily accented, in ordinary language of the realm, that they drive out the strangers they were sheltering. After a brief, vicious battle, mounted bowmen had rounded up surviving refugees, including women and children, most with some injury. Disarming the men and binding their arms, they led all away at sword's point, and vanished into the west, leaving behind nine either dead or too near death to be moved, even in malevolence.

Worse, they had killed three and wounded ten villagers, burned to the ground a hut where many of the fugitives had been sheltered, and finished by carrying off not only food, but anything else of value they took a fancy to. The account of Idmas concluded with his report that he had also sent word to Captain Bradhinal at Drin Navuna, and on his own authority had reinforced the regular patrol to two squadrons, and directed it to the scene of this appalling incident.

Dolvid recalled himself; he was standing in the high transverse front hall of the Great House, messenger, expectant nearby, still unrefreshed. After summoning a servant to take the man for food and drink, he stood, head bowed, dismay flooding in to drown his first anger. On the double scale he had once proposed to Âna, he recognized he must have become a better *Bôdhrai*, having declined so much as a human being. Not that he had lost all compassion; he could vividly imagine the lives of impoverished yet obviously hospitable villagers broken into by the raiders, the fear, pain and then grief — yet almost before outrage, he had gone to assessing the effect on others, on the *rabhsai*, to the posturing the incident would justify, larger dangers inherent in either underestimating or exploiting its effects.

Not able to guess what had saddened him, Aëlu, having left their guests to find him, came and took his hands. "What is it?"

"War," grimly. "Unless — " he could not say, unless what. As before, with Shudarr's prisoners, there could be no reasonable doubt the mounted archers were Kamin-Tolagh's men.

"The first were deserters, obviously," Shudarr said. "From the famous tribal squadrons, like the lot we captured." There had been no object in concealing from the two guests a border-violation the whole Colony, the entire realm, would shortly be discussing.

"Their desertion, if such it was," testing feelings here, "Is no justification for the attack."

"None, *Asai*."

"Not *Asai*," for the thousand-and-second, and perhaps last time. He noted Orbanak's grin, and wondered whether he had been informed about the proposed *nimum*.

"Master, I meant to say, Master. This would be an open act of war, wouldn't it?" Like others of his age and calling, the prospect did not daunt Shudarr.

"With a friendly neighbor," Orbanak pondered, "the correct course, where lawbreakers or deserters cross a border, would be to ask through an embassy for their arrest and return."

Dolvid agreed, though he knew of no such case in long memory. "If it were the Hrin, for example, who made the request, before handing back fugitives, we would try to determine for ourselves whether those who had sought refuge with us had broken laws, or whether a private vengeance was being pursued."

"Not entirely Kamin-Tolagh's fault," Aëlu, quietly, "he does not have that recourse. He has approached us for a treaty."

"Not to say, that justifies killing of the innocent, or the destruction of their property," Orbanak said, and Aëlu nodded, aware he was not rebuking her, but merely developing her thought, which was not far from his own `if I were rabhsai' remark of two days ago.

"Well," Shudarr pronounced. "The Army of the West is ready."

Let him think so. Bradhinal, true, could put forty squadrons in the field within five days, and Shudarr's eminent father had recently assured Dolvid that in the event of war the Mainland could build to a fully-equipped strength of twenty-five mounted regiments in less than two weeks. But those numbers assumed a defensive war; for the kind of retaliation Shudarr anticipated, numbers would have to be tailored to their capacity to supply themselves and their mounts across the harsh breadth of Landegh, pack-trains would need to be assembled, and at this lean time of year stocks brought from the Mainland; by the time that was accomplished, it would be too near full heat of summer to think of launching a campaign where water was always scarce. A war against Kamin-Tolagh with practical objectives was six months away, at the least.

Orbanak was still very reflective. "Monstrous, men and women under our protection have been killed and injured; a realm is nothing if it cannot keep its subjects safe. To violate our borders under arms is a crime in itself. But it is strange to me thousands could die in our desire to right those wrongs."

"What, then?" Shudarr challenged. "You say yourself, weakness makes us a nothing. If Kamin-Tolagh isn't taught we're able to punish crime, he'll hold us in contempt, and worse will come."

"When worse comes, I am ready to fight, but Kamin-Tolagh's opinion means nothing to me."

"You're a soldier. You've sworn oaths to guard the realm and its people."

"Soldiers are our people, too. Is it guarding the realm to charge like a goaded bull, headlong into a war where who-knows-how-many of our best men — "

Dolvid, at a glance from Aëlu, rapped a knuckle on the table. "Your pardon, *Asai*, but we do not permit controversy at our meals. To sum up: it is clear Kamin-Tolagh must be shown he cannot violate our borders and assail our subjects with impunity." He turned to Shudarr. "And we must hope and strive for a way short of war to teach that lesson plainly; war is last resort, not first. Try the lobster."

He wanted to be alone with Aëlu, so he could think out loud, but Orbanak contrived to linger after Shudarr, amply fed, had withdrawn.

"I think we have puzzled your friend. To him, it must seem as if we were all trying to minimize an outrage."

"He never had the pleasure of sleeping at the *Mankh'.*" Orbanak, who had spent two years under the care or restraint of the former Patriarch, was aware both his host and hostess were *Atarlum*-trained. "So his thoughts still go in straight lines. But there will be more than enough voices whipping up anger over this crime. Can we be kept from war?"

"Is it so easy to read my face?" He had tried to mask his gloom, steadily gathering through the meal, but had not thought Orbanak so keen.

The young man laughed. "Your task needs no translation. My brother, whom we honor, is in most things sanest man alive, but Kamin-Tolagh is his madness. You would prefer a way to bring him this news that did not cause armies to march in an hour."

"Kamin-Tolagh, you see, can go to earth among the Hrin, and to ferret him out could be beyond the entire resources of the realm. They have more ships, and may be better seamen. Two realms could bleed to death, in a war that cannot be ended."

Aëlu said, "Is it possible he wants a war? They say he contrived provocations against the Hrin, to make them attack him."

"What Kamin-Tolagh wants is beyond speculation — " invaded by his old vision of *rabhsai* and self-styled emperor gripped in a force that, outside all choice, meant them to duel to the death. "Any conceivable intention of Kamin-Tolagh's in this, beyond the recovery and punishment of fugitives, is a remarkably stupid one."

Orbanak said, "If there is one small gleam in a dark night, this raid will not win new admirers for Kamin-Tolagh within the realm."

A nod. Policies pursued since appearance of the forged letter had done their best to make it come true, and from his rueful expression Orbanak was regretting how Rodlakh's intransigence had only advanced Kamin-Tolagh's cause with the Families.

"Two gleams in the dark, *Asai*. I had not realized till now we were such allies. In our loyalty," he emphasized.

"In our loyalty," fervently, with the beginnings of a blush.

When he had left, Aëlu said, "But Elamirr is going to be all for war."

"First, I think, he will renew his call for repressive measures against Kamin-Tolagh's potential adherents in the Heartland — we are going to hear again about the kin-law. No matter; the day of his influence is practically done." Letting her imagine his source, he told her what had happened, and as he did so, his proper course became clear. "The reason Rodlakh renewed his ban against dealings with Kamin-Tolagh," he said, "was a letter we know to have been a forgery."

"*Know*? Can it be proved?"

"Not perfectly, perhaps, if Altorri will not admit it." The rest of Âna's evidence, while thoroughly convincing to Dolvid, was short of the objective ideal: her informant at the Old Bronze Residence was Orimat, unashamedly one of Dolvid's loyalists, whose dislike for Elamirr and the new men he had brought in was no secret.

"By your reading, Rodlakh seized on the letter only as an excuse for doing what he wanted to anyway."

"But he could not admit that."

Aëlu frowned on, till she saw where this was leading. "No," decisively. "You are not going to the West."

"I must."

"Too dangerous. If Kamin-Tolagh out of some whim let you survive, Rodlakh never would. Not in office, that is."

Dolvid explained: he was counting on the *rabhsai* being abashed when he learnt the truth about Elamirr, and on Kamin-Tolagh's men having gone beyond their orders in attacking the Lunu Tezh' hamlet. If Kamin-Tolagh could be convinced it was the only way to save his fragile empire from ruinous war, he might be induced into a written apology, and the giving of monetary compensation, as well as assurances for the future. Rodlakh could privately condemn such a settlement as unauthorized (as it would be), but with the opinion of the Families to consider after exposure of Elamirr, he could not risk a public repudiation. "I think, in any case, this is going to be my last act as *Bôdhrai*."

"Oh, now — " she leaned to him to kiss his temple.

"I was never suited for it. I do not have stomach for the hard decisions — for making men die."

Aëlu's only answer was a steady gaze, but at last she said, "What is Kamin-Tolagh's reward for giving you what you ask him?"

"Freedom from threat of imminent war. I can't say; it could be the necessary condition before negotiation — before any chance of being recognized as ruler over his conquests."

"Recognition by Rodlakh? You would consider making concessions in his name, without his express sanction? Dolvid."

"Who else is there with the smallest hope of making it work? I have dealt with Kamin-Tolagh before; he knows I do not try trickery, and Rodlakh — " He silenced himself.

"Owes debts, which as a last tile you would remind him of."

"Something like that."

"No," after considering. "Too many risks."

"Against one far worse danger." Perhaps a muddled memory from history, Saidhan and Tobhsila settling the War of the Widowed, but he saw their two descendants, Rodlakh and Kamin-Tolagh, sword to sword in a morning meadow, and could not glimpse the outcome.

"What makes you think you are the one man appointed to save us all?" she taunted, virtually echoing words of Khalú, many years ago, and here the beginning of a rare quarrel. Aëlu additionally accused him of courting danger for its own sake, of wanting the year always to be 2942, with its intoxication of great and desperate deeds, reminding him that then he was childless and divorced, with the right to gamble with his unconnected life. Dolvid's counter-arguments, that there was no real personal danger, and it was worth any risk to prevent war, tended to weaken rather than complement each other, but this was a pointless dispute; his mind was made up, and Aëlu abandoned her objections when she saw they would not change it. She ended in his arms, with only the faintest detectable residue of reproach in her tender provocations.

His attempt at sleep kept many themes churning in his head, till he rose early, convinced there was a way to prove the Market Gate forgery. While morning mist was undisturbed, an inscrutable blank where the view to harbor and estuary should be, he rode to wake Arvat, now leasing the pleasant house built by Sett, Âna's uncle, when he was a frequent visitor to Kamsilat on trading trips. There, Dolvid excited a small, shrill dog, and woke a small child with his hammering at the door, before a sleepy girl-servant came grumbling to answer, her mouth dropping open when she saw who their caller was. Behind, in lamplight, the slight figure of Arvat was tilted over for a view of the entrance, and behind him, in the door to what must be the main bedroom, his small wife had stooped farther to see past him. She was a quiet, precariously pretty, painfully bashful woman, part-Froghuli in heritage. She was pregnant again.

Arvat found a dressing-gown, and came forward, pulling it on. "Master. Is there trouble?"

Dolvid did not waste time. "The letter from Elamirr," as Arvat led the way to a comfortable room next to the enclosed courtyard. "When he had made use of Altorri's forgery — you still have it?"

"Forgery?" his bewilderment was, in a sense, genuine: those engaged in saving the realm from suicidal dreams of sharing did not in their private minds make use of forgeries.

"The document," Dolvid clarified, "Elamirr had manufactured to depict Kamin-Tolagh's true intentions when he talked about peace and friendship; `half-ape advisors to a mongrel lord,' that letter."

"Lavsila's letter."

A nod. "Yes, the one Lavsila omitted to write for himself."

That brought tentative beginning of a smile, though quickly cancelled, as if Arvat had thought for one instant Dolvid was joining the conspiracy. Then: "Master, all Elamirr's letters dealing with policy I destroy." He recognized this constituted an admission, and began to make the best of it. "At his behest. Not that there is anything to hide, Master, it's only discretion. I burn them all."

"You do not." Here, he was quite confident. With the assistance of men like Arvat, Elamirr was going to make himself

Bôdhrai, but he had to promise his helpers some reward, and Arvat was too canny not to hold on to documents that would make sure those promises were kept.

Though taut with anxiety over this strange morning visit, Arvat had not yet seen the seriousness of the game he had been playing, and Dolvid's part was to enlighten him; use of a false document to influence critical policy was undoubtedly treason, and in failing to protest against or expose the deception, Arvat made his own guilt equal. Inasmuch as no death-penalty had been carried out in the reign of Rodlakh, or of his entire House, except for the brief Ban-Sila years, the punishment would be no worse than life-imprisonment on the Island as laborers, but Arvat could yet mitigate his offense. "The man who actually penned the forgery is, as I am sure you know, already a condemned prisoner, but once he begins to tell his story, nothing can prevent justice taking its course — nothing, certainly, can save Elamirr. You, however, just have time to escape the worst."

"We have known each other so many years, Master." They had, and a cold stare silently advised him not to pursue that theme. Largely because of whose son and whose brother he was, Dolvid had taught Arvat, employed him, overlooked his failings, his fits of petulance, shielded him from his father's murderers and personally seen to his smuggling off to safety of the Colony and a post with Saidhan; at the end of the Jinzai War had given him his fervent wish to be brought back to Kadon Dinul — in return for which Arvat had worked to help Elamirr supplant Dolvid as *Bôdhrai*. "This time, I can help you only so far as you allow me to, if you assist me, withholding nothing."

Almost at once, from a hiding place in the back room, he had much more than he wanted, packets of letters, kept in order by date, composed, in Elamirr's familiar, spiky writing, using the simplest of all replacement-cyphers, which a practised eye could take in at a glance.

Ignoring lurid and tempting bypaths, Dolvid rapidly found two letters on the right subject, either completely damning, penned with an arrogance eventually pitiable: everywhere apparent was Elamirr's contempt for all those who failed to share his belief in the universal Owani conspiracy, his horribly genuine, poisoned conviction he was serving the best interests of the realm. In the letter describing his use of the Market Gate document, he referred to '*the dream-world of one you know better than I, which can ruin us all, with the willing help of the*

Rabhsayu, *though she is of our blood.* The earlier letter actually enclosed a text approximating the forgery, asking Arvat to suggest improvements.

Oddly, exposed to all the insulting references to himself, Dolvid's anger began to shift away from the purely personal. "Why?" he asked Arvat, who, unable to sit still, was palely pacing. "Why have you made yourself a part of this hatred?"

The small man reached for some dignity. "You are forgetting, Master. Your people killed my father."

"No people did," angrily. "A man called Zhinladh did. My race was the same then as it is now; I was your father's friend, and I helped you then. Faëdhal was endlessly generous with his time, from Saidhan you had nothing but kindness; Aëlu has treated you well, and your sister married Rhunilat. Am I supposed to condemn all your people, because Bolan was a false friend to me?"

"It is no crime to receive letters," with a sullen shift of his ground.

"In most cases, that is true — " going on to suspend Arvat from his duties at the Great House, and warn him not to attempt to leave Kamsilat, nor communicate with Elamirr.

The pile of letters remained, containing, who could say what other treasons; clearly his duty to the realm was to seize them and have them sifted through, line by line.

"If I were you, I would burn these now, as you promised. But do not count on Elamirr being any more true to his word; we may well find he has preserved all your replies."

Nothing had been so devastating to Arvat. Leaving him shaken, Dolvid remounted his waiting horse, perplexed whether he was satisfied with his day so far, or disgusted with himself.

"You will need an escort." Shudarr left no doubt as to his candidate for the post of its commander.

"A small one, a half-squadron, I think. But you are expected at Kadon Dinul."

"So are you, Master."

"Your father would not forgive me for taking you into such unnecessary danger."

"To Lady Aëlu, you said there was no danger."

"I meant, for me," unconvincingly. "I am not going to tempt Kamin-Tolagh with Shudarr, son to the Captain of Armies, for a prize hostage."

"If he wants a hostage," with a laugh, "I think it would hard to do better than *Bôdhrai* to the Realm — unless you're going to take Orbanak instead of me."

"I am not." Aside from other considerations, he wanted Orbanak to go to Kadon Dinul, and use what moderating influence he possessed in softening the news.

"At my age," pugnaciously. "As I have not ceased to hear, the Captain of Armies had already singlehanded saved our realm from certain destruction in more ways than can be counted. He says I shirk responsibility, but, Hrafi! the Captain of Armies didn't do it all alone. Someone had to trust him with the task, before he could amaze the world with his prowess."

"Do not make any mistake," gently. "Your father deserves his fame."

"Yes, I know," Shudarr disarmingly confessed. "He is a true hero. But he was not denied the chance to be. I am coddled as a child, and then rebuked for childishness."

"Come with me, then," he abruptly conceded. "Choose the best and strongest of your men, and those with good mounts." It would be a lonely ride; Shudarr was good company, and Dolvid, too, was tired of hearing Shumat's carping about the boy.

The decision was accepted with a resigned envy by Orbanak, who acceded to his less adventurous part with a warning for Dolvid, not to let Shudarr try to overcome the Empire of Kargusai singlehanded. Notwithstanding their newfound alliance, it would be improper to make Orbanak into a private courier to his brother's wife, but Aëlu, without prompting, offered to place evidence taken from Arvat in Âna's hands and no others. There was a brief covering note, necessarily impersonal, explaining their provenance and how they might be used, and a message for the Patriarch asking that the prisoner Altorri not be dispatched to the south of the Island, but kept safe at the *Mankh'* for the time being, or in near-impregnable Drin b'Afon if he had already been sent to the Island. A letter, almost certainly ineffectual, for Rodlakh, laying out a version of the reasoning behind this journey to the Farther West; hardly possible to write, `*I am going,* Rabhsai, *because afraid you will do something ill-considered and disastrous if I do not.*'

Parting with Aëlu was unstrained and affectionate, with no shadow remaining from their quarrel; she said wryly, forbidding herself tears, "I should be able to manage this farewell, after so many years of practice — " a rare reference to her first marriage, to Sebhal.

With Shudarr's half-squadron, they had reached First Bridge before noon, setting as hard a pace as they dared, Dolvid's mind moving ahead, to brief rests on the road, to spare mounts and supplies at the Frontier, hardships of Landegh, to the once-known, inscrutable figure at far end of the journey. After seven years, who could tell what was left of the old, gallant Kamin-Tolagh?

35.

Kamin-Tarú said, "This is not a time of moon for me to ride so far."

"You will miss good sport," her brother cajoled. A party of Heartlanders, of whom many had come back to the Abu for Halving Day, were riding down to the Laughing Owl country for the executions. Kamin-Tolagh had been obliged to postpone them till after the spring ceremonies, but the spectacle would be worth the wait. Of men who were the twelve original deserters, eight had survived pursuit, capture and the journey back, and their deaths, extended over three days, were going to be a lesson for any man of the tribes who thought he could walk away from military service when he was tired of its hardships and dangers.

"Iruvakh," Lavsila was casual, "was asking about your intentions. He may be there."

"We shall have to outdo ourselves. I am going to begin by having the wives thoroughly flogged." Wives and near-wives, that was; two at least were choices of younger men not yet married. Of seven in all who had gone with their men, one, wounded in the fight, had died on the return journey.

"What have the wives done?" Kamin-Tarú wanted to hear.
"With those tribes, they are no different from their husbands' goods — they would have no choice whether they went or stayed, if their men were setting out for the moon."

She would never learn, he resigned himself, to think first in terms of the Empire. Here, admittedly, he had been at fault, wooing her with what she might be entertained by, failing to emphasize the underlying import. "Everything I do has a purpose. Armies are ruled by greed and fear — "

"Or honor," Lavsila suggested, "where such terms have meaning. Soldiers have to be taught to fear the consequences of cowardice or desertion above their dislike of what their duties bring, hunger, thirst, battle, the chance of wounding or death. For men bred in our heritage, of course, it should be enough they take an oath, and have their comrades beside them, but with the tribes there are no such traditions."

"Exactly." The congratulation was sardonic, though Lavsila's thoughts would have been apposite enough, if the man had ever seen battle. "Here, we have to use what they do understand, and chiefly that means pain. Some heroes of the tribes willing to risk it for their own sake may think again if desertion means pain for their women as well — and their women might do more to dissuade them."

Lavsila grunted assent. "As it is with most clans, a widow is better off than an unmarried girl, and may do better in her second marriage — where is the incentive for her to be much concerned what happens to a husband chosen for her?"

"In Hunghi's hand — " though his sister was not won over. Evidently, she enjoyed watching a flogging only with a young man under the lash.

"You have a ruler's right to discourage disloyalty," Lavsila conceded, but there was a qualification on its way: "Iruvakh says g'Asalladh' Himself has been disturbed by rumors of excesses here."

Could the Patriarch have heard about annihilation of the Hwenala? Kamin-Tolagh dismissed the thought. "Excesses? Iruvakh, when he was at the *Mankh'*, must have had his beatings, and with less object. If g'Asalladh's minions want to remain welcome, they and their Master had better learn who rules here. I have signed no treaty."

"Very true," grudgingly, and the next remark was not as much a change of subject as it seemed. "In the Paowan, maybe in all the realm, your name, I am told, is heard more and more. When Rodlakh brought in his new selective taxes, there was open talk of yours as a realm where to be Owani was not to be disfavored." Since final expulsion of Iolfrant, an added handful of young Heartlanders had arrived at Hyolenstr, but Kamin-Tolagh had heard too often about his mounting popularity with Lavsila's imagined host of allies.

"Are you telling me Owanil care what punishments I inflict on tribesmen of the Froghushei?"

"Not in the least, but they would be unhappy to hear protests of the *Mankh'* had been ignored."

"When Iruvakh, *at*-Iruvakh, has a protest, he had better make it to me, and he knows his answer. A condition of his appointment was that I alone decide what is good and necessary for the Empire. If, through softheartedness — " in a gesture of solace, he covered Tú's hand with his — "we fail to make desertion too terrifying to contemplate, what fields are *ga-Yalil* will cease to be a question, and your Heartlanders will be lucky to escape back to Rodlakh's terrible realm." A complacent house-bred pigeon, taken to the wilds, could not be taught in time to fear hawks, but Lavsila at least should recognize how precarious his safety was, and how much more so since Zelu Bablakhi. These punishments were also going to express part of what he had been obliged to suppress for the sake of policy, the anger he felt over the failure of his expedition.

The action against the Hwenala had been a regrettable piece of severity, necessary in his judgment for the wellbeing of the Empire, but not easily understood by those without his responsibilities. This, by contrast, either as just punishment or exemplary warning, was a public event, its effect improved by the size of its audience.

The site chosen was not far from the main settlement of the Laughing Owl people, the same place where the squadrons had reassembled on the day of the great firesetting. Troops on duty were drawn from all tribes, so the tale of Kamin-Tolagh's wrath would be carried everywhere; besides holiday-makers from the Abu, numbers of Laughing Owl and its neighbor tribes on each side helped enclose the wide, dusty level, where three stakes had been erected, man-high.
At these, in three batches, women first, several of them pretty enough to add zest to the spectacle, were stripped and lashed, whimpering, by Hunghi with a single apprentice. While this occupied only part of the first morning, and the whippers took care to use punishing but not killing force, Kamin-Tolagh was then obliged to postpone the start of executions for a day, to let the wives recover enough to witness the sufferings of their men. After initial disappointment, the spectators from the Abu decided they did not really mind. They had plenty of food, drink and servants with them, the rainy season, a little wetter this year, was come and gone, weather warm but not oppressive, and in these conditions, like most people who seldom have to, they made a pleasure of spending some nights under canvas. Iruvakh, after all the talk, was not among those in attendance; perhaps recalling

how at-Sholidu had been unwillingly associated with the near-flogging of Valubran, he had expressed cautious disapproval twice, first with a note to Kamin-Tolagh questioning the necessity of protracted executions, and then by leaving on an abrupt journey to the southern empire.

For the next phase, Tau-Suaka not only directed but relished taking part, as the first three condemned men were subjected to long-drawn ingenuities of torment and mutilation. The pace was unhurried, allowing each victim to regain his senses each time he fainted, but the day was marred by the death, near noon, of one man, weakened by wounds suffered at his recapture. Tau-Suaka was abjectly apologetic over the miscalculation, for which he atoned by his later inventiveness, keeping all spectators profoundly interested; some of the witnesses from the Laughing Owl had been escorted here by soldiery, but once in place there was no wavering of their attention. At the end of an instructive day, it surprised Kamin-Tolagh about half the Heartlanders said they had seen enough, and would set out for the Abu first thing. Most cited their neglected southern estates as excuse, but he suspected the otherwise ineffectual disapproval of Iruvakh had acted on weaker stomachs — what Tau-Suaka would call 'women's hearts.' Although wives were in fact prominent among those continuing to be diverted by the spectacle, and while during the day there had been some covering of faces, there were Heartland women for whom the display or the idea of pain had an effect betrayed by flared nostrils and ripening lips; the pretty, sybaritic Ondhayu, who, in he absence of Niburai, left at the Abu, had to murmur her suggestions at the ear of her husband. They absented themselves for above an hour; composing the anecdote for his sister's amusement, Kamin-Tolagh invented the detail that when they returned, Ondhayu looked much fresher than Pranúdhanai.

Yet he was once more disappointed with the Heartlanders. He did not mind their being entertained, he had invited it, but hoped at the same time for some counterbalancing solemnity, in recognition of the purpose and the lesson behind the spectacle; more might have seen it through as a necessary and instructive ritual.

Those who failed to stay a second day missed comedy, when one of the prisoners, his hamstrings deftly cut, was unbound, and tried to run away on legs that kept toppling like the stack of blocks used as a target for practise with lances; some of the soldiers laughed till they cried. Another full day was to follow, but in mid-afternoon a fast-messenger rode in from the north with a dispatch from Lavsila, containing bewildering news, a thunderbolt. Cancelling the third day's entertainment, giving Hunghi instructions to finish the executions with his whip, he made plans to ride at dawn, and scribbled a message to precede him, all the while wondering how it could be true, and what it meant: Dolvid (how was it possible?) was at the Abu.

To be exact, he was camped at the rim, or just outside its containing-wall. Freighanai, an old acquaintance from the Jinzai War, had apologetically refused permission to enter without Kamin-Tolagh's authority, and when Lavsila, returning from Larghamit, countermanded the order, it was only for Dolvid, who declined to go on alone, not through fear, but because he was not going to see his escort humiliated.

For that matter, a *Bôdhrai*, he kept telling himself, had to maintain dignity appropriate to the majesty of an offended realm. When, with a shrug, he resigned himself to one more night, at best, of sleeping on the ground, Shudarr remarked it was as well they had not brought Orbanak, who would not have been so patient. "But I told him last year, Master, even the *rabhsai*'s brother can't always sleep where he wants to."

This, a sly reference to the Morulis episode, complete with sidelong glance, Dolvid let pass without comment. He despaired of ever being an authentic dignitary; a boy young enough — exactly young enough — to be his son was breezily comfortable with him, nor did he want respect due his rank at the cost of that ease. He was not certain he had earned it; here on the gravest of errands, camped with his tiny band in sight of uncounted potentially hostile troops, and actually enjoying himself, as he had on Landegh, the campfires and crowded stars, the juddering chill of morning and its penetrating sense of life. The third day out of Drin Navuna, by what he had been told was the one unfailing source of water, they had spotted and cautiously approached the rough, untidy encampment of some hundred-odd members of a clan or small tribe, men, women, children and their dogs and goats.

Understanding no language Dolvid spoke, however slightly, they recognized the words *Army of West* and the name *Sebhal*, and after wary greetings communicated by signs and actions that they were a northern tribe returning from their winter pastures days to the south, having waited, as always, only for the blossoming of a small yellow flower; whether this was simply a sign for them of the changing season, or they had a use for the plant, Dolvid was unable to ascertain. They were pleased *jinzal* — an idea easily mimed — had become rare, and conveyed a description of their homeland as densely grassed uplands with plenty of game, and especially birds; as well as skilled linen weave, some of them wore loose waistcoats, caps or capes evidently and exquisitely made of feathers, for which thousands of birds must have paid with their lives. When Dolvid's company rode on, these people, who called themselves something like Skâbh-brao, were preparing to resume their northward trek. This glancing encounter with an unknown people from an unknown land, who in their turn knew nothing about Rodlakh, Kamin-Tolagh's empire, or disputes of rulers, an occurrence outside time, with neither prologue nor consequence, curiously gladdened him with its vivid reminder about the vastness and variousness of the world; as Shudarr thoughtfully remarked, "Plenty of room for everyone, if there wasn't any greed."

"Or envy."

Lavsila came again to bring food and solicitude, and probe ineffectually into Dolvid's purpose in coming. He had changed from the callow young man once a leader of the Heartland faction opposed to Dolvid, but his face had not aged a dozen years since then; an odd dislocation to see the pampered Heartlander here in this scoured and unordered land, odder to think of him as Khalú's husband. He showed off his intimate grasp of the realm's current affairs, remarkable in view of his long absence; baiting Dolvid a little with Elamirr's rise in esteem, and commiserating gratuitously with the difficulties of overseeing policy at Kadon Dinul from a place so distant as the Colony.

Clearly, the implication here was that Rodlakh, under Elamirr's influence, had used the vacancy at Kamsilat to exclude Dolvid from the center of power, but getting nowhere with those veiled taunts, he tried the theme of the Heartlanders who had quit Rodlakh's realm to be with Kamin-Tolagh. Dolvid responded blandly, all should be free to choose where they lived 'without coercion,' and let him make what he would of it. All the while,

Lavsila appeared to be waiting for something additional, and Dolvid was reminded of the mysterious message that had reached him about the time of those first defections, almost an offer to betray Kamin-Tolagh.   Conjectural whether the inconstant Lavsila would now repudiate or repeat that offer, and he was given no encouragement to do either.

Half an hour behind him there was a fresh arrival, a knot of soldiery that must be the Hill Froghul' tamed by Kamin-Tolagh, short, broad-shouldered men with decorated tunics and shaggy hair, bows slung at their backs. From their midst emerged a tall and graceful rider, hair burnished in early sun.   Kamin-Tarú dismounted with all her old, lithe ease, and to the apprehension of her bodyguard, the rasping displeasure of Lavsila, walked directly to Dolvid, gave him a slender hand, then slipped inside his guard to brush his cheek with soft lips.

"Well met, *Asayu*," honorific validated by Rodlakh's stubbornness over her outlawry. "The air of the West agrees with you." When he had first met her, in what was surely another life, a former age of the world, he was drawn to her, as all men were, but had not seen her as a great beauty; she had been, rather, a large-eyed sort of child-woman of powerful physical appeal. None of that had vanished, and glints of teasing still showed green in her eyes as she inclined her head to acknowledge the compliment, but she was completely a woman now, and an arresting one; Shudarr, nearby, was too well-trained to goggle, but when introduced had contracted a new stammer, while among the men of his half-squadron, the avoidance of staring was loud.

Dolvid said, "I had not appreciated by how much the realm is poorer, *Asayu*, for your continued absence."

"No flattery, now," with a quick, vanishing frown.   He noticed discontent lurking at the corners of her mouth, and wondered how long her brother had been away.

"We choose strange places for our reunions," smile returning. "How is little Orbanak?"

She was thinking of a cold and rainy day, seven years ago, when she had come across Arnan in a fishing boat, and first met the *rabhsai*'s brother. "Not little any more; he has his squadron in the Army of the West."

It was not to be imagined she would again help him reach an understanding with her brother, and yet she enjoyed skirting the edges of her old games. Lavsila making plain with his fidgeting it was time to depart, she swept Dolvid with her eyes. "Is it not cold for you by night, Master? Is a straw mattress enough between you and the hard ground?"

Very aware of the Hill Froghul' guard with their unblinking vigilance, Dolvid said, "A soft bed, *Asayu*, would only distract me from a hard purpose."

"Purpose and all, we shall make you comfortable when you come to the Abu. It will be good to have you as our guest."

"A double joy, to renew friendship," with a mute face.

When she had gone, leaving a faint scent in the warming air, Shudarr, voice held to the over-neutral, said, "So, Master. That is the lady of Kargul."

"It is very important to be cautious in our dealings here, with both men and women. We have a case to make, and while we should be civil, we must also be firm, and avoid excess of friendliness."

Shudarr, trying to steer a similarly diplomatic course, reminded he had instructed him to much that effect when they began their journey, and again when they made their last camp on the edge of Landegh.

"Yes, but I have to keep it in mind myself," with a laugh.

After two nights, and tediously inactive days, Freighanai came again at midday with a couple of tribal squadrons, not Hill Froghul', to say Kamin-Tolagh was expected before nightfall. The fast-messenger who had brought that word also had instructions Dolvid and his company were to be accommodated within the Abu, and supplied with anything they needed.

For the entry, a show of strength had been mustered outside the arched gateway at the western end, a further half-dozen squadrons, so Dolvid's small escort rode in an avenue of lances that closed behind them.

"Well, but some," Shudarr muttered, "don't shape as well as the best of them — those levies there — " indicating with slightest tilt of his head a squadron more motley than the rest, slouched in the saddle with lances held at every angle. "To say nothing about their nags."

"Silent," Dolvid said. Freighanai, who rode at head of the lead squadron, had pulled aside and was waiting so he could ride beside them and point out the sights of the Abu.

His tale of miraculous transformations had to be accepted on trust by one who had not seen this place as Lunu Jinzalladhiyu.

The day was dull, warm but lead-skyed, and the long barracks buildings at the near end, which Freighanai said had been improved beyond recognition, still seemed gloomy to Dolvid; on the dusty flat nearby, more cavalry in the rudimentary stages of training were being exercised, and the growing plots beyond, intersected by little irrigation ditches, were not seen at their best, though there was no need to doubt Freighanai's word they were a valuable advance over the tough and useless scrub that had formerly covered most of the valley floor.

"Over by the south wall," with a wave, "Iruvakh — at-Iruvakh, that would be — has grapes started. Here, you see, *Bôdhrai*, as he says, it's not finding the sun as much as a few hours' shade from the worst of it. He's got his water, thanks to Lavsila's contraptions."

A moment later he pointed out white buildings, flat-roofed, on the approaches to the enclosed mound, saying they housed servants, and had once been the women's quarters, and Dolvid with a strange shiver realized they were quarters of *the* women, the *jinzai*-mothers; the obscene place where Dorrmas had let his men run mad, site of the massacre.

As they made the climb up to the gateway, Dolvid asked whether the settlement on higher ground had a separate name.

"Kargusai Tâl," Freighanai, with half a shrug. "Some of the men call it — " and he broke off, as if recognizing impropriety. Then, because he and Dolvid had campaigned together, he finished the thought: "They call it Kaminú-Kamilá, only to have a nickname for it, *Bôdhrai*."

Where main ways crossed, outside the most imposing of the buildings, there was a formal address of welcome from Lavsila to be endured, in two minutes contriving to make four separate mentions of Kamin-Tolagh's absolute sovereignty here, implying his permitting this visit was an unprecedented example of omnipotent condescension. That done, less momentously, though still flanked by the Hill Froghul' guards, he informed Dolvid this was the official residence here in the north, and a suite of rooms was available for Dolvid's use. Alternatively, having shown a preference for remaining with his escort, he with his entire party could be housed in another comfortable building nearby, until recently that of Captain Kambanal, become the *Sranim'* Kambanal, and permanently resident in the Southern Empire, his province.

Without hesitation, ignoring the gibe directed against his presumed nervousness, Dolvid chose the second alternative. Already he had been repelled by first inklings of a strangeness here, both a presence and a lack he could not identify or define, only wanting to keep a distance from his hosts, and in contact with men like himself.

The house to which they were conducted was not a hundred paces from the official residence, but faced the east-west axis; there were stables, and ample accommodation for two dozen men sleeping six to a bedroom, with Dolvid and Shudarr sharing a fifth. With most of the older and larger buildings here, it was constructed to a style recalling those of Kadon Dinul before the rebuildings of Plakhsila *Kímukoi*, and many of its furnishings, though evidently made locally, also preserved the somewhat somber and overwrought fashion from the reign of Plakhat II and his son Plakhan. Other than light screens well-made of woven rushes, and a few crude but curiously attractive earthen pots, there was nothing incontrovertibly of tribal manufacture, but there were four tribal servants who said they were Gudi-la, and, though they did not understand ordinary language of the realm, astonishingly spoke a form of the Owanilú they called *Hwanió*, rudimentary and corrupt, yet more of the Old Tongue than was understood by all but three or four of Shudarr's men. The servants made available light food, drinks and baths; the men of Shudarr's squadron scrubbed hands, faces and upper bodies in the warmed water provided, but besides Dolvid, only Shudarr and a young file-leader named Varromar actually immersed.

Freighanai had said Kamin-Tolagh was expected before nightfall; after food, Dolvid, wearying of Shudarr's inexhaustible speculation as to the significance of everything they had seen and heard, withdrew to a small private room, comfortably appointed for reading or writing, and passed time making needless refinements in the four closely-written pages he had prepared for Kamin-Tolagh, but which might never be seen; they would have no point if, as was possible, he flatly rejected all responsibility for the assault on the Lunu Tezh' village. Mid-afternoon, Varromar, who had been using an upper side-window to keep watch on the official residence, came to report the arrival of riders. His description of the chief one adequately resembled

Kamin-Tolagh, but although there was considerable subsequent coming and going, no message arrived.

Evening arrived early under the shadowing walls of this great depression, and as light was fading the summons came, brought by a man Dolvid knew, the roundfaced Pivrekhan, young, but permanently bent and hobbling from the dangerous wounds received in the Jinzai War; enforced lack of exercise had made him paunchy, but he was otherwise much the same; peculiarly disappointing a man could come so close to death, and emerge from the experience no more grown-up than before. Though he obviously could no longer hope, as once he had tried, to imitate everything Kamin-Tolagh did, Pivrekhan still spoke the name of his master as a spell to keep off all harm. He would, if convenient, meet with the *Bôdhrai* now.

Moderately cordial, Dolvid thought; if Kamin-Tolagh had wanted to keep a distance he would have waited overnight, but to come here in person would have been a genuinely friendly gesture. He matched equivocations by sending Pivrekhan back with the reply he would be there in half an hour.

"Master, have you decided how we're to address him?" Shudarr asked while, fully ready, they wasted some time.

A question pondered for days, without finding an ideal answer. "Quite proper to call Kamin-Tarú `*Asayu*,' but her brother, as one outlawed, can hold no rank in our realm — not a point I would throw in a man's face where he is plainly master. Yet as an official and a soldier of Rodlakh's *rabhsayum*, which does not recognize his overlordship here, we cannot use whatever title he has given himself."

"They call him the *Lord* Kamin-Tolagh. But I may not have to address him. He will speak to you, Master."

"Your father and he were friends. Well," deciding heavily. "We shall say *Asai*, on the grounds he has had no opportunity to dispute the justice of his outlawry."

A groan of bemusement. "I am glad I'm only a soldier."

Any parallel question about deferences was solved, for the time being, by Kamin-Tolagh himself. As through dusk, with a two-man escort, Dolvid and Shudarr approached the double-doors of the official residence, he appeared, and came down four low steps, arms outspread. "Welcome, *Bôdhrai*." He seized his hand in a warm grasp. "It has been too long."

"In every sense, *Asai*," aware nothing was spontaneous where rival powers jockeyed.

Kamin-Tolagh led the way into a well-lighted transverse great hall in the Owani style, and a half-dozen of the Hill Froghul guards were nearby.

"You will remember Shudarr Shumats-son, *Asai*."

A quick turn. "I would not have known him. You are twice the size. And a squadron-leader!" He cuffed Shudarr's shoulder. "A brave *péfrapravádai* you've turned into."

"My thanks, *Asai*."

"And why not? Your father is the best I'll ever ride with."

Shudarr, without apparent shyness, thanked him again. Kamin-Tolagh looked very fit, face deeply tanned, frame taut and supple as ever. The light eyes were more mobile than remembered, glancing all about, not apprehensively, but like a rope-walker or a juggler just about to do his best trick, making sure his entire audience is attentive, although here there were no others but the two escorts.

"How is Shumat, then — not yet bored to madness keeping books and counting blankets? Your own work, *Bôdhrai*, how does that go?" not disposed to wait for answers. "Your writings, I mean. Well, we have old things and new things to catch up with — there is plenty here to interest an historian."

"I am eager to learn, *Asai*. But we are here on matters of grave urgency. We have to avert war."

Kamin-Tolagh stopped dead, eyebrows up, then gave a reassuring laugh. "We are at peace, so far as neighbors can be who never talk. *Bôdhrai*, the Abu is waiting to greet you. We could not manage a banquet at such short notice, but we can feast in the fashion of the Hrin. Come."

As he turned away, Dolvid put a hand on his forearm, and noted how swiftly the nearest of the Hill Froghul', their evident chief, went to his hilts. He was a menacingly ugly man, with a creased face and dark, baleful eyes, his action exactly a watchdog raising its hackles and giving a low growl.

"*Asai*, this cannot be put off. A violation of the sovereign territory of Arbhal is no occasion for a feast."

The eyes came back, and they were wary; instantly obvious the breezy good fellowship had been a planned tactic. "We have had no report of such a violation. You must be mistaken."

Dolvid had his own strategy formed. "You have never heard of officers named Antighal and Drusilakh? They tell us they are in your service, *Asai*, and I am carrying a letter from Drusilakh to his wife, here at the Abu. Could he be mistaken?"

"Antighal and Drusilakh... " The relief on Kamin-Tolagh's face was absurdly plain. "They have had escort duties, as I recall. I suppose they could have strayed into your territory."

"I have in my possession a written admission, signed by both officers, that they were in the Lunu Tezh' knowingly and under orders, *Asai*. We have also captured the landing-place you have maintained on the shore of Arnan, as well as a band of tribal auxiliaries."

"If what you say is true," slowly. "Someone will have to be admonished. But war, *Bôdhrai*? you see a cause of war? Not on my side. Unless my men were tortured to get their signatures? Let us take it up in the morning."

"But a much graver — " Dolvid began, but this time was unable to detain Kamin-Tolagh, at whose sign the inner doors were thrown open. There was the sound of animated voices and strange but lively music, abruptly hushed.

"*Bôdhrai*. Shudarr — " extending his arm.

The dining hall, a high, beamed space, was brightly lit with both *ôthu* and candlelight, walls hung with rich examples of Heartland weave, a pure — but costly — decoration here, where warmth was not a consideration. A long, broad central table had lavish quantities of varied foods and drinks spread and heaped, but there were no seats drawn up to it; presumably the Hrin style cited by Kamin-Tolagh was for guests to sit, lounge and sprawl on couches and cushions, though none were doing so at present, all having risen at Kamin-Tolagh's entry.

About two dozen, Dolvid quickly estimated, some Heartlanders, others Kargul', soldiers' wives easy to tell by the relative drabness of their dress; they formed, besides, a tight-knit, separate group, practically ignored by the Family guests. Besides Freighanai and Pivrekhan, he knew other soldiers by sight, but none of their wives, whereas all the Heartlanders were known to him, by their kinships if not face to face. Lavsila's wife was most familiar of all.

Shudarr was gazing at the serving-girls, some six or eight, with the attraction of their youth, all in what must be their tribal dress, which bared one honey-skinned shoulder. They were surely not of the Hrin, as the five musicians on a low platform in a shallow alcove certainly were, with their slight-chinned faces. Their instruments were like none Dolvid had seen, reminiscent of unknown weapons or farm tools, but once accept the strange shapes and it could be seen they made music in the same familiar ways, the sounding and stopping of pipes, plucking or rubbing of stretched strings, striking of bells, bars, blocks or taut skins.

Kamin-Tolagh steered Dolvid to a group which, at a Residence Quarter dinner, would have been head of the table; his sister was there, and beside her, almost a head shorter, Khalú, with Lavsila. Among younger Heartland couples, the full-lipped woman, Ondhayu, was related in various ways to, for example, Rhunilat and Faëdhal, and had been one of Kamin-Tolagh's throng of bed-friends in his brief time with the Household at Kadon Dinul, and her new husband's family connections were familiar.

To a currently rather provincial eye, the women were stylish enough, except he had heard long sleeves had come back in fashion at Kadon Dinul since the wedding of Morulis. Here, all others were easily outshone by Kamin-Tarú, in a simple robe obviously inspired by tribal dress; one shoulder was naked, and she had gathered the rich red-gold of her hair to hang on that same side. The fashion, as with the serving girls, had obviously originated for convenience when working, but Kamin-Tarú's version was hardly made for drudgery, being of finest teased and glazed linen, costliest of all stuffs, except gold brocade. Cunningly fitted to her body, it triumphantly achieved the presumed intent of making her resplendent while at the same time causing the other women to look over-elaborate.

The feast, at such short notice, was surprisingly sumptuous, Hrin influence again detectable in elusive spicings, ostentatious in the bewildering array of fruits, cooked and preserved as well as fresh, some occasionally seen on tables of the wealthy at Kadon Dinul, at least one, pear-shaped, but with the flesh of a luscious golden melon, altogether new to Dolvid. There were also Hrin wines, scented and soft, though Kamin-Tolagh proudly filled his cup with a dark wine unmistakably Peframi Gorge, full and mellowed enough to have been born before its pourer.

Other guests showed lavish hospitality towards Shudarr, so that mid-evening Dolvid quietly suggested he not permit his cup to be filled quite so often. Everywhere was a determined effort to be cheerfully inconsequential, entailing a strange absence of curiosity over the reasons for this arrival; as eating tapered down to the nibbling of delicacies, with much sauntering to and fro, it became clear he was being kept from serious talk. He had begun an exchange with Fretasi, a solemn woman in middle life, plain-faced and plain-dressed, treasurer or keeper of accounts, who told him how trade was expanding, and what great returns were expected from newly planted acreage in the South. But when he wondered about covering the high cost of importing food and crafts from the Hrin lands, and Fretasi's frown deepened, Lavsila swooped in with a remark about the succulence of the roast boar, and turned it into a Residence Quarter conversation, polite and negligible. Again, when the plain soldier, Freighanai, was about to expand on variance in fighting-qualities between tribe and tribe, Lavsila was there to speak about measures for overcoming drought.

It was Kamin-Tolagh who hovered close by, when Dolvid and Shudarr together spoke with the young officer, Niburai. He, for a change, was permitted to talk, and prompted, both with words and admiring gazes, by young women, especially Ondhayu, he recounted stirring events from a recent campaign. Geography and tactics were unclear, but Niburai loftily lectured Shudarr on the difficulties of holding men together where weather, terrain and large enemy numbers all conspire against it; he described the fording of a forest stream in spate, and it could not be made out whether the men he led were advancing or retreating. Here, Kamin-Tolagh drifted in, and improbably charged Niburai with excessive modesty, going on to vaguely describe other exploits against heavy odds. Shudarr appeared enraptured, perhaps at the idea of a living hero near his own age, not a dead one, such as Saidhan or Sebhal, nor ancient, like his father. Even Kamin-Tolagh, just thirty, must be virtually an historical figure for one only a child during the Jinzai War.

When Dolvid tried to place these actions more exactly than "away south," Niburai said he would have to talk to Dubovai. "He is mending, I'm told," he said, and abruptly fell silent, eyes on Kamin-Tolagh.

Who shook his head ruefully, and explained Dubovai, their excellent mapmaker, had sustained a wound in the same campaign where Niburai had so distinguished himself. Passing, this left, with so much else, a faint, inexplicable menace, a wisp of smoke in the air. Except for glancing mention of Iruvakh's facility with languages, mapmaking was, so far as Dolvid could remember, the only reference he had heard to a skill not directly connected with war or agriculture, and he caught himself wishing he had brought a couple of copies of the lyrics of Bronal, and perhaps Tellis's book, to remind these self-exiles about civilized life. The music was no different from weave for the walls, a furnishing.

The three soldiers engaged in a highly technical conversation to do with weights and the effectiveness of *pefral*, and Dolvid felt free to wander off for a closer look at the musicians. From the formidable instruments he would have expected jagged and jarring noises, but the Hrin music he had heard up to now was like Hrin wines, smooth, inoffensively pleasant, with not much for memory to hold on to.

By the musicians' platform he found himself next to another of the Kargul' officers, Luzhan, said to be a specialist in training tribal levies. His face, plain and serviceable, was not as aggressively Owani as some, and if he'd had dark eyes, Kamin-Tolagh's mother would have had a ready explanation for the man's ability with the tribes. Affably, he made motions with his hands as if to imitate stopping and plucking of the largest stringed instrument, resembling a small, flat loom, with a thrumming bass voice. In this he was a little hampered by a stiff or sore left elbow. "Yaënsilat," softly, "wishes to be remembered."

"I am surprised not to see him here. A fine soldier."

"Soldier no longer." It came to Dolvid this was a very confidential conversation, and Luzhan was a born conspirator, continuing to gesture as if the subject was music.

Dolvid now mimed motions of playing the thick, curved Hrin flute, with plungers for changing pitch. "You have a message?"

"He wants private talk. You will be here tomorrow night?"

"It would appear so."

"Fifth house north of the crossways, the small one of dark stone. Yaënsilat will leave the back door open after nightfall."

"What — ?" and loudly, as the music paused: " — but they have only small pipes and their finger-drums. I have seen a very old treatise on the music of the Vrobanil, which speaks — "

"A pity," Kamin-Tolagh, as he came up. "We have no Hrin dancers with us at present. My sister, in particular, is fond of their performances, not matched by anything you have seen in the realm. What do you say, *Bôdhrai*," in an intimate tone. "Are we going to let the boy have his wish?"

"As I have tried to tell you, *Asai*. we are here on the gravest of business, not to make holiday — " but following Kamin-Tolagh's gesture to where Shudarr, flushed, while ostensibly talking to Freighanai, was intently watching his favorite among the serving-girls, not older than sixteen, with rounded but sinuous hips.

"These," Kamin-Tolagh ignored the rebuff, a little drunk himself. "These are girls of the Gudi-la. Fine, willing girls, and pleasing to the eye, as you see." Another of the girls was passing by, and he caught at her arm to display her to Dolvid. In the other hand the girl carried a bowl of fruit-sauce, and as she was swung around, stumbling a little, she nearly lost the bowl, some of its contents splashing on Kamin-Tolagh's breeches. A dead pause, and then he laughed, with a careless wave, using the crude *Hwanió* to tell the girl it was nothing.

Yet the blank instant before he spoke, an extraordinary fury had flashed across Kamin-Tolagh's face, and the other feasters had held their breath, as if in expectation or fear of — what? The girl, who had recoiled, touched by the same terror, was not reassured by Kamin-Tolagh's speech, and had to be led away, whimpering.

"At Kadon Dinul," with a chuckle. "A girl makes less fuss over causing a stain on a man's breeches." All his jokes brought a thunderclap of laughter from the guests, who evidently tried to keep not less than one ear apiece cocked in his direction.

Without knowing how, Dolvid was very near Khalú. "I hear there are children," she said, with no preamble.

"Three. Two are mine; Sedukh is Sebhal's son."

After a pause she said, "I am glad you have found a woman who can give you what you wanted most."

He made a slight bow.

"They say there is a rift between you and the *rabhsai*."

"Not," pointedly, "as there was with Ban-Sila. Nothing patience cannot heal — and goodwill."

"I am glad." She lightly touched the back of his hand.

"Are you content?" he felt obliged to ask, not really caring about any part of this exchange.

"Why not? I have everything here I could wish for." Curiously, in speaking this blatant untruth her eyes went not to her husband, but to Kamin-Tolagh: yet how could one whose chief diversion had always been shared amusements of polite society make such a claim in this harsh and sparsely gentled place?

Lavsila, having captured Shudarr, bore down unctuously. "While in the West, *Bôdhrai*, you must make time, I have been telling the boy here, to ride the ancient Moon's Road down to Larghamit. The ruins there would interest you, though there's new building, too."

He waited, and Khalú, with prompting, told about the splendid new house Lavsila had built, still incomplete, overlooking the ancient harborage, the many drawings he had made for the guidance of Hrin masons, tapping of deep underground springs which he hoped would bring orchards and water-gardens to that arid country. Only, perhaps, because he knew her so well, he could detect in Khalú's recital the dutiful tones of someone trying to believe half the delights she was describing. At a guess, notwithstanding her husband's preening enthusiasm, she did not want to live at Larghamit: if the Abu, when the visiting Heartlanders went back to the South, was starved for company, what must it be at the edge of the world, an outpost surviving from a thousand years ago?

That thought made Dolvid wish he could indeed ride the old road, enjoy the delicious, limited responsibility of being just an historian, in service only to accuracy, becoming, as he was sure would be true, only living man to have seen both Narn and Larghamit, eastern and westernmost cities of the First Empire. "My business here," he told Lavsila, reprimanded himself, "is too urgent to leave time for sightseeing."

After being cautioned, Shudarr had sipped very sparingly at his wine, and while he did a little weaving when first struck by cool night air on their short walk back to quarters, he was sober enough to want answers to many questions before sleeping. Why, for an important example, had Dolvid begun by bringing up the earlier and less deadly violation of the Lunu Tezh'? Ruefully, he explained it had been a tactic, which could not now be as effective as if he had been able to pursue his point without interruption. "Kamin-Tolagh was bound to protest innocence of either incursion; if I could get him to use all his vehemence denying one we can document, his protestations would have had a hollow sound when we came to the real charge, where we have no evidence to show."

"Can there be doubt, Master?" frowning owlishly. "Especially now, having seen these brutes who serve him."

"That we are convinced is no proof. Although, in fact, with this case, proof is nothing; what matters is, Kadon Dinul will see as we do, a crime that is self-evident. My job is to get Kamin-Tolagh to realize exactly that."

This, very properly, was a little overcomplicated for a straightforward young cavalry officer, already assailed by wine and fatigue; Shudarr paused in the painstaking unlacing of boots, stared at Dolvid, and took a new path. "You'd think," as if personally aggrieved, "he could find men of his own for a bodyguard, not those uncouth faces. They could dampen any feast. He's got men of Kargul here."

Dolvid agreed the oddly brooding nature of the feast came in part from the gloomy, unwinking guards, who were, however, a symptom, not a cause. "As we see, the provincial cavalrymen have all become squadron-leader, *kímukan*, under-captain, to command tribal troops."

Shudarr had one boot off. "That Niburai tells a fat story. Still, it would be something to be in a fight like that, eh?"

Possibly he was considering his personal chances for rapid promotion. "Can you tell me what his campaign or his war accomplished?"

"Master?"

"Victories have objects, defeats only heroes." For his histories, Dolvid had read hundreds, perhaps thousands of military dispatches, and in all ages, regardless of language, there was a certain unmistakable tone, a strident insistence on glorious examples of individual courage and self-sacrifice, invariably used to distract attention from the futility or failure of the enterprise in general. Niburai was also a symptom, and somewhere, Dolvid was convinced, Kamin-Tolagh's forces had suffered a serious setback.

Ready for his bed, predictably for distending dreams of tribal women with polished shoulders, Shudarr knotted his face in ultimate bafflement. "Master — what is it we're doing here?"

"I am here — " fighting off the sharp pang of guilt — "To seek peace. You and your men are guarding me, that is all. Tomorrow, when I have to drive tough bargains, you will be with me for the sake of what you can learn; you will have no part in negotiations, and no opinion about their outcome — is that understood?" Among dangers, it seemed increasingly likely Rodlakh would see this action as treasonable; it might well be the end of Dolvid's career; no need to associate Shudarr in that.

"Very well, Master," but puzzled by the unwonted flourish of authority. As he settled to sleep, his last perplexed word was, "But there's *something* wrong here — " as good a summation as could be found; something was so badly wrong it was hard to see; there was a madness not readily given an exact location, a conspiracy to madness, as if everyone here had to keep saying what they knew was not true — to become mad so as to make Kamin-Tolagh sane.

"What is his purpose here?" Kamin-Tolagh demanded.

Lavsila studied two half-empty cups, and combined their contents. "Not, you can be certain, what he has given us so far. He has always been full of tricks."

Kamin-Tarú raised a sleep-blurred face. "Were our men in the Lunu Tezh'?"

"But Dolvid would be last to bring that up," impatiently. "I have been told he quarreled with the *rabhsai* over the attempt, illegal attempt, to keep the *Mankh'* from sending its envoys here. That itself, naturally, was only a trick, to make the Families think he cares about the rights of religion. However, he would be the last to make an issue of our escorting of *atarlal*. My best guess is, he is here as a spy, and thinks talking about the threat of war will help him judge how ready we are for it."

"Shumat, or some other military leader, would have been better for that," skeptically. Well, but the son of Shumat was with Dolvid, and Zelu Bablakhi had left signs of weakness everywhere for a discerning eye and ear: Niburai's vaunting tale was no exception. Had news of the disastrous campaign reached Kadon Dinul — from Hrin traders, perhaps? But a revelation of his sudden weakness would logically have resulted in an ultimatum from Kadon Dinul, delivered, with insulting intent, by some obscure low-level official or squadron officer. Arrival of so high a dignitary was made ambiguous by poverty of his retinue; no servant, minimal comforts, and an ordinary, youthful half-squadron from the Army of the West — although that, again, was changed by its having Shudarr Shumatike'ati as its commander. The first command Kamin-Tolagh had issued on learning of Dolvid's arrival had been to increase and extend patrols eastward of the Abu: normally a squadron would go slightly beyond the head of the cliffs marking the rim of Landegh; for the past few days they had been venturing a half-day out on the plateau, but the *Bôdhrai*'s small riding had not been shadowed, as he had feared, by a much larger force of cavalry; nothing was moving on Landegh.

An insult to good sense, to accept the embassy at face-value, but Lavsila's talk of plots within plots was not convincing, and Kamin-Tarú's weary suggestion he wait and see what they had to say all the more exasperating for being the only practical course he could follow.

Dolvid said, "You must understand, *Asai*, I do not speak in my capacity as an official of Rodlakh's *rabhsayum*, and have no instructions from the *rabhsai*.   I am here without his foreknowledge, much less permission."   Though carefully worded, nonsense; *bôdhrayum* could not be omitted from his baggage, like spare boots.

Kamin-Tolagh sought enlightenment: "Then you are here as a private person, is that it?"

Lavsila murmured, "Private, but prominent." Dolvid would willingly have sacrificed Shudarr's presence for an hour alone with Kamin-Tolagh, or Kamin-Tolagh with his silent, watchful sister, but the meeting had been allowed to develop out of a late breakfast, in a bare, not unpleasant hall of the official residence, at a heavy oaken table with matching chairs which must have required a whole pack-train to transport, if they had been brought here during the *jinzai*-breeding years; a low sideboard of the same massive construction held fruits, cold meats and bread, but the servants had been sent away, and of guards only the vigilant Tau-Suaka, and another man ugly enough to be a close kinsman, remained.

"I am here, as I have already said, to prevent the war that is almost unavoidable consequence of recent events in the Lunu Tezh'."

"Not a popular war at Kadon Dinul," Lavsila said. "Not if your *rabhsai* is going to fight over the escorting of *atarlal*, which true Children of Yoëlladhu — "

"That is a minor matter. The shipping of goods through our territory under armed guard without authorization was an unnecessary provocation, but by chance no one was harmed by it, and it is finished now."

"It will be finished, when my officers and men are returned unharmed. You have no right to hold them."

"Nor, as you are well aware, to imprison *atarlal* of the *Mankh'*," Lavsila contributed.

"No one of the *Mankh'* is being held by us," irritated by this attempt to be the injured party. "Uniformed men of a foreign power, captured in arms on our territory, we have every right to hold. As to the officers, if the *Nim'* of Kargul knew of their existence, he would demand they be given to him for trial as deserters, but I have taken it upon myself not to inform him of the incident. Both officers are well, and Drusilakh will be returned to you and to his family as soon as we can reach accommodation. The other, Antighal, with three of the tribal troops, has expressed a desire to remain in the Colony."

"So," Lavsila said. "You are using these men as your hostages."

Dolvid appealed to Kamin-Tolagh. "Must we go through this trifling mock-combat, *Asai*? Would I come here, put myself wholly in your hands, so as to announce we are holding two junior officers hostage? Subsequent to our interception of that company, *Asai*, other troops under your command illegally pursued fugitives across the borders of the Lunu Tezh', and in capturing them, inflicted damage, injury and death on peaceful subjects of Rodlakh *Rabhsai*. That is not a minor matter."

"It is decidedly not a minor charge, *Bôdhrai*," Lavsila said.

"True." He sat back, fairly certain he had taken them by surprise, but anticipating a tedious, unmeaning process of denial.

Kamin-Tolagh said, "Let us be clear. There has been an incident, you say, on the borders of Lunu Tezh', in which troops of mine, you say, have been involved — "

"What I say does not matter, *Asai*. They were uniformed troops, and yours is the only power westward of our borders to maintain regular formations. What matters is that at Kadon Dinul, the question of proof will not come up; there will never be the smallest doubt about who is responsible for this outrage."

"And?" waving Lavsila to silence.

"Rightly or wrongly, it will be seen as a cause for war. That is what I have come to prevent."

"Yet you say you are not here to represent the views of your *rabhsai*."

"The moment I heard this news, *Asai* — " grateful, as he had been seven years ago, that Kamin-Tolagh's intelligence made it possible to cut swiftly to the heart of the business — "I saw what it would mean. In the Jinzai War, I learned a great deal about the prowess and pride of two without whom that war would have been lost. The *rabhsai*, who, with cause, already believes he has been wronged, is not going to stop to consider whether troops of yours have exceeded their orders — orders, I have to say, which were unwise on the face of it."

"If there ever were such orders — "

"Ssh!" Kamin-Tolagh hissed sharply, gesturing for Dolvid to continue.

"*Asai*, I knew the *rabhsai* would be likely — is likely — to demand satisfaction from you in terms you may well find unacceptable. To your standing," he appended, though the word in his mind was another. "This might be the beginning of a process that could only end in war, and needless death of thousands, perhaps."

"I thought you were his *Bôdhrai*," with ponderous irony. "If you had to urge restraint on someone, you could have done so at Kadon Dinul, and saved your crossing of Landegh. I have my own advisors."

"Yes, but I could not hope to influence the *rabhsai*, when in all essentials I agree with him; the realm has suffered intolerable injury, and Rodlakh has every right to be angry. I am not sure that can be changed, whether or not I win concessions here."

He was congratulating himself on complete candor, when Lavsila gave a sneering laugh. "What is this but a threat at second hand? I have heard much the same at a cattle market, where a man will come and say he is not sure his master would sell his stud-bull at any figure, but will negotiate with him, if you will make an offer that will not offend him — a way of bidding up the price while masquerading as an ally."

Dolvid clamped down hard on annoyance, not wanting to do worse than Kamin-Tolagh, who had shown remarkable ability not to take offense at anything said; even Shudarr had cringed slightly when he asserted Rodlakh's anger would be just, but Kamin-Tolagh was not wasting time with side-issues. "What concessions are you seeking?"

Reaching inside his outshirt for the sheaf of paper, Dolvid again noted the bristling alertness of Tau-Suaka. "My notion, *Asai*, is that we need at last to put our lands on a better footing.

We have numerous differences to discuss, but everything must begin with a full apology for the incident in the Lunu Tezh', and compensation for death, injury and damage."

"Money?" Lavsila pretended astonishment. "The just wrath of your *rabhsai* can be assuaged with *money*?"

Kamin-Tarú raised her head, and made her first contribution: "What a stupid thing to say."

So it was, and Dolvid recounted how, since becoming chief magistrate for the Colony, he had heard as many as two hundred claims for compensation, and at least half those who brought suit, when asked to justify their damages, began by saying what they had lost was dear to them beyond replacement, beyond any price. "Which may well be true, but as I tell them, the law has only money to award. Unless we want a world of eternal vengeance, we have to find a price."

"The price for the life of some mongrel creature, living on the borders of nowhere," Lavsila said, "cannot be all that great."

Still declining to be baited, he remarked generally, as much to Shudarr as anyone, "I would not want the task of holding together an empire, where high officials see more than nine-tenths of the people as worthless."

Before Lavsila could make his sneering rejoinder, Kamin-Tarú asked her brother why he had this silly man as part of their discussions; "No wonder poor Khalú always looks so bored."

"He amuses me," Kamin-Tolagh replied instantly, as if to a question he had asked himself, and turning back to Dolvid, "What else? What is this? — " reaching a hand for Dolvid's documents.

"A treaty?" The unsubdued Lavsila half-stood to crane over the top page.

"Not a treaty. It cannot be so much as draft for one; I have told you, no part of my mission here has been approved by the *rabhsai*. But on the journey, and while waiting in camp, I made notes on items which must be considered if there is to be friendship, or no less than mutual tolerance, between Kadon Dinul and the Abu. Several of these points I have raised with the New Residence in the past, but this is in no way an authorized proposal." Also where ground under his feet was least solid: most of his points were only common sense, but a common sense Rodlakh had not shown in his approach to Kamin-Tolagh's adventure; complete agreement in principle here could turn Dolvid, in his eyes, into an advocate for the enemy.

After perfunctorily riffling pages, Kamin-Tolagh passed the sheaf to Lavsila. "Very fine, but we have made proposals, friendly proposals, to Kadon Dinul, and have not been honored with a reply.

"Except for your letter, *Bôdhrai*," he amended. "But that is some years in the past, now."

"For my part, our silence is to be regretted, *Asai* — " resolving he would not be drawn any nearer criticism of Rodlakh. "My thought was, if you and I reached agreement, if only to subjects needing to be discussed, I would have a secure starting-place for my next meeting with Rodlakh *Rabhsai*."

"An ambitious undertaking," Lavsila, recovering with insensate swiftness from Kamin-Tarú's slap. "To represent each side in turn with the other. Has your voice enough weight left at Kadon Dinul?"

Shudarr shifted in his seat. Obeying instructions, he had kept his silence, and may have failed to follow the subtler fencing, but was reacting as a proper escort commander, to what he heard as a slight to the importance of his charge. Dolvid put a soothing hand on the young man's wrist; since Khalú's question last night he had known Lavsila must have had reports, probably highly colored ones, about Dolvid's loss of influence, and the rise of Elamirr.

"I do not wish to conceal — " remaining focused on Kamin-Tolagh — "my allegiance is, and will remain, with the *rabhsai*, and his decisions must be my law."

"But those decisions can be influenced by others with less than your goodwill, your stated goodwill for us. You must be aware, *Bôdhrai*, there is a strong faction at Kadon Dinul openly advocating war, against not only Kargusai, but on subjects of your own *rabhsai* who are thought to be less than ideally hostile to Kamin-Tolagh *Deghi* — "

"All parts have their lunatic immoderates," blandly. "We suspect there is a faction here, openly urging subjects of the *rabhsai* to conspire at his deposing." He leaned over to indicate a paragraph on his second page. "That is the reason for this."

Lavsila read aloud, in a voice carefully emptied of meaning, "`*unimpeded access for the* Atarlum — ' a generous concession, but, `*Kargusai will agree to refrain from unauthorized incursions into our territory, as also from all interference in internal affairs of Rodlakh's realm.*'"

"As we would undertake to in yours," Dolvid explained to Kamin-Tolagh, who was showing only marginal interest.

"The servants of Rodlakh's *rabhsayum* would also have to refrain from attempting to whip up feeling against Kargusai with false accusations of interference in Rodlakh's realm. A document used for this purpose was plainly a forgery."

"That is true," startling him with agreement. "But believed, only because it resembled other, plainly authentic documents, arguing, if more discreetly, to the same treasonable purpose."

"`*To renounce all claim to title or inheritance within the realm of Arbhal* — '" Lavsila read.

"The realm in which I am a declared outlaw?"

"Which can be nullified by simple recognition of your standing as a foreign ruler — although that," he quickly amended, for Shudarr's benefit, "is not the present intention of the *rabhsai*."

"But you, for a price, would advocate — " Lavsila began, but Kamin-Tarú interrupted.

"Are there towns in the Lunu Tezh' Protectorate?" she asked.

"In the eastern part, down south by the shores of En'tesh, *Asayu*. Kamin-Tolagh *Asai* will remember our disembarking there in the War — a number of lakeside settlements have grown together, though the town, as far as I have heard, has taken no single name. Elsewhere, *Asayu*, there are only small huddles of huts — not unlike the hamlets of your valley tribes, I would imagine."

"As they were," Kamin-Tolagh corrected. "I wish you had time, and had come at a cooler season, for visiting the tribal country. We have improved the roads, and the villages are beginning to prosper, now they are free from fear of attack."

"Yes," with grinding emphasis. "A peaceable village should not have to fear sudden, murderous attacks."

Kamin-Tarú was pursuing her own line. "And Rodlakh, you think, would make war for the sake of such a place?"

"There is a principle here, *Asayu*. The *rabhsai* has to be able to protect those in his allegiance."

"Kargusai, so it's said," Shudarr at last failed in his effort to keep silent, but was cunning enough to address Dolvid only, "made war over a counterfeit candlestick."

"Not because of the threat of war," she proclaimed, "but in simple justice, if our men did what is said, we ought to pay compensation."

"You have no shred of proof — " Lavsila predictably protested.

"Not under threat of war," Kamin-Tolagh echoed his sister. "I do not fear war with the realm, *Bôdhrai*."

"As *Bôdhrai*, I do not fear anything. As *Bôdhrai*, I am satisfied the realm is too strong to be overcome by any other power, or imaginable combination of powers. But as a man who knows history, and has lived long enough to see how the chief product of war, no matter how just, will always be death and suffering, there is nothing I fear worse."

"But without war, *jinzal* would have overcome the realm. Without war, I could not have united the tribes, or made them safe from raiders."

"Plainly, *Asai*, you have accomplished a great deal here, in so short a time," Dolvid said, and not in flattery. "All the greater reason, then, not to waste it all in a ruinous war you could not win."

"Will you ride with me?" Kamin-Tolagh abruptly asked.

"When, *Asai*?" startled.

"Now. Well, in half an hour. At this season, the heat is tolerable before mid-afternoon."

"We have settled nothing here."

Kamin-Tolagh took Dolvid's notes from Lavsila, then handed them back. "These proposals of yours; Lavsila will give them the benefit of his closest perusal, and he and I will consider them before dinner. I can tell you, as to your primary complaint, the men responsible for the incursion into your lands, which I did not order, have already been punished."

This with a flickering glance to Lavsila, and Dolvid was conscious of unsaid words, a joke shared. Nevertheless, to have Kamin-Tolagh admit the offense, to negotiate at the fringes of so many touchy issues, with no tempers lost, was extraordinary progress,.

"Certainly I'll ride with you, *Asai*." What harm could it do?

"You and I," Kamin-Tolagh told his sister, who had half-risen in hopes of being included, "can have our ride later."

She remained discontent, and Lavsila, too, was uneasy; perhaps the insults were rankling — or he feared in private talk Dolvid might mention his long-ago overtures to the *rabhsai*.

With Shudarr, he walked back to the house that had been Kambanal's, to change into riding-boots. He thought Kamin-

Tolagh meant to ride alone, but when Varromar, maintaining his vigil, reported a dozen of the Hill Froghul' bodyguard in the saddle outside the official residence, awaiting Kamin-Tolagh's emergence, delighted Shudarr by asking him to ready one file of his half-squadron for escort.

Kamin-Tolagh raised eyebrows, but made no comment when Dolvid's company came up to his; with only small talk about changes here since Lunu became Abu, they rode sedately to the western end. Having made the winding climb to the rim, Kamin-Tolagh said, "My intention was to go unescorted — unless the West makes you nervous, *Bôdhrai*?"

Dolvid waved the thought away. Evidently Tau-Suaka and his men meant to remain here; Shudarr was acutely unhappy with the orders for him to return to their quarters, evidently suspecting an elaborate ruse to simplify assassination of the *Bôdhrai*. Not impossible, but hardly Kamin-Tolagh's style — and if that was what he wanted, he had no need to get Dolvid alone; he had the numbers to overwhelm or massacre the entire escort as well. Of available dangers, Dolvid was most immediately concerned with the enormous antipathy Shudarr had contracted for Tau-Suaka and his Hill Froghul', and the opportunities for taunts and insults between two bands of idling soldiery. Firmly, he repeated his order; disconsolately, Shudarr turned back.

Once beyond the gate, Kamin-Tolagh suggested they ride westward, but his thoughts were directed south, to the tribes whose lives his coming had changed forever.

"Do you have, or will you promulgate, a code of law?" and Dolvid was astonished and a little disturbed at how newly the question came to Kamin-Tolagh.

"Tribes," offhandedly, "have differing traditions. When they serve in my armies, they are under military law, but most other questions I leave in the hands of their head-men, who know they can be deposed and replaced if they go too far."

Precisely the diversity of those people had prompted the question. "But now I suppose they have dealings with each other, tribe to tribe, intermarriage, trade, exchanges and barters — whose tradition rules if disputes arise?"

"I have settled a few such cases. Good and evil live here, as everywhere, and if you cannot tell one from the other, no library of law can help."

Late morning, but odd ragged strands of mist were clinging under a pewter sky. They rode through a drab landscape, way mounting and descending a series of identical, low, bare ridges, while Kamin-Tolagh spoke about the increase of traffic between the Abu and Larghamit, a living port once again. He laughed. "Lavsila wanted to change its name to *Elva Tolaghit*, but I shall save that for some place as-yet unnamed — unbuilt, maybe. We must respect our history, eh?"

Dolvid, he remarked, could have a glimpse of *Zhanurai bi-Nímuraibákimai*, the Great Imperial Road, though, sadly, not of the ancient city itself, where there was much to interest an historian.

"Have inscriptions been found?" Dolvid and Faëdhal were on opposite sides of a long-standing dispute about usage, which would be settled by finding a text definitely datable as belonging to the time of Shâl IV, but earlier than 1384, the 56th year of that immense reign.

"Iruvakh could talk about those things. A pity you could not meet with him — you and he would history each other to untimely death. He is also skilled in languages."

"Any skill I ever had is like Larghamit before you restored it, crumbled away with disuse."

"Your work, Dolvidhai, your histories — how does that go?"

"I have had little time for writing."

"You are wasted there. By the shores of Arnan, all history is in the past. What can be chronicled at Kadon Dinul? A fourthing rise in the price of firewood, and the *rabhsai* wore a Household tunic when he rode down to Owan Sai. Here we still have real deeds to record — the ordering of lands kept in poverty by their ignorance and by petty squabbling, bringing of water and green growth to a dusty wilderness, the making of a new empire with its chief glories yet to come — is that not history?"

"Indeed, *Asai* — " embarrassed by the transparency of his desire for lasting fame. "But history can be an unkind judge."

"Lavsila would tell you, that depends on who wins the battles. The victorious can hire their historians, who manage to praise those great objectives for which any cruel deed can be forgiven. Unforgivable acts belong only to the losers, so the sole real crime is failure."

"If I believed that, *Asai*," not sure whether Kamin-Tolagh did, "I could not be either historian or *Bôdhrai*."

"With me," pulling up his *pefrai*; having turned northward across a bone-hard salt flat, they were at the margin of a well-marked road. "With me, you could be both, and more. Good men are needed — oh, fighting-men I have in plenty, and they can be trained; it is administrators, governors I have to find. Out beyond Flamûrai, there are lands beyond lands to be put in order — or southward, the Hrin country, we have hardly begun there, and the plowshares, almost, are made of gold. I could make you wealthy, as ruler over provinces where the Siv'loi Banner is going to fly, but I would have it so there was time for you to use your pen, and give you deeds worth recording. You are a young man, but the realm with its drudgery will make you old before your time. Come with us here, where mornings still bring news."

This was mostly a kind of game, no doubt, but in some sense Kamin-Tolagh seemed genuinely to mean his offer. Dolvid half-stood in his stirrups to sketch half-deference. "I am flattered, *Asai*, but I am Rodlakh's man, too set in my loyalties to change."

"But is he fixed in his?"

"No matter what rumors have come here," rather stiffly, "Rodlakh *Rabhsai* and I have an understanding that goes beyond day-to-day agreement or difference of viewpoint." Once, he would have been quite certain that was true.

"Yet here you are, seeking peace, when Rodlakh, you say, wants war."

"If the *rabhsai* wanted war," patiently, "he would have made an excuse for it long before, when your strength, *Asai*, was considerably less. The raids into the province of your birth, which is also a part of Rodlakh's realm; your landing of armed men at Ninkufu, when you ended your lady sister's betrothal — or activities of Lavsila's pen, which could justly be called provocative. Your father the *Nimu* has urged armed action against you — no; what I have said is, Rodlakh, contrary to his best desires, may be driven into war, unless he can be reassured the murders in Lunu Tezh' were an aberration, sincerely regretted, with steps taken to prevent any recurrence."

For an instant the face registered an affront akin to the fleeting spasm of anger with the serving-girl last night. Abruptly, "And the *rabhsayu*? What does she think?"

"Of what, *Asai*?" caught on the wrong foot.

"Of this — " with an inclusive wave.

"Like the *rabhsai*," Dolvid ventured awkwardly, "Âna is far from happy. She regrets this gulf that has come between two she has admired."

"Does she?" Kamin-Tolagh spent too much time pondering this milksop of an answer. "Well — " he gave a short laugh. "I am not forgotten."

Rather aimlessly, in gathering heat, they took the road up to the col where it crossed the highest of the ridges, but visibility was poor, and there was little to see in this brown country of endless low hills.

"Not for years," mildly, "has there been anyone to dare addressing me as you have today, *Bôdhrai*. Lavsila is sifting through your notes, trying to discover what double or treble layers of deceit there are in your apparent candor, but I am inclined to accept that you are telling the truth about your reasons for coming here. You have always been sentimental as well as shrewd."

"If it is sentimental to prefer peace and productive labor to arson and rape, crippling and untimely death, then I am."

"But you have learned to make your tears serve your purpose, as others do their cynicism," reflecting rather than accusing. "So: the *Bôdhrai* fears war, the *rabhsayu* fears war, and the *rabhsai*, you say, has no taste for war he may be compelled to order, and you come to me to prevent it. I have lived with the hardships of war, and, yes, its disfigurements — " fingering the scar on the left side of his jaw. "Life is not everlasting, and there have been many very long lives that in the end meant absolutely nothing; I shall not rust my harness weeping for brave deaths that achieve some object — my own, if it comes to that."

Though far from ignoble, and unquestionably sincere, this was deficient in logic; clearly, with no successor, the only object achieved with Kamin-Tolagh's death would be instant collapse of all he had worked for here.

"Well — " he could be seen to determine on one of his flamboyant gestures. "My sister says I should pay your compensation, give you what you ask for. I believe the men think I indulge her too much."

As expected, Lavsila was completely opposed to all concessions. "You have only his word, the word of a lifelong trickster, for any of this — that the *rabhsai* will make the incident into a cause for war, or anything we do would change his mind; it could as easily be a plan hatched between Rodlakh and Dolvid."

"No. The border-incident is not invention; it happened, as we know. Count on your fingers — after hearing about it, there was no time for him to have visited Kadon Dinul, or to have exchanged dispatches, before leaving to come here; as it is, he could hardly have delayed a half-day. If there is a plot, it is his own."

"To win his way back into favor," adaptive as ever. "And if we send him home empty-handed, it might well be the end of the Dolvid era. The Families would thank you for that."

"Again?" in angry sarcasm; only a week ago, Lavsila had assured him his Heartland support was steadily growing, once again promising an imminent time when he could count on enough disaffection within the realm to bring him victory in a war with Rodlakh. But the great wave of feeling that was to call him back as its rescuer remained the same unattainable distance away.

"When Elamirr, champion of the illiterate, succeeds him, there will be nothing to stand in the way of his war against the Families, and no remedy except to depose Rodlakh and the entire House Arbhai-Navu."

Not for the first time, Kamin-Tolagh was shocked more than he should be by this callous prescription of suffering for friends and kin, as a desirable element in his plans.

"Unfortunately, I am going to give Dolvid the compensation and written regrets he came for. My sister says I should."

Lavsila did not quite dare to call it a frivolous reason, nor doubt out loud it was the real one. Which, of course, it was not; the fact was while Kamin-Tolagh was irked by the idea of apologizing, it would be foolish to risk war when he was least prepared for it. At some later time, when he had been able to replace the losses of Zelu Bablakhi, he would take his chances in a war, especially one where Rodlakh, by taking the offensive, gave up his great advantage in numbers; it would be a fight, not against the realm of Arbhal, but the fragment of it that could be put in the field six lean days riding from its base. Kamin-Tolagh envisaged a two-phased war with an interval of truce; a series of heavy defeats on the armies Rodlakh sent allowing him to make an advantageous peace, including recognition, and ceding of the westward marches of the Lunu Tezh' Protectorate, which he could then use to gather his forces and their supplies for the second and decisive round; all this was within reach if Rodlakh could be provoked into an attack a year hence, or a little beyond, the autumn after next, and (Lavsila's part), if the *rabhsai* also had to deal with dissension at home.

Lavsila disconsolately riffled the pages of Dolvid's notes. "The danger, as I see it; any concession will be seen, rather, as a confession of weakness, and encourage instead of deter an assault. Many of these stipulations are insulting."

"They will never come to anything," Kamin-Tolagh predicted. "We can assent to them in the same spirit as they were given, as theoretical basis for imaginary discussions."

"He speaks about fixing northern and eastern boundaries of Kargusai — of your domains. Here: `*Landegh to be considered as free, except the armed forces of the* rabhsai *only will be permitted there —* ' can that be called neutral, where his army can go, and not yours?"

He took the page, and read the passage marked. "That we must except; Shumat could bring an army and store its supplies less than a day's ride from here. Dolvid must know that is out of the question. He included it as a test; if we allow it, he will conclude we want peace at any price."

"We can agree to none of this, and still send him home a hero, by giving him his apology."

"Then he will have the greater height to fall from. You will have to find other ways to advance the cause of Elamirr."

"The *rabhsai*, it is true, may feel he has no choice but to endorse a settlement brought home by Dolvid, but he is not going to love him for it. Some bad feeling there — I hear from a man at Kadon Dinul who says the *rabhsayu* from time to time gets in bed with Dolvid."

"Oh, come — " in utter, angry disbelief; this went beyond even Lavsila's permissible limit of foolishness. "You are talking about treason. It is absurd; Âna is not one of your Residence Quarter wives."

"But those Mixed women, once let loose, can have appetites no one man can satisfy."

"You — " he mastered himself. "Stories your Residence Quarter champions recite while measuring themselves? Dolvid, besides, is married to Aëlu, and she must be quite enough for him; does your wife tell you nothing?"

"Difficult, naturally, to prove."

"What is not true often is."

"Well," placatingly. "No need for that. What would be thought if, a month or two after his triumphant return, he was discovered in possession of gold, stamped with the head of Kamin-Tolagh?"

"That I had bribed him to make peace," thoughtfully, reflecting on the notorious simplicity of the *Bôdhrai*'s life. "If believed. Wait, though — his exile under Ban-Sila — was that not on a charge of peculation? A false charge, as later claimed."

"Khalú's brother helped provide the evidence, and my father had a part in it, too. Nevertheless, a conviction of that kind, it can be disproved a thousand times, and still leave suspicions; there will be plenty of knowing nods if it happens again." He was settling it with himself. "It can be contrived, I think, but I shall have to come to you for a large enough sum in gold."

"And Fretasi to you, for a complete accounting." One day, Lavsila was going to *contrive* his own downfall. If disgraced under Rodlakh, Dolvid might be persuaded to come here to the West, an irony Lavsila would enjoy, till he saw the result: his displacement.

"Your task," he said meanwhile, "give me the Families. Any chance of an uprising in the Heartland, led by the private armies, will tie at least one of Shumat's hands."

"Elamirr will deliver them to us."

"And I must have the cavalry — " he began, and broke off. Of Kargul, had been in his mind, but Lavsila did not have to know everything. Restored tribal armies, dissent and threat of dissent in the Heartland, Rodlakh provoked into taking the offensive, all that was needed, but the invasion with which the wars would finish was going to need first-class cavalry, *péfrapravádal*. With those of Kargul, he was still admired, he believed, above their titular captain, his father, and his most ardent admirers, forced into retirement in Tovakh's reorganization, could be called back to the colors in a week. Those squadrons, the best cavalry anywhere, could be his for a march on Kadon Dinul. Here, he needed no help from Lavsila.

By nightfall, Dolvid was wondering whether he should risk taking up Luzhan's quiet invitation of the night before. Beyond his best reasonable hopes in coming here, he had a small bag of gold pieces, a written expression of regrets at the incursion, and treaty notes with interlinear comments from Kamin-Tolagh.

However improbably, he had won, and had made his intention of an early start on the journey home his excuse for leaving the cordialities of the official residence, with Kamin-Tolagh hospitably protesting there was a last unopened bottle of the perfectly-matured Peframi Gorge wine. Dolvid warned himself it would be foolhardy to gamble unexpected victory on the boyish skulk demanded by a meeting with Yaënsilat, yet was enormously intrigued by the furtive manner of Luzhan's approach, its hints both of important secrets and genuine danger.

In the little writing-room he continued in doubt, while making a detailed record of his observations and impressions, where the personal warmth of Kamin-Tolagh made a sharper contrast with the indefinable atmosphere of dread that hung as an invisible fog over the Abu. He was interrupted by the discreetest of taps on the door; Shudarr.

"Not yet — " for some hours he had wanted to recount his adventures during Dolvid's longer-than-expected excursion with Kamin-Tolagh.

"No, Master — there is a lady to see you."

Not, as momentarily feared, Kamin-Tarú; no, Khalú, cloaked, but unattended; he had said farewell less than an hour ago, not expecting to see her again before leaving.

She confessed, with a remembered mischievous air, she was `supposed to be' home and on her way to sleep, but Lavsila, she expected, would stay drinking with Kamin-Tolagh well past midnight. If there was a suggestion in all this, it meant nothing to Dolvid; with most of his life he was the one who found it hard to close a chapter, but nothing was so completely over as the feeling he had once had for Khalú. Whether or not she expected him to want her, that clearly was not what she had come for, and he was struck by her freedom from concern over being observed; if clandestine, her visit was anything but secretive in its manner; soldiery and others were about in the small settlement.

Seated, cloak thrown back from her shoulders, eyes gravely on him, she made what he assessed as a token feint at sentiment, asking who would have expected to find them together, here, of all places in the world, after so much shared and separate time? He poured her wan Hrin wine, and before long she came to her subject.

"This treaty the *rabhsai* may sign with Kamin-Tolagh — "

"There is nothing approaching a treaty as yet, not the draft of one, only the vaguest notes."

"I understand, but if there is a treaty, if Rodlakh recognizes Kargusai, would that mean everyone would have to make a final choice?"

"Everyone, who?" He did not trouble to re-emphasize how far Rodlakh was from such an act.

Khalú displayed impatience with him. "Us, the ones who came here; should we have to renounce all allegiance to Arbhal?"

He was slow to understand what she wanted. "Kamin-Tolagh, I am sure, will demand allegiance; one excludes the other."

"Irrevocably?"

"Well — " and then he saw the question she was afraid to ask, *What if this empire fails?* Yet the worry was unlike Khalú's normal blithe assumption of privilege, which in this case would surely not fail her; she was from an enormously wealthy and highly influential family, and would obviously be reinstated without much difficulty. "You have not committed any crime in Rodlakh's realm."

She lowered her eyes as if at a sudden onset of alien modesty. "Yes, but I am married to a man who — " she turned up opened palms.

Who had reasons to fear *rabhsai*'s justice. At last it came to him Khalú had come here, not merely with Lavsila's permission, but at his behest. Angrily, he said, "Your husband is going to have to find how to hedge his own bets, not send his wife."

"In his position," pleading for sympathetic understanding, "he has to be careful to maintain an appearance. But he wanted me to tell you — " Not at her best dealing with large affairs, Khalú paused here to make sure she had the words right, her lips moving in a silent rehearsal, as she closed her eyes to concentrate, just as Dhunival had with an earlier message from Lavsila. "He would not want the language of robust debate to be mistaken for his true feelings, and his admiration for you remains unimpaired."

"His what for me? How can you recite such nonsense; you better than anyone know Lavsila, for fifteen years, has had nothing but contempt for me as a renegade Owani, and for my *evil dream-world of mingled races*." The last was a quotation from a dozen years ago, the day of the foolish duel with Khalú's brother, but could as easily be a phrase from one of the intercepted letters.

Khalú flushed; old experience instructed him her innate incapacity for being caught in the wrong would soon transform embarrassment into anger, or bitter tears.

"Acts have consequences," not a particularly new thought, unless you were, in the words of Tellis, a house-pet bred by the Families. "I can do nothing for Lavsila; he will stand or fall with Kamin-Tolagh."

On the other hand, it might yet be possible to save Ghuradh, and it came to her as a novel and shocking idea her brother's games with Lavsila could constitute treason.   He would predictably experience a sense of betrayal, if he knew his confederate in the West was trying to keep open a line of retreat with *rabhsayum* they were busy vilifying.

"*Rabhsayum* has been reluctant to dignify these plotters by moving against them, but the killings in the Lunu Tezh', despite my success here, make support for Kamin-Tolagh not as good a joke as it was."

Khalú's confusion was complete; she became angry with Lavsila, recognizing for the first time the extent and implications of his duplicities, at the same time fearing she had botched his errand, of which a further part, she confided, was the bizarre offer to keep Dolvid covertly informed as to developments in the West affecting the interests of the realm.

"I was supposed to tell you that — " she was near tears, "only if your response was a friendly one — if you could be trusted not to betray him to Kamin-Tolagh. You won't, Dol, will you?"

He was shocked — and then surprised he could be — to recognize her husband had expected and perhaps encouraged Khalú to bed with him. "You can tell Lavsila, truthfully, I said only a fool would rely on information, or any other offer, from such a source. I have known for a long time what he is, and Kamin-Tolagh cannot have many illusions left. Who he chooses to trust is no business of mine."

"What about Ghuradh?" She was remarkably untroubled by his assessment of her husband.

Her brother, he told her, would have to do better; Kamin-Tolagh might succeed well enough to keep Lavsila safe, and still be no worse than a nuisance for Rodlakh's realm, if not a complete irrelevancy. Chances of his ever collecting the armed strength to be a serious threat were remote, and Ghuradh must by now see for himself the yet slighter possibility of a Heartland uprising in Kamin-Tolagh's favor.

"Why say all this to me? I cannot advise Ghuradh. You can see I have no way to write him a confidential letter."

"You could, if I carried it." He did not blame her for caution, and in the end asked her to write and sign only a recommendation Ghuradh listen to what Dolvid had to say. Distraught now, she would guess later he meant to turn her brother into a more reliable version of what Lavsila had offered, a source of information about Kamin-Tolagh's intentions. That would entail deception of her husband by her brother, but Dolvid did not think Khalú would interpret it in exactly that way; the issues meant nothing to her, for whom it was a *zhabhu* game, where players, no matter how friendly, sought, and expected each other to seek, every available advantage.

Terse note written, he saw her gratitude was about to bring on a sentimental nostalgia less calculated than the earlier attempt, and with a familiar strain of self-pity; eyes moistening, she murmured nothing in her life had gone right since parting from him.

"Life is so cruel here," rising from her seat, "Will you kiss me?"

He compromised by grasping her shoulders and kissing her forehead, an instant addition to his long catalogue of insults.

When he saw her to the door, the moon had set, and lighted windows were few; she did not object when he gave her Varromar for her escort on the brief walk to her house and Lavsila's, largest on the farther side of the crossways. Though guards remained all night outside the house where Kamin-Tolagh and his sister slept, there were no observed patrols in the few streets. In minutes, Varromar returned. Noting everything was perfectly still, Dolvid told Shudarr he would be going out for an hour or two, and the back door beyond the kitchens should be kept unlocked.

"No," he rebuked the ghost of a smirk on the young man's face. "Not a woman." Briefly, he told about the overtures of Luzhan, and Shudarr at once said he would go in his place. If accosted, he could hint with half-drunken winks and nudges he was on his way to or from an hospitable bed. This connected in some fashion with the tale he had been trying to tell, but Dolvid again put him off, regretfully declining his offer. True, the nocturnal wanderings of youth might be treated more indulgently than those of a *Bôdhrai* no longer twentyish, but would Yaënsilat willingly tell his tale to a complete stranger?

Necessary, also, to refuse Shudarr's substituted suggestion he accompany Dolvid; in the midst of several hundred potential enemies, the slight added protection did not justify the increased risk of being observed. Finally, Shudarr was strictly forbidden to go out, or send men out, in search of Dolvid if he was delayed.

"Black as a hole in nothing," Shudarr commented, as, with kitchen-light covered, they stood by the back door, which only memory told them opened on a pleasant little garden, with sweet herbs, small trees, and a rippling thread of a stream. Dolvid agreed, wondering whether there was light enough for him to find his way without noisy bumpings and stumblings.

Half a minute standing beneath some sort of ornamental maple was enough to change his mind; the moon was gone, but sky over the Abu was extravagantly thronged with sharp stars, and the ground itself seemed to breathe out a faint luminescence; he could almost imagine he cast a shadow as he went. Uneasy about his visibility, he scaled a low wall as quietly as he could, and crept between dark buildings to the edge of the street that ran east and west.

Shudarr, in defiance of orders, was about to take a half-file in search of him when he returned, having been over twice the hour he had forecast. What he had heard from Yaënsilat had left visible signs of shock, or so he judged when Shudarr's first words, drawing his blade, were, "Are you being pursued?"

"No, no. There is no danger. No immediate danger," he modified, and found a rough kitchen chair to sit on. He had been mad to make this journey, criminally mad to bring two dozen good men, including the son of his oldest friend. "I know now what caused the strangeness we could feel at the feast."

Since he was not yet ready to expand on that conclusion, Shudarr took it as an appropriate moment for the story Dolvid had been too preoccupied to hear. Coming back from the western end of the Abu in the morning, and passing near the women's quarters, he had glimpsed, hanging out laundry, the pretty girl he had admired so ardently at the feast.

"I thought, Master, pardon me, I had time for a word with her," sheepishly. "But by the time I'd seen the men to the mound here, she had gone inside. Those girls aren't house-servants; they live there in the large white building."

More than half in love, at that age Dolvid vividly remembered, when such yearnings can feel as absolute as need for air or water, Shudarr had gone inside, and come to a kind of washroom, filled with steam.

"I could not see the girl I was looking for, but that other one was there — that one who splashed fruit on Kamin-Tolagh. She was washing herself. Naked, Master."

"Spare me the haft-boning stories," irritatedly.

Shudarr flushed. 'Haft-boning' was camp slang, in origin a reference to the practice of rubbing down the thick end of a lance with a meat bone boiled bare, to make the wood less liable to cracking. "No, Master, her back; she was marked with a terrible flogging, fresh weals, and there was blood. I tried to question her, but I can't do much with that *Hwanió* talk; besides it made her frightened just my being there, so I came away. Servants need whipping sometimes, if they steal or tell lies, but would Kamin-Tolagh have a girl whipped so viciously, for an accident, where he himself was the cause?"

"*Have* her whipped? I do not doubt he gave himself that pleasure." No need to harrow Shudarr with the detailed stories he had heard from old Yaënsilat, supported for a time by Luzhan, who came and went like a wraith. The village-burning incident that had ended Yaënsilat's military service, ferocious treatment of captured rebels, many individual instances of cruelty, down to the recent disastrous campaign and its grisly aftermath, recapture of the deserters, their brutally prolonged deaths — everything went to illustrate a growing appetite for inflicting pain, and a growing satisfaction in witnessing it. Recalling the lingering executions, Luzhan, an eye-witness, had been obliged to leave the room to retch in private. Beyond all that, haunting imagination, was the reported cold extermination of virtually an entire and ancient tribe, casually, like throwing away boots that pinched. Khalú's tearful remark, *it is so cruel here*, had not been as self-pitying as he had assumed.

"These are things," Yaënsilat had said, voice trembling, and not with age, "enough to revolt any honest soldier. I didn't flinch, killing a man in battle, so long as he meant to fight, but where's honor in this murderer's work?" But his horror kept lapping over into practical concerns: "Plenty of others beside Luzhan feel it as I do — not as many as there were; this bloody madness down south killed sixteen men of Kargul, not to mention those like Dubovai who'll never mend aright. And this giddy place is feasting Niburai as if he was young Sebhal. A soldier's a soldier, *Bôdhrai*, ready to take his chance for an honest purpose, but who wants to die or be maimed? But it's going on, war after war, battle after battle, another thousand miles of rock and sand won; nobody's luck can hold against too many tosses of the coin. Some of the young idiots think they'll fill their pockets with Hrin gold, but will that buy back what they miss the most? their homes, I mean to say, and the grass valleys of Kargul."

So the old soldier came to the chief reason he had asked for this meeting: there were, he claimed, a score at least of cavalrymen who wanted to renounce their allegiance to Kamin-Tolagh — many more, maybe, but in this spy-ridden place a dangerous sport was to enquire into a man's true feelings; everyone was afraid of the bodyguard led by Tau-Suaka, tough and ruthless men, who did not question orders. There was, moreover, the problem of where they could escape. "Here, they are dying, one by one, and in their home, they're condemned rebels."

Dolvid could have said they had made their choice and taken new oaths; there had been a time when they were offered the chance of going home, and many had come with Kamin-Tolagh after. But those who had stayed, surely, had been unable to envision the atrocities they would be party to. "Kargul is out of the question unless a time comes when Tovakh *Asai* can be persuaded to offer amnesty. But there are other green places in the realm, and if my voice still has influence at Kadon Dinul — " He broke off, remembering his new powers. "On my own authority, I can extend the hospitality of the Colony, if only as a resting-place. I cannot guarantee assistance for your escape, beyond instructing the Army of the West to watch for you on Landegh." Rodlakh could countermand this offer of sanctuary, but Dolvid did not think he would want to be outshone in clemency, nor to be trapped, as others of his House had been, in a dispute with the Colony. If Yaënsilat and his friends could once reach the Frontier, he doubted they would ever face trial; Tovakh himself might be shamed into a magnanimous gesture.

"The answer to your question," to Shudarr, having given only bare bones of Yaënsilat's long tale. "Why does Kamin-Tolagh rely on an alien bodyguard? If you were an officer of Kargul, longing for his home, how would you purchase a pardon from Tovakh *Asai*?"

He considered. "If I had allies, I would try to arrest Kamin-Tolagh, and bring him home as a prisoner."

"Exactly."

"But he has given you the apology and the compensation you came here for."

"Not because his sister said he should," tartly. "Nor because he was swayed by my *sentimentality*." A long time would have to pass before he could get rid of the bitter aftertaste from that amicable ride; with a pomposity embarrassing to contemplate, he had put in his notes that he had, perhaps, been privileged to see a genuine Kamin-Tolagh rarely displayed to those for whom he had to maintain the implacable dignity of an overlord. If he, Dolvid, had to have a weakness, he supposed it could be worse than this lifelong habit of wishing to find true virtue in improbable places, but Elamirr would make a feast of deriding his gullibility here.

"Why, then?" Shudarr persisted.

"I suppose, simply, because he is afraid of war, after the losses in the south — a thousand of his best-trained tribal troops, according to Luzhan, and he was there. An overestimate, maybe, but the lengths he has gone to to disguise defeat argue a seriously weakness."

"Then we ought to make war on him at once."

"We, you and I and our puny two dozen ought to remove ourselves while we can from this place where life is so cheap, and death so easy. I should not have brought you here."

35.

Kamin-Tarú said, "This is not a time of moon for me to ride so far."

"You will miss good sport," her brother cajoled. A party of Heartlanders, of whom many had come back to the Abu for Halving Day, were riding down to the Laughing Owl country for the executions. Kamin-Tolagh had been obliged to postpone them till after the spring ceremonies, but the spectacle would be worth the wait. Of men who were the twelve original deserters, eight had survived pursuit, capture and the journey back, and their deaths, extended over three days, were going to be a lesson for any man of the tribes who thought he could walk away from military service when he was tired of its hardships and dangers.

"Iruvakh," Lavsila was casual, "was asking about your intentions. He may be there."

"We shall have to outdo ourselves. I am going to begin by having the wives thoroughly flogged." Wives and near-wives, that was; two at least were choices of younger men not yet married. Of seven in all who had gone with their men, one, wounded in the fight, had died on the return journey.

"What have the wives done?" Kamin-Tarú wanted to hear. "With those tribes, they are no different from their husbands' goods — they would have no choice whether they went or stayed, if their men were setting out for the moon."

She would never learn, he resigned himself, to think first in terms of the Empire. Here, admittedly, he had been at fault, wooing her with what she might be entertained by, failing to emphasize the underlying import. "Everything I do has a purpose. Armies are ruled by greed and fear — "

"Or honor," Lavsila suggested, "where such terms have meaning. Soldiers have to be taught to fear the consequences of cowardice or desertion above their dislike of what their duties bring, hunger, thirst, battle, the chance of wounding or death. For men bred in our heritage, of course, it should be enough they take an oath, and have their comrades beside them, but with the tribes there are no such traditions."

"Exactly." The congratulation was sardonic, though Lavsila's thoughts would have been apposite enough, if the man had ever seen battle. "Here, we have to use what they do understand, and chiefly that means pain. Some heroes of the tribes willing to risk it for their own sake may think again if desertion means pain for their women as well — and their women might do more to dissuade them."

Lavsila grunted assent. "As it is with most clans, a widow is better off than an unmarried girl, and may do better in her second marriage — where is the incentive for her to be much concerned what happens to a husband chosen for her?"

"In Hunghi's hand — " though his sister was not won over. Evidently, she enjoyed watching a flogging only with a young man under the lash.

"You have a ruler's right to discourage disloyalty," Lavsila conceded, but there was a qualification on its way: "Iruvakh says g'Asalladh' Himself has been disturbed by rumors of excesses here."

Could the Patriarch have heard about annihilation of the Hwenala? Kamin-Tolagh dismissed the thought. "Excesses? Iruvakh, when he was at the *Mankh'*, must have had his beatings, and with less object. If g'Asalladh's minions want to remain welcome, they and their Master had better learn who rules here. I have signed no treaty."

"Very true," grudgingly, and the next remark was not as much a change of subject as it seemed. "In the Paowan, maybe in all the realm, your name, I am told, is heard more and more. When Rodlakh brought in his new selective taxes, there was open talk of yours as a realm where to be Owani was not to be disfavored." Since final expulsion of Iolfrant, an added handful of young Heartlanders had arrived at Hyolenstr, but Kamin-Tolagh had heard too often about his mounting popularity with Lavsila's imagined host of allies.

"Are you telling me Owanil care what punishments I inflict on tribesmen of the Froghushei?"

"Not in the least, but they would be unhappy to hear protests of the *Mankh'* had been ignored."

"When Iruvakh, *at*-Iruvakh, has a protest, he had better make it to me, and he knows his answer. A condition of his appointment was that I alone decide what is good and necessary for the Empire. If, through softheartedness — " in a gesture of solace, he covered Tú's hand with his — "we fail to make desertion too terrifying to contemplate, what fields are *ga-Yalil* will cease to be a question, and your Heartlanders will be lucky to escape back to Rodlakh's terrible realm." A complacent house-bred pigeon, taken to the wilds, could not be taught in time to fear hawks, but Lavsila at least should recognize how precarious his safety was, and how much more so since Zelu Bablakhi. These punishments were also going to express part of what he had been obliged to suppress for the sake of policy, the anger he felt over the failure of his expedition.

The action against the Hwenala had been a regrettable piece of severity, necessary in his judgment for the wellbeing of the Empire, but not easily understood by those without his responsibilities. This, by contrast, either as just punishment or exemplary warning, was a public event, its effect improved by the size of its audience.

The site chosen was not far from the main settlement of the Laughing Owl people, the same place where the squadrons had reassembled on the day of the great firesetting. Troops on duty were drawn from all tribes, so the tale of Kamin-Tolagh's wrath would be carried everywhere; besides holiday-makers from the Abu, numbers of Laughing Owl and its neighbor tribes on each side helped enclose the wide, dusty level, where three stakes had been erected, man-high.

At these, in three batches, women first, several of them pretty enough to add zest to the spectacle, were stripped and lashed, whimpering, by Hunghi with a single apprentice. While this occupied only part of the first morning, and the whippers took care to use punishing but not killing force, Kamin-Tolagh was then obliged to postpone the start of executions for a day, to let the wives recover enough to witness the sufferings of their men. After initial disappointment, the spectators from the Abu decided they did not really mind. They had plenty of food, drink and servants with them, the rainy season, a little wetter this year, was come and gone, weather warm but not oppressive, and in these conditions, like most people who seldom have to, they made a pleasure of spending some nights under canvas. Iruvakh, after all the talk, was not among those in attendance; perhaps recalling how at-Sholidu had been unwillingly associated with the near-flogging of Valubran, he had expressed cautious disapproval twice, first with a note to Kamin-Tolagh questioning the necessity of protracted executions, and then by leaving on an abrupt journey to the southern empire.

For the next phase, Tau-Suaka not only directed but relished taking part, as the first three condemned men were subjected to long-drawn ingenuities of torment and mutilation. The pace was unhurried, allowing each victim to regain his senses each time he fainted, but the day was marred by the death, near noon, of one man, weakened by wounds suffered at his recapture. Tau-Suaka was abjectly apologetic over the miscalculation, for which he atoned by his later inventiveness, keeping all spectators profoundly interested; some of the witnesses from the Laughing Owl had been escorted here by soldiery, but once in place there was no wavering of their attention. At the end of an instructive day, it surprised Kamin-Tolagh about half the Heartlanders said they had seen enough, and would set out for the Abu first thing. Most cited their neglected southern estates as excuse, but he suspected the otherwise ineffectual disapproval of Iruvakh had acted on weaker stomachs — what Tau-Suaka would call `women's hearts.' Although wives were in fact prominent among those continuing to be diverted by the spectacle, and while during the day there had been some covering of faces, there were Heartland women for whom the display or the idea of pain had an effect betrayed by flared nostrils and ripening lips; the pretty, sybaritic Ondhayu, who, in he absence of Niburai, left at the Abu, had to murmur her suggestions at the ear of her husband. They absented themselves for above an hour; composing the anecdote for his sister's amusement, Kamin-Tolagh invented the detail that when they returned, Ondhayu looked much fresher than Pranúdhanai.

Yet he was once more disappointed with the Heartlanders. He did not mind their being entertained, he had invited it, but hoped at the same time for some counterbalancing solemnity, in recognition of the purpose and the lesson behind the spectacle; more might have seen it through as a necessary and instructive ritual.

Those who failed to stay a second day missed comedy, when one of the prisoners, his hamstrings deftly cut, was unbound, and tried to run away on legs that kept toppling like the stack of blocks used as a target for practise with lances; some of the soldiers laughed till they cried. Another full day was to follow, but in mid-afternoon a fast-messenger rode in from the north with a dispatch from Lavsila, containing bewildering news, a thunderbolt. Cancelling the third day's entertainment, giving Hunghi instructions to finish the executions with his whip, he made plans to ride at dawn, and scribbled a message to precede him, all the while wondering how it could be true, and what it meant: Dolvid (how was it possible?) was at the Abu.

To be exact, he was camped at the rim, or just outside its containing-wall. Freighanai, an old acquaintance from the Jinzai War, had apologetically refused permission to enter without Kamin-Tolagh's authority, and when Lavsila, returning from Larghamit, countermanded the order, it was only for Dolvid, who declined to go on alone, not through fear, but because he was not going to see his escort humiliated.

For that matter, a *Bôdhrai*, he kept telling himself, had to maintain dignity appropriate to the majesty of an offended realm. When, with a shrug, he resigned himself to one more night, at best, of sleeping on the ground, Shudarr remarked it was as well they had not brought Orbanak, who would not have been so patient. "But I told him last year, Master, even the *rabhsai*'s brother can't always sleep where he wants to."

This, a sly reference to the Morulis episode, complete with sidelong glance, Dolvid let pass without comment. He despaired of ever being an authentic dignitary; a boy young enough — exactly young enough — to be his son was breezily comfortable with him, nor did he want respect due his rank at the cost of that ease. He was not certain he had earned it; here on the gravest of errands, camped with his tiny band in sight of uncounted potentially hostile troops, and actually enjoying himself, as he had on Landegh, the campfires and crowded stars, the juddering chill of morning and its penetrating sense of life. The third day out of Drin Navuna, by what he had been told was the one unfailing source of water, they had spotted and cautiously approached the rough, untidy encampment of some hundred-odd members of a clan or small tribe, men, women, children and their dogs and goats.

Understanding no language Dolvid spoke, however slightly, they recognized the words *Army of West* and the name *Sebhal*, and after wary greetings communicated by signs and actions that

they were a northern tribe returning from their winter pastures days to the south, having waited, as always, only for the blossoming of a small yellow flower; whether this was simply a sign for them of the changing season, or they had a use for the plant, Dolvid was unable to ascertain. They were pleased *jinzal* — an idea easily mimed — had become rare, and conveyed a description of their homeland as densely grassed uplands with plenty of game, and especially birds; as well as skilled linen weave, some of them wore loose waistcoats, caps or capes evidently and exquisitely made of feathers, for which thousands of birds must have paid with their lives. When Dolvid's company rode on, these people, who called themselves something like Skâbh-brao, were preparing to resume their northward trek. This glancing encounter with an unknown people from an unknown land, who in their turn knew nothing about Rodlakh, Kamin-Tolagh's empire, or disputes of rulers, an occurrence outside time, with neither prologue nor consequence, curiously gladdened him with its vivid reminder about the vastness and variousness of the world; as Shudarr thoughtfully remarked, "Plenty of room for everyone, if there wasn't any greed."
  "Or envy."

  Lavsila came again to bring food and solicitude, and probe ineffectually into Dolvid's purpose in coming. He had changed from the callow young man once a leader of the Heartland faction opposed to Dolvid, but his face had not aged a dozen years since then; an odd dislocation to see the pampered Heartlander here in this scoured and unordered land, odder to think of him as Khalú's husband. He showed off his intimate grasp of the realm's current affairs, remarkable in view of his long absence; baiting Dolvid a little with Elamirr's rise in esteem, and commiserating gratuitously with the difficulties of overseeing policy at Kadon Dinul from a place so distant as the Colony.
  Clearly, the implication here was that Rodlakh, under Elamirr's influence, had used the vacancy at Kamsilat to exclude Dolvid from the center of power, but getting nowhere with those veiled taunts, he tried the theme of the Heartlanders who had quit Rodlakh's realm to be with Kamin-Tolagh. Dolvid responded blandly, all should be free to choose where they lived `without coercion,' and let him make what he would of it. All the while,

Lavsila appeared to be waiting for something additional, and Dolvid was reminded of the mysterious message that had reached him about the time of those first defections, almost an offer to betray Kamin-Tolagh.   Conjectural whether the inconstant Lavsila would now repudiate or repeat that offer, and he was given no encouragement to do either.

Half an hour behind him there was a fresh arrival, a knot of soldiery that must be the Hill Froghul' tamed by Kamin-Tolagh, short, broad-shouldered men with decorated tunics and shaggy hair, bows slung at their backs. From their midst emerged a tall and graceful rider, hair burnished in early sun. Kamin-Tarú dismounted with all her old, lithe ease, and to the apprehension of her bodyguard, the rasping displeasure of Lavsila, walked directly to Dolvid, gave him a slender hand, then slipped inside his guard to brush his cheek with soft lips.

"Well met, *Asayu*," honorific validated by Rodlakh's stubbornness over her outlawry. "The air of the West agrees with you." When he had first met her, in what was surely another life, a former age of the world, he was drawn to her, as all men were, but had not seen her as a great beauty; she had been, rather, a large-eyed sort of child-woman of powerful physical appeal. None of that had vanished, and glints of teasing still showed green in her eyes as she inclined her head to acknowledge the compliment, but she was completely a woman now, and an arresting one; Shudarr, nearby, was too well-trained to goggle, but when introduced had contracted a new stammer, while among the men of his half-squadron, the avoidance of staring was loud.

Dolvid said, "I had not appreciated by how much the realm is poorer, *Asayu*, for your continued absence."

"No flattery, now," with a quick, vanishing frown.   He noticed discontent lurking at the corners of her mouth, and wondered how long her brother had been away.

"We choose strange places for our reunions," smile returning. "How is little Orbanak?"

She was thinking of a cold and rainy day, seven years ago, when she had come across Arnan in a fishing boat, and first met the *rabhsai*'s brother. "Not little any more; he has his squadron in the Army of the West."

It was not to be imagined she would again help him reach an understanding with her brother, and yet she enjoyed skirting the edges of her old games. Lavsila making plain with his fidgeting it was time to depart, she swept Dolvid with her eyes. "Is it not cold for you by night, Master? Is a straw mattress enough between you and the hard ground?"

Very aware of the Hill Froghul' guard with their unblinking vigilance, Dolvid said, "A soft bed, *Asayu*, would only distract me from a hard purpose."

"Purpose and all, we shall make you comfortable when you come to the Abu. It will be good to have you as our guest."

"A double joy, to renew friendship," with a mute face.

When she had gone, leaving a faint scent in the warming air, Shudarr, voice held to the over-neutral, said, "So, Master. That is the lady of Kargul."

"It is very important to be cautious in our dealings here, with both men and women. We have a case to make, and while we should be civil, we must also be firm, and avoid excess of friendliness."

Shudarr, trying to steer a similarly diplomatic course, reminded he had instructed him to much that effect when they began their journey, and again when they made their last camp on the edge of Landegh.

"Yes, but I have to keep it in mind myself," with a laugh.

After two nights, and tediously inactive days, Freighanai came again at midday with a couple of tribal squadrons, not Hill Froghul', to say Kamin-Tolagh was expected before nightfall. The fast-messenger who had brought that word also had instructions Dolvid and his company were to be accommodated within the Abu, and supplied with anything they needed.

For the entry, a show of strength had been mustered outside the arched gateway at the western end, a further half-dozen squadrons, so Dolvid's small escort rode in an avenue of lances that closed behind them.

"Well, but some," Shudarr muttered, "don't shape as well as the best of them — those levies there — " indicating with slightest tilt of his head a squadron more motley than the rest, slouched in the saddle with lances held at every angle. "To say nothing about their nags."

"Silent," Dolvid said. Freighanai, who rode at head of the lead squadron, had pulled aside and was waiting so he could ride beside them and point out the sights of the Abu.

His tale of miraculous transformations had to be accepted on trust by one who had not seen this place as Lunu Jinzalladhiyu.

The day was dull, warm but lead-skyed, and the long barracks buildings at the near end, which Freighanai said had been improved beyond recognition, still seemed gloomy to Dolvid; on the dusty flat nearby, more cavalry in the rudimentary stages of training were being exercised, and the growing plots beyond, intersected by little irrigation ditches, were not seen at their best, though there was no need to doubt Freighanai's word they were a valuable advance over the tough and useless scrub that had formerly covered most of the valley floor.

"Over by the south wall," with a wave, "Iruvakh — at-Iruvakh, that would be — has grapes started. Here, you see, *Bôdhrai*, as he says, it's not finding the sun as much as a few hours' shade from the worst of it. He's got his water, thanks to Lavsila's contraptions."

A moment later he pointed out white buildings, flat-roofed, on the approaches to the enclosed mound, saying they housed servants, and had once been the women's quarters, and Dolvid with a strange shiver realized they were quarters of *the* women, the *jinzai*-mothers; the obscene place where Dorrmas had let his men run mad, site of the massacre.

As they made the climb up to the gateway, Dolvid asked whether the settlement on higher ground had a separate name.

"Kargusai Tâl," Freighanai, with half a shrug. "Some of the men call it — " and he broke off, as if recognizing impropriety. Then, because he and Dolvid had campaigned together, he finished the thought: "They call it Kaminú-Kamilá, only to have a nickname for it, *Bôdhrai*."

Where main ways crossed, outside the most imposing of the buildings, there was a formal address of welcome from Lavsila to be endured, in two minutes contriving to make four separate mentions of Kamin-Tolagh's absolute sovereignty here, implying his permitting this visit was an unprecedented example of omnipotent condescension. That done, less momentously, though still flanked by the Hill Froghul' guards, he informed Dolvid this was the official residence here in the north, and a suite of rooms was available for Dolvid's use. Alternatively, having shown a preference for remaining with his escort, he with his entire party could be housed in another comfortable building nearby, until recently that of Captain Kambanal, become the *Sranim'* Kambanal, and permanently resident in the Southern Empire, his province.

Without hesitation, ignoring the gibe directed against his presumed nervousness, Dolvid chose the second alternative. Already he had been repelled by first inklings of a strangeness here, both a presence and a lack he could not identify or define, only wanting to keep a distance from his hosts, and in contact with men like himself.

The house to which they were conducted was not a hundred paces from the official residence, but faced the east-west axis; there were stables, and ample accommodation for two dozen men sleeping six to a bedroom, with Dolvid and Shudarr sharing a fifth. With most of the older and larger buildings here, it was constructed to a style recalling those of Kadon Dinul before the rebuildings of Plakhsila *Kímukoi*, and many of its furnishings, though evidently made locally, also preserved the somewhat somber and overwrought fashion from the reign of Plakhat II and his son Plakhan. Other than light screens well-made of woven rushes, and a few crude but curiously attractive earthen pots, there was nothing incontrovertibly of tribal manufacture, but there were four tribal servants who said they were Gudi-la, and, though they did not understand ordinary language of the realm, astonishingly spoke a form of the Owanilú they called *Hwanió*, rudimentary and corrupt, yet more of the Old Tongue than was understood by all but three or four of Shudarr's men. The servants made available light food, drinks and baths; the men of Shudarr's squadron scrubbed hands, faces and upper bodies in the warmed water provided, but besides Dolvid, only Shudarr and a young file-leader named Varromar actually immersed.

Freighanai had said Kamin-Tolagh was expected before nightfall; after food, Dolvid, wearying of Shudarr's inexhaustible speculation as to the significance of everything they had seen and heard, withdrew to a small private room, comfortably appointed for reading or writing, and passed time making needless refinements in the four closely-written pages he had prepared for Kamin-Tolagh, but which might never be seen; they would have no point if, as was possible, he flatly rejected all responsibility for the assault on the Lunu Tezh' village. Mid-afternoon, Varromar, who had been using an upper side-window to keep watch on the official residence, came to report the arrival of riders. His description of the chief one adequately resembled

Kamin-Tolagh, but although there was considerable subsequent coming and going, no message arrived.

Evening arrived early under the shadowing walls of this great depression, and as light was fading the summons came, brought by a man Dolvid knew, the roundfaced Pivrekhan, young, but permanently bent and hobbling from the dangerous wounds received in the Jinzai War; enforced lack of exercise had made him paunchy, but he was otherwise much the same; peculiarly disappointing a man could come so close to death, and emerge from the experience no more grown-up than before. Though he obviously could no longer hope, as once he had tried, to imitate everything Kamin-Tolagh did, Pivrekhan still spoke the name of his master as a spell to keep off all harm. He would, if convenient, meet with the *Bôdhrai* now.

Moderately cordial, Dolvid thought; if Kamin-Tolagh had wanted to keep a distance he would have waited overnight, but to come here in person would have been a genuinely friendly gesture. He matched equivocations by sending Pivrekhan back with the reply he would be there in half an hour.

"Master, have you decided how we're to address him?" Shudarr asked while, fully ready, they wasted some time.

A question pondered for days, without finding an ideal answer. "Quite proper to call Kamin-Tarú `*Asayu*,' but her brother, as one outlawed, can hold no rank in our realm — not a point I would throw in a man's face where he is plainly master. Yet as an official and a soldier of Rodlakh's *rabhsayum*, which does not recognize his overlordship here, we cannot use whatever title he has given himself."

"They call him the *Lord* Kamin-Tolagh. But I may not have to address him. He will speak to you, Master."

"Your father and he were friends. Well," deciding heavily. "We shall say *Asai*, on the grounds he has had no opportunity to dispute the justice of his outlawry."

A groan of bemusement. "I am glad I'm only a soldier."

Any parallel question about deferences was solved, for the time being, by Kamin-Tolagh himself. As through dusk, with a two-man escort, Dolvid and Shudarr approached the double-doors of the official residence, he appeared, and came down four low steps, arms outspread. "Welcome, *Bôdhrai*." He seized his hand in a warm grasp. "It has been too long."

"In every sense, *Asai*," aware nothing was spontaneous where rival powers jockeyed.

Kamin-Tolagh led the way into a well-lighted transverse great hall in the Owani style, and a half-dozen of the Hill Froghul guards were nearby.

"You will remember Shudarr Shumats-son, *Asai*."

A quick turn. "I would not have known him. You are twice the size. And a squadron-leader!" He cuffed Shudarr's shoulder. "A brave *péfrapravádai* you've turned into."

"My thanks, *Asai*."

"And why not? Your father is the best I'll ever ride with."

Shudarr, without apparent shyness, thanked him again. Kamin-Tolagh looked very fit, face deeply tanned, frame taut and supple as ever. The light eyes were more mobile than remembered, glancing all about, not apprehensively, but like a rope-walker or a juggler just about to do his best trick, making sure his entire audience is attentive, although here there were no others but the two escorts.

"How is Shumat, then — not yet bored to madness keeping books and counting blankets? Your own work, *Bôdhrai*, how does that go?" not disposed to wait for answers. "Your writings, I mean. Well, we have old things and new things to catch up with — there is plenty here to interest an historian."

"I am eager to learn, *Asai*. But we are here on matters of grave urgency. We have to avert war."

Kamin-Tolagh stopped dead, eyebrows up, then gave a reassuring laugh. "We are at peace, so far as neighbors can be who never talk. *Bôdhrai*, the Abu is waiting to greet you. We could not manage a banquet at such short notice, but we can feast in the fashion of the Hrin. Come."

As he turned away, Dolvid put a hand on his forearm, and noted how swiftly the nearest of the Hill Froghul', their evident chief, went to his hilts. He was a menacingly ugly man, with a creased face and dark, baleful eyes, his action exactly a watchdog raising its hackles and giving a low growl.

"*Asai*, this cannot be put off. A violation of the sovereign territory of Arbhal is no occasion for a feast."

The eyes came back, and they were wary; instantly obvious the breezy good fellowship had been a planned tactic. "We have had no report of such a violation. You must be mistaken."

Dolvid had his own strategy formed. "You have never heard of officers named Antighal and Drusilakh? They tell us they are in your service, *Asai*, and I am carrying a letter from Drusilakh to his wife, here at the Abu. Could he be mistaken?"

"Antighal and Drusilakh... " The relief on Kamin-Tolagh's face was absurdly plain. "They have had escort duties, as I recall. I suppose they could have strayed into your territory."

"I have in my possession a written admission, signed by both officers, that they were in the Lunu Tezh' knowingly and under orders, *Asai*. We have also captured the landing-place you have maintained on the shore of Arnan, as well as a band of tribal auxiliaries."

"If what you say is true," slowly. "Someone will have to be admonished. But war, *Bôdhrai*? you see a cause of war? Not on my side. Unless my men were tortured to get their signatures? Let us take it up in the morning."

"But a much graver — " Dolvid began, but this time was unable to detain Kamin-Tolagh, at whose sign the inner doors were thrown open. There was the sound of animated voices and strange but lively music, abruptly hushed.

"*Bôdhrai*. Shudarr — " extending his arm.

The dining hall, a high, beamed space, was brightly lit with both *ôthu* and candlelight, walls hung with rich examples of Heartland weave, a pure — but costly — decoration here, where warmth was not a consideration. A long, broad central table had lavish quantities of varied foods and drinks spread and heaped, but there were no seats drawn up to it; presumably the Hrin style cited by Kamin-Tolagh was for guests to sit, lounge and sprawl on couches and cushions, though none were doing so at present, all having risen at Kamin-Tolagh's entry.

About two dozen, Dolvid quickly estimated, some Heartlanders, others Kargul', soldiers' wives easy to tell by the relative drabness of their dress; they formed, besides, a tight-knit, separate group, practically ignored by the Family guests. Besides Freighanai and Pivrekhan, he knew other soldiers by sight, but none of their wives, whereas all the Heartlanders were known to him, by their kinships if not face to face. Lavsila's wife was most familiar of all.

Shudarr was gazing at the serving-girls, some six or eight, with the attraction of their youth, all in what must be their tribal dress, which bared one honey-skinned shoulder. They were surely not of the Hrin, as the five musicians on a low platform in a shallow alcove certainly were, with their slight-chinned faces. Their instruments were like none Dolvid had seen, reminiscent of unknown weapons or farm tools, but once accept the strange shapes and it could be seen they made music in the same familiar ways, the sounding and stopping of pipes, plucking or rubbing of stretched strings, striking of bells, bars, blocks or taut skins.

Kamin-Tolagh steered Dolvid to a group which, at a Residence Quarter dinner, would have been head of the table; his sister was there, and beside her, almost a head shorter, Khalú, with Lavsila. Among younger Heartland couples, the full-lipped woman, Ondhayu, was related in various ways to, for example, Rhunilat and Faëdhal, and had been one of Kamin-Tolagh's throng of bed-friends in his brief time with the Household at Kadon Dinul, and her new husband's family connections were familiar.

To a currently rather provincial eye, the women were stylish enough, except he had heard long sleeves had come back in fashion at Kadon Dinul since the wedding of Morulis. Here, all others were easily outshone by Kamin-Tarú, in a simple robe obviously inspired by tribal dress; one shoulder was naked, and she had gathered the rich red-gold of her hair to hang on that same side. The fashion, as with the serving girls, had obviously originated for convenience when working, but Kamin-Tarú's version was hardly made for drudgery, being of finest teased and glazed linen, costliest of all stuffs, except gold brocade. Cunningly fitted to her body, it triumphantly achieved the presumed intent of making her resplendent while at the same time causing the other women to look over-elaborate.

The feast, at such short notice, was surprisingly sumptuous, Hrin influence again detectable in elusive spicings, ostentatious in the bewildering array of fruits, cooked and preserved as well as fresh, some occasionally seen on tables of the wealthy at Kadon Dinul, at least one, pear-shaped, but with the flesh of a luscious golden melon, altogether new to Dolvid. There were also Hrin wines, scented and soft, though Kamin-Tolagh proudly filled his cup with a dark wine unmistakably Peframi Gorge, full and mellowed enough to have been born before its pourer.

Other guests showed lavish hospitality towards Shudarr, so that mid-evening Dolvid quietly suggested he not permit his cup to be filled quite so often. Everywhere was a determined effort to be cheerfully inconsequential, entailing a strange absence of curiosity over the reasons for this arrival; as eating tapered down to the nibbling of delicacies, with much sauntering to and fro, it became clear he was being kept from serious talk. He had begun an exchange with Fretasi, a solemn woman in middle life, plain-faced and plain-dressed, treasurer or keeper of accounts, who told him how trade was expanding, and what great returns were expected from newly planted acreage in the South. But when he wondered about covering the high cost of importing food and crafts from the Hrin lands, and Fretasi's frown deepened, Lavsila swooped in with a remark about the succulence of the roast boar, and turned it into a Residence Quarter conversation, polite and negligible. Again, when the plain soldier, Freighanai, was about to expand on variance in fighting-qualities between tribe and tribe, Lavsila was there to speak about measures for overcoming drought.

It was Kamin-Tolagh who hovered close by, when Dolvid and Shudarr together spoke with the young officer, Niburai. He, for a change, was permitted to talk, and prompted, both with words and admiring gazes, by young women, especially Ondhayu, he recounted stirring events from a recent campaign. Geography and tactics were unclear, but Niburai loftily lectured Shudarr on the difficulties of holding men together where weather, terrain and large enemy numbers all conspire against it; he described the fording of a forest stream in spate, and it could not be made out whether the men he led were advancing or retreating. Here, Kamin-Tolagh drifted in, and improbably charged Niburai with excessive modesty, going on to vaguely describe other exploits against heavy odds. Shudarr appeared enraptured, perhaps at the idea of a living hero near his own age, not a dead one, such as Saidhan or Sebhal, nor ancient, like his father. Even Kamin-Tolagh, just thirty, must be virtually an historical figure for one only a child during the Jinzai War.

When Dolvid tried to place these actions more exactly than "away south," Niburai said he would have to talk to Dubovai. "He is mending, I'm told," he said, and abruptly fell silent, eyes on Kamin-Tolagh.

Who shook his head ruefully, and explained Dubovai, their excellent mapmaker, had sustained a wound in the same campaign where Niburai had so distinguished himself. Passing, this left, with so much else, a faint, inexplicable menace, a wisp of smoke in the air. Except for glancing mention of Iruvakh's facility with languages, mapmaking was, so far as Dolvid could remember, the only reference he had heard to a skill not directly connected with war or agriculture, and he caught himself wishing he had brought a couple of copies of the lyrics of Bronal, and perhaps Tellis's book, to remind these self-exiles about civilized life. The music was no different from weave for the walls, a furnishing.

The three soldiers engaged in a highly technical conversation to do with weights and the effectiveness of *pefral*, and Dolvid felt free to wander off for a closer look at the musicians. From the formidable instruments he would have expected jagged and jarring noises, but the Hrin music he had heard up to now was like Hrin wines, smooth, inoffensively pleasant, with not much for memory to hold on to.

By the musicians' platform he found himself next to another of the Kargul' officers, Luzhan, said to be a specialist in training tribal levies. His face, plain and serviceable, was not as aggressively Owani as some, and if he'd had dark eyes, Kamin-Tolagh's mother would have had a ready explanation for the man's ability with the tribes. Affably, he made motions with his hands as if to imitate stopping and plucking of the largest stringed instrument, resembling a small, flat loom, with a thrumming bass voice. In this he was a little hampered by a stiff or sore left elbow. "Yaënsilat," softly, "wishes to be remembered."

"I am surprised not to see him here. A fine soldier."

"Soldier no longer." It came to Dolvid this was a very confidential conversation, and Luzhan was a born conspirator, continuing to gesture as if the subject was music.

Dolvid now mimed motions of playing the thick, curved Hrin flute, with plungers for changing pitch. "You have a message?"

"He wants private talk. You will be here tomorrow night?"

"It would appear so."

"Fifth house north of the crossways, the small one of dark stone. Yaënsilat will leave the back door open after nightfall."

"What — ?" and loudly, as the music paused: " — but they have only small pipes and their finger-drums. I have seen a very old treatise on the music of the Vrobanil, which speaks — "

"A pity," Kamin-Tolagh, as he came up. "We have no Hrin dancers with us at present. My sister, in particular, is fond of their performances, not matched by anything you have seen in the realm. What do you say, *Bôdhrai*," in an intimate tone. "Are we going to let the boy have his wish?"

"As I have tried to tell you, *Asai*. we are here on the gravest of business, not to make holiday — " but following Kamin-Tolagh's gesture to where Shudarr, flushed, while ostensibly talking to Freighanai, was intently watching his favorite among the serving-girls, not older than sixteen, with rounded but sinuous hips.

"These," Kamin-Tolagh ignored the rebuff, a little drunk himself. "These are girls of the Gudi-la. Fine, willing girls, and pleasing to the eye, as you see." Another of the girls was passing by, and he caught at her arm to display her to Dolvid. In the other hand the girl carried a bowl of fruit-sauce, and as she was swung around, stumbling a little, she nearly lost the bowl, some of its contents splashing on Kamin-Tolagh's breeches. A dead pause, and then he laughed, with a careless wave, using the crude *Hwanió* to tell the girl it was nothing.

Yet the blank instant before he spoke, an extraordinary fury had flashed across Kamin-Tolagh's face, and the other feasters had held their breath, as if in expectation or fear of — what? The girl, who had recoiled, touched by the same terror, was not reassured by Kamin-Tolagh's speech, and had to be led away, whimpering.

"At Kadon Dinul," with a chuckle. "A girl makes less fuss over causing a stain on a man's breeches." All his jokes brought a thunderclap of laughter from the guests, who evidently tried to keep not less than one ear apiece cocked in his direction.

Without knowing how, Dolvid was very near Khalú. "I hear there are children," she said, with no preamble.

"Three. Two are mine; Sedukh is Sebhal's son."

After a pause she said, "I am glad you have found a woman who can give you what you wanted most."

He made a slight bow.

"They say there is a rift between you and the *rabhsai*."

"Not," pointedly, "as there was with Ban-Sila. Nothing patience cannot heal — and goodwill."

"I am glad." She lightly touched the back of his hand.

"Are you content?" he felt obliged to ask, not really caring about any part of this exchange.

"Why not? I have everything here I could wish for." Curiously, in speaking this blatant untruth her eyes went not to her husband, but to Kamin-Tolagh: yet how could one whose chief diversion had always been shared amusements of polite society make such a claim in this harsh and sparsely gentled place?

Lavsila, having captured Shudarr, bore down unctuously. "While in the West, *Bôdhrai*, you must make time, I have been telling the boy here, to ride the ancient Moon's Road down to Larghamit. The ruins there would interest you, though there's new building, too."

He waited, and Khalú, with prompting, told about the splendid new house Lavsila had built, still incomplete, overlooking the ancient harborage, the many drawings he had made for the guidance of Hrin masons, tapping of deep underground springs which he hoped would bring orchards and water-gardens to that arid country. Only, perhaps, because he knew her so well, he could detect in Khalú's recital the dutiful tones of someone trying to believe half the delights she was describing. At a guess, notwithstanding her husband's preening enthusiasm, she did not want to live at Larghamit: if the Abu, when the visiting Heartlanders went back to the South, was starved for company, what must it be at the edge of the world, an outpost surviving from a thousand years ago?

That thought made Dolvid wish he could indeed ride the old road, enjoy the delicious, limited responsibility of being just an historian, in service only to accuracy, becoming, as he was sure would be true, only living man to have seen both Narn and Larghamit, eastern and westernmost cities of the First Empire. "My business here," he told Lavsila, reprimanded himself, "is too urgent to leave time for sightseeing."

After being cautioned, Shudarr had sipped very sparingly at his wine, and while he did a little weaving when first struck by cool night air on their short walk back to quarters, he was sober enough to want answers to many questions before sleeping. Why, for an important example, had Dolvid begun by bringing up the earlier and less deadly violation of the Lunu Tezh'? Ruefully, he explained it had been a tactic, which could not now be as effective as if he had been able to pursue his point without interruption. "Kamin-Tolagh was bound to protest innocence of either incursion; if I could get him to use all his vehemence denying one we can document, his protestations would have had a hollow sound when we came to the real charge, where we have no evidence to show."

"Can there be doubt, Master?" frowning owlishly. "Especially now, having seen these brutes who serve him."

"That we are convinced is no proof. Although, in fact, with this case, proof is nothing; what matters is, Kadon Dinul will see as we do, a crime that is self-evident. My job is to get Kamin-Tolagh to realize exactly that."

This, very properly, was a little overcomplicated for a straightforward young cavalry officer, already assailed by wine and fatigue; Shudarr paused in the painstaking unlacing of boots, stared at Dolvid, and took a new path. "You'd think," as if personally aggrieved, "he could find men of his own for a bodyguard, not those uncouth faces. They could dampen any feast. He's got men of Kargul here."

Dolvid agreed the oddly brooding nature of the feast came in part from the gloomy, unwinking guards, who were, however, a symptom, not a cause. "As we see, the provincial cavalrymen have all become squadron-leader, *kímukan*, under-captain, to command tribal troops."

Shudarr had one boot off. "That Niburai tells a fat story. Still, it would be something to be in a fight like that, eh?"

Possibly he was considering his personal chances for rapid promotion. "Can you tell me what his campaign or his war accomplished?"

"Master?"

"Victories have objects, defeats only heroes." For his histories, Dolvid had read hundreds, perhaps thousands of military dispatches, and in all ages, regardless of language, there was a certain unmistakable tone, a strident insistence on glorious examples of individual courage and self-sacrifice, invariably used to distract attention from the futility or failure of the enterprise in general. Niburai was also a symptom, and somewhere, Dolvid was convinced, Kamin-Tolagh's forces had suffered a serious setback.

Ready for his bed, predictably for distending dreams of tribal women with polished shoulders, Shudarr knotted his face in ultimate bafflement. "Master — what is it we're doing here?"

"I am here — " fighting off the sharp pang of guilt — "To seek peace. You and your men are guarding me, that is all. Tomorrow, when I have to drive tough bargains, you will be with me for the sake of what you can learn; you will have no part in negotiations, and no opinion about their outcome — is that understood?" Among dangers, it seemed increasingly likely Rodlakh would see this action as treasonable; it might well be the end of Dolvid's career; no need to associate Shudarr in that.

"Very well, Master," but puzzled by the unwonted flourish of authority. As he settled to sleep, his last perplexed word was, "But there's *something* wrong here — " as good a summation as could be found; something was so badly wrong it was hard to see; there was a madness not readily given an exact location, a conspiracy to madness, as if everyone here had to keep saying what they knew was not true — to become mad so as to make Kamin-Tolagh sane.

"What is his purpose here?" Kamin-Tolagh demanded.

Lavsila studied two half-empty cups, and combined their contents. "Not, you can be certain, what he has given us so far. He has always been full of tricks."

Kamin-Tarú raised a sleep-blurred face. "Were our men in the Lunu Tezh'?"

"But Dolvid would be last to bring that up," impatiently. "I have been told he quarreled with the *rabhsai* over the attempt, illegal attempt, to keep the *Mankh'* from sending its envoys here. That itself, naturally, was only a trick, to make the Families think he cares about the rights of religion. However, he would be the last to make an issue of our escorting of *atarlal*. My best guess is, he is here as a spy, and thinks talking about the threat of war will help him judge how ready we are for it."

"Shumat, or some other military leader, would have been better for that," skeptically. Well, but the son of Shumat was with Dolvid, and Zelu Bablakhi had left signs of weakness everywhere for a discerning eye and ear: Niburai's vaunting tale was no exception. Had news of the disastrous campaign reached Kadon Dinul — from Hrin traders, perhaps? But a revelation of his sudden weakness would logically have resulted in an ultimatum from Kadon Dinul, delivered, with insulting intent, by some obscure low-level official or squadron officer. Arrival of so high a dignitary was made ambiguous by poverty of his retinue; no servant, minimal comforts, and an ordinary, youthful half-squadron from the Army of the West — although that, again, was changed by its having Shudarr Shumatike'ati as its commander. The first command Kamin-Tolagh had issued on learning of Dolvid's arrival had been to increase and extend patrols eastward of the Abu: normally a squadron would go slightly beyond the head of the cliffs marking the rim of Landegh; for the past few days they had been venturing a half-day out on the plateau, but the *Bôdhrai*'s small riding had not been shadowed, as he had feared, by a much larger force of cavalry; nothing was moving on Landegh.

An insult to good sense, to accept the embassy at face-value, but Lavsila's talk of plots within plots was not convincing, and Kamin-Tarú's weary suggestion he wait and see what they had to say all the more exasperating for being the only practical course he could follow.

Dolvid said, "You must understand, *Asai*, I do not speak in my capacity as an official of Rodlakh's *rabhsayum*, and have no instructions from the *rabhsai*. I am here without his foreknowledge, much less permission." Though carefully worded, nonsense; *bôdhrayum* could not be omitted from his baggage, like spare boots.

Kamin-Tolagh sought enlightenment: "Then you are here as a private person, is that it?"

Lavsila murmured, "Private, but prominent." Dolvid would willingly have sacrificed Shudarr's presence for an hour alone with Kamin-Tolagh, or Kamin-Tolagh with his silent, watchful sister, but the meeting had been allowed to develop out of a late breakfast, in a bare, not unpleasant hall of the official residence, at a heavy oaken table with matching chairs which must have required a whole pack-train to transport, if they had been brought here during the *jinzai*-breeding years; a low sideboard of the same massive construction held fruits, cold meats and bread, but the servants had been sent away, and of guards only the vigilant Tau-Suaka, and another man ugly enough to be a close kinsman, remained.

"I am here, as I have already said, to prevent the war that is almost unavoidable consequence of recent events in the Lunu Tezh'."

"Not a popular war at Kadon Dinul," Lavsila said. "Not if your *rabhsai* is going to fight over the escorting of *atarlal*, which true Children of Yoëlladhu — "

"That is a minor matter. The shipping of goods through our territory under armed guard without authorization was an unnecessary provocation, but by chance no one was harmed by it, and it is finished now."

"It will be finished, when my officers and men are returned unharmed. You have no right to hold them."

"Nor, as you are well aware, to imprison *atarlal* of the *Mankh'*," Lavsila contributed.

"No one of the *Mankh'* is being held by us," irritated by this attempt to be the injured party. "Uniformed men of a foreign power, captured in arms on our territory, we have every right to hold. As to the officers, if the *Nim'* of Kargul knew of their existence, he would demand they be given to him for trial as deserters, but I have taken it upon myself not to inform him of the incident. Both officers are well, and Drusilakh will be returned to you and to his family as soon as we can reach accommodation. The other, Antighal, with three of the tribal troops, has expressed a desire to remain in the Colony."

"So," Lavsila said. "You are using these men as your hostages."

Dolvid appealed to Kamin-Tolagh. "Must we go through this trifling mock-combat, *Asai*? Would I come here, put myself wholly in your hands, so as to announce we are holding two junior officers hostage? Subsequent to our interception of that company, *Asai*, other troops under your command illegally pursued fugitives across the borders of the Lunu Tezh', and in capturing them, inflicted damage, injury and death on peaceful subjects of Rodlakh *Rabhsai*. That is not a minor matter."

"It is decidedly not a minor charge, *Bôdhrai*," Lavsila said.

"True." He sat back, fairly certain he had taken them by surprise, but anticipating a tedious, unmeaning process of denial.

Kamin-Tolagh said, "Let us be clear. There has been an incident, you say, on the borders of Lunu Tezh', in which troops of mine, you say, have been involved — "

"What I say does not matter, *Asai*. They were uniformed troops, and yours is the only power westward of our borders to maintain regular formations. What matters is that at Kadon Dinul, the question of proof will not come up; there will never be the smallest doubt about who is responsible for this outrage."

"And?" waving Lavsila to silence.

"Rightly or wrongly, it will be seen as a cause for war. That is what I have come to prevent."

"Yet you say you are not here to represent the views of your *rabhsai*."

"The moment I heard this news, *Asai* — " grateful, as he had been seven years ago, that Kamin-Tolagh's intelligence made it possible to cut swiftly to the heart of the business — "I saw what it would mean. In the Jinzai War, I learned a great deal about the prowess and pride of two without whom that war would have been lost. The *rabhsai*, who, with cause, already believes he has been wronged, is not going to stop to consider whether troops of yours have exceeded their orders — orders, I have to say, which were unwise on the face of it."

"If there ever were such orders — "

"Ssh!" Kamin-Tolagh hissed sharply, gesturing for Dolvid to continue.

"*Asai*, I knew the *rabhsai* would be likely — is likely — to demand satisfaction from you in terms you may well find unacceptable. To your standing," he appended, though the word in his mind was another. "This might be the beginning of a process that could only end in war, and needless death of thousands, perhaps."

"I thought you were his *Bôdhrai*," with ponderous irony. "If you had to urge restraint on someone, you could have done so at Kadon Dinul, and saved your crossing of Landegh. I have my own advisors."

"Yes, but I could not hope to influence the *rabhsai*, when in all essentials I agree with him; the realm has suffered intolerable injury, and Rodlakh has every right to be angry. I am not sure that can be changed, whether or not I win concessions here."

He was congratulating himself on complete candor, when Lavsila gave a sneering laugh. "What is this but a threat at second hand? I have heard much the same at a cattle market, where a man will come and say he is not sure his master would sell his stud-bull at any figure, but will negotiate with him, if you will make an offer that will not offend him — a way of bidding up the price while masquerading as an ally."

Dolvid clamped down hard on annoyance, not wanting to do worse than Kamin-Tolagh, who had shown remarkable ability not to take offense at anything said; even Shudarr had cringed slightly when he asserted Rodlakh's anger would be just, but Kamin-Tolagh was not wasting time with side-issues. "What concessions are you seeking?"

Reaching inside his outshirt for the sheaf of paper, Dolvid again noted the bristling alertness of Tau-Suaka. "My notion, *Asai*, is that we need at last to put our lands on a better footing.

We have numerous differences to discuss, but everything must begin with a full apology for the incident in the Lunu Tezh', and compensation for death, injury and damage."

"Money?" Lavsila pretended astonishment. "The just wrath of your *rabhsai* can be assuaged with *money*?"

Kamin-Tarú raised her head, and made her first contribution: "What a stupid thing to say."

So it was, and Dolvid recounted how, since becoming chief magistrate for the Colony, he had heard as many as two hundred claims for compensation, and at least half those who brought suit, when asked to justify their damages, began by saying what they had lost was dear to them beyond replacement, beyond any price. "Which may well be true, but as I tell them, the law has only money to award. Unless we want a world of eternal vengeance, we have to find a price."

"The price for the life of some mongrel creature, living on the borders of nowhere," Lavsila said, "cannot be all that great."

Still declining to be baited, he remarked generally, as much to Shudarr as anyone, "I would not want the task of holding together an empire, where high officials see more than nine-tenths of the people as worthless."

Before Lavsila could make his sneering rejoinder, Kamin-Tarú asked her brother why he had this silly man as part of their discussions; "No wonder poor Khalú always looks so bored."

"He amuses me," Kamin-Tolagh replied instantly, as if to a question he had asked himself, and turning back to Dolvid, "What else? What is this? — " reaching a hand for Dolvid's documents.

"A treaty?" The unsubdued Lavsila half-stood to crane over the top page.

"Not a treaty. It cannot be so much as draft for one; I have told you, no part of my mission here has been approved by the *rabhsai*. But on the journey, and while waiting in camp, I made notes on items which must be considered if there is to be friendship, or no less than mutual tolerance, between Kadon Dinul and the Abu. Several of these points I have raised with the New Residence in the past, but this is in no way an authorized proposal." Also where ground under his feet was least solid: most of his points were only common sense, but a common sense Rodlakh had not shown in his approach to Kamin-Tolagh's adventure; complete agreement in principle here could turn Dolvid, in his eyes, into an advocate for the enemy.

After perfunctorily riffling pages, Kamin-Tolagh passed the sheaf to Lavsila. "Very fine, but we have made proposals, friendly proposals, to Kadon Dinul, and have not been honored with a reply.

"Except for your letter, *Bôdhrai*," he amended. "But that is some years in the past, now."

"For my part, our silence is to be regretted, *Asai* — " resolving he would not be drawn any nearer criticism of Rodlakh. "My thought was, if you and I reached agreement, if only to subjects needing to be discussed, I would have a secure starting-place for my next meeting with Rodlakh *Rabhsai*."

"An ambitious undertaking," Lavsila, recovering with insensate swiftness from Kamin-Tarú's slap. "To represent each side in turn with the other. Has your voice enough weight left at Kadon Dinul?"

Shudarr shifted in his seat. Obeying instructions, he had kept his silence, and may have failed to follow the subtler fencing, but was reacting as a proper escort commander, to what he heard as a slight to the importance of his charge. Dolvid put a soothing hand on the young man's wrist; since Khalú's question last night he had known Lavsila must have had reports, probably highly colored ones, about Dolvid's loss of influence, and the rise of Elamirr.

"I do not wish to conceal — " remaining focused on Kamin-Tolagh — "my allegiance is, and will remain, with the *rabhsai*, and his decisions must be my law."

"But those decisions can be influenced by others with less than your goodwill, your stated goodwill for us. You must be aware, *Bôdhrai*, there is a strong faction at Kadon Dinul openly advocating war, against not only Kargusai, but on subjects of your own *rabhsai* who are thought to be less than ideally hostile to Kamin-Tolagh *Deghi* — "

"All parts have their lunatic immoderates," blandly. "We suspect there is a faction here, openly urging subjects of the *rabhsai* to conspire at his deposing." He leaned over to indicate a paragraph on his second page. "That is the reason for this."

Lavsila read aloud, in a voice carefully emptied of meaning, "`*unimpeded access for the* Atarlum — ' a generous concession, but, `*Kargusai will agree to refrain from unauthorized incursions into our territory, as also from all interference in internal affairs of Rodlakh's realm.*'"

"As we would undertake to in yours," Dolvid explained to Kamin-Tolagh, who was showing only marginal interest.

"The servants of Rodlakh's *rabhsayum* would also have to refrain from attempting to whip up feeling against Kargusai with false accusations of interference in Rodlakh's realm. A document used for this purpose was plainly a forgery."

"That is true," startling him with agreement. "But believed, only because it resembled other, plainly authentic documents, arguing, if more discreetly, to the same treasonable purpose."

"`*To renounce all claim to title or inheritance within the realm of Arbhal* — '" Lavsila read.

"The realm in which I am a declared outlaw?"

"Which can be nullified by simple recognition of your standing as a foreign ruler — although that," he quickly amended, for Shudarr's benefit, "is not the present intention of the *rabhsai*."

"But you, for a price, would advocate — " Lavsila began, but Kamin-Tarú interrupted.

"Are there towns in the Lunu Tezh' Protectorate?" she asked.

"In the eastern part, down south by the shores of En'tesh, *Asayu*. Kamin-Tolagh *Asai* will remember our disembarking there in the War — a number of lakeside settlements have grown together, though the town, as far as I have heard, has taken no single name. Elsewhere, *Asayu*, there are only small huddles of huts — not unlike the hamlets of your valley tribes, I would imagine."

"As they were," Kamin-Tolagh corrected. "I wish you had time, and had come at a cooler season, for visiting the tribal country. We have improved the roads, and the villages are beginning to prosper, now they are free from fear of attack."

"Yes," with grinding emphasis. "A peaceable village should not have to fear sudden, murderous attacks."

Kamin-Tarú was pursuing her own line. "And Rodlakh, you think, would make war for the sake of such a place?"

"There is a principle here, *Asayu*. The *rabhsai* has to be able to protect those in his allegiance."

"Kargusai, so it's said," Shudarr at last failed in his effort to keep silent, but was cunning enough to address Dolvid only, "made war over a counterfeit candlestick."

"Not because of the threat of war," she proclaimed, "but in simple justice, if our men did what is said, we ought to pay compensation."

"You have no shred of proof — " Lavsila predictably protested.

"Not under threat of war," Kamin-Tolagh echoed his sister. "I do not fear war with the realm, *Bôdhrai*."

"As *Bôdhrai*, I do not fear anything. As *Bôdhrai*, I am satisfied the realm is too strong to be overcome by any other power, or imaginable combination of powers. But as a man who knows history, and has lived long enough to see how the chief product of war, no matter how just, will always be death and suffering, there is nothing I fear worse."

"But without war, *jinzal* would have overcome the realm. Without war, I could not have united the tribes, or made them safe from raiders."

"Plainly, *Asai*, you have accomplished a great deal here, in so short a time," Dolvid said, and not in flattery. "All the greater reason, then, not to waste it all in a ruinous war you could not win."

"Will you ride with me?" Kamin-Tolagh abruptly asked.

"When, *Asai*?" startled.

"Now. Well, in half an hour. At this season, the heat is tolerable before mid-afternoon."

"We have settled nothing here."

Kamin-Tolagh took Dolvid's notes from Lavsila, then handed them back. "These proposals of yours; Lavsila will give them the benefit of his closest perusal, and he and I will consider them before dinner. I can tell you, as to your primary complaint, the men responsible for the incursion into your lands, which I did not order, have already been punished."

This with a flickering glance to Lavsila, and Dolvid was conscious of unsaid words, a joke shared. Nevertheless, to have Kamin-Tolagh admit the offense, to negotiate at the fringes of so many touchy issues, with no tempers lost, was extraordinary progress,.

"Certainly I'll ride with you, *Asai*." What harm could it do?

"You and I," Kamin-Tolagh told his sister, who had half-risen in hopes of being included, "can have our ride later."

She remained discontent, and Lavsila, too, was uneasy; perhaps the insults were rankling — or he feared in private talk Dolvid might mention his long-ago overtures to the *rabhsai*.

With Shudarr, he walked back to the house that had been Kambanal's, to change into riding-boots. He thought Kamin-

Tolagh meant to ride alone, but when Varromar, maintaining his vigil, reported a dozen of the Hill Froghul' bodyguard in the saddle outside the official residence, awaiting Kamin-Tolagh's emergence, delighted Shudarr by asking him to ready one file of his half-squadron for escort.

Kamin-Tolagh raised eyebrows, but made no comment when Dolvid's company came up to his; with only small talk about changes here since Lunu became Abu, they rode sedately to the western end. Having made the winding climb to the rim, Kamin-Tolagh said, "My intention was to go unescorted — unless the West makes you nervous, *Bôdhrai*?"

Dolvid waved the thought away. Evidently Tau-Suaka and his men meant to remain here; Shudarr was acutely unhappy with the orders for him to return to their quarters, evidently suspecting an elaborate ruse to simplify assassination of the *Bôdhrai*. Not impossible, but hardly Kamin-Tolagh's style — and if that was what he wanted, he had no need to get Dolvid alone; he had the numbers to overwhelm or massacre the entire escort as well. Of available dangers, Dolvid was most immediately concerned with the enormous antipathy Shudarr had contracted for Tau-Suaka and his Hill Froghul', and the opportunities for taunts and insults between two bands of idling soldiery. Firmly, he repeated his order; disconsolately, Shudarr turned back.

Once beyond the gate, Kamin-Tolagh suggested they ride westward, but his thoughts were directed south, to the tribes whose lives his coming had changed forever.

"Do you have, or will you promulgate, a code of law?" and Dolvid was astonished and a little disturbed at how newly the question came to Kamin-Tolagh.

"Tribes," offhandedly, "have differing traditions. When they serve in my armies, they are under military law, but most other questions I leave in the hands of their head-men, who know they can be deposed and replaced if they go too far."

Precisely the diversity of those people had prompted the question. "But now I suppose they have dealings with each other, tribe to tribe, intermarriage, trade, exchanges and barters — whose tradition rules if disputes arise?"

"I have settled a few such cases. Good and evil live here, as everywhere, and if you cannot tell one from the other, no library of law can help."

Late morning, but odd ragged strands of mist were clinging under a pewter sky. They rode through a drab landscape, way mounting and descending a series of identical, low, bare ridges, while Kamin-Tolagh spoke about the increase of traffic between the Abu and Larghamit, a living port once again. He laughed. "Lavsila wanted to change its name to *Elva Tolaghit*, but I shall save that for some place as-yet unnamed — unbuilt, maybe. We must respect our history, eh?"

Dolvid, he remarked, could have a glimpse of *Zhanurai bi-Nímuraibákimai*, the Great Imperial Road, though, sadly, not of the ancient city itself, where there was much to interest an historian.

"Have inscriptions been found?" Dolvid and Faëdhal were on opposite sides of a long-standing dispute about usage, which would be settled by finding a text definitely datable as belonging to the time of Shâl IV, but earlier than 1384, the 56th year of that immense reign.

"Iruvakh could talk about those things. A pity you could not meet with him — you and he would history each other to untimely death. He is also skilled in languages."

"Any skill I ever had is like Larghamit before you restored it, crumbled away with disuse."

"Your work, Dolvidhai, your histories — how does that go?"

"I have had little time for writing."

"You are wasted there. By the shores of Arnan, all history is in the past. What can be chronicled at Kadon Dinul? A fourthing rise in the price of firewood, and the *rabhsai* wore a Household tunic when he rode down to Owan Sai. Here we still have real deeds to record — the ordering of lands kept in poverty by their ignorance and by petty squabbling, bringing of water and green growth to a dusty wilderness, the making of a new empire with its chief glories yet to come — is that not history?"

"Indeed, *Asai* — " embarrassed by the transparency of his desire for lasting fame. "But history can be an unkind judge."

"Lavsila would tell you, that depends on who wins the battles. The victorious can hire their historians, who manage to praise those great objectives for which any cruel deed can be forgiven. Unforgivable acts belong only to the losers, so the sole real crime is failure."

"If I believed that, *Asai*," not sure whether Kamin-Tolagh did, "I could not be either historian or *Bôdhrai*."

"With me," pulling up his *pefrai*; having turned northward across a bone-hard salt flat, they were at the margin of a well-marked road. "With me, you could be both, and more. Good men are needed — oh, fighting-men I have in plenty, and they can be trained; it is administrators, governors I have to find. Out beyond Flamûrai, there are lands beyond lands to be put in order — or southward, the Hrin country, we have hardly begun there, and the plowshares, almost, are made of gold. I could make you wealthy, as ruler over provinces where the Siv'loi Banner is going to fly, but I would have it so there was time for you to use your pen, and give you deeds worth recording. You are a young man, but the realm with its drudgery will make you old before your time. Come with us here, where mornings still bring news."

This was mostly a kind of game, no doubt, but in some sense Kamin-Tolagh seemed genuinely to mean his offer. Dolvid half-stood in his stirrups to sketch half-deference. "I am flattered, *Asai*, but I am Rodlakh's man, too set in my loyalties to change."

"But is he fixed in his?"

"No matter what rumors have come here," rather stiffly, "Rodlakh *Rabhsai* and I have an understanding that goes beyond day-to-day agreement or difference of viewpoint." Once, he would have been quite certain that was true.

"Yet here you are, seeking peace, when Rodlakh, you say, wants war."

"If the *rabhsai* wanted war," patiently, "he would have made an excuse for it long before, when your strength, *Asai*, was considerably less. The raids into the province of your birth, which is also a part of Rodlakh's realm; your landing of armed men at Ninkufu, when you ended your lady sister's betrothal — or activities of Lavsila's pen, which could justly be called provocative. Your father the *Nimu* has urged armed action against you — no; what I have said is, Rodlakh, contrary to his best desires, may be driven into war, unless he can be reassured the murders in Lunu Tezh' were an aberration, sincerely regretted, with steps taken to prevent any recurrence."

For an instant the face registered an affront akin to the fleeting spasm of anger with the serving-girl last night. Abruptly, "And the *rabhsayu*? What does she think?"

"Of what, *Asai*?" caught on the wrong foot.

"Of this — " with an inclusive wave.

"Like the *rabhsai*," Dolvid ventured awkwardly, "Âna is far from happy. She regrets this gulf that has come between two she has admired."

"Does she?" Kamin-Tolagh spent too much time pondering this milksop of an answer. "Well — " he gave a short laugh. "I am not forgotten."

Rather aimlessly, in gathering heat, they took the road up to the col where it crossed the highest of the ridges, but visibility was poor, and there was little to see in this brown country of endless low hills.

"Not for years," mildly, "has there been anyone to dare addressing me as you have today, *Bôdhrai*. Lavsila is sifting through your notes, trying to discover what double or treble layers of deceit there are in your apparent candor, but I am inclined to accept that you are telling the truth about your reasons for coming here. You have always been sentimental as well as shrewd."

"If it is sentimental to prefer peace and productive labor to arson and rape, crippling and untimely death, then I am."

"But you have learned to make your tears serve your purpose, as others do their cynicism," reflecting rather than accusing. "So: the *Bôdhrai* fears war, the *rabhsayu* fears war, and the *rabhsai*, you say, has no taste for war he may be compelled to order, and you come to me to prevent it. I have lived with the hardships of war, and, yes, its disfigurements — " fingering the scar on the left side of his jaw. "Life is not everlasting, and there have been many very long lives that in the end meant absolutely nothing; I shall not rust my harness weeping for brave deaths that achieve some object — my own, if it comes to that."

Though far from ignoble, and unquestionably sincere, this was deficient in logic; clearly, with no successor, the only object achieved with Kamin-Tolagh's death would be instant collapse of all he had worked for here.

"Well — " he could be seen to determine on one of his flamboyant gestures. "My sister says I should pay your compensation, give you what you ask for. I believe the men think I indulge her too much."

As expected, Lavsila was completely opposed to all concessions. "You have only his word, the word of a lifelong trickster, for any of this — that the *rabhsai* will make the incident into a cause for war, or anything we do would change his mind; it could as easily be a plan hatched between Rodlakh and Dolvid."

"No. The border-incident is not invention; it happened, as we know. Count on your fingers — after hearing about it, there was no time for him to have visited Kadon Dinul, or to have exchanged dispatches, before leaving to come here; as it is, he could hardly have delayed a half-day. If there is a plot, it is his own."

"To win his way back into favor," adaptive as ever. "And if we send him home empty-handed, it might well be the end of the Dolvid era. The Families would thank you for that."

"Again?" in angry sarcasm; only a week ago, Lavsila had assured him his Heartland support was steadily growing, once again promising an imminent time when he could count on enough disaffection within the realm to bring him victory in a war with Rodlakh. But the great wave of feeling that was to call him back as its rescuer remained the same unattainable distance away.

"When Elamirr, champion of the illiterate, succeeds him, there will be nothing to stand in the way of his war against the Families, and no remedy except to depose Rodlakh and the entire House Arbhai-Navu."

Not for the first time, Kamin-Tolagh was shocked more than he should be by this callous prescription of suffering for friends and kin, as a desirable element in his plans.

"Unfortunately, I am going to give Dolvid the compensation and written regrets he came for. My sister says I should."

Lavsila did not quite dare to call it a frivolous reason, nor doubt out loud it was the real one. Which, of course, it was not; the fact was while Kamin-Tolagh was irked by the idea of apologizing, it would be foolish to risk war when he was least prepared for it. At some later time, when he had been able to replace the losses of Zelu Bablakhi, he would take his chances in a war, especially one where Rodlakh, by taking the offensive, gave up his great advantage in numbers; it would be a fight, not against the realm of Arbhal, but the fragment of it that could be put in the field six lean days riding from its base. Kamin-Tolagh envisaged a two-phased war with an interval of truce; a series of heavy defeats on the armies Rodlakh sent allowing him to make an advantageous peace, including recognition, and ceding of the westward marches of the Lunu Tezh' Protectorate, which he could then use to gather his forces and their supplies for the second and decisive round; all this was within reach if Rodlakh could be provoked into an attack a year hence, or a little beyond, the autumn after next, and (Lavsila's part), if the *rabhsai* also had to deal with dissension at home.

Lavsila disconsolately riffled the pages of Dolvid's notes. "The danger, as I see it; any concession will be seen, rather, as a confession of weakness, and encourage instead of deter an assault. Many of these stipulations are insulting."

"They will never come to anything," Kamin-Tolagh predicted. "We can assent to them in the same spirit as they were given, as theoretical basis for imaginary discussions."

"He speaks about fixing northern and eastern boundaries of Kargusai — of your domains. Here: `Landegh to be considered as free, except the armed forces of the* rabhsai *only will be permitted there — ' can that be called neutral, where his army can go, and not yours?"

He took the page, and read the passage marked. "That we must except; Shumat could bring an army and store its supplies less than a day's ride from here. Dolvid must know that is out of the question. He included it as a test; if we allow it, he will conclude we want peace at any price."

"We can agree to none of this, and still send him home a hero, by giving him his apology."

"Then he will have the greater height to fall from. You will have to find other ways to advance the cause of Elamirr."

"The *rabhsai*, it is true, may feel he has no choice but to endorse a settlement brought home by Dolvid, but he is not going to love him for it. Some bad feeling there — I hear from a man at Kadon Dinul who says the *rabhsayu* from time to time gets in bed with Dolvid."

"Oh, come — " in utter, angry disbelief; this went beyond even Lavsila's permissible limit of foolishness. "You are talking about treason. It is absurd; Âna is not one of your Residence Quarter wives."

"But those Mixed women, once let loose, can have appetites no one man can satisfy."

"You — " he mastered himself. "Stories your Residence Quarter champions recite while measuring themselves? Dolvid, besides, is married to Aëlu, and she must be quite enough for him; does your wife tell you nothing?"

"Difficult, naturally, to prove."

"What is not true often is."

"Well," placatingly. "No need for that. What would be thought if, a month or two after his triumphant return, he was discovered in possession of gold, stamped with the head of Kamin-Tolagh?"

"That I had bribed him to make peace," thoughtfully, reflecting on the notorious simplicity of the *Bôdhraï*'s life. "If believed. Wait, though — his exile under Ban-Sila — was that not on a charge of peculation? A false charge, as later claimed."

"Khalú's brother helped provide the evidence, and my father had a part in it, too. Nevertheless, a conviction of that kind, it can be disproved a thousand times, and still leave suspicions; there will be plenty of knowing nods if it happens again." He was settling it with himself. "It can be contrived, I think, but I shall have to come to you for a large enough sum in gold."

"And Fretasi to you, for a complete accounting." One day, Lavsila was going to *contrive* his own downfall. If disgraced under Rodlakh, Dolvid might be persuaded to come here to the West, an irony Lavsila would enjoy, till he saw the result: his displacement.

"Your task," he said meanwhile, "give me the Families. Any chance of an uprising in the Heartland, led by the private armies, will tie at least one of Shumat's hands."

"Elamirr will deliver them to us."

"And I must have the cavalry — " he began, and broke off. Of Kargul, had been in his mind, but Lavsila did not have to know everything. Restored tribal armies, dissent and threat of dissent in the Heartland, Rodlakh provoked into taking the offensive, all that was needed, but the invasion with which the wars would finish was going to need first-class cavalry, *péfrapravádal*. With those of Kargul, he was still admired, he believed, above their titular captain, his father, and his most ardent admirers, forced into retirement in Tovakh's reorganization, could be called back to the colors in a week. Those squadrons, the best cavalry anywhere, could be his for a march on Kadon Dinul. Here, he needed no help from Lavsila.

By nightfall, Dolvid was wondering whether he should risk taking up Luzhan's quiet invitation of the night before. Beyond his best reasonable hopes in coming here, he had a small bag of gold pieces, a written expression of regrets at the incursion, and treaty notes with interlinear comments from Kamin-Tolagh.

However improbably, he had won, and had made his intention of an early start on the journey home his excuse for leaving the cordialities of the official residence, with Kamin-Tolagh hospitably protesting there was a last unopened bottle of the perfectly-matured Peframi Gorge wine. Dolvid warned himself it would be foolhardy to gamble unexpected victory on the boyish skulk demanded by a meeting with Yaënsilat, yet was enormously intrigued by the furtive manner of Luzhan's approach, its hints both of important secrets and genuine danger.

In the little writing room he continued in doubt, while making a detailed record of his observations and impressions, where the personal warmth of Kamin-Tolagh made a sharper contrast with the indefinable atmosphere of dread that hung as an invisible fog over the Abu. He was interrupted by the discreetest of taps on the door; Shudarr.

"Not yet — " for some hours he had wanted to recount his adventures during Dolvid's longer-than-expected excursion with Kamin-Tolagh.

"No, Master — there is a lady to see you."

Not, as momentarily feared, Kamin-Tarú; no, Khalú, cloaked, but unattended; he had said farewell less than an hour ago, not expecting to see her again before leaving.

She confessed, with a remembered mischievous air, she was `supposed to be' home and on her way to sleep, but Lavsila, she expected, would stay drinking with Kamin-Tolagh well past midnight. If there was a suggestion in all this, it meant nothing to Dolvid; with most of his life he was the one who found it hard to close a chapter, but nothing was so completely over as the feeling he had once had for Khalú. Whether or not she expected him to want her, that clearly was not what she had come for, and he was struck by her freedom from concern over being observed; if clandestine, her visit was anything but secretive in its manner; soldiery and others were about in the small settlement.

Seated, cloak thrown back from her shoulders, eyes gravely on him, she made what he assessed as a token feint at sentiment, asking who would have expected to find them together, here, of all places in the world, after so much shared and separate time? He poured her wan Hrin wine, and before long she came to her subject.

"This treaty the *rabhsai* may sign with Kamin-Tolagh — "

"There is nothing approaching a treaty as yet, not the draft of one, only the vaguest notes."

"I understand, but if there is a treaty, if Rodlakh recognizes Kargusai, would that mean everyone would have to make a final choice?"

"Everyone, who?" He did not trouble to re-emphasize how far Rodlakh was from such an act.

Khalú displayed impatience with him. "Us, the ones who came here; should we have to renounce all allegiance to Arbhal?"

He was slow to understand what she wanted. "Kamin-Tolagh, I am sure, will demand allegiance; one excludes the other."

"Irrevocably?"

"Well — " and then he saw the question she was afraid to ask, *What if this empire fails?* Yet the worry was unlike Khalú's normal blithe assumption of privilege, which in this case would surely not fail her; she was from an enormously wealthy and highly influential family, and would obviously be reinstated without much difficulty. "You have not committed any crime in Rodlakh's realm."

She lowered her eyes as if at a sudden onset of alien modesty. "Yes, but I am married to a man who — " she turned up opened palms.

Who had reasons to fear *rabhsai*'s justice. At last it came to him Khalú had come here, not merely with Lavsila's permission, but at his behest. Angrily, he said, "Your husband is going to have to find how to hedge his own bets, not send his wife."

"In his position," pleading for sympathetic understanding, "he has to be careful to maintain an appearance. But he wanted me to tell you — " Not at her best dealing with large affairs, Khalú paused here to make sure she had the words right, her lips moving in a silent rehearsal, as she closed her eyes to concentrate, just as Dhunival had with an earlier message from Lavsila. "He would not want the language of robust debate to be mistaken for his true feelings, and his admiration for you remains unimpaired."

"His what for me? How can you recite such nonsense; you better than anyone know Lavsila, for fifteen years, has had nothing but contempt for me as a renegade Owani, and for my *evil dream-world of mingled races*." The last was a quotation from a dozen years ago, the day of the foolish duel with Khalú's brother, but could as easily be a phrase from one of the intercepted letters.

Khalú flushed; old experience instructed him her innate incapacity for being caught in the wrong would soon transform embarrassment into anger, or bitter tears.

"Acts have consequences," not a particularly new thought, unless you were, in the words of Tellis, a house-pet bred by the Families. "I can do nothing for Lavsila; he will stand or fall with Kamin-Tolagh."

On the other hand, it might yet be possible to save Ghuradh, and it came to her as a novel and shocking idea her brother's games with Lavsila could constitute treason. He would predictably experience a sense of betrayal, if he knew his confederate in the West was trying to keep open a line of retreat with *rabhsayum* they were busy vilifying.

"*Rabhsayum* has been reluctant to dignify these plotters by moving against them, but the killings in the Lunu Tezh', despite my success here, make support for Kamin-Tolagh not as good a joke as it was."

Khalú's confusion was complete; she became angry with Lavsila, recognizing for the first time the extent and implications of his duplicities, at the same time fearing she had botched his errand, of which a further part, she confided, was the bizarre offer to keep Dolvid covertly informed as to developments in the West affecting the interests of the realm.

"I was supposed to tell you that — " she was near tears, "only if your response was a friendly one — if you could be trusted not to betray him to Kamin-Tolagh. You won't, Dol, will you?"

He was shocked — and then surprised he could be — to recognize her husband had expected and perhaps encouraged Khalú to bed with him. "You can tell Lavsila, truthfully, I said only a fool would rely on information, or any other offer, from such a source. I have known for a long time what he is, and Kamin-Tolagh cannot have many illusions left. Who he chooses to trust is no business of mine."

"What about Ghuradh?" She was remarkably untroubled by his assessment of her husband.

Her brother, he told her, would have to do better; Kamin-Tolagh might succeed well enough to keep Lavsila safe, and still be no worse than a nuisance for Rodlakh's realm, if not a complete irrelevancy. Chances of his ever collecting the armed strength to be a serious threat were remote, and Ghuradh must by now see for himself the yet slighter possibility of a Heartland uprising in Kamin-Tolagh's favor.

"Why say all this to me? I cannot advise Ghuradh. You can see I have no way to write him a confidential letter."

"You could, if I carried it." He did not blame her for caution, and in the end asked her to write and sign only a recommendation Ghuradh listen to what Dolvid had to say. Distraught now, she would guess later he meant to turn her brother into a more reliable version of what Lavsila had offered, a source of information about Kamin-Tolagh's intentions. That would entail deception of her husband by her brother, but Dolvid did not think Khalú would interpret it in exactly that way; the issues meant nothing to her, for whom it was a *zhabhu* game, where players, no matter how friendly, sought, and expected each other to seek, every available advantage.

Terse note written, he saw her gratitude was about to bring on a sentimental nostalgia less calculated than the earlier attempt, and with a familiar strain of self-pity; eyes moistening, she murmured nothing in her life had gone right since parting from him.

"Life is so cruel here," rising from her seat, "Will you kiss me?"

He compromised by grasping her shoulders and kissing her forehead, an instant addition to his long catalogue of insults.

When he saw her to the door, the moon had set, and lighted windows were few; she did not object when he gave her Varromar for her escort on the brief walk to her house and Lavsila's, largest on the farther side of the crossways. Though guards remained all night outside the house where Kamin-Tolagh and his sister slept, there were no observed patrols in the few streets. In minutes, Varromar returned. Noting everything was perfectly still, Dolvid told Shudarr he would be going out for an hour or two, and the back door beyond the kitchens should be kept unlocked.

"No," he rebuked the ghost of a smirk on the young man's face. "Not a woman." Briefly, he told about the overtures of Luzhan, and Shudarr at once said he would go in his place. If accosted, he could hint with half-drunken winks and nudges he was on his way to or from an hospitable bed. This connected in some fashion with the tale he had been trying to tell, but Dolvid again put him off, regretfully declining his offer. True, the nocturnal wanderings of youth might be treated more indulgently than those of a *Bôdhrai* no longer twentyish, but would Yaënsilat willingly tell his tale to a complete stranger?

Necessary, also, to refuse Shudarr's substituted suggestion he accompany Dolvid; in the midst of several hundred potential enemies, the slight added protection did not justify the increased risk of being observed. Finally, Shudarr was strictly forbidden to go out, or send men out, in search of Dolvid if he was delayed.

"Black as a hole in nothing," Shudarr commented, as, with kitchen-light covered, they stood by the back door, which only memory told them opened on a pleasant little garden, with sweet herbs, small trees, and a rippling thread of a stream. Dolvid agreed, wondering whether there was light enough for him to find his way without noisy bumpings and stumblings.

Half a minute standing beneath some sort of ornamental maple was enough to change his mind; the moon was gone, but sky over the Abu was extravagantly thronged with sharp stars, and the ground itself seemed to breathe out a faint luminescence; he could almost imagine he cast a shadow as he went. Uneasy about his visibility, he scaled a low wall as quietly as he could, and crept between dark buildings to the edge of the street that ran east and west.

Shudarr, in defiance of orders, was about to take a half-file in search of him when he returned, having been over twice the hour he had forecast. What he had heard from Yaënsilat had left visible signs of shock, or so he judged when Shudarr's first words, drawing his blade, were, "Are you being pursued?"

"No, no. There is no danger. No immediate danger," he modified, and found a rough kitchen chair to sit on. He had been mad to make this journey, criminally mad to bring two dozen good men, including the son of his oldest friend. "I know now what caused the strangeness we could feel at the feast."

Since he was not yet ready to expand on that conclusion, Shudarr took it as an appropriate moment for the story Dolvid had been too preoccupied to hear. Coming back from the western end of the Abu in the morning, and passing near the women's quarters, he had glimpsed, hanging out laundry, the pretty girl he had admired so ardently at the feast.

"I thought, Master, pardon me, I had time for a word with her," sheepishly. "But by the time I'd seen the men to the mound here, she had gone inside. Those girls aren't house-servants; they live there in the large white building."

More than half in love, at that age Dolvid vividly remembered, when such yearnings can feel as absolute as need for air or water, Shudarr had gone inside, and come to a kind of washroom, filled with steam.

"I could not see the girl I was looking for, but that other one was there — that one who splashed fruit on Kamin-Tolagh. She was washing herself. Naked, Master."

"Spare me the haft-boning stories," irritatedly.

Shudarr flushed. `Haft-boning' was camp slang, in origin a reference to the practice of rubbing down the thick end of a lance with a meat bone boiled bare, to make the wood less liable to cracking. "No, Master, her back; she was marked with a terrible flogging, fresh weals, and there was blood. I tried to question her, but I can't do much with that *Hwanió* talk; besides it made her frightened just my being there, so I came away. Servants need whipping sometimes, if they steal or tell lies, but would Kamin-Tolagh have a girl whipped so viciously, for an accident, where he himself was the cause?"

"*Have* her whipped? I do not doubt he gave himself that pleasure." No need to harrow Shudarr with the detailed stories he had heard from old Yaënsilat, supported for a time by Luzhan, who came and went like a wraith. The village-burning incident that had ended Yaënsilat's military service, ferocious treatment of captured rebels, many individual instances of cruelty, down to the recent disastrous campaign and its grisly aftermath, recapture of the deserters, their brutally prolonged deaths — everything went to illustrate a growing appetite for inflicting pain, and a growing satisfaction in witnessing it. Recalling the lingering executions, Luzhan, an eye-witness, had been obliged to leave the room to retch in private. Beyond all that, haunting imagination, was the reported cold extermination of virtually an entire and ancient tribe, casually, like throwing away boots that pinched. Khalú's tearful remark, *it is so cruel here*, had not been as self-pitying as he had assumed.

"These are things," Yaënsilat had said, voice trembling, and not with age, "enough to revolt any honest soldier. I didn't flinch, killing a man in battle, so long as he meant to fight, but where's honor in this murderer's work?" But his horror kept lapping over into practical concerns: "Plenty of others beside Luzhan feel it as I do — not as many as there were; this bloody madness down south killed sixteen men of Kargul, not to mention those like Dubovai who'll never mend aright. And this giddy place is feasting Niburai as if he was young Sebhal. A soldier's a soldier, *Bôdhrai*, ready to take his chance for an honest purpose, but who wants to die or be maimed? But it's going on, war after war, battle after battle, another thousand miles of rock and sand won; nobody's luck can hold against too many tosses of the coin. Some of the young idiots think they'll fill their pockets with Hrin gold, but will that buy back what they miss the most? their homes, I mean to say, and the grass valleys of Kargul."

So the old soldier came to the chief reason he had asked for this meeting: there were, he claimed, a score at least of cavalrymen who wanted to renounce their allegiance to Kamin-Tolagh — many more, maybe, but in this spy-ridden place a dangerous sport was to enquire into a man's true feelings; everyone was afraid of the bodyguard led by Tau-Suaka, tough and ruthless men, who did not question orders. There was, moreover, the problem of where they could escape. "Here, they are dying, one by one, and in their home, they're condemned rebels."

Dolvid could have said they had made their choice and taken new oaths; there had been a time when they were offered the chance of going home, and many had come with Kamin-Tolagh after. But those who had stayed, surely, had been unable to envision the atrocities they would be party to. "Kargul is out of the question unless a time comes when Tovakh *Asai* can be persuaded to offer amnesty. But there are other green places in the realm, and if my voice still has influence at Kadon Dinul — " He broke off, remembering his new powers. "On my own authority, I can extend the hospitality of the Colony, if only as a resting-place. I cannot guarantee assistance for your escape, beyond instructing the Army of the West to watch for you on Landegh." Rodlakh could countermand this offer of sanctuary, but Dolvid did not think he would want to be outshone in clemency, nor to be trapped, as others of his House had been, in a dispute with the Colony. If Yaënsilat and his friends could once reach the Frontier, he doubted they would ever face trial; Tovakh himself might be shamed into a magnanimous gesture.

"The answer to your question," to Shudarr, having given only bare bones of Yaënsilat's long tale. "Why does Kamin-Tolagh rely on an alien bodyguard? If you were an officer of Kargul, longing for his home, how would you purchase a pardon from Tovakh *Asai*?"

He considered. "If I had allies, I would try to arrest Kamin-Tolagh, and bring him home as a prisoner."

"Exactly."

"But he has given you the apology and the compensation you came here for."

"Not because his sister said he should," tartly. "Nor because he was swayed by my *sentimentality*." A long time would have to pass before he could get rid of the bitter aftertaste from that amicable ride; with a pomposity embarrassing to contemplate, he had put in his notes that he had, perhaps, been privileged to see a genuine Kamin-Tolagh rarely displayed to those for whom he had to maintain the implacable dignity of an overlord. If he, Dolvid, had to have a weakness, he supposed it could be worse than this lifelong habit of wishing to find true virtue in improbable places, but Elamirr would make a feast of deriding his gullibility here.

"Why, then?" Shudarr persisted.

"I suppose, simply, because he is afraid of war, after the losses in the south — a thousand of his best-trained tribal troops, according to Luzhan, and he was there. An overestimate, maybe, but the lengths he has gone to to disguise defeat argue a seriously weakness."

"Then we ought to make war on him at once."

"We, you and I and our puny two dozen ought to remove ourselves while we can from this place where life is so cheap, and death so easy. I should not have brought you here."

36.

The parting ceremonies became an agony for Dolvid, who wanted only to be gone. He was aware all through a last meeting at the official residence, where bread and meat were shared with Kamin-Tolagh, that Shudarr, a youth not yet twenty, who had no ambition to be other than a good soldier, now knew a great deal too much for his experience. Dolvid had solemnly warned him once again individual feelings had no place in diplomacy, and what they had learned about Kamin-Tolagh, both cruelties and defeat, would not change their smiles and courtesies, and once again he was instructing himself as much as the youth; painfully hard to maintain the cordial atmosphere in the teeth of lies and hypocrisies.

Even the drinking of *raminat* did not end it; Kamin-Tolagh insisted on mounting a part of his bodyguard, to accompany the homebound guests as far as the gate at the eastward end of the Abu.

"A pity, *Bôdhrai*, you will not stay another day or so. Iruvakh is bound to return from the south any day."

Dolvid gestured to his pocket where notes were for the treaty. "Now we are on speaking terms, there may be other opportunities."

"Come to us again when we are staying in the south, among the Hrin. It is very pleasing, by the river there. You have seen hardly any of our lands."

He bowed his thanks, ready to shout with impatience.

"You, too, warrior — " reaching a hand to cup Shudarr's neck. "Like the *Bôdhrai*, you will always be welcome — next time, you must come and watch our squadrons train."

"As much as I have seen, *Asai* — " Shudarr did well, not to shrink from the unwanted caress. "Is more than I ever expected."

"I shall be awaiting word from your *rabhsai*. Please convey my warmest personal regards to him. And to — to others who have been friends."

Shumat, Âna; in his face there was a shading of regret. Dolvid, unable to see circumstances in which they would meet again, remembered with sorrow their great ride together in the Jinzai War, how much he had come to admire about this man. Over the past seven years he had observed and sometimes regretted changes in Rodlakh, but if the habit of power was a deforming disease, then Rodlakh's case was a couple of sneezes compared to the plague that had seized Kamin-Tolagh. True, the powers of the *rabhsai*, hedged in by laws, balanced by those of the provinces, armies, *Mankh'*, were not to be compared to those wielded by Kamin-Tolagh, with his unquestioning bodyguard, his abject followers, his airy conviction his own will or whim was all the law his empire needed. Not since legendary times had the realm groaned under a lord so absolute: even the imperial Shâls had sometimes to contend with a spirited provincial governor, an assertive Patriarch.

The legality of power was not the entire answer; Kanavakh the Bloody had achieved his notorious cruelties nominally under many of the same limitations as Rodlakh was subject to — and a Rodlakh given unrestricted power could never become a Kamin-Tolagh; despite arbitrary fits, he lacked the terrible certainty needed; when Rodlakh was unyielding it was out of inner doubts which demanded he make a stand somewhere. His natural inclination would be to imitate his father and amble away from hard questions, but his sense of duty was too active; issues without a clear right or wrong muddled him, and so he took refuge in obstinacy. Having bent his nose against that mood, Dolvid could not keep perpetually in mind the agonized good intentions behind it, but would try not to forget a ruler could display far worse faults than confusion. Kamin-Tolagh, it seemed, always knew exactly what to do, if it was to murder an entire tribe.

As their small riding with its pack-animals breasted the first rise, Dolvid turned in the saddle, to see Kamin-Tolagh still in the same place. He raised a hand, but his tribal guard had drawn in close about him.

The day, Shudarr remarked, would be a warm one, sun glaring in their faces as they settled to the ride. "Master," after a glance behind. "I see we're going to have company." A sizeable force, four squadrons or so, was following at a mile's distance.

"Only to where the trail climbs up to Landegh. A normal patrol, so Kamin-Tolagh says." For reply, there came a grunt.

Minutes later, on the road ahead where it wriggled among great boulders, a further body of troops began coming into view, moving towards them. Shudarr put the tip of his tongue between dry lips, and looked for orders or reassurance to Dolvid, who had neither to give. The new company, not yet entirely in view, numbered at least fifty: if, after all, Kamin-Tolagh had made up his mind on a massacre, here where none of his close circle at the Abu need know about it, he had provided ample numbers against their two dozen. The only hope for any of them to live would be an attempt to break through the men ahead, but that would mean being the ones to initiate hostilities, which would be stupid even if it could be done.

About to give bleak instructions that if fighting began, every man must try to save himself, he saw the approaching force was not one any sane ruler would assign to murder, consisting of rawest recruits with untipped lances carried at all angles, formations ragged, the riding itself less than expert; a double-squadron of new levies out learning the paces. The officer at their head was Luzhan, allowing himself to be no more than slightly handicapped by a left arm wounded, as Dolvid now knew, in the Zelu Bablakhi bloodbath.

When the companies met, Luzhan called a halt, and achieved a jostling one; his subordinate half-squadron and file officers were all men of the tribes. Luzhan, with the slightly forced cheerfulness of one saying farewell to brief acquaintances, said, "I had hoped to see you, that's why I brought the geese this way. If we laugh and so forth, Master, they won't guess what we're saying." He chuckled. "The old soldier was wrong to bring you into our troubles, Master," and Dolvid understood he was also omitting use of a name the tribal soldiers would recognize. Not easy to hold in mind that here, contrary to all experience, some words of the Owanilú were understood where ordinary language was not.

He reached out and grasped Luzhan's hand warmly. "Why?"

"His neighbor, a Heartlander," Luzhan continued cheerfully. "Asked him, first thing this morning, was that not the *Bôdhrai* came to see him last night?" A gesture that might mean it would be a hot day. "How he could recognize you by night, I can't say. The old one told him he was mistaken, but he was not convinced."

Dolvid threw back his head to give a loud guffaw, and punched at the shoulder of Shudarr, who, if belatedly, joined in. Still shaking with laughs, Dolvid said, "Can something be done to help?"

For less than a second the officer was unable to prevent his expression matching his despondent thoughts. "We must hope." The grin was forced back in place. "My fear is, you will be in danger yourselves if... "

If Yaënsilat was unable to resist determined questioning. "We should outdistance any pursuit. Do you want to come with us now?"

Luzhan drew back and gave a jocular salute. "I have a wife, Master, and my daughter."

"In autumn," returning the salute in kind, "ten days past Halving, the Army of the West will hold exercises on Landegh. The exiled Heir from your home province has been forewarned." He meant to convey, it would be a prime time for an attempt at desertion.

"I thank you," Luzhan said.

"I hope the other will be able to take advantage of this."

"We must hope," Luzhan repeated, in exactly the singing tone of a reiterated farewell.

Continuing to display ostentatious high spirits, they led their companies past each other, slouching beginners, disdainful men of the Colony.

"This other rabble following us is not much better," Shudarr remarked. "They're not a threat to us."

Dolvid admired the spirit, but did not like odds of eight to one no matter what the difference in quality. "Kamin-Tolagh, if he hears and credits the news from Yaënsilat's neighbor, may send better troops after us, the best he can find."

Pointing out they would have a good start on any such fresh pursuit, Shudarr spoke of camping in the same place they had on the outward journey, a wind-sheltered cleft, a few hours the other side of the broken edge of Landegh, at this season possessing a small, cool stream, but Dolvid, knowing that resting-place to be predictable, meant to be well beyond there by nightfall. "A cold night, I am afraid, on the open plain."

"We're going to feel some wind, Master."

"I want to go on, after four hours of rest, as quietly as we can, and leaving our watchfires burning. There will be the third of a moon — can we manage that?"

"If we stick to the trail — " frowning in thought, very much his father. "But, Master, the going will be slow, and we'll have to rest again. If we move by night and rest by day, they'll soon catch us."

"If we are followed, I want to discourage them, to make them feel they are outdistanced. Tomorrow about midday, we can rest briefly again, except for you and three or four of your youngest and strongest who can go without sleep — with strong horses, also."

"Master?"

"I am going to give you a message for Captain Bradhinal, at Drin Navuna. You will press forward, with one pack-animal, the best we have, and set a new record for crossing Landegh."

"My place is with you," setting his chin stubbornly. "If you want to send word ahead, I'll pick men for you, but I am staying at your side."

"I am not putting you out of danger," a quarter-truth; he was in fact glad to have a creditable reason for sending the youth to safety. "I must have one I can rely on to carry my message swiftly — and also one who, when he reaches the Drin, can ask to be taken straight to Bradhinal, without long haggling with some *kimukan*. Whose son you are will help that."

"The men need my leadership if there is to be a fight."

How well he remembered the boy's father in this mulish mood. "Are you so bad a field-officer, have you trained your squadron so poorly they cannot fight without you? If you were disabled in a fight, would they have to surrender?"

"No, but you made me commander of your escort, and my only duty — "

"You will be doing more to protect me, I swear, carrying my message. It will ask Bradhinal to ride out to meet us, with as many squadrons as he can assemble in an hour. He will let you ride with him, I am sure, if you are not asleep in the saddle."

"Would you — could you find room in your message to tell him that, Master?" His yielding was not yet complete, but this wistfulness was a good sign.

After a silent quarter-mile, he said suddenly, "If the Captain Bradhinal rides out — if there is a battle with some of Kamin-Tolagh's funny companies — we'll kick them clear off Landegh, no question, but — ?"

"Yes?"

"Isn't that start of the war we, you, came here to prevent?"

"If Kamin-Tolagh led the pursuit in person," jokingly, never believing he would, "it could be the end of it."

After seeing off the visitors, Kamin-Tolagh, pleased with how it had gone, returned to bed, getting up again when Kamin-Tarú did for the first time. Over a breakfast which was his second, she wished he had wakened her for the farewells. "Dolvid does not change."

"Could he be bedfriend to the *rabhsayu*?" That absurdity of Lavsila's refused to vanish entirely.

"Now, you mean to say, or before? Before, she was bedfriend to Sebhal," Kamin-Tarú hedged, not comfortable with speculation on this subject. She had a tender thought for Dolvid, and pleasant memories of being with him in at Kamsilat, again in those baths Khalú was so proud of — in and beside them. Something her brother knew nothing about, and for no explicable reason she had encouraged the idea of Dolvid's coldness. "At Kadon, as you know very well, anyone can be anyone's bedfriend."

"Âna?" letting his skepticism show. "With Dolvid?"

"Who says so?"

"Lavsila."

"No," genuinely decided. "Dolvid is too correct. Besides, he has Aëlu."

"Is that truly what you think?" It coincided remarkably with his own opinion.

She bridled. "Why would I say it just to please you? I do not know what you want to hear."

The effect of this teasing answer was unpredictably profound; he could feel solid ground shift under his feet. "Never," half-rising, "never do that. I don't mean here, where our thoughts are much the same, but you must always tell me truly what you think, not what you think I would like."

"I do — " but she was not really sure. Last year she would have been.

"We must have this between us, you and I." Bafflingly hard to tell when he was being informed and when cosseted; that men and women dependent on his goodwill became fearful of speaking their minds was at the same time a measure of his power, and a limitation on it. He would not have wanted a whole entourage of underlings like Dolvid, whose candor could be offensive, nor had he lapsed into imagining an empire could be ruled by good fellowship, but he was maddened by dissembling. Worse now he learned that to show his irritation only made deception more likely: Freighanai he could count on, and in a paradoxical way, Lavsila, whose maze of machinations could safely be ignored, so long as their interests coincided. But Kamin-Tarú was indispensable: for her to hide her thoughts would be to have hands he could not trust to do his will.

Lavsila came in unannounced, with the ridiculous question whether Kamin-Tolagh had heard about a meeting between Dolvid and Yaënsilat.

"There was no such meeting."

"Valubran says yes. I asked him to keep an eye on comings and goings at Yaënsilat's house, now he lives nearby." The youthful goldsmith had not hesitated to claim the small dwelling of a man of Kargul lost in the Zelu Bablakhi disaster.

"Very late last night, when Yaënsilat opened his back door, the light fell for a moment on the face of his visitor, and Valubran is almost sure it was Dolvid. Foolishly, he asked this morning, and Yaënsilat denied it." Valubran had then gone as usual to his forge, and had only sought out Lavsila with the tale when unable to rid himself of his conviction.

"How would Valubran know Dolvid well enough?" Kamin-Tarú asked.

"His family is all Craft, both sides. All those people recognize the guild-smasher, and the whole Abu witnessed his arrival. Besides, at Kadon Dinul, he was often pointed out to Valubran by his mother, who as a girl was Dolvid's special friend."

"But why would there be such a meeting?" Kamin-Tolagh demanded, though recognizing reason might matter less than result.

He could not resist delaying an answer with the reminder he had suggested the dwelling of Yaënsilat should be watched as potential center of undesirable intrigues. Another soldier, he said, not identified by Valubran, had been there last night; maybe there was a conspiracy hatching, with covert support of the *rabhsai*, or of Dolvid acting alone.

"For what? To murder me, and rejoin the realm?"

"Or put Dolvid in your place — " as always carrying counterplot past the brink of the credible.

"Perhaps they just wanted to talk," Kamin-Tarú said, and then her brother saw clearly a danger realler than Lavsila's dreams, the strong possibility Yaënsilat, learning from his army friends the true magnitude of the Bablakhi disaster, had given Dolvid information greatly more valuable than the compensation-gold he was carrying back to the realm.

"Yaënsilat," Lavsila objected, "has no way of verifying numbers lost, not with any accuracy."

"Dolvid is not stupid. He does not need numbers; he can see it was a reverse grave enough for us to conceal from him." Kamin-Tolagh's annoyance began to grow, in realization Dolvid could have been privately mocking his lofty willingness to make concessions. "He would now assume his victory here was due, not to his persuasions, but our weakness."

Lavsila wanted more. "Why not a scheme to concert an attack by the Army of the West with a mutiny here, led by Yaënsilat? Dolvid may have brought gold from Rodlakh as an inducement."

"Old Yaënsilat lead a mutiny?" Kamin-Tarú reproached. "No."

"All the same," grimly. "We have been too lenient with him. I have respected his standing with the cavalry, but if he is going to misuse that influence, I may remember how he came to his retirement. He is going to tell us what he said to Dolvid, every word, and if needed I shall let Tau-Suaka do the questioning." Another bridge he had thought never to cross, to have a man of Kargul threatened with torture, but need here was imperative, like so much else, a question of survival.

His sister's eyes were very wide, but Lavsila, expected to raise racial demurs, was happily carried along by events. "He might at the same time wish to reveal names, those he considers his allies — there is no need to speak of mutiny, the officers whose support he would ask if seeking favors, reinstatement to active service, for example."

Tau-Suaka was not in immediate attendance, but one of his trusted deputies, another cousin-by-marriage, Humi, was told to take a dozen men to Yaënsilat's house, and bring the old soldier back here forthwith, using as little or as much force as was needed, but beginning with a polite request.

"I have pampered the men of Kargul. These men who would have been lucky, at Inilun Barabhi, to be file-leaders by their fiftieth birthdays, leading squadrons or *kímukol* here, with gold in their pockets, farms waiting for them in the south, and suddenly they flatter themselves I cannot do without them. Freighanai is valuable to me, and Kambanal; Dubovai has been, but otherwise, who? Who is indispensable? I have tribal officers who can train tribal levies. Because a man is of my province, am I supposed to be indulgent with treachery? I have Tau-Suaka and his men for unquestioning loyalty." For protection, also, if need be against his own Kargul'.

"Yaënsilat could not be plotting against you. I will not believe it." She had kept silent, not liking the talk about questioning the old soldier, with its hints of yet more pain, but all at once she was frightened by a vision of the West without either Kargul' or Heartlanders, where she would be surrounded by nothing but shabby, jabbering little men and women with crooked teeth. Even better-class Hrin, who knew enough to keep their bodies clean, did not smell (except of their cloying spices), and used some color in their dress, still had boring, incomprehensible beliefs and customs: it was good to be free to love her brother, but the prospect of year after year surrounded by people who would always be strangers was bleak beyond endurance.

"We shall have an answer, soon enough," Lavsila, in his condescending way.

But they would not. Tau-Suaka came with news of events he had not witnessed, but which, evidently, his underling had been afraid to deliver; the Hill Froghuli chieftain himself was hesitant in giving the report. After posting half his men at the back door of Yaënsilat's house, Humi had knocked at the front; Yaënsilat had looked out a small window to see who was there, and had called out, without apparent alarm, asking them to wait. After minutes, with no response to renewed knocking, Humi had gone inside, to find the elderly officer lying on the floor in a great deal of blood. He was alive, but died within minutes, having, with a will Tau-Suaka marvelled at, driven a small, sharp game-knife into the large artery of his throat.

"Oh." Kamin-Tarú had scarcely known the man, but his dignified and courteous bearing had reminded her of old-fashioned virtues — what her mother called *the priceless legacy of Old Owan*, although when she tried to think of a model for her idea of Yaënsilat, there was no one of Kargul, and she ended with *like Saidhan*, which would outrage Petakoi.

"The fool," Kamin-Tolagh, angered by the implications of this desperate act, as if he had ever treated the men of Kargul as anything but his comrades. "I would not have harmed him. He was a file-leader of the escort, when our father married."

Lavsila took it the suicide was confirmation of their worst suspicions, and unfortunately left them with no clue as to who else had been part of the conspiracy. "To let them think they are unsuspected, I can put out the story Yaënsilat had become despondent over his lack of duties."

"The fool," still incredulous. "If he was allowed to live, after defying my direct order in battle, his gratitude alone should have taught him better."

"And he ends as a coward," Lavsila said. All the same, Kamin-Tolagh, remembering the charge Yaënsilat had mounted to win the real battle, after refusing to make war on women and children, a wrongheaded but not contemptible choice, unwillingly perceived something creditable in the man's end. He did not accept Lavsila's over-elaborated theory — Dolvid's tale of coming here without the *rabhsai*'s consent was too simple-minded not to be true, and if not, how could he come prepared to bribe men he had no idea existed? Far likelier was that Dolvid had guessed he was not being told the truth, and had by some process found his way to Yaënsilat in search of a fuller story. A man other men would trust with their discontents, and if Yaënsilat had killed himself to avoid revealing names of those who confided in him, rather than incipient revolt, it proved only the exaggerated fears of too much solitude. A mistake to send the Hill Froghuli bodyguard to arrest him; such a mind would have gone instantly to the thought of torture.

Still, what he had caused could be more dangerous than phantom mutinies, Dolvid riding for home with news the Empire had suffered a defeat and lost fully a third of its battle-ready troops. Rodlakh was full of malice for the Empire, and had desisted from an attempt to destroy it only because that would cost too many lives; he would be thirsting for blood once he heard it could be done at bargain prices.

As indeed it might, for the Abu, at least, and the northern Froghushei; the Hrinani was another question, difficult to invade by land against determined defenders, hardly assailable by sea for the existing resources of the realm. Yet, as he had told Kamin-Tarú, he needed the tribal lands as breeding-ground for his armies; hemmed in among the Hrin with remnants of those armies, he would be in constant decline, with each skirmish costing men he could not replace: worse, Shumat would have the opportunity to levy auxiliaries from the northern tribes, who gave Kamin-Tolagh no particular allegiance, except for the Man-mani of Noh-Sra-Lal-Hin, and Tau-Suaka's contingent of Hill Froghul. Long before being worn down by the forces of the realm, he might lack the troops to discourage a general Hrin uprising. They were useless as fighters, but knew how to murder.

Not to be permitted. "Dolvid," abruptly, "must be stopped," but he declined to discuss military details with Lavsila, who immediately asked *how?* His sister was biting her lip.

The decision to act cleared his mind. At this moment, Dolvid's riding was five or six hours down the trail, moving with slow pack-animals that doomed them to six full days on Landegh at best. It should be easy to catch them; he already had troops detailed to see them off, led by Niburai, the Bablakhi hero. He could be reached with message-riders, cancelling his orders to turn back where the ascent to the plateau began, instructing him to shadow Dolvid as far as supplies allowed. They were not provisioned for a crossing of Landegh, but Kamin-Tolagh meant to assemble a further and more effective force, including Tau-Suaka with fifty of his best, whose spare mounts, faster than pack-ponies, could carry water, food and feed to supply both themselves and Niburai's force, when overtaken. Water would have to be rationed out; in all there would be three hundred men, and there was the return journey to consider.

Left out, Lavsila waited till Kamin-Tolagh had issued most of the needed orders before he commented again. "No doubt, your men can catch up with the *Bôdhrai*, but to what purpose? If you attack his company, that is going to bring the same war you fear would come from our present weakness being known."

He thought it through. The party could be wiped out to a man, and all signs of the battle removed, but no matter how hurriedly Dolvid had decided on this venture, he must have left word of his intentions; for Kamin-Tolagh to protest that he had not seen them, had no knowledge of their whereabouts, would not satisfy Kadon Dinul. News of the extraordinary visit would already be in letters from Owanil of the Abu, his Heartlanders, to their friends and kin in the South, and that tale would come back to Rodlakh's realm with Hrin trading-vessels.

"Dolvid and Shudarr must be taken prisoner." The others could die; the bodies would be burned or concealed, captives taken south to the Hrin lands. Kadon Dinul could be put off for a while with denials, giving Kamin-Tolagh time to fortify the main villages of the northern Froghushei, and prepare them for siege with stocks of food and arrows; he would also initiate training for a war Rodlakh was going to find too costly to fight, with no battles, but hundreds of small actions, ambushes, harrying of supply-trains, arrows from cover, but if the armies of the realm did come, two better hostages than the *Bôdhrai*, close friend to the *rabhsai*, and a son of the Captain of Armies, could hardly be found.

Lavsila had the temerity to say, "Good, but you had better be sure your men understand the orders. As we saw in the Lunu Tezh', in fights, harm can come to men not meant to be killed."

"I am leading the pursuit in person." There could be no room for mistakes this time.

By the time supplies were collected, all the horses well watered, Dolvid's lead had lengthened to nine hours under a sun already westering. No matter; Kamin-Tolagh was with hard-riding men, and ahead there were others who would keep the quarry in sight. A few good hours before dark, a dawn start tomorrow; he had no fear they would fail to catch up.

On what should be a spring day, cold rain beating down, Âna and Aëlu matched its gloom together in the *rabhsayu*'s suite at the Residence.

"It is useless, worse than useless to defend Dolvid until the *rabhsai*'s anger cools." The *rabhsai*! Absurd she had not said *Rodlakh*, but she was always stiffer than she wanted to be with Aëlu, whose self-possession still made her shy.

"I have not seen him so angry."

"Not many have." Alone with Âna, Rodlakh had never forgotten himself as he had on hearing about Dolvid's journey to the West. The scene must have been alarming indeed for Aëlu, with whom he generally adopted a courtliness quaint by standards of the day. "You understand, though I could not tell him so, his fury is half fear for Dolvid's safety."

As soon as this was out, Âna saw it as tactless; while Aëlu already knew the dangers, and could not be more anxious than Âna was, as wife to Dolvid and mother of his children she was entitled to conventional consideration.

She said, "You know Kamin-Tolagh. Would he harm Dolvid?"

"They reached understanding in the Jinzai War. Unless Kamin-Tolagh has changed altogether, he will receive him with high hospitality — he loves a lordly gesture, more than life."

"Not quite, perhaps," with the faintly mysterious smile.

Further discussion was set for later in the day, with Elamirr and Shumat in attendance: it would be a difficult meeting, but Âna found slight comfort in reflecting Rodlakh's anger over violation of the Lunu Tezh' had not been quite enough to have him, as he had threatened, instruct Shumat to make immediate war. Though hard to see, she told Aëlu, her bringing both pieces of news in person rather than leaving it to a dispatch may have worked to moderate the *rabhsai*'s wrath.

So Dolvid had hoped, Aëlu said, but his chief reason for asking her to make the crossing was to bring Âna documents he did not dare entrust to ordinary couriers; she handed over the package, containing an account of the questioning of Arvat, transliterations and the originals of Elamirr's two cyphered letters dealing with the Market Gate forgery, including the rough draft in his own hand.

Âna only just repressed a triumphant war-cry, and was dismayed how much she had come to hate Elamirr. Minutes ago, Rodlakh had been threatening to dismiss Dolvid from his *bôdhrayum*, which could only mean the dismal prospect of Elamirr's promotion, but Âna recognized the virulence of her feeling went well beyond the young man's determination to displace Dolvid: she and Elamirr had a great deal in common, Mixed of moderately comfortable origin who had first obtained education, then attained rank unthinkable a few generations ago for those of their blood. In him she saw all the resentments and sweeping condemnations once hers, but which she had left behind as she grew up, and came to meet real Owanil, to observe they were as various as any other people, and conclude no race had a monopoly on either virtue or greed. But in retaining his grudge against Owan, Elamirr had kept with it the narrowness of outlook, male arrogance and punishing instincts she had loathed in her own circle of birth.

Quieting her emotions, she asked, "You know about this?" a question where personal and official awkwardly overlapped.

"We discussed the whole affair."

"What action has been taken against Arvat?"

"For his part in this shabby business? None. None invoking law, that is — Arvat is no longer privy to Great House discussions, and is confined to Kamsilat." She seemed to think Dolvid's forbearance needed explaining: "Arvat's wife is with child again. She is not much beyond a child herself, once outside her kitchen."

"Elamirr also has a young wife. Not with child, but her wellbeing is a concern of mine. Her family at Burantal, and Elamirr's kin, too, were kind to me — to us all."

"I have heard the story. They did what they could to save Sebhal. But, Madam — " Aëlu's astonishing use of formal address was, and was meant to be, a trumpet-call — "The cases are not the same, are they? No one wants to cause misery to any wife, but Arvat at most has been a useful but malcontent clerk in a provincial Great House."

The *whereas* was unneeded; Elamirr was at the center, more influential than ever, willing to use forged documents to advance a dangerously divisive policy. "Yes, yes, he must be curbed. I meant only it would cause less grief to those I owe gratitude if the damage he does could be undone without need of public disgrace."

"Madam, it seems to me you have that power." Aëlu's eyes were on the bundle of documents in Âna's hands.

Aëlu was right; together with Âna's discovery of the link with Altorri, the forger, there was enough to hamstring Elamirr. On his way to the new meeting, Âna managed to intercept him, and draw him aside into an unused room.

"Madam, the *rabhsai* is waiting for me," measuring her in a manner she could easily find offensive.

"I shall have a voice there, too. What will you have to say about your master's journey to meet with Kamin-Tolagh?"

He did not care for *master*, she noted. "Madam, the *rabhsai* has strongly condemned the action. As Madam is aware, he has explicitly forbidden all dealings with the outlaw. Would you have me quarrel with the *rabhsai* for the sake of Dolvid's standing?"

She made herself take three measured breaths before speaking again. "If you are insolent, I shall give the *rabhsai* proof his decision to ignore Kamin-Tolagh's offer of friendship was based in part on misinformation. Much better if you were to advise him you no longer accept the authenticity of the Market Gate Letter — if I have to tell the story, I shall tell it all."

He was divided between discovering what she meant, and his defense against the charge of insolence — less his than his people's, *her* people's difficulty in allowing a woman any part in mannish matters, such as government. Curiosity won the struggle: "What story, Madam?"

"Your dealings with the forger, Altorri — "

"A confessed felon, a liar, Madam."

"Exactly. And I have other incontrovertible evidence you fabricated the letter passed off as Lavsila's." The nature of the evidence she would keep close for the present; let Elamirr sweat: he would have some anxious days when he failed to hear from Arvat.

At the moment, his near-condescension had changed to wariness, a crouched fox in inadequate cover. "Madam, I can explain — "

"No, you cannot, not to me, certainly not to the *rabhsai*. It explains itself; you influenced policy using a false document, and have tried to exploit for your own advantage the suspicions of race against race this *rabhsayum* has worked to be free of."

"The particular letter, Madam, may or may not have come from Lavsila," anger under the reasonable tone. "But it does not misrepresent his policies, nor the sentiments of those it addressed — the ones who want to turn time around, and make *us* slaves again. The Old Blood, they call themselves; the *Bôdhrai* means well, but he is living in a dream when he says Owani exclusion is all in the past. At bottom, he, too, is one of them, and thinks we lesser beings should be happy with our table-scraps."

"Be silent — " she was furious, then passed through that to a cool contempt, examining Elamirr like a doubtful fish she was deciding not to buy. "I have offered you a chance to save yourself, and now I wonder if I should. Caught in lies, like a child you tell me they ought to be true. We are holding up a meeting to decide the realm's policy, where no one will be of Owani blood unmixed — I do not say it should be, only that it happens to be so. Is it a table-scrap to be *rabhsai, rabhsayu,* Captain of Armies? No — " she forestalled fresh rancors, which were beginning to bore her. "This ends here, today. There will be no further talk treating all the Families as potential traitors — "

"Madam, the safety of the realm — "

"Your realm? Not ours, where whole races are seen as criminal. At this meeting, you are going to inform the *rabhsai* it has been proved to your complete satisfaction the Market Gate Letter was a forgery, apparently designed to discourage reconciliation with Kamin-Tolagh, and the *Bôdhrai* had this information when he set out on his journey. You are going to admit it now seems to you the influence of Lavsila with the Families has been grossly overestimated."

"How will it appear, Madam, if I suddenly reverse myself?" For the second time, Elamirr glanced darkly at her under his brows; it reminded her of her childhood, of a boy her brother had just outwrestled, picking himself up and refusing to accept the proffered hand of the victor, on whom he later tried to take revenge in various sly and petty ways. But also appraising, as if Elamirr was actually wondering whether — and beyond that, why — she had secretly sold herself to the Families. In a strange, almost occult way, his cynical opportunism, she saw, did not exclude, worked perfectly in harness with, a genuine, fanatical belief in the Owani conspiracy.

"As if you are attaining wisdom, at last. But you have the choice. Either you tell the *rabhsai* about the forgery, or I shall, presenting all the evidence."

Advancement for Others would never placate Elamirr, who desired the extinction of the Owanil, and she wondered, after, why she had spared him, when in the end he would have to be brought down, or permitted, rather, to destroy himself. More than Ana's regard for his lovely wife, for his Burantal kin, was keeping him in his post; there was also her fear of adding yet another element to the *rabhsai*'s anger: given full truth, Rodlakh would instantly dismiss Elamirr, and perhaps have him tried for treason, but he would not be grateful in his heart to Âna for depriving him of his newer counsellor, just when the elder had, as he put it, gone mad.

That assessment immovable with the sense of wrong behind it, she realized she had exaggerated in her mind the effect Elamirr's forced revelations might have on policy. Shumat, taking them as a cue to suggest merit, after all, to the idea of a parley, was peremptorily silenced by Rodlakh, standing on rank as never before. It became only a passing episode in what turned into a discussion of how and where a retaliatory blow for the Lunu Tezh' incident could be struck.

Elamirr, with need to reassert himself, was not slow to observe the *Bôdhrai*, though with all good intentions, had in one sense tied the hands of the realm, since, for the sake of his safety, no action could be taken while he was there in the West. This Shumat dismissed, saying it made no tactical difference; assembly of forces for an effective expedition would take far longer than Dolvid's mission to complete.

Rodlakh was ruminative. "In the days of the First Empire, if there was a raid from beyond the frontiers, policy was to send a punitive force to the country of the invaders. If they had burnt a village, ten of their villages would be razed, if they had stolen cattle, ten times that number would be confiscated or destroyed. A counter-raid, in essence, with no idea of occupation, or of overcoming Kamin-Tolagh's main formations — could we not draw the squadrons for this, with their supplies, almost immediately, from the Army of the West?"

"To strike at the Lunu — what they call Abu Kargusai, *Deghi*? — " Shumat was gravely dubious.

"No, no, to avoid it. The tribal country Kamin-Tolagh claims as his empire is, as we understand it, southward of there."

"What they call the Froghushei."

Âna wondered if she had gone mad. Not counting Elamirr, everyone here had gone through the bloodiest episodes of the Jinzai War, and she could not imagine how anyone would willingly endure or impose more of those killings and manglings, the nightmare and the pain of warfare, unless, as then, defending lives against marauders; she remembered reminding Dolvid he had told her that at the moment of triumph Rodlakh, this same man, had wept bitterly over all the good men lost. Yet her horror of what was proposed here was much greater. "You would order a raid against peaceful villages, against old men, women, children?"

"Ours was a peaceful village of the Lunu Tezh'."

"And we have called Kamin-Tolagh's acts an outrage. And so our civilized realm, the home of justice, is going to descend to vengeance? If there is a crime, we punish the guilty, not the innocent."

For the first time today, Rodlakh faltered a little. "In the days of the First Empire, this policy often won freedom from fresh attacks for a year or longer."

"The First Empire! When did we start to take the cruelties of Old Owan as our model?"

Shumat, she sensed, approved, but added practical doubts. "We would not be striking back at a single tribe, but at part of what calls itself an empire, with a standing army. In all likelihood our counter-raid would be answered with another and more damaging one against the Lunu Tezh', which, as one who is absent has not ceased to remind us, we cannot adequately defend. For a such a piecemeal war, Kamin-Tolagh may be better-prepared than we are; most of his tribesmen have had some training now, and I don't doubt his villages are fortified. A direct assault on the Abu would be a bloodbath, but less costly, maybe, in the end, than many little wars."

Rodlakh's temper was rising again. "Yet you say we do not have enough men under arms to be sure of overthrowing Kamin-Tolagh."

"Not if we want to keep the realm's roads safe from robbery." Some time past, Shumat had given six thousand as the smallest number with which he would attempt the task, and eight thousand as desirable, either figure for only the first year of a war he thought could take three campaigning seasons.

"I cannot believe this great and powerful realm can be humiliated by a handful of savages, and have no recourse."

Whether he was invited, which Âna doubted, Orbanak came in and heard the last. "I do not believe, *Deghi*," he told his brother with an odd, earnest humor, "anyone has yet found a way to humiliate this great and powerful realm."

Though the presence of Orbanak, for no explicable reason, had a curiously muting effect on controversy, the meeting broke up with Shumat instructed to produce by morning plans and estimates both for full-scale war, and for lesser engagements. A small delay for precipitate action, but for Âna darkness did not abate, and she was obsessed with the dream there must be a word, a little act of hers, that could bring Rodlakh back to reason. At further cost to herself she had just managed to persuade him not to announce Dolvid's dismissal, arguing no irrevocable step should be taken before he came back from the West with opportunity to explain his actions, but she could not risk open opposition to the naming of Elamirr as acting-*Bôdhrai*. The words of moderation she had crammed into the man's mouth had the unlooked-for effect of confirming Rodlakh's high opinion; obviously Elamirr had matured, and could see all sides of a question. Except emblematically, it did not matter; if he succeeded, or was about to succeed, in advising some lunatic policy, she would make use of the high tile, his indiscreet letters to Arvat — though it was hard to see how he could advocate a course more dangerous, more repugnant, than the one Rodlakh had chosen for himself.

After the *rabhsai's* solitary departure, she followed Shumat out of the room, struck by the sudden idea he had not heard his son was with Dolvid.

"Yes, Madam, the Lady Aëlu took time to inform me. All to the good, really. I can't say how much use the boy will be to Dolvid, but it's time he saw real service. Besides — " he slowly rubbed his nose. "However. Concern for Shudarr may do more to curb his rashness than regard for his own skin. Between us, Madam, our prudent *Bôdhrai* with his blood up is worse than any young *jinzai*-eater in the Army of the West.

"Sorry — " quickly, seeing her face darken.

The first completely unguarded word between them; she had admired Shumat's competency and good sense, but not had anything resembling friendship with Dolvid's oldest friend. Now she perceived an ally she could trust without reserve. "This is a bad dream."

"Madam, it must pass."

"To judge our readiness for war, you will need to visit the Colony?"

He was puzzled. "If there is war, I'll command in person. I'll have to assess the Army of the West first hand, yes."

"As Captain of Armies, at Drin Navuna, you could make decisions Bradhinal could not — more would be left to your discretion. If you were ordered to make this punitive raid, for example, and news came back from the Farther West to alter the circumstances, you could call a pause, pending the *rabhsai*'s reconsideration."

"That is true, Madam." The face was impossibly bland.

"Or if you merely had a good reason to expect a change in the situation — word might come from Dolvid — "

"Let it come soon," with fervor, and she could have hugged him for being anxious.

Twice, she decided at the end of the day in all her life she would least want to live over, twice today she had shown concern over Dolvid beyond what was wise. Shumat, she would suppose, if he knew or guessed anything, would be discreet, but the first of Elamirr's baleful looks of deferred retribution had come when she let herself be angered by his slighting assessment of his master and original sponsor, the *Bôdhrai*. She must be careful; crazy but inescapable, what seemed entirely personal and private became muddled with large events. Her uncertainty with Aëlu was an example, but with Elamirr it could be catastrophe.

"We are not going to lose our shadows," Shudarr, shading his eyes to squint back the way they had come, sun low in the west. They had reached the climb up to the edge of Landegh, but Kamin-Tolagh's followers had not turned back, as promised. Here where, to make the ascent, the way twisted and wrapped back on itself, an accurate count could be made, five tribal squadrons, and Shudarr suddenly recognized the tall Owani officer leading them.

"Niburai," in simulated awe. "A pity, Master, we don't have a stream in spate to cross; he could show us the hero's way to lead men through it."

"What else?" having given the youth his grin.

"No pack train, they are only carrying saddle-supplies. We'll soon lose them on Landegh."

"If we press forward. They may be resupplied, if Kamin-Tolagh keeps stores of food and water concealed near the trail." Too early to conclude Niburai's persistence reflected new orders, in turn meaning Kamin-Tolagh had heard about the meeting with Yaënsilat, and drawn deadly conclusions. A strange flight, from a host they had parted from in ostensible cordiality, pursued now only by the idea of a threat.

Near midnight Kamin-Tolagh with his company made camp in a gully by the road, next to the stream, a place counted as halfway between the Abu and the beginning of Landegh. Within an hour, his sentries on the road halted a message-rider, and he discovered Niburai, instead of being close to where Dolvid must be camped, was only a few miles up the road. He had watched the *Bôdhrai* begin the crossing of Landegh, and then, obeying his original orders, had turned back with brief daylight left, to be met by Kamin-Tolagh's new orders only at nightfall.

He had decided to halt. While he had put some hours distance between himself and a riding which had, as Niburai admitted, made better speed than expected, he was quite confident with a start at first light he could easily catch Dolvid's company tomorrow, probably in early afternoon.

When he did, his orders were to keep them in sight. If Niburai's estimate was correct, Kamin-Tolagh in turn could count on overtaking when he camped tomorrow night, close behind Dolvid, and next morning they could envelop and destroy the escort, which they would outnumber more than ten to one; daylight was needed to be sure no one escaped, and the two he wanted for hostages were not harmed.

On that, Kamin-Tolagh slept, and in the morning felt a new sense of imminent success. He was in the saddle among trusty if taciturn companions, and the outcome, as it should be, was in his own hands. After rest and food they climbed in full day past the ruined outworks of another empire whose failure began when its rulers delegated their battles to others, but Kamin-Tolagh had learned the lesson of Zelu Bablakhi.

Still before attaining the level plateau, they were met by another fatigued message-rider with a dispatch. Puzzling, because unless Dolvid had been unexpectedly slowed or halted, it was too soon for word; now was the earliest Niburai could be coming in sight of the quarry.

Opening the folded sheet, Kamin-Tolagh cursed, but waved away Tau-Suaka's quick curiosity. Their quarry, Niburai apologetically wrote, had not made camp in the usual place. He must have continued his ride well into the night, which meant he was farther ahead than expected. The message was only four hours old, but by now Niburai, who had written his dispatch from the place where Dolvid had in fact spent the night, was some eight hours' riding away, with the *Bôdhrai*'s company an unknown distance beyond that.

The start of a dream-pursuit, Niburai urging thirsty men after an unseen fugitive, Kamin-Tolagh with the swifter and hardier Hill Froghul very gradually closing in on Niburai. The small and unsatisfying information there was passed only one way; so long as Niburai continued the chase, there was no sense to killing horses in an attempt to reply to his terse messages.

One reliable fact was that the prudent Dolvid would not risk leaving the trail, sometimes ill-defined, often branching into a fainter web of trails; outside sheer chance, the only hope of encountering water at a couple of widely separated places was to stay with this way made with *jinzai* labor, and on either side the bafflement of Landegh stretched, rocky, broken, forbidding and dry. But not till late on the second day was there remotely encouraging news; a message-rider appeared to say Niburai had come upon horse-droppings only hours old; here, such leavings soon dried, crumbled and were blown away by the gusting winds. Less happily, Niburai's force was near the end of its water, and would have to halt before darkness, in one of the places where a small stream was accessible from the trail. Doubling riding-time for the messenger put him four hours ahead, but Kamin-Tolagh, with darkness coming, decided not to press on and make junction; even Tau-Suaka's tough riders were showing strain, and he had to have them ready for a fight at the end of this chase. He did send back one of Niburai's men, with word food and water were not far behind.

Another cold night came, and another dawn of swinging, stiff and chilled, into the saddle, to spur his men to renewed hard effort. This was not a hunt where sight of the quarry gave a lift to the heart and sent blood pumping through muscles, this drudging pursuit of the invisible across unchanging harshness. Morning passed wearily, and in the afternoon another message came from Niburai, glad at last to know he had support in his rear, but incredulous he'd had no sight of Dolvid; his men would soon have to stand and wait for supplies to catch up with them. Kamin-Tolagh's men, eking out their water, were thirsty too; this year for some reason the stream they passed near had been a disappointing trickle, and Kamin-Tolagh had not dared use the time for letting the mounts drink their fill. With each step away from safe base, the return journey was a thought that nagged at him, and he elbowed it away, focussing fiercely to the front.

Not long after dispatching this most recent message, Niburai must have come upon the discarded pack-train, which Kamin-Tolagh reached as evening approached. The corpses of five ponies were being disputed by carrion-birds, and had just been discovered by several of the lean, tattered doglike creatures which mysteriously came slinking out of the surrounding emptiness whenever dead meat was to be had. Nearby were signs more ponies had been butchered, and a ransacked heap of straw mattresses, oddments of bedding and spare clothes.

Tau-Suaka dismounted, waving off birds, contemptuously kicking aside grey, snarling dogs. "The ponies had their throats cut. This lord of the realm wanted us not to have his animals, Lord."

He considered. "No. This means he thought he was being pursued, but was not yet sure. Unless he suspected, he would not have given up his slower animals — though, Hrafi! with them he has moved faster than he should. If he had been certain he was followed, he would not have had them killed. Being softhearted, he did not want to leave them to hunger and thirst."

"From the way of this other bleeding, Lord," with a wave and a sagacious jut of the lower lip. "Can be seen there was butchery done long after the ponies were dead. Captain Niburai's men are having a meat-feast tonight."

Kamin-Tolagh made a disgusted face, but as things stood he most likely would be obliged to order use of spare animals for food on the return journey.

Despite their proclaimed exhaustion, and the time Niburai must have lost here, he had made up little ground on that company for the whole day; it was exasperating to know that whether they were closer to Dolvid could not be said.

Another distance was beginning to worry. Drin Navuna must be well over two days' riding away, or as much as three, but the Army of the West regularly sent out squadron-strength patrols a dayride beyond the Frontier. Reinforcement of Dolvid's small force by a squadron, even a *kímuko*, would leave odds overwhelmingly in Kamin-Tolagh's favor, but make it harder to be certain no one escaped to tell the tale. Tomorrow, or early the next day at latest, he must finish this business, or have to consider abandoning it.

He was awakened deep in the night to hear news brought by a man who had picked his way here in darkness. In the space of a few words Kamin-Tolagh changed from bleared bad temper to eager anticipation: at last light Niburai had caught a glimpse of Dolvid's band. He was confident his forces had not been seen, and was camped in a place overlooking the *Bôdhrai*'s small watchfires.

Even with this to hearten them, the Hill Froghul required rest, and Kamin-Tolagh did not send them stumbling forward through the dark. As the first paling came to the sky, they were all in the saddle, grimed faces taking on the narrowed look of a hunting-beast that scents prey.

The sun, sidling up from a distant, broken line of heights, reminded Kamin-Tolagh this was the fourth day; that mountain country must be the beginning of the approaches to Drin Navuna, still far off, but too near. Looping over the shoulder of a low ridge, the trail for once brought them to where they could see for some distance ahead; nothing was there except rocks, gravelly flats, scarce tufts of pallid vegetation. Then Tau-Suaka's extraordinary eyes picked up movement, and soon a horseman was plainly in sight, drooping in the saddle, weary on a weary mount. When they met, he was surprised to be with Kamin-Tolagh so soon; not much above an hour had passed, he thought, since he had left Niburai.

His news was devastating; Niburai's hasty scrawl admitted he had again lost contact with their quarry. Last night's watchfires had been a feint; it was now apparent Dolvid had piled them high, and left them to burn out, resuming his march after midnight. Yet plainly, Niburai insisted, they could not have made much ground by darkness, and must be within reach.

Hope disappointed, the day became another like the last, except the country was becoming increasingly difficult, the trail less level, balks and pinnacles of rock rising all around, the way ahead seldom offering a long prospect, as it snaked among tilted slabs and huge split boulders. Late in the afternoon, when it had become clear there would never be an end to this barren hunt, another message-rider waylaid Kamin-Tolagh, having merely waited till he was overtaken. There had been, he said, a fresh sighting of the fugitives. Though near the end of their resources, Niburai's men were plodding on, and he implored his lord to do the same, and to reach them with water.

The sun swung down at their backs, cool stars came out, dusk arrived with no sight of Niburai. Determined to unite his forces, Kamin-Tolagh groped on after nightfall. Dark deepened, mounts slithered and checked, men let out soft curses in their own tongue. Not much short of midnight they came to the brink of a folded gully splashed with light, the watchfires of Niburai.

Who, in a voice scoured by the dust of Landegh, reported Dolvid was camped in the next low ground, Niburai having scouts up on the intervening ridge to watch for repetition of last night's trick. "But even these sons of Draha must need rest sometime, Lord," and Kamin-Tolagh detected, and found he shared, a grudging admiration for the hardiness of their quarry.

More than half the water left to the combined force was consumed in the hour after their junction, men rousing from loggish sleep to wet cracked lips. Dangerous to deplete their stocks, but there should be one more source not far ahead, and tomorrow Kamin-Tolagh was going to call on these men for a last great effort; here, the trail, improved by *jinzal* so their siege-weapons could be trundled towards Drin Navuna, was as good as some byroads in mountainous Kargul: Tau-Suaka, remembering this place from his years of service in the Army of the West, said they were two dayrides from the Frontier, one midsummer dawn-to-dusk on a strong mount. Not likely patrols ventured so far at this time, but clearly capture of Dolvid and Shudarr, extermination of their escort must be accomplished tomorrow.

If the unceasing flight often seemed madness to him, to his men it must be worse, soldiers trained for fighting here in full retreat from an enemy they never glimpsed. The hushed resumptions in the middle of the night, after heaping what fuel they could find on the watchfires, were a joke soon worn thin, and his order, on an unconfirmed sighting of pursuers, for a ruthless lightening of loads, destruction of the pack-animals, had met with an approach to open dissent.

The doubt was gone. Varromar, the quiet, reliable young file-leader in charge since Shudarr's departure, his mount fresher than most, had volunteered to stay behind in one of the places where, from cover, he could keep watch on a couple of miles of trail; when he caught up it was to report a force not smaller than three full squadrons was still behind them, still led by Niburai. Like Shudarr, Varromar added a disparaging estimate of their quality as fighters, but with his company down to a bare twenty, Dolvid was not going to test that thesis; ten slept their brief two hours while the rest watched. Another midnight departure; doubtful the trick could work again, but each step forward was so much nearer Drin Navuna and the hope of help.

Sums had too many conjectured numbers. Shudarr with a little band of the youngest and hardiest had begun his dash three days ago, but with an absolute minimum of rest could hardly reach the Frontier sooner than tomorrow morning, that presuming no unforeseen checks, such as a horse lamed or ridden out. Unless there was a regular patrol to be encountered — and that might not add sufficient strength to survive an attack — tomorrow near sunset would be soonest hope of rescue by the Army of the West, perhaps too late.

It assumed, moreover, Shudarr would without delay argue his way to Bradhinal, who could immediately deploy not less than five and preferably a dozen squadrons. Yet once he reached the Drin, the larger game was over; he was carrying a written account of the information Kamin-Tolagh wanted to keep from the realm, so whether or not he killed or captured Dolvid became a side-issue.

Not to me, Dolvid thought, as, once again, he estimated miles and counted hours, doubting he would have a chance to convince Niburai his pursuit was futile, *and not to my companions*; in the flicker of firelight he scanned the young faces masked with dust, too weary for emotion, and hoped he had not led these men out to an unnecessary death.

Niburai had wanted a night attack, but while Tau-Suaka's Hill Froghul had discarded many of their traditional ways, their old superstitions remained strong, and they would fight by darkness only at absolute need. Without that, Kamin-Tolagh would have waited for day; all the men, nearly spent, would fight better after rest, and by daylight there would be less danger of mistakes, failing to account for all of the escort, or accidentally killing one of the prize hostages. With Tau-Suaka and Niburai, he was emphatic on the point; in particular the bowmen must take care who they shot at, and Kamin-Tolagh vowed the man who shot either Dolvid or Shudarr would be a long week dying. Better if the attack could come in a more open place, where the enemy could be completely surrounded; better yet if they then surrendered, and could be killed in an orderly manner.

Later the fugitives had again resumed their march by feeble moonlight, but this time they were observed, and while it took time to have his men awake and in the saddle, Kamin-Tolagh soon followed, after sending scouts ahead to maintain contact. Dawn came, and a flurry of near-panic, as he found he had lost touch with the advance riders, and feared they had been ambushed in this broken country, ideal for concealment. An anxious hour, but then he came up to his scouts, who reported the tail of the retreating column had just disappeared, little above a mile ahead, where the trail mounted a narrow, ascending cleft between masses of rust-colored rock. Above, according to Tau-Suaka, was just the terrain they wanted for their attack, a broad, bare level, with a single isolated hillock, which used to be overnight place of bivouac for patrols one dayride out from the Drin.

A tedious, dispiriting climb, with nowhere room for more than three to ride abreast. Cursed on by Kamin-Tolagh and his officers, weary troops toiled in the declivity for two hours before they mounted to the final stretch, where the way widened again.

At the abrupt brink, Kamin-Tolagh was looking out across a rubbled plain, which mounted only gradually to where stark and forbidding heights rose mountain-high, deceptively near in the clear air. Not two miles ahead, a small knot of riders crept across the tableland.

The situation was ideal; with his overwhelming numerical advantage Kamin-Tolagh had no need of surprise, and the trail here was only a recommended course, with nothing to prevent riders from spreading out to either side. Except for minor outcrops of stone and scattered shocks of tough, sparse vegetation, there was no cover. Urging his forces to a shambling trot, Kamin-Tolagh moved out onto the plain, Niburai extending his squadrons wide.

With fresh mounts, they could have been up with Dolvid in minutes, but here the gap closed with a maddening, nightmare slowness, and a full half-hour passed before it was clear the fugitives had no choice but to stand and fight. Any doubt they were aware of pursuit was ended when they turned aside from the trail to make for the low eminence Tau-Suaka had mentioned, only available higher ground. The slope would be slight impediment to a serious attack, but there the fugitives would make their stand; as they climbed they were spreading into a ring of lances, and Kamin-Tolagh thought he could discern the helmless head of Dolvid.

But for his desire to keep that head whole, he could have trusted the task to unaided bows. Two hundred paces short of the hillock, he paused, and Tau-Suaka, coming up alongside, pointed up the trail. Some distance away there was a glitter of breastplates, a new band of horsemen coming at a brisk trot. "Not two squadrons," Tau-Suaka estimated. "Lances, followed by bows."

Possessing rested cavalry the equal of the Army of the West, Kamin-Tolagh would not have hesitated; the odds were still near three to one in his favor, and he would have sent Niburai's five squadrons against the newcomers, leaving Dolvid to Tau-Suaka. That was the order Niburai seemed poised to hear, but the approaching cavalry was on *pefral*, from an army Kamin-Tolagh had seen at work in the Jinzai War, and with mounts and riders relatively fresh, not gasping for thirst, wearied by long days and nights of pursuit. He would have to fight, but it was not his choice.

A signal-trumpet sounded from the new squadrons, answered, to Kamin-Tolagh's astonishment, not from the little band huddled on the hillock, but faintly from far off. Tau-Suaka waved again, and out of the dark background of mountains emerged the gleam of many breastplates, ripple of lances like a forest. The Army of the West was here.

No need of waiting to count numbers, obviously more than equal his. The chase was over; such a body of cavalry must mean Dolvid, as could have been guessed, had sent word ahead of him. Whatever secrets the *Bôdhrai* had learned from Yaënsilat had already reached the Frontier, and could no longer be kept from the *rabhsai*.

But was the chase over, or had he merely changed from hunter to quarry? His squadrons would not have the speed or endurance to elude a determined chase by fresh troops; he called back Niburai, and told him to withdraw with all speed. If Kamin-Tolagh could reach the place where the narrow trail descended, there was a chance he could hold off a hunt, using the mounted bows for rearguard. His hope was that in haste to rescue the *Bôdhrai*, the main enemy squadrons had not waited to equip themselves except for a couple of days on Landegh, but his not having seen a supply-train did not mean it might not be following, at the slower pace of pack-ponies.

For a moment, as Tau-Suaka swung his guard around to follow Niburai's men, Kamin-Tolagh was alone in the space between bows and lances, and a man riding near the rear of a tribal squadron abruptly wheeled out of formation, and rode in his direction. Just time to register the oddity, when he saw the man's lance come up level, as he kicked his half-*pefrai* into the best pace it could still achieve.

Kamin-Tolagh had no lance, and had barely time to draw blade to ward off the attack, hauling his *pefrai* to face the oncoming soldier, and sweeping the thrust lance aside. He had the brief impression of a face from the Froghushei twisted in anger or hatred, before the man, not quick enough in releasing his lance, was jolted clean off his horse. Jarred, Kamin-Tolagh swung from the saddle, and almost before his assailant hit ground had buried his blade in the exposed abdomen below the breastplate.

The assailant's squadron was frozen in shock, or perhaps cowering in fear of what the consequences for them might be. Tau-Suaka's men swiftly ringed Kamin-Tolagh, bows ready, as he wiped first one then the other side of his stained blade on the breeches of the dying man, and had leisure to regret he had not merely disarmed him to experience an agonizingly longer death.

Tau-Suaka, as if in apology for failure to guard his lord, said several times, the man was mad, the Landegh madness, there had been such cases in the Army of the West.

"Ride on," with a gesture, as, sheathing his sword, he remounted, ostentatiously turning his back on the traitor's squadron.

Watching from the rim of the plain, it seemed there was not going to be a pursuit; the Army of the West was content, like a well-trained watchdog, to see off the intruder, leading squadrons coming on at a walk, while later arrivals made a halt near where the *Bôdhrai* had taken his stand. Still, Kamin-Tolagh would have to keep a watch to his rearward, and not delay on the long journey home, near five added days of fatigue, thirst, and growing hunger; the spare horses were doomed.

For Kamin-Tolagh, too, new anxiety over events at the Abu, in the tribal country, during his absence. Zelu Bablakhi, beyond simple military arithmetic, had come to appear a wrong turning, a crucial choice after which nothing had gone right; more immediately troubling than danger of an assault by the realm was this sudden epidemic of disloyalty. The man who had tried to kill him, whether or not he could be called mad, was one of the remnant Hwenala, mistakenly spared to ride in honor with a mixed tribal squadron, but most of the men were of the same Laughing Owl tribe whose desertion had led to the Lunu Tezh' incident. Someone had said actual members of that same family at the heart of the defection could still be found in his armies: no telling how many of those, insufficiently taught by the lingering deaths awarded their kin, were of the same mind as his would-be assassin, till now lacking only the insane courage to act as he had.

There remained the death of Yaënsilat, another upon whom clemency had in the end been wasted. For Lavsila that suicide confirmed a dangerous infection among the men of Kargul, and here, days from safety, still unsure whether he had escaped the Army of the West, wrist and forearm muddied with the blood of a traitor, he could believe in any disloyalty. But these Kargul' were men like the ones he had first ridden with at sixteen, whose dangers, discomforts and triumphs in time of war he had shared, as he had their camp food and fireside talk, bawdy songs and rough jokes, and Lavsila was jealous of the love he had fairly earned. In any event, if there was widespread disaffection, it would have manifested itself before now; the Abu could easily have been seized during one of his absences with Tau-Suaka's men, or his sister taken hostage in a hundred possible places; why mutiny now, when they must see their reward was at hand, with conquest of the Hrin lands?

Remembering how his sister had longed for deep grass, green trees and flowing waters, he made up his mind the duty rosters would be arranged so every man of Kargul would have a spell of duty in the south with Kambanal, a chance to experience the valley of the Hflen where the farmland of his honorable retirement would be waiting. In the end, perhaps, Yaënsilat had died of homesickness.

For Dolvid, too exhausted to do anything but stand next to his spent horse in dazed silence, the joy of rescue was made more unreal by added incredulity; the Army of the West was here with its Captain, Bradhinal, all huge grins, keeping his youthful looks though three times a father, but here too, beyond explaining, was the Captain of Armies, his oldest friend. They greeted gravely, Shumat shaking his head. "I thought you had outgrown your taste for mad adventures." Could it be twenty years Dolvid wondered — as much as twenty years, only twenty years — since the three of them, all hardly more than boys, had gathered like this, after sharing victory at the Pass of Perus?

Each year of Rodlakh's reign, just over three weeks past Spring Halving, there was a commemoration, not of his actual accession, which would have been to celebrate the murder of his brother, Ban-Sila, but of his acclaiming, eight days later, at the Frontier, where he had first learned he was *rabhsai*. This year Âna half-expected and wholly hoped the occasion would be let pass unremarked; of those who had brought Rodlakh to power,

Dolvid was absent, in disgrace, possibly dead, and Âna, who had carried the news to Drin Navuna, was in despair.

Yet Rodlakh, grim in these days, unsmiling, still prone to fits of temper followed by depression and desire for solitude, insisted on the holiday; there would be the usual trinket-sellers and puppet-shows on the Avenue, feasts in the Residence Quarter, general emptyheadedness. With bad grace, Âna submitted to fittings for a new gown; her pregnancy was too new to make her existent wardrobe unwearable, but the *rabhsayu* was a part of the spectacle for these occasions, and, as she remarked to Tellis, she did not doubt the realm would be damaged beyond recovery if she were to appear again in her once-worn Halving Day gown.

The weather, which had been cool and wet, turned suddenly to brilliant spring, leaves and orchard-blossoms and the random wildflowers coming in such a rush they practically stumbled over one another. For no sustainable reason Âna felt the stirring of hope, just seasonal change, she told herself contemptuously, of a farmer's daughter, whose moods went with the weather.

Returning from a final session with imperious women who spoke through mouthfuls of pins, agony softened by a dressmaker's compliment on the unaltered slimness of her waist, she was overtaken by her brother, Konir, who asked for a private word. He was overdue, he remarked with rare acidity, for a meeting at which Rhunilat would instruct each *bôdh'loiki* where he must stand on the Steps for the forthcoming ceremonies.

"These distractions help keep us from too much thinking. Honest people do it with work."

"No word of Dolvid?" They walked together, her stride lengthening, as when she was ten.

"No," bleakly.

In her ante-chamber, he would neither accept refreshment, nor sit. "You know you have made yourself an enemy, don't you?"

"More than one, I'm sure."

"Most of them do not matter." Konir was over-casual, a manner she knew well. "As you know, I do not concern myself with your doings."

True, which was why Âna was so attentive. She did not doubt the enemy was Elamirr.

"A man I talk to told me this enemy you have made is all of a sudden very generous buying drinks and little trinkets for servants here at the Residence. He is looking for a scandal involving — one who is absent."

"It's not hard — " Âna admired her own composure, "to find bad things to say about the absent."

"Almost exactly what my informant said. He also said if enough people are offered rewards to say horses have wings, there are bound to be those who have seen them flying. Being a loyal subject, he perhaps wanted this conveyed to my exalted sister, which is now accomplished."

"Ah, but the horse cannot deny he flew."

"I have delivered my message," Konir, making for the door.

"Another thing," turning. "Yesterday, I went to the Old Bronze Residence for a treatise on dye-woods, and a useless thing it is, too. There is a scribe, Orimat, one of Dolvid's men. He is not an Owani."

"Yes, I know him. He comes from Kanzan Tâl."

"I mention his Mixed blood," innocently, "only because the Acting *Bôdhrai* likes to have it that the Other Races are all in his pocket, and only Owanil with Dolvid. This Orimat tells me the Acting *Bôdhrai* has been having confidential talks with the Acting Captain of your Household."

"They are friends, I have heard," Âna said, but not dismissively; her brother did not prattle.

"According to Orimat, the subject between Elamirr and Dorrmas has been, how the Household will act, in case of war with Kamin-Tolagh."

"In war, in peace," a little pettishly. "The Household is the *rabhsai*'s personal guard, and will act as the *rabhsai* orders."

Konir nodded serenely. "Well, Elamirr probably feels the *rabhsai* would be too preoccupied to issue some of the needed orders."

"What orders?"

"Is Orimat trustworthy as a witness?"

"He has been in the past." He was the one who had first told Âna about Elamirr's meeting with the Market Gate forger. "Granted a strong aversion to the Acting *Bôdhrai*."

"According to him, the orders Elamirr is afraid the *rabhsai* may fail to give would be for arrest and detention of all men and women of Family who, having cousins or nephews or remoter kin serving Kamin-Tolagh, might be expected to favor him in a war."

"*Be expected to*? Expected by whom? Everyone in the Residence Quarter and all the Families of the Heartland are more or less related to the idiots who joined Kamin-Tolagh — old Faëdhal, Rhunilat." Brief, sour amusement to reflect if the measure extended to kin by marriage, Elamirr's ally at Kamsilat, Arvat, would have to be included. Âna could not see why her brother was so calm. "We have not had talk of preventive detention since the worst days of Ban-Sila. Why has Dorrmas not reported these talks with Elamirr? No one has questioned his loyalty." His judgment, she reflected, was a different question.

Konir shielded himself with a raised arm. "Peace. I'm no good at riddles. A marvel to me anybody wants to spend his time, or her time, chewing at such gristle."

Meant as an affectionate compliment, but Âna, dizzied with too much news, answered fervently, "Anybody who wanted to would have to be mad."

Left to herself, she soon decided these meetings, notwithstanding their somewhat clandestine nature, were no reflection on the loyalty of Dorrmas. She herself, alone with Dolvid, more recently Shumat, had conspired at policies not, or not yet, Rodlakh's; an advisor was entitled to ideas on what was for the realm's good, and to advance them till they were rejected by *rabhsai* or Council, or banned by existing law. Dorrmas, a man of stubborn convictions, was at fault for not submitting the lunatic contingency plan for consideration, but would only be outside law if a war actually came, and he proceeded with the arrests on his own authority.

But that was dangerous, because Dorrmas was just such a man, convinced he was in the right, going forward till told to stop; he was the one, she abruptly recalled, who had ordered the massacre of the women at Lunu Jinzalladhiyu — that was seven years ago, but Shumat never failed to mention it when there was a suggestion Dorrmas be advanced from acting-captaincy to be full and unconditional Captain of the Household. A promotion Elamirr might promise, for when he came to his full power.

He was the one at fault; understandable if his friends assumed he had become *Bôdhrai* in everything but title, and Dorrmas could be forgiven the belief his best chance to lose the galling prefix to his captaincy was with a rising sun. But Elamirr had no right to establish with a soldier a far-reaching policy unsanctioned by the *rabhsai*, particularly one so recklessly unfair. Though countermanded immediately, it would win more adherents for the enemy than all Lavsila could do — or Elamirr fabricate: if convinced *rabhsayum* held nothing for them but repression, the Families would naturally turn to Kamin-Tolagh, and might well be supported by the provincial aristocracy; the realm would be split apart.

With her established prejudice against Elamirr, she was not well-placed to denounce this proceeding; she could not expose the scribe, Orimat, as her source for the meetings with Dorrmas, which Elamirr could deny.

No, not deny, that would risk contradiction by Dorrmas; his best defense would be to say preventive arrests had been among contingencies, some obvious, others far-fetched, he had speculated about with Dorrmas, without any intention of establishing a plan. That ought to kill this particular scheme, but if this was his answer to the reprieve she had given him by not exposing the Market Gate forgery, Elamirr was incorrigible. He could no longer be permitted to conduct a kind of conspiratorial secret government, with its chief object the fostering of distrust and conflict among races. In the realm at large, despite Lavsila on one side and Elamirr on the other, there was less observable disharmony than ever before; intermarriage had become so common, and the laws, till now, so evenhanded, the new *Mankh'* so unexpectedly popular with the formerly excluded, that except in a few obdurate minds, the distinctions were fading away. Not faded; it would be another generation, not less, before men who wanted to rekindle old hatreds ceased to be dangerous.

She had to play high tile, produce her evidence for the forgery — in private, she thought, with Rodlakh, where she could explain her reasons for not doing so before. The end of Elamirr, and for the sake of Morulis, Âna now wished she had not helped to have Orbanak sent off to the Colony; the brother of the *rabhsai* could have been consolation for a woman whose husband faced disgrace, even exile. In his brief period back at Kadon Dinul, Orbanak had shown no signs of renewing his connection with Morulis, but had spent time with two or three others, as if the demonstration he could live without her had alerted him to his advantages of youth, looks, and high rank.

Yesterday, Âna would have hesitated less over denouncing Elamirr — or today, if her brother had brought her only one piece of gossip. But she was not completely convinced no servant could tell about her beddings with Dolvid; she had implied to

Konir she could deny an accusation, but confronted with dates, times and places, with Rodlakh's eyes on her, she could not be so confident. If Elamirr came to her and threatened exposure, offered to buy her silence with his, she would be tempted. An unstable trade, where only the death of Elamirr could make her secure, and a very bad bargain for the realm, her safety and Dolvid's, at the price of Elamirr left in a position of influence — once again, grotesque how what was so self-contained and private as Âna and Dolvid could come to tilt a whole world: how could she see the realm led towards civil war for the sake of keeping that secret? But if she acted at once, showed Rodlakh the incautious letters Elamirr had written, he would be finished, and could not save himself by accusing the *rabhsayu*; if he then counter-denounced her it would only be for vengeance.

The sour smile, nowadays her nearest approach to joy, came back; *only* for vengeance! In the book by Tellis, a main character lamented the trials in the romances men and women would undergo for love were far exceeded in real life by the hard work they put into revenge; she thought sadly of how a man like Rodlakh who had wept over deaths in battle was contemplating murder of peaceful villagers because Kamin-Tolagh had offended his pride.

Rodlakh; internally she experienced a jump, as if someone unheard had come up behind and tapped her on the shoulder; she had been trying to disregard what was the dominant unknown in all her calculations and conjectures, her inability to predict responses of the stranger who had taken the place of her familiar husband. To the *rabhsai* as an impersonal function, her lovemaking with another was plain treason; legitimacy of the succession could not be in doubt — although in fact her children were Rodlakh's beyond any question, she had made sure of that. To him, revelation of her unfaith (as her father's people called it) would once have been a mixture of disbelief, anger, sadness and understanding, and she could have hoped the last two would in the end come uppermost. She was no longer sure about the understanding, and was unable to guess what the frightening new Rodlakh would do, with her or to Dolvid.

Âna had never been able to imagine calculated murder: killing in hot blood she could understand, but to take a life as part of a plan had seemed to her inhuman, even when proposed by Sebhal, whom she had loved. But she could not bring her charges against Elamirr, not without Dolvid's consent; for herself she would brave the consequences, hoping merciful traces of the old Rodlakh lingered, but the danger for Dolvid — if he was still alive — was as great or greater, and she had no right to expose him to the fury of an unpredictable *rabhsai*. The alternative, to allow Elamirr's ambitions and follies to destroy everything they had worked for, was equally unthinkable, and without her leave the thought came to her his abrupt death would neatly solve all problems. Morulis, after mourning, would be better off as a lovely young widow than yoked to either Elamirr ascendant or Elamirr disgraced.

In the Household, to judge by admiring eyes, there were officers who would do anything for their *rabhsayu*, not hoping for any practical expression of her gratitude. If she were to tell one of them in private she had been insulted by the Acting *Bôdhrai* —

Here, a servant came to give her the information the *rabhsai* was in the Private Audience Chamber. With newer misgivings there persisted a long-standing petty irritation with this habit of his; he did not summon her, but pretended not to by letting her know where he was, though to send the servant back with the news she was in her ante-chamber would plainly not be adequate.

He was alone, face in torment, so her mind jumped first to the fear he had been given incontrovertible proof of his wife's recreations. He said, "Elamirr has been at the Bronze Residence; he should be here soon. Look at this — " thrusting at her several sheets of the newly-commonplace paper.

When subjugated nerves let her eyes focus, she saw a long dispatch from Shumat, beginning with particularly appropriate anniversary greetings, '*from here at Drin Navuna, where the realm first learned of its good fortune.*' In his opinion, he went on to say, forces available in the Colony were fully adequate for carrying limited action such as the *rabhsai* had proposed.

What followed was curious indeed. Ostensibly, Shumat, with memories of how the massacre at Lunu Jinzalladhiyu had come about, simply wanted his orders to be unambiguous, therefore listing every contingency he could imagine for the proposed punitive raid, asking for a decision by the *rabhsai* for each case: if resistance had to be overcome, should they kill only those under arms, or others as well? Should men only be killed, or women too? Children? If children, children of both sexes? Small infants? If huts or storehouses were to be burned, should troops ascertain whether anyone had taken refuge inside? What amount of damage in property and lives would be considered fitting? The list was exhaustive.

"What is this?" peevishly. "Shumat has his own judgment; he spent fifteen years at Narn making life-and-death decisions."

Âna was not going to say what she really thought; if she was right, Shumat was a subtler strategist than she would have credited, with a shrewder sense of his *rabhsai*'s real nature. "He never had a task quite like this."

"He does not have it now — " still irascible. "You were right. We cannot answer Kamin-Tolagh with crimes of our own."

Nothing yielded in his manner towards Âna, yet it cheered her a little to see Shumat (as she believed) had guessed right; there was a difference between waving a hand and saying, `*do the same to them*,' and being required to imagine exactly what *the same* would entail, and for Rodlakh, that difference was decisive. The husband she had loved was not dead.

When Elamirr came, exchanging wary looks with her, he did not attempt to reverse a decision clearly made. Riffling pages of the dispatch, he commented, "The Captain, with all respect, would have been well-advised to use cypher. If this had fallen into the wrong hands, Kamin-Tolagh's friends within the realm would have something to exploit."

At state ceremonies, a secondary amusement for Kadon Dinul's street-corner sages was judging who was in and out of favor, by how near they stood on the Steps to the *rabhsai*, and whether smiled on, engaged in conversation, or ignored by Rodlakh or Âna. On the anniversary it was widely noted and thoroughly chewed-over that while, as at Halving, the acting-*Bôdhrai*, Elamirr, was very prominent, confirming rumors of Dolvid's decline, his wife, the admired Morulis, was not beside him. If she had been absent altogether, illness would have been an acceptable explanation, but spectators with superior eyes or better vantage-points spotted her, well back in the shadow of the

Residence with lesser dignitaries, where, a disappointment for those who followed her lead in fashion, little detail could be discerned about her new gown the color of ripe peaches.

That was an oddity, but odder for those who participated was the failure of Morulis to attend the gathering in the Oak Wall Chamber. Her husband, level-eyed as if to defy any query, took his leave after the loyal toasts were proposed and drunk, not staying for food, nor for the second, less formal appearance on the Steps, when the crowd, with ritual out of the way, could cheer without restraint for their favorites. Curious, Âna sought out Tellis, who, in court circles as in the world of her celebrated book, generally managed to have the reasons for what happened.

A little later, Rodlakh was by the stone canopy that overhung the chair of state, unbuckling the sword he had borrowed at the last moment from a Household officer, when a servant approached. After low words, the *rabhsai* followed the man to the doors at the far end of the thronged hall.

He slipped outside, leaving a door ajar, and everyone was startled by the sudden loud whoop that surely could not have come, but then, could only have come, from the *rabhsai*.

He reappeared with dignity regathered, holding up his hands for attention already his. "You will all be gratified," he announced, "to hear we have news from Captain Shumat at Drin Navuna. Our friend Dolvid is alive and safe."

All? Âna questioned, as a ragged applause swept the hall, but her sardonicism was for the sake of her self-control; behind her measured smile was a tongue pressed hard against bottom teeth, as she struggled to prevent her particular *gratification* from spilling over in large tears. Rhunilat stooped over her to observe the news could scarcely have come at a more fitting time, and she could manage only a quick nod, maintaining a frozen, decorous joy, certain Rhunilat's observant wife was making notes for her next book.

Discreetly, Rodlakh gestured Âna should join him in the adjacent Private Audience Chamber, and she went, though she would have liked time to compose herself.

She was promptly hugged. "Shumat wrote in haste. We should have Dolvid's own report by morning, and he will be here in the flesh within — " a quick sum on his fingers — "three days, now. I do not have the story, but Shumat led out troops to assist Dolvid, though there was no fight; his son is also safe. He, quite properly, is riding back with Dolvid — Shumat, I mean to say, not wanting to proceed till we have heard the full story." Rodlakh, himself again after too long an absence, rubbed his hands together.

"You may have noticed," becoming sober, "I did not give Dolvid any title except *friend* when I made my announcement. I am going to demand his resignation, as a formality — an expression of my authority, a sign he is not to be treated with special favor."

She had no trouble guessing the origin of this formality. "But Dolvid is treated with special favor, or should be."

"It has to be seen he is not free to conduct independent policies. Just as a formality, he must ask my pardon, and then I shall reinstate him."

The phrasing was pure Elamirr. "Suppose he declines reinstatement? He often wishes for time with his family, and for writing."

"Then I suppose we shall have to survive without his advice," with an onset of pride. "I do not think Elamirr would fear that."

"Elamirr would attempt the Patriarchate, if it were open."

"Oh, come," in mild reproof. "Where is he, do you know?"

"Watching his wife, I expect," tartly.

"When did Morulis vanish? I scarcely saw her."

No? But next week, if asked, she reflected, he would recall the color of Morulis's gown, though not hers. "There were marks on her face," she said, having learnt enough from Tellis to guess the rest. "Bruises. She, or her husband, were afraid they would be noticed."

"Bruises?"

"Others on her body, probably, but they would not matter."

"A fall?" ignoring the increasingly acerbic tone; her most ardent worshippers could not deny Morulis was a somewhat erratic horsewoman.

"I expect that is going to be the story."

"But not true? What, then?"

"Leaving aside what I have heard surmised, I am told she has been friendly with Badh-Kizhai, the son of Kizhunai."

"Friendly?"

"As two filberts in one shell."

A grimace. "Morulis has taken sash. She is aware Elamirr is not one of our Residence Quarter husbands."

"As I told her when she chose him. I am reliably informed he was hunting his wife the day before yesterday, and found her, alone with Badh-Kizhai, at that summer-house in the meadows east of Shufloi Kadonu." It belonged to Rhunilat, but was used by young men and women of the Residence Quarter. "He all-but bodily dragged her away. Later, the sounds of blows and cries were heard coming from Elamirr's house. Her friends say she did not show herself till late morning, and the bruises were plain to see."

"Elamirr beat her, beat Morulis?"

"At Burantal, it would be the expected thing."

"He is not at Burantal," anger mounting. "And Morulis — "

"Morulis is another Chalice of Tûl, a treasure of the realm." A quick glance took note of her irony, but he was genuinely angry.

"Weren't you her protector?"

"When she was a girl," bitterly. "Now Elamirr is supposed to be her protector."

"This is not the first time?"

"No." She was going to remind him of another occasion Morulis had failed to appear for a dinner with Hrin ambassadors, but Rodlakh was recalling they had guests.

He rebuttoned his Household tunic. "Elamirr," he decided, "can no longer be an official of the *rabhsayum*. I am not going to give such brutes the sanction of high rank. We shall give Morulis protection from him — she can come back to her former post, if you both would want that, but Elamirr — I do not want to see his face. Dolvid is going to have to put his histories aside, we cannot spare him. He will have to give half the year to Kadon Dinul, at the least."

Before he had heard a word about the mission to the Farther West, almost before Dolvid could answer the ritual enquiry as to his health, Rodlakh was telling him the reasons for Elamirr's abrupt dismissal. "In the heat of the moment, I forgot he had been your assistant, appointed by you. In courtesy, I ought to have consulted you."

After days of riding where debate about possible conduct of more than possible war was relieved only by warnings from Shumat about the *rabhsai*'s implacable anger, the triumphant dominance of Elamirr, Dolvid was bewildered by apologies on this subject; he was speechless. His unbelieving eyes met a privately amused Âna, who told Rodlakh, "It cannot have escaped your notice Elamirr, for some time, has not been in accord with Dolvid."

"You knew about his cruelty to his wife?" Rodlakh asked sharply.

Dolvid assured him, no, and began to feel old, or weary. Morulis was lovely, but the realm was not going to stand or fall because of her bruises. Not the worst, however, if a ruler was going to be obsessed with brutality, for him to be against it.

With that thought, after handing over Kamin-Tolagh's gold and his now hollow-sounding letter of regret, Dolvid began his account with the truths he had heard from Yaënsilat, not merely the disastrous recent campaign, but the mounting cruelties of Kamin-Tolagh; Âna showed revulsion, but Rodlakh was unexpectedly dispassionate. "That house teaches the use of pain as other children learn their letters."

He was unemotional, too, about potential there had been for the start of war in the chase across Landegh, saying it was good there had been no loss of life, and the pursuers had retreated without a fight on the appearance of Shumat with his squadrons.

"Unless — " Dolvid began, then was reluctantly compelled to complete the thought: the file-leader, Varromar, who had excellent eyes, had been convinced he saw Kamin-Tolagh himself among their pursuers, and if so, the *rabhsai*'s forces had let slip a chance unlikely to come again. He added there was no intent to blame Shumat, who had rightly limited his mission to the rescue.

"It must be said, *Rabhsai*," Shumat offered, "Kamin-Tolagh's present weakness may be another opening that won't come again. He can't replace his losses in trained men overnight."

"Are you advocating war?"

"No. I am a soldier, *Rabhsai*, not a policy-maker. I'm only saying, if we're going to have to fight him, this may be the least costly time." On their long ride, he had glumly concurred with Dolvid that in honesty they must advise Rodlakh to that effect;

the relentlessness of the pursuit across Landegh argued strongly for a vulnerability Kamin-Tolagh would do anything to conceal, the short-term opening for defeating him decisively, in a war neither of them wished to see fought; though with higher stakes, the same opportunity they had let pass six years ago, after Kamin-Tolagh ignored Dolvid's letter.

"Less costly by comparison, that is; there's no time when the cost in lives will not be heavy. Looked at another way, the time could not be worse; Kamin-Tolagh, with all his tribes to play with, can raise and train replacements for his losses in six months — not squadrons for a battle, maybe, but numbers, with weapons, and he's got his Hrin to feed them; burning their crops and barns is no answer. So, to take advantage of his weakness, we would have to begin tomorrow, and that would mean fighting a summer campaign where most of the rivers stop running by Shu'sai."

"At this moment, in what they call their rainy season, or just past, it is a parched country."

Shumat gained in animation. "Yes, and water's just an example for what will always be true in a war fought over a distance; the defender has all the advantages — as attacker, except for quality of fighting-men, we give everything away to the enemy. We would have to maintain a large army in the field, a six-day journey, no water, from its source of supply and reinforcement, and once down in the tribal country all our lines of communication are subject to attack; to keep one squadron in the field could take four on escort-duty. Down there, you see, he can arm every man — women and children, too, if he can convince them they're fighting for their lives; anybody with a bow can kill from cover. I've been hearing, *Rabhsai*, for five years now, this war has to come, sooner or later. Well, the army will attempt what you command, but as a soldier I'd say, let him come to us; if we have to fight, let it be where we can levy the men we need, and he has the headache of supply."

Though all his points had been discussed before, Dolvid had never heard Shumat so eloquently cogent, but their talk on the subject had constantly assumed a *rabhsai* whose hunger to avenge the Lunu Tezh' incursion would only be added to by subsequent events.

Another consideration had been discussed at length without reaching a wholly satisfactory resolution, Shumat eventually taking refuge in his standing as, his words, a simple soldier: did the realm have a moral duty to crush Kamin-Tolagh, ending the barbarities of his reign in the West? If he had been a provincial overlord, inflicting his cruelties on subjects of the *rabhsayum*, the question would answer itself, and the realm had a four-hundred-year-old precedent, with Kanavakh `Vakh'biSegh', for joint-action including the army to depose a *rabhsai* guilty of monstrous misuse of his power. In that case, aside from a small personal bodyguard, opposition to the ruler had become so nearly unanimous, his removal had cost few if any lives. If that had not been so, Dolvid held it would still have been a duty for men of conscience to attempt ending a reign so filled with atrocities.

"*At Kadon Dinul,*" Shumat had emphasized. "*A few dozen nasty deaths, including some people of good blood. In the back-country, I doubt they saw much difference; we've had reigns that killed and tortured more Mixed-blood provincials. Who cared about* them? *They were nobodies.*"

The historical point was well taken, but Dolvid reminded his friend that more recently, to bring about downfall of a *rabhsai* whose rule harmed mainly the Others, there had been those risking and in some cases giving their lives, some what Shumat called people of good blood; Saidhan, Sebhal who was killed, Faëdhal. Whatever it was in Kanavakh's time, the issue for men of conscience had become moral, not racial. Now, the question was whether war was to be waged, lives lost, not to save people of the realm from suffering, but to end the reported cruelties of a man of the realm against both obscure tribes and his own followers.

"*Followers, men and women who chose to go with him.*"

Again, a good distinction, but not sufficient. Through the attempted neutrality of Shumat's comments, where he stood was easy to perceive; neither in relative strength and weakness, nor in provocations to the realm, were there any imaginable conditions for an offensive war against Kamin-Tolagh's Kargusai, and much greater and nearer threats to the realm were needed to change his sane professional opinion. Again, the answer was clear reduced to its simplest human terms: would they want to reach into, for instance, central Nîv, the dark hills where the Nibhfoi had its source, grab up some plowboy who had never seen Kadon Dinul or the Arnan, tell him he had to cross the water and ride dry days to the west, so as to be killed for the sake of utterly alien tribes? To this side, though uneasily, Dolvid could add the argument that they could not judge whether the so-called empire had in sum increased the pain of the tribes beyond what they would have suffered in their small wars, raiding of the folk Kamin-Tolagh had recruited for his unpleasant bodyguard, from the hunger which he had obviously done much to alleviate. For that matter, the Man-mani had evidently been cruelly oppressed by their own head-man, Sra-na-*something*, and what other home-grown despots, breech-clout Kanavakhs, had been displaced or forestalled by Kamin-Tolagh was beyond knowing. In the world, there might be a hundred rulers, or hundreds, just as vicious, a thought chiming seductively with Shumat's, that their realm could not right every wrong, and had plenty of work ensuring justice and saving lives within its borders.

All true, and still Dolvid was gnawed by the fact that this *rabhsayum* had sent Kamin-Tolagh to the West, and failed to enforce its demands for his return; to whatever extent he persecuted the northern tribes or the peaceable Hrin, he would not have been there to do so without Rodlakh's orders. Like Shumat, his instincts were against any war for less than absolute survival, but he would not be able to give an unequivocal *no*, if the *rabhsai* asked him whether the realm had a duty to remove Kamin-Tolagh.

Rodlakh said, "*What* this Yaënsilat had to say is interesting — "

"And terrible," Âna reminded.

"And terrible, but is it not equally interesting he did talk to you, and in secret?"

"I am afraid he may be dead," Dolvid said.

"But if these acts of cruelty were provoked by desertions among the tribal armies, and if the men of Kargul are tired of him, this empire of his is doomed. Should we not let it die of internal dissension, rather than rally his men back to him by an attack? Why should we spend lives bringing together for mutual defense what may be crumbling apart?"

Dolvid was glad there was no Elamirr to urge the equally arguable case a swift assault now might cause dozens of Kamin-Tolagh's men to desert, and find just as many unwilling to fight; without absolute certainty it would undo an evil, Dolvid was not willing to counsel war. If the Empire could be destroyed at the cost of ten lives, or two, it was too many. He could not guess what had brought about the complete change in Rodlakh, but welcomed it, so long as wishes were not taken for facts.

"At the same time, *Rabhsai*, we must improve our defenses, especially in the West, and to watch the borderlands of Lunu Tezh'." He had a plan for recalling to the colors for one month each year each man of the Colony (except the aged) who had ever served, giving a rotating force of up to thirty added squadrons.

"Do as you think best — *Asai*," a slight pause making clear the title was no mistake.

"I would also wish to renew our attempts at a working alliance, or an understanding, with the Hrin from parts not under Kamin-Tolagh's control. As I said last year, we may be able to support, or help arm, an uprising there against the foreign usurper. That will take money, but a great deal less than the cost of raising and equipping new troops of our own."

"Let me have estimates. Young Shudarr did well, I hear." The question was to be shared.

Shumat grunted. "Well enough. There could have been better discipline in that detachment of his. As its leader, he should not have let you send him ahead."

"He disputed with me, but I wanted the best riders to go."

"At his age, an official whose escort I led would have to do more than dispute to make me leave his side." Not exactly what Dolvid remembered, but he did not reply, letting the *rabhsai* gently reproach Shumat for underpraising his son's fine service.

"Your days may have been worse than mine."

"Not as thirsty," with a caress for his spurious self-effacement.

"What changed Rodlakh?"

She told how Shumat's request for detailed orders had shaken him. "Having seen himself at the brink, he is in full retreat from a face he was repelled by."

Dolvid was still bewildered the ethical question over which he had spent so many gnawing hours had apparently not crossed Rodlakh's mind; at the same time as relieved he was a little disappointed with the *rabhsai*, but from one brief interjection knew Âna had seen the dilemma, and decided to let it sleep.

"What is going to become of Elamirr?"

"Rodlakh says he'll make him a provincial tax-gatherer, but that cannot be permitted, with his views about race. The truth about the forgery is going to have to come out — if it comes from you, by way of the letters to Arvat, there will be no need to explain why I did not speak out."

"What about Elamirr's tales?"

"He can't prove anything, he has no evidence. Just his conviction everyone of Mixed blood should hate as he does; if I do not it must be because I am bedding with an Owani. Rodlakh told me when he summoned Elamirr and questioned him about Morulis's bruises, he muttered something mysterious, about not being like his betters, a tame cuckold, but would not say what he meant. I said he must have been railing at the Residence Quarter. He lost his nerve."

Dolvid concurred. "He had enough wisdom to see the conditions for making his charges safely had been reversed; he needed Rodlakh pleased with him and angry with me."

"And me."

"What about Morulis?" He felt a stab of guilt over the predictable sorrow of her parents, his old friends.

"She will remain here at the New Residence." The mocking gaiety was a little forced. "Even if she wants to, she is not allowed to return to Elamirr for half a year. She is under the *rabhsai*'s personal protection."

"And...?"

"Everyone is going to think so, whether it is true or not, so I suppose he might as well have the pleasure," determinedly uncaring. "Probably a good thing; a *rabhsai* who keeps to one bed becomes something of a joke, like Lambarr. Morulis will add glory to his renown."

Despite the shrug in her voice, despite where she was, Âna minded, but he guessed she would mind more his perceiving that. "Elamirr. An historian would see the reason for his fall as frivolous. Not for Morulis, no, but a man might be cruel to his wife and still give good advice — or be worse for the realm than Elamirr, and hold on to power by keeping his vices private. He could have been midwife to civil war."

Âna made a desolate noise. "What are we doing? I was forced to stand by and watch his tricks, because of us. I love Rodlakh — I do, my love, and I admire Aëlu more than ever — you love her, and love your children, you are the best friend Rodlakh has. What are we doing?"

He kissed her. "Could we not be here?" All she said was true, and he had no better idea than she about how Rodlakh would behave if this technical treason came to light; she was not first to have been troubled by how private fulfillment suddenly came to affect public business. Paradoxically, he had never felt so serene or certain, till she voiced his misgivings, and now with a thud that ought to be audible, he saw this was going to have to end. Not now, when Rodlakh's adoption of Morulis would make Âna feel doubly deserted, but quite soon, and by common, hard consent.

Alarmingly, she was weeping. "Dear Dolvid. I could not have borne it if you had been lost."

"A foolish attempt."

"Not entirely." After moments of clinging, she was her familiar self, seldom unready to be serious. "Rodlakh has Kamin-Tolagh's apology to make public. We can keep the peace without discredit."

"This time. We must not let the *rabhsai* go back to pretending Kamin-Tolagh does not exist."

"You still see war coming?"

"I may be wrong," feeling the old chill settle on his shoulders. "We have to keep working to make me wrong."

A week ago, Aëlu had asked the same question after a glad reunion at Kamsilat, where he had stayed only briefly before going on to Kadon Dinul.

"Why? Why must they try to destroy each other, Kamin-Tolagh and Rodlakh?"

Why, that was, did he believe so, and of any number of possible answers, none entirely explained his clinging conviction. He thought about the ride with Kamin-Tolagh, and despite a great deal intended to deceive, there remained the revelatory moment when he had asked what Âna thought about his accomplishments. "For one reason, he wants to prove to her she chose the wrong man."

"What, Âna? But she did not choose Rodlakh because he was powerful, because he was a warrior, because he was *rabhsai*."

"No. But if he had not been *rabhsai* — " In a belated spasm of diplomacy, he did not finish.

"You mean, she would rather have taken you," Aëlu shockingly said. "But you were too much *rabhsayani*."

"Did Âna tell you that?"

"Of course she did not," chidingly. "My eyes tell me."

Dolvid wrenched the discussion back. "I am only saying, Kamin-Tolagh is the kind of man whose victories please them for a day, but who cannot forget their defeats. If he survives his present weakness, rebuilds in the West, brings all the Hrin under his rule, founds a great and prosperous empire, he will still resent that the *rabhsai* has one thing he once desired."

"But he has his sister-bride, and he desired that far longer. Are you saying, any man who loves Âna must love her for ever?"

"I did not say he loved her," carefully ignoring any other implication. "Only that she has become his emblem of incomplete success."

End of the Fifth Part

Kamin-Tolagh

VI

37.

"Luzhan," Lavsila announced. "I have questioned him about the death of Yaënsilat." Aware of the vigilance of Tau-Suaka's men, he went into the Owanilú, an imperfect precaution, since the Hill Froghul could be assumed by now to have picked up some of the *Hwanió*. "He knew the man well, used to ride in his squadron. He, if anyone, would have been deep in any schemes."

"How did you *question* him? We have already given out a reason for the suicide." They were in the same bare but not uncomfortable room where the news had first come to Kamin-Tolagh, but the death was already a month in the past.

"I have not forgotten. I did nothing to alarm Luzhan. Actually, I asked him only if he had heard or could guess any specific reason for the sudden act of Yaënsilat, an immediate event, some connection with the *Bôdhrai*'s visit, for example."

"I am glad you did nothing to alarm him," corrosively.

"His answer was long in coming. He may be a good man, but there is something shifty about his face — some off-blood there, no? No doubt it helps him with the tribes. In the end, he admitted Yaënsilat spoke very often of his home near Inilun Barabhi, his desire to die there. Luzhan allowed, departure of the *Bôdhrai* might have reminded him of his own exile."

"Exile?" deeply disliking the word. "Luzhan said, exile? This man was one of the first to bring his wife here. His daughter was born at the Abu. When, before, did he sleep under a roof he could call his own? In his old squadron, he was a file-leader, and now he wears the badge of an under-captain, and draws pay as a *kímukan*, rank enough for a decent holding in the south when time comes. How many of our new captains are longing for barracks life, and soft service with my father?"

The demand was purely rhetorical, and he scarcely listened to Lavsila's sweeping answer, which hinted Luzhan, if properly persuaded, could tell a great deal. Though the notion of widespread disaffection was hardly comforting, it was good to have confirmation of his guess about Yaënsilat's homesickness; he was not the first such sufferer to have brooded his way into a state of mind where every shadow is a threat.

"Perhaps I caught the barest hint, that your Kargul' men retain, if you will pardon me, some resentment of *those you have chosen to be your personal guards —* " ending in a conspiratorial mutter.

"Freighanai knows, the others should, it is a compliment to their usefulness. A man who can lead a squadron of tribal cavalry is wasted as my personal guard, whereas these... " With a shift of his eyes alone, he indicated the unwinking Hill Froghul. Lavsila gave a small, quick nod, and as usual it was impossible to tell whether he was actually in agreement, or assenting to what would be the official story; perhaps for him there was no effective distinction.

It remained a complicated question, not least for Kamin-Tolagh; between the two occasions when he had permitted, encouraged men of Kargul not fully with him to return home he had chosen Tau-Suaka's Hill Froghul' for a bodyguard — a time, that was, when he first admitted he could not count on the unswerving loyalty of every *péfrapravádai* of his home province. His recent thought of those men as his campfire comrades, then, could be nothing but a sentimental ideal, a vision he had needed after the tribal soldier's attempt to kill him.

Yet days before that, while Dolvid was still at the Abu, he had been dreaming of taking back the entire provincial cavalry from his father, using those squadrons to give his armies a point of steel, enabling him not merely to defeat but to supplant Rodlakh, become ruler over two realms, old and new. But if there were some he could not trust among his own Kargul', men who had chosen to stay, or freely chosen to join him here, how could he hope to win over a force from which Tovakh had assiduously weeded his sympathizers?

He did not, in fact, need the heart of every trooper; if he could win over officers, squadrons would follow, as they were trained to do. No matter what Tovakh did to purge the cavalry, many of the younger officers would still choose Kamin-Tolagh the admired over his father who was merely feared.

Was that preference enough to break the chain of obedience descending from Tovakh, their *nimu*, to whom their oaths were sworn? The two first under-captains, after the reorganization, were Gremnivai, and the dry, effective Talfoyan, and if one was ineffectual, the other a competent rather than inspiring leader, both had made clear their hostility to Kamin-Tolagh's aspirations. Their new Captain, Ulvidhai, was not Karguli at all, but another of Petakoi's Islanders.

Without that cavalry he could not hope, for years to come, to challenge Rodlakh, not if Lavsila could put every one of his cousins, his kinsmen to the remotest degree, into the Avenue of Treaties to shout for him. A return to Kargul: he was certain it would have to come, but if only Rodlakh would hold his hand, there was no such urgency as he sometimes felt. At other, perhaps saner times, he was convinced his energies would be better spent completing conquest of the Hrin.

Then, his base secure, would be a time for bending his thoughts back to the land of his origins — and yet it could equally be said that with the resources of the realm at his disposal, he could digest the Hrin with ease.

Out of this dense tangle of conflicting thoughts a plan began murkily to emerge, not one he was going to share with Lavsila; not yet, if ever.

"We are making too much of this," startling and affronting him with the abrupt change of mood, and of language. "No army without its grumblers, and it is said they fight the better for it. When all the men have had a chance to see Hyolenstr and the valley of the Hflen, the ones who still find themselves homesick can be permitted to depart."

"Depart? Depart where?" regathering himself, to recall that Tovakh had sworn to treat any man who had followed Kamin-Tolagh as a traitor, and would assert his rights over a Karguli soldier found in any part of the realm.

"As is clear from the case of Antighal and Drusilakh, where Dolvid admits he made no move to inform my father of their capture, our out-of-favor *Bôdhrai* wants to improve his reputation as the one man of moderation, by making the Colony a place of refuge. Those who wish to leave us can do so here in the north." In autumn, he was thinking, when, as he had been courteously warned, the Army of the West would hold exercises on Landegh. If the drills were a ruse to disguise the beginning of an attack on him, the defections would make no difference.

"It could be Dolvid's final downfall, if he shelters accused deserters, Tovakh is bound to raise the matter in Council."

A conceivable side-benefit, but scarcely the point Kamin-Tolagh was making. "My father's folly has its limits." He would, also, have Petakoi advising him. "If these men return to the realm in what passes for remorse, renouncing their error, it would be idiocy to come down on them with full force of law. If Tovakh wanted to, the *rabhsai* would not let him; he will say, grant them amnesty, encourage others to follow them."

The face, despite every effort, made no secret of Lavsila's bewilderment; if the *rabhsai* said that, he obviously thought, it might be a valid point, and beyond that, it baffled him why Kamin-Tolagh cared what happened to the men, once they decided to leave him. At last, he decided the offer must be made plausible. "No matter what you say," he cautioned, "the homesick ones are going to suspect it is just a trap, to get the disaffected to declare themselves." He suspected it himself.

"With what object? What, other than let them go, would I do to them if they did?" He wished Freighanai were here; this man understood nothing about the soldier's mind.

"Well... " turning back to the Owanilú, and trying to be jocular and confiding at once. "They know you have been, shall we say, less than tolerant of the same disease, even the incipient disease, among ordinary soldiery of the Empire."

"The tribal squadrons?" incensed by the comparison. Since the fruitless and nearly-disastrous chase across Landegh, he had identified remaining members of the disloyal Laughing Owl family, and ordered them executed, and was now having a count made of all remaining Hwenala under arms, to see whether, in his present weakened state, he could afford to weed them out, but in all the years of Empire, the only men of Kargul who had died had been lost in battle, and in retribution for one of them he had carried out a punishing raid.

"The cases are quite different," hastily retrenching. "But, Lord, as we see in the affair of Yaënsilat, nervousness — "

"Yaënsilat became an old woman, hearing robbers each time the wind blew." Yet it had to be admitted there was evidence for an apprehensiveness more general than the bloated fears of one solitary and underoccupied soldier. To the body of the Kargul' men, perhaps, he had become a remote and therefore daunting figure, an unpredictable master. To an extent, that was desirable, but at the same time he had to have their trust — the same trust he had easily regained in a few moments of encouragement and banter before the battle at Hyolenstr.

"I shall talk to them. They will see I have no wish to harm, certainly not detain, any man who simply misses his home, and cannot put down new roots here in the West. I shall tell them how I believe my father is bound to behave, to those whose repentance is sincere." Sincere in some cases, but when they left, the defectors were going to have inserted among them a few of his most faithful servants, well-paid, who would sound out his latent friends in Kargul, and perhaps prepare the way for his own less abject return.

"Tell me your means — " once again, in ordinary speech — "for winning over Kadon Dinul."

Lavsila, unsatisfied with what had gone before, blinked. "Then you do not after all expect the *rabhsai* to begin a war?"

Kamin-Tolagh laughed at compound confusion. "The Army of the West, if they had known I was there, could have begun and ended it in ten minutes. But if war comes tomorrow, it will be a long one, and as the *rabhsai*'s losses mount, support for me at Kadon Dinul will be all the more valuable. We must prepare, get on with our business, and if they come, they come." In reality, while he was keeping the tribal country ready to fight, the early attack he had feared when word of his weakness reached Kadon Dinul was fading in likelihood; already summer was too near.

"If they do come," trying to huff up embers, "you must be sure of your officers — "

"Are you short of work? Hounding the men of Kargul is the best way to create the discontent you are trying to uncover. The question of Yaënsilat and his supposed clandestine meetings is closed."

"For the present."

"For all time. If you want to say a word beyond `good morning' to any of my officers, get my permission first."

After a covertly affronted moment, Lavsila found refuge in sententiousness. "It galls me, for your sake, that so much energy and so much treasure must be spent on preparedness for war. Perhaps the *rabhsai* is not ready to attack, but men of his blood can never lose a grudge. How can it ever be fully your own free empire, Lord, so long as Rodlakh has vengeance in his heart — so long as he continues to regard you as a revolted vassal?"

Long past a protracted dinner and another evening of talk which, like the inadequate rushlights, would flare up for a moment, then settle back to inconsequence, he sat in silence, pondering. He could no longer ignore it, nor pretend to be reassured by her denials: his sister was unhappy. She had been unwell, he recalled, at the time of the desertions, but before then, since returning to the north, unsmiling and silent too much of the time. During Dolvid's brief presence she had recaptured or put on much of her normal animation; her boredom with the small circle here was no secret, and the story Luzhan had told to help explain Yaënsilat's suicide could apply equally to her discontent; maybe the departure of Dolvid had left her wishing she could be riding for a world more various and stimulating than this.

Unexpectedly, because his sister was outside any comparisons, he found Âna in his thoughts. Like everyone who had come here from the Heartland, recent arrivals from the *Mankh'* had joined in the chorus of continuing wonder that the *rabhsayu* let no issue go undebated, and on questions of government, notwithstanding childbearing, spent as much time and energy as Rodlakh. With Lavsila's Heartlanders, the comment was invariably prelude to sneers about the farm-girl who thought herself a new Laluvoi, though no one who made it could cite an actual instance where Âna had been deficient in knowledge — nor indeed, name one thing other than flawless breeding they approved in Laluvoi, supposed betrayer of her race.

Kamin-Tarú, though it amused her to pose as ingenuous, had no shortage of acumen, and it might be her passionate desire to be nothing like their mother that kept her from more than fitful interest in the workings of empire. But Petakoi, and probably Âna, too, had never known what boredom was.

A new guest tonight had been at-Dhanurai, first from the *Manadilum* to visit the Empire, and a man of considerable learning. He was one of the two *atarlal* briefly detained in the Colony, but beyond conceding Dolvid had remained narrowly within law and the Treaty, at-Dhanurai was silent about the incident. He was readier to pass along gossip from the *Mankh'*, where Petakoi had again solicited help of the Patriarch on the question of succession. Having gone so far, at-Dhanurai had to be encouraged past his fluster, but assured of Kamin-Tolagh's contempt for outlawry in a realm he no longer acknowledged, went on to recount talk was Rodlakh, with proposals pending that could be blocked by five votes in Council, was being forced to drop opposition to Kamin-Tarú's formal removal as titular Heir in Kargul, in favor of Pedh-Sivai, Petakoi's nephew.
Mild derision maintained an indifferent stance, and Petakoi's choice for heir was no surprise, but all the same a curiously poignant moment for Kamin-Tolagh, as he unrolled in his mind the scroll of his patrilinear heritage; Tebadh, Talbhan, Tolat, Tolvan, martyred Tobhsila, the adoptive Tobhan his grandfather; *nimul* of Kargul had always been warriors worthy to captain the finest of all provincial cavalries, and now at last Petakoi could achieve perfect expression of her contempt for their *clanking about with swords*, by willing the province to a soft and slack-armed Islander, who could recite the eighty-two names in the Patriarchal succession, but would fall off his horse if handed a lance to carry. This, moreover, with the blessing of Tovakh: it had taken thirty-two years, but the mountain-lion was tamed and clawless, an Island captive, unless Kamin-Tolagh should return.

Late, there was word from Kambanal in the south, perplexed, chiefly, over the religious concerns pressing in on him, the still ungauged potential in the popularity of *Hridveyuth*, who drew his crowds throughout the six *onhrid*, never saying anything that could be read as a direct challenge to authority, leaving behind the restlessness of vaguely wakened hopes. Then, presence of *edhradul*, and the risk there for trouble with the pious Hrin; here, Kambanal had a specific point, the question of continued access to the many places a sect or faction considered in some way holy, as against assertions of domain by the new Owanil landowners. He urged the need of defining rules, which could only emerge from an agreement subscribed-to by at-Iruvakh but dictated by Kamin-Tolagh himself.

He reached to light a candle at the copiously smoking rushlight, which he then blew out. With a nod to Tau-Suaka he went out and made his way to his sister's bedroom. As often lately, she did not wake; though he now permitted it, she seldom came to his sleeping-quarters; it seemed a very long time since they had seen in grey dawn together, refreshing with cool wine.

When he grasped her shoulder she wakened as a child, eyes huge and fearful in the small light of the candle. "What is it?"

"We are going to the south." He had intended to take her back to Hyolenstr when the summer heat set in here, but at-Dhanurai was leaving almost at once, with the last of the Heartlanders left over after Spring Halving and subsequent amusements.

"When?" Tú asked, as she comprehended.

"Soon. The day after tomorrow."

"Very good." Pulling up covers, she turned to sleep.

"I thought you would be glad."

A silence, before she said, "I am. It is good news," as if in concession to an entreaty.

"We shall have those dancers back, the ones you enjoyed, with the high shoes and the bells."

"In the morning," drowsily querulous. "Could this not have waited till morning?"

"In the days of my youth," Oyestri conceded, as Kamin-Tolagh tried and failed to imagine this evil old walnut had ever been young. "Poison was a high art of the Hrin, most now lost.

As spices with our cooks, poisons are a skill needing practice and — ah — "

"Experience?" Kambanal offered.

"The very word." Oyestri's command of either language of the conquerors would falter at unexpected places, oftener as he went on drinking. Wine made him no less personally repellent, yet he could be a fascinating drinking-companion, downing cup after cup of the bland wine, smacking his lips over a sweeter vintage, and recounting histories sworn to by Hrin mariners, distant islands that teemed with articulate and prophetic snakes, men three feet tall, fierce as weasels and black as tar, a lost country ruled by naked, ample women who lusted perpetually, but butchered and ate men unable to satisfy them; Oyestri was especially fond of salacious adventures. Fond, rather, of the effect he hoped to produce, grinning lasciviously as he filled in extravagant details, but all the while keeping sly watch from corners of his dark, narrowed eyes.

Nearer to home, his scenes were more recognizable, though even here, a world of wonders seemed to have passed away just before Oyestri's birth, or when his father was a child; birds had wisdom and men arose who had the stride of giants. But the intrigues of Oyestri's own youthful time most interested Kamin-Tolagh, gold and trading-rights mingled with treachery and murder, all wrapped in a fine, confusing weave of religious doctrine, mostly incomprehensible, mattering even less than it meant, much less than Oyestri thought: beliefs might be sincere with some, but in most cases they more resembled devices on the banners of opposing armies, allegiance and emblem, that was all. Wherever he went, he heard strange tales about ways of the local gods, but men struggled in the same familiar way for food, land, mates, wealth, power over others: Sranadatta with his convenient god-thoughts, Iolfrant and the *dveyust-ranga-hrindan*, harbored and served the same desires as Petakoi and Tovakh.

"The other lord of your realm, Lords, who has no sword, Lavsila — he, too, had interest in our old art. Not, I guess, not well-famed in lands where Rodlakh rules."

"We do not think it an honorable means of settling a quarrel," Kambanal, with commendable restraint.

"Ah. In that realm, so I have been taught, when two lords have disagreement, or hatred, each for the other, each gathers up all his fighting men, and sends them against the other's, and when enough men have been killed, or one has none left able or willing to fight for him, the quarrel is finished. Poison, when it was being done, caused less dying — men who tasted for lords, if the grudge was a long one, but then one lord or both were dead, or else they became weary of their plots and defenses, and ended their difference. Few common lives were wasted in a cause not theirs, lords."

"Saving men, so you could starve them, or work them till they dropped. The Hrin are a thrifty people."

"So," the old man agreed, ignoring or oblivious to sarcasm.

Oyestri went on to give some idea of the complexities of the poisoner's art. The *hrithust* preceding the one supplanted by Iolfrant, for example, had been disposed of, despite all precautions, with use of two substances, each harmless alone. The first, a nearly tasteless powder made from seeds of a rare foreign fruit, was retained in the body for several days, becoming a fast-acting poison when the second, a liquid from an altogether different source, was introduced. Having obtained access to the kitchens, the poisoner — at a guess, Oyestri himself — had fed the first component to his victim for most of a week, without harming either him or his taster. The taster was then removed by means of a commonplace poison, easily traceable to an under-cook, and the new taster, unharmed by food containing the second element of the latent poison, confidently passed it on to its intended victim, who died instantly.

These arts, Oyestri insisted, had always been confined to the priest-goldsmith class, and had been ended at Hyolenstr when Iolfrant began his rule by seizing all those suspected of having practised poisoning, and, with one obvious exception, executing them in the traditional and unpleasant manner, by means of a slow-acting, agonizing poison of no known antidote. Oyestri described with relish the latter stages, when, still alive and conscious, the victim could watch and smell the putrefaction of his own extremities.

Hard to imagine such decisive toughness in the irresolute Iolfrant, harder to believe so developed a craft had been extinguished with the death of leading exponents — again, with an exception. As Kamin-Tolagh later remarked to Kambanal, for nearly two centuries when the laws of Preference were at their most stringent, Gabhanil of the realm had been barred from following their traditional skill, carpentry, yet to this day, two further centuries on, it was among those with a strong line of Gabhani descent the master-carpenters were found: lore that was useful did not die out. As *hrithust*, and therefore inducted into Hrin traditions, Kambanal had every right to his uneasiness. Probably, Oyestri was never drunk enough to be indiscreet, and doubtless he paraded his learning so as to advertise his usefulness to Kambanal's establishment; who better to defend them than one who had used all the tricks?

And he had plenty to tell, poisons that mimicked common diseases, apparent antidotes that killed, poisons masked by nutmeg, by overcooking, methods of introducing a poison into a sealed bottle, into fresh fruit without breaking the skin. Notwithstanding a reluctant admiration for what must be a lifelong study, Kamin-Tolagh, more keenly than when he was word-fencing with Dolvid, or turning disaster at Zelu Bablakhi into a mild setback redeemed by acts of courage, felt a yearning for simpler worlds where peace and war were what they seemed, men settled their differences with keen steel, and loyalty was given where owed — for the clean mountain breezes of Kargul. Yet, revolted by the cunning smiles and self-congratulatory chuckles of Oyestri, he saw he could get back to that world not by retreat, but only by going forward, through subtleties, strategies, deceits, by making use of maggot-people any soldier would despise.

"Poison," was Kambanal's morning-after summation, a trace of his youthful bookishness lingering. "Worse, even, than an arrow shot from hiding. To bend a bow needs some resolve, but to put a pinch of powder into food — what does that take? No merit we ever looked for in a man."

True, and neither were those qualities, sinew, courage, resolve, a firmness in the face of danger and pain, of any use against poison; Kargul had bred warriors because the feeble and cowardly died, but poison could kill a hero as soon as a weakling; no wonder the Hrin were as they were.

Lavsila, unbidden, arrived from Larghamit with news which, coming from Kadon Dinul by way of Thenimala, had already passed silently once through Guodvestr. A setback to his hopes of winning adherents through mistreatment of the Owanil;

Elamirr, chief advocate of openly discriminatory measures, was dismissed and in disgrace.

Kamin-Tarú asked, "Why disgraced?" They were still seated after an open-air breakfast, Hflen full as they had never seen it. Spring in this great valley was yielding to early summer, but from mountainsides far away to the north and west, melting snow feeding the river had caused it in many places to overspill its banks, and here, brown and cloudy, it lapped within a handspan of the terrace.

"Reasons have not been made public," but with the wise half-smile. "Manufactured reasons, they may be; it is no secret the *rabhsai* has taken a fancy to the dark rose of Burantal, Elamirr's wife."

"This is gossip, not news," in irritation.

"Rodlakh," his sister said dogmatically, "would not use his position in that way."

"Lady," with a grating tolerance for her innocence. "There are scant limits to what a man, even a man of honor, can do when he wants a woman." His proprietary expression must refer to the absent Khalú.

"That is stupid. If the *rabhsai* wants to enjoy a married woman for an hour or a week or till he is bored, he does not need to get rid of her husband. What could Elamirr say?"

Though admiring his sister's victorious counter, Kamin-Tolagh had small interest in this aspect. "Then Dolvid is not going to be replaced yet awhile by your favorite Owani-baiter."

"He is high in favor again," showing no embarrassment over his discredited predictions. "It was announced, when he returned from his visit to the Abu, he is to be raised to *nimum*. Sweating on top of Morulis must have addled the *rabhsai*'s brain; the man is son of the Residence librarian."

"Yet his father did not fail to win service with that *rabhsayum*. He was not rejected for a magistracy because of his doubtful reputation."

Lavsila flushed deeply. "Mongrel lies. Half-apes at court persuaded Laluvoi to promote one of the same kind." He had been taken off-guard: Kamin-Tolagh, having heard the story in the week he first met Lavsila, had hoarded his knowledge all these years, for use in just this moment.

The blow was inadequate to keep Lavsila subdued for long. Soon, he was seeing actual advantages in altered conditions at

Kadon Dinul; the Families knew Dolvid of old, and would not be deceived. His newer connection with the Colony, besides —

This was ludicrous; after five years at least of gaining him support of the Owanil, Lavsila was still talking about it as a process to be carefully nurtured to slow maturity. In fact it was hard to see how Kamin-Tolagh's popularity could ever be greater at Kadon Dinul, unless he could be there, giving reality to the renown of his deeds in the Farther West. As shown by Ondhayu's foolish remark about old heroes, the Jinzai War, so soon, was becoming dead history, and he had not been long enough at Kadon Dinul to leave any lasting impression, except on girls he had bedded; Petakoi, after all, had been right, he should have spent the time nurturing his alliances. Another of Petakoi's old projects had come back to mind with renewed plausibility, figurehead use of the woman generally held to be nearest legitimate continuation of the ruling house displaced by Banak and Laluvoi, now seventy years ago.

"Have you given any further thought to Finú?" watching his sister's face register facetious distaste.

"You said she was soft in the head," Lavsila complained.

"All the better. She could be made *rabhsaëyu*, and declared incompetent all in one day. Kargul has championed her cause in the past; if my swords brought her to her rightful place, who else would be *Maëdhrai*, when the Protectorship is declared?" Not for years had he spoken of himself as representing his native province, but he was thinking ahead now to alliances — or not less than absences of opposition — needed to make his power secure, the Great Families, the *Mankh'*, places where a veneer of legality counted for a great deal; the lawful *Moradhilum* he conjectured would in reality need votes in the Council of Thirteen.

Lavsila, taken doubly by surprise, was no disappointment, adjusting with only the slightest of visible jolts to the new strategy, agreeing that in many of the best houses of the Heartland, Finú was still regarded as true heir to the only authentic ruling dynasty.

"And, of course, a powerful advocacy is easier, and at the same time more convincing, when it comes from a disinterested desire for justice, and the welfare of the realm, with no taint of personal ambition."

"Welfare of the realm?" Kamin-Tarú was ecstatic. "*Finú?*"

"Legitimacy— " a word now haunting Kamin-Tolagh's mind when he turned to the old realm, propelling him to a new consideration of his plans; in law, at this moment, only one life stood in the way of his sister, his other self, becoming ruler in the province of Kargul, the one to hold the oaths of the cavalry officers. Two lives, really; Tovakh's widow would never give them any peace.

He was not astonished to find he could contemplate the death of either parent with virtually no feelings except for the practical results. Given time, it might be contrived; an assassin, for example, might be unsuspected among any who chose to return to the realm during the autumn exercises by the Army of the West.

Too soon and too late; his own armies needed many months of rebuilding, but by that time the succession would be changed by adoption of Pedh-Sivai, the legitimacy he sought a dead issue.

What was to be thought of as a happy event interrupted; Dubovai, who had been brought here to Hyolenstr when his survival was still in doubt, formally reported for whatever service could be matched to his fragile capacities, the first time since his wounding he had been upright beyond a few minutes. Having heard about recent arrivals, his unashamed eagerness to meet with and show his maps to at-Dhanurai, a fellow-geographer, was an admitted element in his determination to be out of bed.

Between two sticks, but disdaining the support of a pair of tribal soldiers, he emerged painfully onto the terrace, and while he held himself at his best approach to attention long enough to declare he was fit for duty, he crumpled with relief into a chair as soon as Kamin-Tolagh offered it, standing to help Dubovai down. Hidden under the breast of the weatherworn but freshly laundered tunic, he knew, was a deep, still raw-looking depression, and the *ramidul* who tended him had expressed wonder he lived through such an injury, and the arduous, harried retreat through the forest, long journey before help could be found. He had been struck, also, in the face, and the flushed lips of an arrow-wound moving from scab to scar were like a freakish diagonal elongation of his mouth, giving him a lingering, lopsided smirk.

Kamin-Tarú urged fruit and cool *raminat* on Dubovai, asked sweetly about his pain, but soon remembered there was a hairdresser waiting for her, and went inside. She was never comfortable in the presence of deformity, disease or disability, a speech-impediment or a palsied twitch, no less than a humped shoulder or goiter, but this distress, her brother maintained, denoted an excess of feeling rather than a lack.

Into the pause following her departure, Lavsila injected as afterthought what should have been his first news, soon to be confirmed by the Hrin traders; it was no longer possible to buy Dakbân steel at Thenimala, the *rabhsai* having forbidden export of swords, knives, body-armor, or bars of unworked metal. "This will anger the steelmakers — " as if trying to think of a way their grievance could be exploited, not Kamin-Tolagh's primary concern. A large number of first-class weapons had been lost in the forests above Zelu Bablakhi, left, that was, with the dead who had carried them.

Kamin-Tolagh said wrathfully, "The Hrin swords bend like solder or snap against a Dakbân blade. The *rabhsai* may be willing to endure a little discontent, for the sake of such an advantage."

"Can we not make better steel?"

"Perhaps you would want to try. The best Hrin metalworkers concur, the hardness of Dakbân steel is not entirely due to the forging, nor the tempering, but there is some secret alloying of the actual iron." The craftsmen on the upper reaches of the Dakbân River sent pack-trains into the virtually-abandoned former province of Asekh, but what they brought back was a well-guarded secret.

"I can get an agent at Kadon to purchase us weapons, and have them shipped in boxes as — something else. I would need gold in advance; the price may be high, and bribes will be needed."

"Find me your agent, and then come to me for gold. What will he do, walk into the armorer's shop by Market Way, and ask for five hundred swords, cash down?" Mention of money had depressingly reminded Kamin-Tolagh of Fretasi's imminent arrival. For safety, the treasury had travelled with him, but she had stayed to bring her accounts up-to-date, and would shortly descend, no doubt with gloomier tales than ever.

Dubovai stirred, and asked Lavsila, "You say, arms, armor, and bar steel; do you know, sir, whether the ban includes made things other than weapons — farming-tools, hoes, spades, plowshares, scythes? If those can still be bought, Lord — " turning to Kamin-Tolagh — "blacksmiths at the Abu, or the Hrin have good ironworkers here, who could reforge them into swords. For that matter, last time I saw the warehouse at Zelu Bablakhi, there were quantities of such tools, from those the Hrin brought there to trade. They'll never be as good as a real Dakbân sword, but a lot better than anything from these parts."

Congratulating him on a practical notion, Kamin-Tolagh made sure Lavsila heard the implicit distinction. Dubovai, near weeping with joy to have an opening for useful service, further suggested that in a few days, when he was stronger, he could take ship for the trading-station, and see what was there that could be used in making weapons. Admirable that return held no nightmares for him, and Kamin-Tolagh gave his leave, though with the unspoken reservation that in a week, if this man had not improved a great deal beyond his present frailty, the same would be accomplished by means of a dispatch. Likeliest Dubovai's days of hard travelling were done, and with them his beloved map-making.

A courteous letter in near-archaic Owanilú came from the *Hrithust* Hvrayos, whose *onhritha* was smallest and poorest of all, a narrow, rocky peninsula adjacent to Nestos on the south coast. Not, however, least influential, since there, on a high cliff, was the authentic Place of All Shrines, of which those by Larghamit were lesser replicas. Rusty with the Script of Shâl, in which the letter was written, Kamin-Tolagh required the assistance of at-Dhanurai, who informed him it was an invitation for him and his compatriot *hrithust* to *honor with their esteemed presence this most apt of anniversaries.* There was more, the *atarlai* said, with heavy *Mankh'* disdain, about *sacred places* and a *rite of reconsecration.* With Kambanal's help he realized the date must be an anniversary, the sixth, for dedication at Kafai Zhaëli of the shrine to Noh-Sra-Lal-Hin and Siv'loi, in this one case the original, of which Hvrayos possessed, or harbored, the duplicate.

Waiting for doom-laden Fretasi and filled with his own plans, Kamin-Tolagh decided Kambanal, author of the Siv'loi legend, should go. Assured by Oyestri no Hrin, and particularly not the mild Hvrayos, would make such an occasion part of a hostile plot, Kambanal, taking only a half-squadron, crossed the river and rode away south. On the same day, Lavsila, tasting the novelty of a comfortable ride in one of the smooth-running little horse-drawn wagons of the Hrin, went down to Guodvestr to take a ship back to Larghamit.

In Kambanal's absence from the *hrithust*'s palace, Kamin-Tolagh discovered the beginnings of irritation at how the deputy he had created was wearing his power. Young, likable, he had been a little too much at ease in these airy halls, as if born to a lordly graciousness, and with a growing confidence he attended, went through the motions of officiating at, incomprehensible rites of the Hrin. Still unwed, not for a lack of admirers, but at present his devotion was entirely for his tasks, and for his lord, whose approval, nevertheless, he tended to assume too readily. Though most able of followers, and, with Freighanai, the one whose loyalty was least in doubt, his success at maintaining an impression of mildness and moderation hinted at the chance of a future rival hard to discredit. His present indispensability, with so many other questions, could only be solved by gaining access to the talents of the old realm, where his replacement could be found, should it become necessary later to kill him. As if a joke, which it half was, Kamin-Tolagh told this to his sister, but she did not laugh, and only stared uncomprehendingly. Being back beside the Hflen was not working the same healing magic on her despondency as last year.

Kambanal had given an outline report concerning most vexed of the religious disputes between Hrin and Owani such as his letter had warned about, but his impression he had soothed all sides with reasonable compromise was angrily rejected, in the week following his departure, by Iruvakh, who came to the palace agitated, impatient to voice his grievance.

"The result of excessive coddling of these people and their superstitions. Defiance, insubordination — it all revolves around this arrogant *Hridveyuth*. When are you going to put some restraint on him?"

Not long ago Iruvakh had spoken in deep apparent respect for the holy man of the Hrin — of his existence, not his creed, then only another among many to be examined, including that of the *Mankh'*. Then, all were superstitions, or none were.

The present tale illuminated what had been hinted at in Kambanal's letter. Securing the purchase with family wealth, Pranúdhanai and Ondhayu had acquired one of the biggest and richest of new estates, woodland and pasture, vineyard and orchard, sprawling along the opposite bank of the Hflen eastward of Hyolenstr. Wide acreage of land long disused promised expanding returns.

A lazy backwater of the river provided an accessible place for watering of many cattle, and there were also docks, and a house for summer use, partially supported on pilings set in the water. To westward, a spur of the riverbank threw off a barely detached continuation, partially closing off the shallows, a long spear of islet, thick with rushes, shrubs and spindly trees, breeding-place for multitudes of water-birds, but in particular, swans.

Kamin-Tolagh recalled his guide during the campaign against Iolfrant speaking about this holiest of birds, and of a sect or cult giving it special importance. Now Iruvakh recounted that where the projection of riverbank came nearest the islet, called Swan Eyot in the Hrin language, there was a small, unassuming shrine, a plain circle of squared stones set deep in the turf, but a hallowed place of devotion for those of the Swan cult, who were more numerous than had appeared from the offhand description given last year by Istaluodn. Access was by a deep slot of narrow path, said to have been in use a thousand years, cutting across pasture and dividing tilled fields of the Heartlanders' estate. The eternal trickle of pilgrims across their fields, mainly ragged folk of no consequence, swelling to a spate at times of religious significance, had become an annoyance to Pranúdhanai and Ondhayu, as had the habit among some of their own laborers of breaking off their tasks without warning, to fulfill an observance associated with the swans. Most recently, and more acutely, they objected to use of the shrine by the *Hridveyuth* as a place for addressing large gatherings, which at times spread along the riverbank so as to impede cattle coming down to drink.

According to Iruvakh, Kambanal, with his absurd dual authority as *Sranim'* and *hrithust*, had worsened the dispute by his equivocation: when Pranúdhanai tried with new fences to divert the path around their fields, Kambanal had declined to seek out and punish those who broke down the barriers, and told the Heartlanders to respect the ancient passage. A spring ritual, where the Swan Cult demonstrated its reverence by killing several of the fowl in ways abominable to observe, had led the landowners to appeal to Iruvakh for a religious ruling, but his decision the shrine be dismantled had been overruled by Kambanal, after a protest from the *Hridveyuth*.

"Consider, the path to this place of so-called devotion now divides fields consecrated in *ga-Yalum*, Aëlovoi's Gift."

This was the man who had once defended Man-mani right to beliefs that killed far more than swans. "And have you made any attempt to teach the One Way to these unfortunate Hrin?"

A telling question. The present *Atarlum* of Dozhusai, glad to partake in the new popularity of Zhôl in Rodlakh's realm, was not going to discourage an attempt at enlisting Hrin devotees, but Iruvakh, who, no less than Kambanal, owed double allegiance, to Empire and *Mankh'*, was in danger of letting himself be captive to a third, the old racial exclusiveness Heartlanders still espoused, the creed of an *Atarlum* now in eclipse. The most those unregenerate believers wanted of lesser races was that they acquiesce silently in the necessary superiority of the Owanil.

Iruvakh was evasive. "I have not tried to suppress this cruel cult, though that would be my instinct. There are other islands in the Hflen where swans nest, and the shores can be reached crossing no *ga-Yalil* fields. My solution was, the stones be taken up and conveyed to another site; I invited the *Hridveyuth* to participate in its selection."

That, as suggestion only, had been part of the truce imposed by Kambanal, but the *Hridveyuth* had failed to appear for any further discussions with Iruvakh. Instead, yesterday, another important festival in the Swan calendar, he had again caused his followers to occupy the promontory of the shrine, interfering with running of the estate. Kamin-Tolagh gathered there had been ineffectual beatings dealt out by personal retainers of Pranúdhanai, Hrin from other parts, but arrival of the *Hridveyuth* himself had influenced these men to join the celebrants.

"Rebellion, nothing less. Troops are needed to disperse these wretches and enforce the law."

In some way, Kamin-Tolagh perceived, Iruvakh had helped bring about this crisis, taking advantage of Kambanal's absence to go over his head, in hopes of a more arbitrary settlement.

On evidence, and in view of his instructions not to provoke unrest, more so since the losses at Zelu Bablakhi, Kambanal had in fact acted correctly, but there was at least one other point, one which would come first with Lavsila: the damage it could do to Kamin-Tolagh's reputation as last defender of Old Owan if Kadon Dinul heard he had upheld wicked superstitions of foreigners over the rights of a well-connected Heartland couple, two of their offspring.

That required qualification. Having dispatched one of the Hill Froghul to summon the Karguli duty-officer, Kamin-Tolagh reminded Iruvakh that in permitting consecration of the new estates, he had stipulated there was to be no violation of existent Hrin rites.

"Within reason, yes," still vehement.   "If some Hrin superstition says no cattle can be grazed on a thousand acres of pasture, are we to honor that?"

"That has not happened," admiring his own coolness, determined to keep his mounting anger with Iruvakh in check.

The duty officer was Niburai who had come south with Kamin-Tolagh, his glory somewhat dimmed after the unsuccessful chase across Landegh, the thirsty and disheartened return. Having already heard of the disturbance, he had been about to ferry across the river with two squadrons when Kamin-Tolagh's summons came.

Iruvakh failed to hide dissatisfaction with the careful orders issued: Niburai was to take a Hrin interpreter, and occupy the headland without undue force. The *Hridveyuth* was to be found, and invited to meet with Kamin-Tolagh at Hyolenstr forthwith, but given no opportunity to refuse.

"He may still be there, strutting like the only cock in the barnyard. You would do well to take workmen, and give them protection, while they dig up the stones of the shrine, as I ordered."

"As you presumptuously ordered." Resolve to remain calm snapped, and he moved to glare down on Iruvakh, who hastily stood. Even so, Kamin-Tolagh loomed head and shoulders over him. "Do you think *g'Asalladh'* Himself dares to tell the *rabhsai* how his troops are to be used? You have less power here."

He turned to wave Niburai on his way, but as he reached the door, halted him, in midst of choking anger abruptly reminded of how it had ended when he sent men to *invite* Yaënsilat to meet with him. About the *Hridveyuth*'s life, he cared much less, but he had not the troops to deal with a general uprising his death might bring. Crossing to where Niburai stood expectantly, he also remembered the special friendship with Ondhayu, which might influence his sympathies in this case.

With this man he was eye-to-eye. "The *Hridveyuth* is a reasonable and peaceable man. Your orders can and will be carried out without bloodshed."

"If there is resistance, Lord — "

"A hundred men should be enough. I do not expect the holy man to resist, but if he does, use six men, or as many as you need to secure him without harming him."

"What if there are weapons among the mob, Lord?"

"There will not be. Follow your orders. If you kill anyone, I shall have to look into the question of your subscribing to false reports of actions at Zelu Bablakhi."

Niburai's mouth came open, his eyes giving him a childish look of injustice, as he recalled the origins of the hero he had come to represent so contentedly. He had no viable protest. He could not even complain to his Heartland friends, without exposing his own fraudulence.

"Nothing is fair," paternally. "But I will be served well." He clapped a hand on Niburai's shoulder. The only way to be sure was to go in person, but Empire would fail in any event if he could not find subordinates to trust.

"You," wheeling back on Iruvakh, "are not going to make me a bully to take blame for your follies; if you want to begin a war of religion, your *atarlal* will have to fight it."

"We are speaking *my Lord*, of defiance — "

"Yes, yours. Kambanal followed my instructions to avoid these conflicts."

"Pranúdhanai and Ondhayu hold their lands lawfully. Allow these Guardians of the Swan to succeed, and Hrin everywhere will see they can commit any crime; the lives of the Owanil will be in danger."

"And if they force the Hrin to rise up in defense of their beliefs? Not one Owani will survive; my men cannot be in all places." Just the same, and uncomfortably, there was something to Iruvakh's thesis, and he hated him bitterly for bringing matters to this point, where conciliation could be construed as weakness, strength as oppression.

In a new wave of fury, he took Iruvakh's shoulder in a bruising grip. "Listen to me, *at'ai*. I rule here. Your *Atarlum* is here, not by treaty, but at my pleasure. If there is one further instance, just one — " he held a forefinger an inch away from the startled face — "where an *atarlai* supposes he is free to make policy, I shall expel you all, and leave you to explain your failure to His Enlightenment. Any Child of Yoëlladhu who values discarded doctrine above my law, above his life here of ease and profit, can go with you, and look for gratitude from *g'Asalladh'* — or, better, from his fallen predecessor. Now go. I shall send for you when the *Hridveyuth* comes."

With a cold stare to maintain his dignity, Iruvakh did leave. Tau-Suaka, who could scarcely have followed the complexities of discussion, had the complacency of a dog who knows his master has done a clever thing. Later, Kamin-Tolagh saw he had stumbled onto the word that routed Iruvakh, who had never evinced any fear of discomfort, pain, or death but whose new terror was of failure. At Kamin-Tolagh's instance, the *Mankh'* he had embraced and then rejected had offered him a new chance, and he was afraid for his future. Men who would rather risk death than face disgrace were familiar enough; Iruvakh was now no more complicated than an ordinary soldier.

Notwithstanding Iruvakh's prediction, the *Hridveyuth* had vanished from the Swan shrine. His habit of travelling alone and mainly on foot made his appearances into the splendid, unwarned surfacings of a silent, invisible ocean-dweller, and in this instance meant a long task for Niburai, whose squadrons brought the man back to Hyolenstr on the evening of the third day. Busy with Fretasi, Kamin-Tolagh saw to it the man, who acted unconcerned, was fed and given a bed. They would meet in the morning, as soon as they could be joined by Iruvakh.

Who arrived before noon with confidence restored, enheartened by a curious alliance with Oyestri. While they waited for the *Hridveyuth* the devious old Hrin counsellor explained the Swan cult had never been endorsed by the official priesthood, since they used the birds in place of priests, asking them for special favors, and in foretelling the future. This was, then, a direct challenge to the authority of the *hrithust*, any *hrithust*, including the *Sranim'* Kambanal. The cult could not be abolished outright, but dismantling of the ancient shrine would weaken it, and at the same time demonstrate the powerlessness of the *Hridveyuth*, who was now allied to the Guardians of the Swan.

Kamin-Tolagh wondered how much the Heartlanders had promised Oyestri for his advocacy, while Iruvakh blandly observed that the single solution, removal of some stones, served the interests of important Heartland settlers, while at the same time agreeing with two otherwise divergent orthodoxies.

About to felicitate him on his new-found respect for the *dveyust-ranga-hrindan*, Kamin-Tolagh was halted by the abrupt reappearance of Kambanal, who wore all signs of a man who had ridden without rest.

"Lord," deference mainly to the fact of company. "The *Hridveyuth* must be released at once, and unharmed."

"He is not a prisoner. No one has harmed him. We are about to have a peaceful meeting." The agitation in Kambanal's manner was hard to understand.

"Could he have refused to come? Consider, Lord, how it appears to his followers, when a hundred soldiers surround him, and bring him back here at sunset. The story is already spreading like a brush-fire in the hills and valleys southward. I heard it backwards, an hour past daybreak, a six-hour ride from the Hflen crossing."

"Backwards?"

"Men called out to my Hrin interpreter, wanting to hear whether their *Hridveyuth* had yet been put to death, and from them I got the story of what they called the arrest."

He had since spoken to Niburai, but factual details of the case, he argued, did nothing to alter the larger fact: the common Hrin supposition their holy man was at best a captive. "He must be seen at once, free and unscathed."

"Must?" ignoring Oyestri, who was muttering about the insignificant birth of the *Hridveyuth*'s following. "I decide what must be, and you must obey me."

"Your pardon, Lord, but you did not make me your deputy in these parts to watch in silence while others provoke an uprising." His glance for Iruvakh and Oyestri was eloquent. "Neither former priests, nor *g'Asalladh'*, whom I reverence, are sovereign here. If the *Hridveyuth* is not our prisoner, it should be made known at once, before the crowd becomes too large and unruly to control."

"The crowd?"

"Gathering now in front of the city. So far, only dozens, but hundreds must be making their way here on foot."

Iruvakh stirred. "Where is government, if disputes are to be decided by the size of the mob that musters — "

"My point exactly," Kambanal, one of his unnerving displays of a discrepant sophistication. "If we wait for the mob to grow big enough to have a good opinion of its powers, it is going to seem as if we had no choice but to release their troublesome hero."

"We cannot release what we are not holding," having noted the quiet arrival of the *Hridveyuth*, in his usual plain garb. "The four of us," excluding Oyestri, that was, "are going to ride together to the place of this shrine, and discuss its future as we do. If you are not too exhausted?"

Kambanal shook his head. His distrust of Iruvakh was easy to read, confirming the suspicion the *atarlai* had tried to go behind his back in a question he had thought settled. Iruvakh in turn disapproved of the forthcoming ride, but knew he'd had his full allowance of support from Oyestri, not one for swimming against a current.

"If I guarantee this shrine in perpetuity — " Kamin-Tolagh stooped over slightly, holding his *pefrai* in check to match the pace of the *Hridveyuth*'s lesser mount. "I must have assurances these Guardians of the Swan will do nothing to undermine the authority of the *Sranim'*, or of lawful landowners." Which side he would take had been settled days ago, when he assailed Iruvakh. Lavsila was going to complain about his squandering the goodwill of the Heartland, but while he might someday need support at Kadon Dinul, he would never get there without this Hrin foothold to stand on.

How near they might have come to losing it was brought home by the curious scene when the four principals emerged from the city gate, Tau-Suaka's guard kept at a small distance, though with arrows ready at the string. Rather than a crowd, the gathering they rode through was many small clumps of rough-clad men and women, and the unshackled reappearance of their smiling *Hridveyuth* was cause for satisfaction, not joy, a subdued acclamation made of a multitude of pleased murmurs.

"Of the shrine, and of ancient access to it?"

"If those who use it will keep to the path. Fences will be made."

The holy man considered. "Lord," lightly, "anyone who has the dangers of rule would desire to make gods into his bodyguard."

"What about these swans? Do you yourself hold to this cult? Do they teach obedience, respect for law?"

"The swans are nothing. Being alive, they share in all life, but they can teach only what is already learned."

"Spare me riddles for gaping goatherds. You know what I am asking."

A baffled one-hand gesture. "You ask me, Lord, is this bridge safe to cross? What can I say? It has stood to now, but can I say there will never be a flood or an earthquake to break it? In the islands, where the one who was *hrithust* now is, men carve sticks and dress them in straw, and call those their gods. When fishing is bad, or their crops fail, they throw these dolls down and whip them. But I cannot tell swans which way to fly, and no god is my apprentice."

This circling speech appeared to disclaim responsibility for any effect of his utterances. "On the other hand, you can tell these Swan people they are assured their sacred place by the graciousness of the *Hrithust* Kambanal, whose lord is Kamin-Tolagh."

"That I can say," gravely. "It will be good to hear, after so long."

A sharp glance could detect no sarcasm in the open face.

So as the *Hridveyuth*'s good health could be seen by as many as possible, they had ridden on the populous south side, crossing the Hflen only when opposite the swan islet, a boat having been instructed to keep pace. The *Hridveyuth* remained at the place of the shrine to greet a gradual gathering, while Iruvakh went reluctantly to instruct Pranúdhanai and Ondhayu as to Kamin-Tolagh's disappointing decree.

On the ride back, Kambanal, very weary, gave a sketchy account of his brief stay in the *onhritha* of All the Shrines, and meeting with Hvrayos, described as a very polite and friendly little man, by a wide margin the most impressive Hrin yet encountered, despite his execrable pronunciation of the Owanilú. Never having been a trader or any sort of traveller (he admitted, also, to being an indifferent goldsmith), the minor *hrithust* had learnt the language principally through books; he mysteriously possessed a copy of *Lamalkezhul baKamantanil*, the Island Annals, the *Mankh's* enormously tedious record of the long Exile, where he claimed to have met with wonderful inspiration.

"Stubbornness," Kambanal explained. "Hvrayos would wish the Hrin to have some of our steadfastness as a people, not divided by foolish religious quibbles."

"Our holy man is of the same opinion."

Near sleep enough to be unguarded, Kambanal made a noise like an abortive sneeze. "Lord, I have no more use for the swan business than for this street-juggler, but the Heartland crew forget how few of us there are."

"We are of a mind. The street-juggler made a martyr can be a nuisance beyond anything he is alive. As it is, Oyestri is the one who most needs watching."

"He is old, as old is here."

"With ancient habits, lies, treachery." The man was clearly going to have to be helped to his death, but not until he had no more use in him.

"For me — " he thought better of what probably would have been advocacy of Iruvakh's right to the prize for perfidy. "Lord," he substituted, "I must ask pardon for my earlier abruptness. I was road-weary and angry, having thought the solution to this question already agreed-to."

"Between us, I am tired of cringing men who tell me what they guess I would enjoy hearing. You at least have a mind worth speaking." He might have been less tolerant, however, if he had not agreed with Kambanal.

In all, a good day; earlier, while awaiting Iruvakh's arrival, he had been able to rout, or temporarily repulse, Fretasi, with help of a dispatch from Dubovai at Zelu Bablakhi; against all prediction, and upsetting Fretasi's direst forecasts, small quantities of gold were again being brought in by the river-people. Presumably their unseen rival, Iolfrant, was unable to supply enough of the coveted *sviranth* powder to monopolize the trade, but at the estuary the forest-dwellers had a range of new commodities to offer in exchange for food and woven cloth. In their little boats, the wild men were bringing swords, helms, breastplates, saddles, harness, all the pickings of a defeated army and of despoiled bodies, though not one of those who offered these things had seen a corpse, or taken any part in the late war; everything was simply found, lying in the forest.

The Zelu Bablakhi men, Dubovai wrote, especially those of Kargul, had been understandably infuriated at what struck them as mockery of their losses, and had first declined to offer for what they said was already theirs; some had attempted to seize the gear, and there had been clashes. That was ended; Dubovai had told the men to poultice their wounded pride, and had let the river-people know military gear in good condition would be traded for. Examples had already reappeared, and he expected more, as word spread. Oversupply, and the uselessness of such things to the wild men, were making for bargain prices; his offer of a half-bag of flour for five helms and a pair of good Dakbân blades had been quickly accepted.

"We shall have to see, *Asai*," Fretasi had replied, when asked if this dual news did not change her estimates, either for income or the expense of equipping squadrons newly raised. But she was already gathering up her irrefutable journals and alarming loose pages, and at that moment Dubovai won his full captaincy.

"Shall we ever see Kargul again?" Kamin-Tarú, gazing out on the heron-haunted Hflen from the place where she slept. She had asked the same before, on the day Lavsila had brought his mixed bag of news from Rodlakh's realm. Then, her question had its origin in smells, not sight; the Hflen had been in flood, and on its journey from the hills had brought down much debris, branches, whole small trees, mud, vast shoals of leaves and twigs from last autumn. The banks at the high-water mark, every pool and backwater, had helped fill the air with the rich scent of slow vegetable decay, becoming the reedy fringes of the river near Inilun Barabhi, where they had spent whole summer days in play and long shared thoughts.

"Some of us will, before the end of the year, if I guess right, Luzhan, for one — the *kímukan* who works with tribal levies."

"With the good teeth, I know."

"With a small daughter." That Luzhan would be among those to leave was pure assumption; he had been the one to confirm homesickness as a reason for Yaënsilat's suicide, and surely shared the complaint.

"Lavsila called such men Yaënsilat's accomplices. Accomplices in what? If we are going to call it a crime to long for our clean mountain air, or to think Peframi wine is better than the millet beer of the Gudi-la, then I shall have to begin by condemning myself."

Yet first offer of a release from service for such men had been made a month ago, and Freighanai reported somewhat embarrassedly from the Abu no one had yet spoken up to take advantage of it — he did not dare say, no one dared to. Not believable that suddenly there was no discontent or disaffection in the ranks, and Kamin-Tolagh saw he would have to assemble the men of Kargul in small groups, joke with them, convince them his offer was sincere, taking for text the *Mankh'* rubric *better to rule in one willing heart than over ten thousand slaves.* There would be defectors crossing Landegh in autumn, if more than half were to be spies in his pay: they were needed for a mask. He might be wrong about his father being obliged to offer amnesty to the soldiers, but that no longer counted; on the same day as Kambanal rode south and Lavsila left for the north, Kamin-Tolagh had seen the one answer to the problem in time set by the impending adoption of Pedh-Sivai, a way to make it not matter; how, after all, he could bring together all the indispensable elements for eventual defeat and supplanting of Rodlakh.

Which, prompted by her lament, it was time to unveil for Tú. Like one of Dubovai's fair-copied maps, he laid out the clear logic for her. Avoiding unneeded provocations such as the Swan affair, they could hold on here, and gradually build strength, but for the Empire to expand and prosper, the resources of the realm could shorten every road. Forty first-line squadrons, Kargul, or for that matter Household or General Cavalry, could complete conquest of all the Hrin in a single season; two thousand such men could keep the Empire tranquil while enough fresh troops were raised and trained.

Tú had often complained of how servants here had to be taught the most elementary things, and the same was true at every level; from the old realm, also, and nowhere else, could come the experienced administrators, tax-gatherers, magistrates, authorities on industry and commerce, to secure and exploit his acquisitions; the two domains would become one, greater than their present sum.

"You mean, you and Rodlakh, ruling together?"

"Dual sovereignty could never survive, not that Rodlakh has given us any hope it could ever come to be. Two rulers in eternal negotiation and conflict — no, Tú; Rodlakh must go. A *rabhsai* who has stupidly declined the chance to welcome new territories into his domain; I have no more patience with him. He deserves to lose his inheritance."

"Overthrow him?" turning from the window in distress. "He has many more troops than we have, thousands. Those squadrons you want will fight for him."

"Not all." He reminded her of how, three times when he had gone back, twice to their home province, once to Ninkufu, it had been impossible to find Karguli cavalry to raise a weapon against him. "One hole can sink a great ship. With the *péfrapravádal* of Kargul, I can make that hole."

Here, now, was the heart of his plan, and he would need all his eloquence. She and he, he maintained, lovers defying the rules people and peoples made, were already outlaws in the profounder sense, a pair above all convention, not to be governed by law or allegiance or any other barrier to their union. For them to be together, he had been forced to found a new realm, but she knew now what measures were needed that so it could with certainty endure. To that goal, removal of an implacable enemy, the first and toughest obstacle was their father, whose death would make her *nimu* in Kargul.

"Tovakh will live another thirty years, unless he breaks his neck hunting."

"His death might be hastened."

"How?"

"Poison."

"And Petakoi, too?" Without any hesitation; he could not tell whether Tú thought he was joking.

"Yes, of course. She would try to maintain our precious Island cousin had been lawfully named to the succession."

"Or if he were dead, anyone else she could think of."

"I am serious, Tú."

"Not a subject for laughter," she agreed, still in a dulled, distancing voice.

"Judge them as you would two strangers. A boasting bully, weak at the core, willing captive of a woman who has done nothing but betray him, helped breed *jinzal* — " he suspected he could win his sister's approval readily if Petakoi were the only one meant to die.

"She kept us apart."

"She could again, by standing in our way."

"How would you have them poisoned?" Kamin-Tarú asked, or challenged, then with a quick inspiration, "One of the men that go back across Landegh in autumn? How will he get near enough to them?"

"That has indeed been the puzzle, among several. Until I saw there is one person who could be certain of getting into the Great House at Inilun Barabhi, of having access to food for Tovakh and Petakoi; you."

Before she could say anything, he launched into the details, now fully-formed: some time late in summer, perhaps when they went to Larghamit for Zhôl's Day, he and she would be seen to have a serious disagreement, would publicly quarrel, and afterwards appear to be estranged; when he returned south, she would remain at the Abu. Something requiring his attention here in the south would prevent his being at the Abu, after Autumn Halving, for departure of the homesick. She would then simply join the defectors, and should soon encounter the Army of the West at its exercises on Landegh; no one would dare prevent her.

"You want me to leave you, go away from here?"

"Of course I don't, you know I do not. There is no other way to make us safe."

She gave him her wondering stare. "Do you think any soldier on guard at the Abu, overseeing this departure, would risk your anger, letting me ride away unchallenged? Whatever threats I could make would be nothing; they would respectfully detain me and ask for instructions."

A valid but not insuperable objection. His first answer was, she could dress plainly, use one of the deep-hooded capes women often wore for long journeys in the unrelenting sun, and pass unnoticed among army wives. Better than that, she could give loud advance notice of her intention to leave, and he would airily give permission, as if following a pattern of improbable threat and ostentatious unconcern established in their falling-out. After, it would be clear from his anger he had never believed she would go.

"The estrangement will be hard," he warned them both. "Because of your task, no one must guess it is only pretense — no one. We shall not be able to meet secretly, or send any messages; it must seem completely true."

"You want to be separated from me?"

He quickly took her hands, first time they had touched. "You know I do not; I want to be with you, for all time to come. If I could see any other way — "

"How long?"

"The spring after next, if I can rebuild my armies, and you can make peace at Inilun Barabhi."

"If I could go to Inilun Barabhi."

"When you reach the realm, you must be bitter against me. Say I have become heedless of anyone except myself, I have turned my face finally away from the realm, and you never thought the division would be permanent — do all you can to establish your sincere repentance."

"I might already be too late. If the inheritance has been changed." She was not dredging up difficulties: he had no indication of either rejection or acceptance. It was like one of their childhood inventions, where they would begin with an impossibility, such as men with wings, and soberly work out all the details of such a life.

"Not for Tovakh." Here, he was confident. "What can be changed can be changed back, and the seat in Council is still his. He can be made to accept Pedh-Sivai, but he will never love a man who rides like a plump *ramidu*, and has not learnt which end of a lance to grasp. Once soothe his anger, as you have done before, and he will remember you as his *péfrapravádayu-loi*."

She bit her lower lip; it had been a mistake to mention that pet-name. Tovakh's clumsy approaches to affection were perhaps the more cherished for their rarity. "What about Petakoi?"

"In this, she will not dare go against him. Besides, you can threaten to tell him what we know about her part in the breeding of *jinzal*."

"But poison, Tam?"

"They have no particular right to live. Hundreds with as good a claim on life died in the war Petakoi made. I was nearly one of them."

"Almost two years apart. You might as well say, forever."

"I'll come for you. I did before."

Briefly, a genuine, radiant smile, for the comedy of that lighter-hearted plot that had brought her here. She seemed about to open one of their shared familiar tales, rites rather, every word rehearsed, about the dullness of Taërinat, her betrothed, or what Antiyu said to Pıvrekhan, but impulse ebbed, and she was remote once again. For a moment, he had thought she was about to weep, but the hand that went to her face was only to capture and loop back a stray tendril of red-gold hair.

"What is it you want me to do?"

As with many of Oyestri's favored methods, a two-stage poisoning, although in this case the second and deadly dose would probably be fatal alone, and the first, a chalky white powder, though it did diminish resistance to the other, was mainly for causing symptoms of illness to explain subsequent sudden death. All-but tasteless added to food, it would bring on an attack very like a severe chill or a common summer complaint, with headaches, fever, queasiness and loose bowels. The second, while briefly reestablishing those conditions, acted very swiftly, apparently by simply stopping the heart, a poison so sudden and painless its common name in the Hrin language meant *merciful*. The yellowish crystals had a slight smell, faintly anise, and readily dissolved in a warm liquid, so the poison would be undetectable in the spiced *raminat* which would by custom be given to Tovakh in his illness.

For his sister, Kamin-Tolagh had a small kidskin bag, drawstring-closed, containing amounts of both needed substances, affectionately prepared by Oyestri, with, he said, much boiling and drying, blending and testing, a number of dead dogs and rabbits. Of the white powder, there were ten measured doses, each in a small, sealed parchment envelope. Most victims, he explained, quoting the Hrin authority, would be sick for three or four days after being poisoned, so allowing a brief recovery between bouts, half a dozen doses could be used to make Tovakh recurrently ill over six or seven weeks, before administering the other, deadly poison, of which there were three doses, each in a tiny pouch made of gut.

Kamin-Tarú, with a lemon-taster's face at the thought, asked if it had to take so long. No, he explained, and on professional grounds Oyestri had been dubious about multiple doses of the preliminary compound; of old, best procedure had been one or at most two, to establish illness, and then the killing poison. More, and a longer process, increased the risk of detection.

"Poisoning would be suspected," his sister agreed, "if Tovakh kept falling sick, with no other reason. Petakoi would guess."

"She will also be a suspect." Even with Kamin-Tarú reinstated in the succession, with Tovakh dead, Petakoi could be counted on to attempt having her daughter declared incompetent, or on merely seizing power with the help of her Island allies, and Kamin-Tolagh had considered whether his sister could plant evidence that made Petakoi appear guilty of murdering her husband. Too uncertain, Petakoi too sly, and law in Kargul, in the confusion following Tovakh's death, would belong for a time to whoever could control the soldiery.

Petakoi, he told Tú, must die first, though after Tovakh had been ill for some weeks; a single feeding of the preliminary poison, followed quickly with the killing one, and about the same time, if Tú herself took a dose or a half-dose of the white powder and was sick for a time, it would help foster the notion of a contagious disease.

"You have overlooked nothing," rousing to a recollection of her old admiration. "But wouldn't there be a *ramidu* attending Tovakh?"

"An Island *ramidu*, if Petakoi has anything to say. When she dies, if there is suspicion, it is likeliest to fall on Pedh-Sivai."

But Pedh-Sivai would be negligible without the support of Ulvidhai, the Island captain of the cavalry, and of Talfoyan, whose fear of Kamin-Tolagh could lead him to join resistance to Kamin-Tarú's succession.

None of which mattered, if only Kamin-Tolagh could come to Inilun Barabhi, ostensibly to secure his sister's rights, within days of Tovakh's death, before the other faction could consolidate control: at his bidding the cavalry would arrest or disable the three or four leaders — and would then be ready to follow him anywhere.

That was the reason for protracting the poisoning of Tovakh so long. "I must have word you have begun. Not an open message; there must not be any evidence, here or the old realm."

Their former informant, Antiyu, could not return with Kamin-Tarú; her husband, Pivrekhan, even if fit for the journey, had no hope for amnesty at Inilun Barabhi; Tovakh would not forgive his treacherous command of Kamin-Tarú's personal escort. But Pivrekhan had left a sister behind at Inilun Barabhi, a girl whose skill with fine-sewing made her a frequent part of the circle surrounding the *nimum*. Natural enough if she were to correspond weekly with her cyder-making uncle in Ninkufu, giving innocent Great House news — the same method as had been used to exchange messages at the time of Kamin-Tarú's counterfeit betrothal, letters readdressed, sent to Thenimala, and put on a Hrin trading-vessel.

"Beginning a year from now I shall keep a fleet of ships at Guodvestr, stocked with food and feed and weapons, and maintain an invasion force at readiness — " like a winning game at *zhabhu*, the parts now were going effortlessly into place — "If word Tovakh has fallen sick, with headaches and chills, reaches me in three weeks, I can be ashore in Ninkufu in six." He had to explain, swift seizure of the provincial cavalry was to run in harness with the larger object, deposing of Rodlakh. His invading army, besides ensuring his safety from arrest as *kaël'rolai*, would be able to secure the person of the figurehead Finú, in her home at Kred' Ludhai in southern Ninkufu.

Thoughtful, Kamin-Tarú asked for a few desultory details: at the death of Tovakh, would she assert her *nimum*, if that meant beginning an open struggle for power, or let events take their course, and wait for Kamin-Tolagh's arrival? Would she have any trusted allies?

"You will no doubt find your friends among the cavalry, but in this, there is no such thing as complete trust. No one else can understand, or can be expected to understand the needs of our love for one another. This will always be between us only."

"Oyestri gave you these poisons. He would know."

"Oyestri will be dead before his poisons are ever used." That, too, was a swift plan forming in Kamin-Tolagh's mind.

"Rodlakh," she said. "Is he to be killed, too?"

He remembered she had bedded with him, broken the colt, as she firmly believed, though Kamin-Tolagh could not. A shrug. "Once deposed, he will be of no consequence."

Not in his mind, but as soon as spoken, a lie; Rodlakh could not be left alive as a name to rally resistance to the new government. In this, even for a civilized realm, tribal rules applied; the brother, Orbanak, would also have to be killed. Âna he could let live, but not her children; like the Sranadatta clan, the blood of Arbhai-Navu must be extirpated.

"Meanwhile — " here with his sister, not letting himself think about what place widowed Âna would have in his realm — "We must decide what our quarrel is to be about."

"A woman," she said at once. "If you were to take another woman, or a boy, even better, and flaunt him in my face at a feast, so as to be a humiliation to me. Everyone would understand my anger, but you would say, *I am Emperor, to do as I please* — "

As anticipated from the first, her old love of lets-pretend was taking over, giving her an eagerness quite aside from any doubts about the object of the game. He nodded approval, then was struck by a thought. "Before that, though, you must be seen to annoy me, pestering for your separate bodyguard, which I shall give you, but grudgingly. When we are apart, you will need guarding, and it would seem strange if later, at the height of my exasperation, my first thought was for your safety."

"Not the Hill Froghul, then."

"Why not?"

"I do not like them around me when you are not there. They scowl too much."

"No men are fiercer or more loyal. They would give their lives defending you."

"Not so at the Man-mani village when the raiders came; most of them went off to battle, sooner than guard a *woman*."

"I cannot give you men of Kargul. They are needed as officers with the newer squadrons."

"What, then? Some other uncouth savages?"

This was absurd; they were at the brink of real bickering over the subject for a feigned disagreement. "A tribal half-squadron, one of the better ones. Gudi-la, with a Karguli in command."

"Which Karguli?"

"Drusilakh?" Newly returned to service, doubly eager to reestablish his loyalty, after being forced to sign a confession when detained by Dolvid in the Colony.

"He could be taller," Kamin-Tarú said, a kind of assent.

For him, the worst was to recognize that the prospect of being parted from her so long was not as hard as it should be. Three years ago, half that, he could not have imagined another separation except as final catastrophe — although even then, if he was honest, he had to admit what he had perceived, however serenely, when first they were reunited: the fulfillment she had been for him at eighteen, keeping its entirety through the lost years, was no longer compatible with the restless, adventurous man he had become. Kamin-Tarú remained the goal of a life he wanted to lay at her feet, but *his* life, not a life modified to conform to her experience.

When they were apart, she had bedded many men, and told him now he was all of them, much more, and all she wanted; that touched him, and made him want to say and mean the same about all his women; the truth was he saw no needed contradiction between the encompassing love of being with Kamin-Tarú, and challenging joy, like an ecstatic fear, of young bodies he had not yet stripped, inexhaustible variousness of desire.

Since Tú's arrival, he had sampled half a dozen others, and except for Khalú, as much a political as a carnal episode, had done so, not exactly furtively, but discreetly, he, the Emperor. Tú, as hinted in her suggestion for the staged squabble, could be offended by a public display of his waywardness, or, as she read it, her implied inadequacy. Yet his intimacy with her was inviolably complete — or would be, if her pleasure in sharing his preoccupations could only extend to all his desires, as he would delight in sharing them with her, dedicate them to her as a necessary part of the life she owned and completed.

He would miss her painfully, and yet there was, as he could never have predicted, an element of relief in it, too; another separation might help him strike a balance between two sorts of insatiable yearning.

The Hrin had their own midsummer holiday, but due to a long-ago priestly miscalculation, the observance slipped back a day each year, till the difference reached eleven days, when it was restored to the true longest day. This year, it fell eight days short, so Kambanal would be able to preside at Hrin rites without violating his participation in *Shuda'sai*, for which the Empire's chief gathering would also be at Hyolenstr.

Unlike the ancient Owani celebration, which began with laughter and culminated in an austere but still hopeful solemnity, the Hrin festival had a dark side; the days leading up to its main religious rites were used for the execution ('tidying up,' Kambanal called it) of condemned criminals, kept in dank vaults beneath the great temple.

"Oyestri," Kamin-Tolagh told him, on the eve of the Hrin holidays, "is now more danger than use to us." At his invitation, they were riding beneath trees next to the Hflen, where thistledown drifted, while round white, pink and pale-yellow petals of disintegrating blossom settled on placid waters, and spangled the trodden pathway.

"I have suspected he manages to keep his former *hrithust* apprised, but it seems to do little harm to us."

"He has been plotting our deaths, yours and mine — my sister's, too, I would guess. He is back at his old trade; I am informed he has been cooking up poisons at his own house. A number of dead animals have been taken away for quiet burial." Kambanal would take his word, and he did not want to spend too much time on a subject that might well come back to mind when Tovakh and Petakoi died suddenly in Kargul.

An exaggerated shudder. "Poison. The man must be arrested and charged."

"A trial would only make for dissent; Oyestri will have covered his tracks, and as you are aware, he still has influence among leading men of this *onhritha*. Besides, they have been a race of poisoners. We should be wary of putting in other minds the notion we are vulnerable to an assassin."

"But once they see we are vigilant, if Oyestri is made to pay — "

"Still there is the idea we need vigilance. Besides, after the unrest brought about by mere rumor the *Hridveyuth* might be harmed, it would be far better if Oyestri were to be killed by a Hrin."

Devotion was a stunning force. For his own sake, for hot revenge, Kambanal could never have given room to dishonorable or devious means, but with his lord and the lord's sister said to be in jeopardy, he was avidly willing. Kamin-Tolagh reminded him Oyestri was to take part in ceremonies connected with the forthcoming executions; his task would be to recount each man or woman's crimes as they were brought before the *hrithust*, and to obtain Kambanal's formal assent to the punishment.

Except for abolishing some bizarre uses of the death penalty in what seemed trivial offences, Kamin-Tolagh had not interfered with traditional Hrin justice, which for what they considered the most serious crimes prolonged executions with various apt and agonizing torments and mutilations, using fire, molten lead, pincers, and small, sharp knives. He suggested now that a prisoner destined for such a lingering end, concealing a smuggled weapon and with his shackles surreptitiously loosened, would agree to cut Oyestri's flaccid throat, for the promise of nothing better than a swift death at the hands of Kambanal's guards. This had the added advantage of removing the chief potential witness to the plot.

If Kambanal was shocked he hid it well, only saying to find and arm a prisoner would need help from one of the two main jailers, shabby men said to be minor priests, though they looked and behaved like minor criminals.

"He would be there at the ceremony to lead in the prisoners? When Oyestri is killed, be angry at the jailer's carelessness, put him to death before he can explain. If you kill him with your own hands, you will be very popular with the Hrin leaders." Gratifyingly tidy, and his only faint regret was he would never be able to recount the plan to an appreciative and envious Lavsila.

After, at the modest feast given by Kambanal to mark the opening of *Shuda'sai*, the disturbance at the Hrin ceremonies, three quick deaths, beginning with the murder of Oyestri, was a chief topic among the Heartlanders, though competing against reported arrival at Guodvestr of two ships from another *onhritha*, carrying a cargo of fine fabrics, now being displayed for sale at quayside.

Kamin-Tarú proclaimed she would ride down to the port next day, pointedly asking her brother to provide escort, adding, "If you would let me have my own bodyguard, I would not be obliged to ask your leave each time, as some Gabhani slave-wife."

The unexampled public display of petulance startled and unnerved nearby listeners, who glanced apprehensively at Kamin-Tolagh. Unwarned, he was momentarily annoyed, then had to maintain that appearance so as to hide his joy. Up to now she had given him no answer, but this, he saw, was acceptance of her part in his elaborate plot. It had begun.

Weeks remained before they went north for Zhôl's Day, and with the Abu at its safest from attack across Landegh, and the country west of Flamûrai calm, he could devote himself to creation of precious memories to sustain them over long separation, at the same time a promise, as he told his sister, of what they could be together when all obstacles were removed. She smiled wanly, and said they could also enjoy the pretense of quarreling, when that time came.

Whether intended or not, it proved to be a warning; there would in any event have been an inimical striving about their attempts at exemplary joy; a necessary condition of perfect happiness was not being thought about, simply being. But with that anxious, flawing self-consciousness, there was also the feeling Kamin-Tarú was preparing for loneliness by progressively pushing him away. Not physically; her body was still effortlessly his, but time and again his openings for established jokes and intimacies failed to bring the proper counter from her; he had not understood before how much was nourished by these exchanges, the actual words worn into rote gestures, but sustaining the wondrous warmth of a sharing that, being sufficient, could exclude all other worlds, not to be simulated, or restored by the efforts of one player.

Sooner than he had thought it would be, they arrived at the last night before his departure; he would go north first, to be sure of preparations, and to make a last attempt to convince doubters there would be no retaliation against those who declared their intention of leaving. By having two men covertly in his pay announce out loud they would take advantage of the offer, he had brought a handful of others forward; Luzhan, the only one who was any real loss, had respectfully declined a promotion and other inducements, with the excuse his daughter, and other children yet to come, deserved to know grandparents, and the winter snow-games of his native hill-country, southward of Zelkova.

"I wish it was otherwise." His sister half-sat, half-lay on the bed, dressed in robes of yellow shuzi, his favorite for her. "That the world would leave us to our simple satisfactions. But life cannot shrink, and if you think you can give up everything but the one small joy you desire, that, too, will be taken from you. It is the tale of the First Empire, one after another of the Shâls contracting his frontier to where he thought it could be held, until in the end the old realm itself was invaded, and Night began."

Much of this was prepared, and he could not recall another time since childhood when he had set out to produce an effect with Kamin-Tarú. What was implied, he recognized angrily, was not really true; if it were achievable, he could never be content limited to a little land, no matter how pleasant. Starting to pace, he spoke unconsidered truth; the tribal lands were his; he had led them out of ignorance and their crippling squabbles, and under Rodlakh, if he could come here with his mildness and his irresolution, they would slide back to what they were within a year.

"I do not hate him, I would gladly let him be — "

"Are you having second thoughts?"

She must long to be released from the plan he had made, and he admired the dispassionate way she asked the question, voice giving no indication of the answer desired. He shook his head. "It is the only way. Rodlakh claims all Landegh as his playground, he refuses to sell us what we need. He tried to keep the *Atarlum* from coming here, and has prevented *raminat* from reaching us. His *Bôdhrai* comes and says, let us be friends, but the *rabhsai* wants to be the kind of friend the old cat was to the young mouse in the story. He cannot reach out to crush us, as he would wish, but he can see to it that we strangle. If I must conquer the realm to make the Empire safe, then that is what I must do — what we must do. You will do your part?"

"When have I failed you?"

At Lavsila's ridgetop house, still progressing almost imperceptibly towards completion, Kamin-Tolagh's late arrival at the feast for Zhôl's Day was legend ready-made. He had reviewed all alternatives; Kamin-Tarú's suggestion he take up with a boy was soon dismissed; he could have managed the physical part easily enough, but to furnish grounds for affront to his sister, he would have to display a fawning infatuation, well beyond provoking the quarrel. It would have to be sustained so as to make their estrangement plausible, and that might be beyond his powers, as it surely was outside his inclinations. Both Ondhayu and Khalú were considered, the reigning beauties after his sister, but one was too frivolous for his purpose, the other too earnest for his comfort; a Khalú persuaded he had forsaken Kamin-Tarú for her could become an intolerable encumbrance, and if he had to have her killed, it would alienate Lavsila, who was going to be needed for a year or two more.

He decided instead on a girl of the tribes, a reminder of his celebrated, undying love for Siv'loi. Not, however, of the Man-mani; they were Gudi-la who served him at the official residence of the Abu, and prettiest of all was Chengha-lel — the name was said to mean `morning lark' in her language — who was just seventeen, the girl Shumat's son had such hot eyes for when he came with Dolvid.

With the feast in the Hrin style already well under way, he entered at the wrong end of Lavsila's main hall, and so, with guests hurriedly standing to make deference, he travelled the entire length of the room with Chengha-lel next to him and nestled into his side, though truthfully in fear rather than the tenderness it mimed. The gleaming blue gown she wore, one everybody would recognize as Kamin-Tarú's, ankle-length on its owner, here trailed the floor.

His sister, seated on the low couch or cushioned bench at head of the hall, watched his approach with a persuasive show of mounting outrage and disdain. "If you please," he prompted, giving a flick of his hand to indicate she should cede place of honor to him and his companion. A faint gasp from the company; Lavsila and Khalú, to whose bench Kamin-Tarú swiftly and resentfully moved, were turned to stone. Handing the girl of the tribes down, Kamin-Tolagh stooped to kiss her slender throat, before seating himself.

In reflection next day, he was amused to think the shock he had produced, the tense expectancy of a thunderclap to come, were shared by men and women for whom, officially, he and Kamin-Tarú were nothing beyond brother and sister, a convention that was to handicap officers and advisors in all their later attempts to deal with Kamin-Tolagh's feelings about the rupture. For the feast itself, he was chiefly admiring of how painfully well his sister played the game, keeping her eyes averted, but making increasingly barbed comments on the vulgarity of this display, shrivelling the unfortunate guests she addressed into vague preoccupation or sudden deafness; they could not — and probably did not — disagree, but were infinitely more anxious not to be seen as taking her side.

When she became loud enough for reprimand, he said, "There is only one ruler here, not two. I shall have respect from you."

"So you shall," with an acid smile, "when you earn it, not by parading your weekwives. Does the Empire need a new device for its banner?"

No hearer, including Chengha-lel, would not have been overjoyed to be almost anywhere else. Kamin-Tarú was altogether convincing. and in his reply Kamin-Tolagh's real dissatisfactions could be drafted into service. He kept his disdainful composure.

"You would like to tether me? You cannot be my wife, sister, and if I took one, she would have to be more careful of my pleasure."

"Of your pleasure, or your pleasures?" standing to face him, letting scorn come into her face. "Your wife, if you can find one, will not be envied. Do you think this is manly, clambering aboard any half-grown girl who flaunts her rump? Any husband of the feeble Hrin is better — " but here, Fretasi, who had been virtually invisible in her feed-sack finery, had sufficient courage, lack of breeding, or years serving House baKargul to come from behind and put a restraining hand on the forearm of Kamin-Tarú. Who shook it off angrily, but allowed herself to be turned away.

Everyone was relieved when, tense minutes later, she demanded to be shown to a bed, everyone except Khalú, who, with a limited supply of bedrooms made usable, would have all combatants under her roof tonight, and had to work out the least perilous dispositions. When, in finger-counting consultation with a tribal housekeeper, she ushered Kamin-Tarú from the hall, the silence was like that apprehensive moment watching a favorite horse, back on its feet after a bad fall, take its first, testing steps. Then, tentative at first, carefully inconsequential conversation resumed, and Kamin-Tolagh called for sweet fruit to be served to Chengha-lel.

Kamin-Tarú, with her new guard, started for the Abu at dawn; by the time Kamin-Tolagh had the news she must be at the place where summer travellers rested and waited out full heat of day, and would complete her journey in near-darkness. Letting his mind go to where she was, beneath satisfaction their separation was going as planned, he felt a surge of paralyzing melancholy; *Once started*, he had again warned her, warned himself, that last night at Hyolenstr, *it has to run its course; we cannot even think of secret meetings, or whispered reassurances, not an exchange of glances ; as we live, nothing is entirely safe from observation, and there must never be any rumor, any hint, that I helped contrive your journey back to Kargul.* Just as when assenting to the rules for one of their childhood games, or concurring in a joint lie to be told to their parents, she had nodded once, her face grave, but he saw now this was going to be harder than anticipated in his bleakest imaginings; it was too real, frighteningly real. Aside from the intended objectives, the only satisfaction in the game would be in chuckling with Kamin-Tarú over how well they had pretended, and his sudden uncertainty desired that reassuring joy now, not two empty years in the future. But for her, keeping up the pretence without the distraction of his absorbing responsibilities, must be yet lonelier, and he could not think of comforting her.

Not many days later a riding came from the Abu which included the five remaining Gudi-la serving girls, all in this or that way related, dispatched by Kamin-Tarú, after first having them all whipped, though not to excess. An effective gesture of contempt, but there was another reason Kamin-Tolagh welcomed it. He was already struggling to keep up a show of consuming passion for Chengha-lel, willing but unimaginative in bed, numbingly narrow in her ambulatory interests; after more than a week he had discovered nothing she enjoyed except honey-cakes and bright-colored clothes. No reason, he decided, why six rivals should annoy Kamin-Tarú any less than one.

His hosts treated his new companions and the estrangement with Kamin-Tarú as aspects of some personal disfigurement that must never be mentioned; Lavsila was plainly puzzled, but filled silence with talk about his attempts to revive the cause of Finú as proper ruler at Kadon Dinul. They were together on the evening before Kamin-Tolagh's announced departure for Hyolenstr, when a saddle-weary Freighanai arrived, with news he had ridden hard to bring in person, but was nervous about telling, even when left alone with Kamin-Tolagh.

"The lady your sister, *Asai*... "

"She is well?"

"She's saying, said to me, she means to go, when the others do. Back to the east, *Asai*, with Luzhan and those."

"She is not a prisoner here. Whatever she desires."

Freighanai, not finished with the principal subject, addressed a side-issue. "Young Drusilakh, *Asai*, who leads the lady's escort. He wanted me to tell you, to be sure you knew, he was still loyal to you."

"So I would suppose."

"Well, but in the circumstances, *Asai* — "

"His orders were, to watch over my sister, and that is what he is doing. He does not have to follow her onto Landegh, if that is the question. She would be riding with soldiers, and they should soon meet their friends, the Army of the West."

This thought he followed into a review of the readiness of the Abu against any sudden attack. Several tribal squadrons in training had been moved there from Larghamit, and the homesick contingent, for most of its first two days travel, would have the company of patrols, going farther out on the plateau than ever, but given strict instructions to avoid any provocation to the Army of the West at its autumn exercises. Once again, if not in such stark words, he made plain Freighanai's best contribution to any defense of a besieged Abu would be to lead a successful breakout with all good troops that could be saved.

"I would be there myself, but there is unrest among the Hrin. Besides, I do not want to give the impression I am watching over those who wish to leave us."

Freighanai nodded, and Kamin-Tolagh recognized these were reasons he accepted but did not really believe. As if offering a point previously unconsidered, he said, "Well, *Asai*, if an attack does come, most of us — the ones, I mean, who know duty comes before homesickness, we would just as soon know you were safe there in the south, then the Empire will go on whatever happens here — I'd like to see them try to come at you in the Hrin lands, *Asai*."

Gratified, Kamin-Tolagh slapped the man's shoulder. "If it does come to a breakout, you and the other men of Kargul should make for here. I shall have ships waiting to take you off." It was something he should have thought of sooner. As for Kamin-Tarú's announced intentions, Freighanai still looked as if he would prefer Kamin-Tolagh's indifference in form of a written order, as safeguard against afterthoughts.

When he rejoined his hosts, the offhand annoucement of those plans produced a silence filled with baffled wonder, Lavsila frowning, Khalú moistening her lips, deciding against some conventionalism she had almost uttered.

Lavsila cleared his throat. "Luzhan will be missed. The man's knack with tribal levies was uncanny."

"The fewer unwilling servants," Kamin-Tolagh pronounced, "the stronger the Empire,"

Khalú wistful, said, "One would almost think you wished to encourage the homesick to leave." She became intensely interested in the decorative basket of dried rushes on the table, having belatedly recognized her remark might be applied also to Kamin-Tarú. Like Freighanai, this pair were deeply puzzled by Kamin-Tolagh's unconcern.

It would be otherwise, he foresaw, both in his real feelings, and for those he must display, when she was actually gone. He had not yet decided whether, when given the news, he should let anger show, or maintain this affected nonchalance, allowing his true distress to be seen as anger about everything else.

38.

"When they come," Dolvid told Bradhinal, "it will not be this way." He was standing on the ramparts of Drin Navuna, looking out on the harshness of Landegh. The fortress was clad in memories: behind was the courtyard to the military commander's residence, where the army had assembled to hear Rodlakh proclaimed, and that thunderclap of approval still echoed in Dolvid's mind, an acclamation from the men, not a few of them soon to die warring against the *jinzal*. In that same building he had lain exhausted but unsleeping, wishing for Âna to come to him, guessing at last she was in Rodlakh's bed. Not only private life had hinged on her choice; without that night, chances were Rodlakh would have married Kamin-Tarú, and so changed history; with his sister as *rabhsayu*, Kamin-Tolagh was unlikely to have embarked on his rebellious course.

"You still say the south, do you?" Bradhinal's face was doubtful. "But he is still Karguli, and Kargul is cavalry. I think he would sooner trust horses than ships." Bradhinal, not forty, still recognizably the youth who had fought with distinction in the Narn Campaign of '28, had a constant struggle to keep fat off his large frame, and in his smooth face nothing could be seen of either father or mother, who were first cousins, and very much alike in their fine, angular boning.

"Trust is not the whole question. Ships can carry ample provisions for their riders, and themselves consume neither feed nor water. Commanding seamen as good as the Hrin, a man would be a fool to march armies across Landegh."

He did not mention Finú, who made her home in Ninkufu, and whose claim, worn threadbare, to be legitimate pretender, had lately been revived in discreet murmurs. Kamin-Tolagh might also like his chances of finding allies in that predominantly Owani enclave. These were speculations to share with Shumat, but he at the last moment had decided against the journey to the Colony to oversee the autumn exercises; as if in reminder there were dangers in the world apart from Kamin-Tolagh, word had come from the far Northeast of renewed problems with sea-raiders, first such outbreak in a decade. Territory where Shumat had spent a dozen years as military commander, its army was the one he had made; understandably he took particular interest in its troubles, at once talking about going there in person. Persuaded only a serious threat of invasion could justify the Captain of Armies being so many days from the capital at a time when war might erupt on Landegh, he was instead culling from various garrisons the reinforcements that might be needed, allowing himself to set up headquarters as far to the north as central Dramal, where news would reach him days sooner, and he could conduct his campaign by dispatch.

Dolvid would have preferred him here, to share responsibility, if it came to that, for starting a war. Officers commanding troops out on Landegh had orders to do all they could not create incidents with any forces of Kamin-Tolagh's, and they had received the unreliable news those who wanted to leave him would be permitted to do so freely; if true, that meant there would be no pursuit of deserters to increase chances of conflict.

Just possibly, however, entire squadrons of Kamin-Tolagh's troops would defect along with their officers, and if such mass desertions occurred, Rodlakh had agreed it would be foolish, with their own troops assembled and well-supported by supplies, not to seize the opportunity of striking at a weakened Abu. Not likely they would capture Kamin-Tolagh, who was last heard of in the south, but it would obviously be a serious blow if his northern headquarters could be taken from him.

Whether to attempt it was entirely in Dolvid's hands, good sense since it would depend on rapidly changing factors, and yet there remained the feeling Rodlakh was shying away from the decision — or that he was often somewhat detached just now from the realm's business; besides recent birth of another son, he was distracted, it was embarrassingly clear for those close to him, by Morulis. His juxtaposition with her, rather, a predictable source of confusion for a married man of Rodlakh's sensibilities. Elamirr, disgraced, was back in Burantal, Morulis at Kadon Dinul, but while Rodlakh had followed established protocol by moving her out of the Residence into a small house nearby where he could discreetly visit, he would never be one to regard such a friendship lightly, or keep from questioning what it *meant*. He should have borrowed humor from his younger brother, who had remarked laconically, "For once in a lifetime, I had the pleasure of preceding the *rabhsai*."

Orbanak, at this moment, was one of the officers who had taken their squadrons farthest to the south and west on Landegh, those, if any, who would make contact equally with defectors or with forces sent to challenge. The risk was unwise, another opportunity for Kamin-Tolagh to take a valuable hostage, but Orbanak bitterly envied the exploit of his friend Shudarr, and was eloquent in scorning his own service as merely decorative soldiering. He was, in fact, a good officer, well-liked by the men he led, lacking his brother's height and powerful shoulders, but possessing the family skill with weapons, and he had added wiry muscle over the past few years.

The West had toughened him in other ways: on first hearing of Elamirr's fall, and its unpredicted cause, he had shrugged, "The man was always a brute, but she would try anybody's patience." It seemed only weeks since they had used the Army of the West to wrench Orbanak away from a deathless love, but time, certainly, was different for the young; Dolvid himself had lived out three lifetimes between sixteen and twenty. With friends, Orbanak at times appeared uncertain whether to be sage or clown, but Dolvid thought he would do very well with a few years of seasoning.

His squadron on Landegh had been augmented by what were called *special troops*. True, the mounted bowmen, Noldar with his brother Guthdar, and other veterans of the squadron once Galt's, were very experienced in Frontier service, but on this occasion they were made special by their covert order to act, above all, as a personal bodyguard to the young prince.

"Troops, a half-file," Bradhinal, squinting, and pointing to where a loop of rough road was visible between crags. "Some word, let us hope."

More; those men were only vanguard of a substantial company led by the Under-Captain Idmas. Between detachments of horse moving at a walk there was a mixed riding, with women and children, pack-animals burdened to near their limit, a dozen disarmed cavalrymen whose tunics from Kargul had been refaced after the fashion of Kamin-Tolagh's armies. Bringing up the rear was the squadron led by Orbanak, and beside him as he rode at the head of his men was a tall and slender woman, whose easy posture and animated gestures contrasted sharply with the weariness of most others.

"As you would expect," Bradhinal, halfway between disapproval and amusement, "the *Valrabh'* has found a deserter to his liking. He could try to be a little more military, in sight of the Drin."

Just before being lost to view behind rocks, the woman half-rose in the stirrups to loosen her shoulders in a quick, fluid movement Dolvid with a catch at his heart instantly knew, instantly eclipsing his eagerness to hear soldiers' tales. She shrugged off the deep hood of plain linen she had worn to keep sun from her face, and the rich gleam of burnished hair confirmed it.

"Kamin-Tarú," he told Bradhinal in absurd disbelief.

Still, in the fortress courtyard, he made himself speak first to Idmas, while horses too tired to paw blew in their nostrils, but lifted their heads at the sense of nearby water. Men and women dismounted, and a small child wailed, while Idmas, a conscientious officer, gave barest report of having encountered *these*, for whom he had no adequate collective name, some four-and-a-half days ago. In accordance with his orders, which coincided with their own desire, he had brought them here to the Frontier.

Luzhan approached, giving Bradhinal a sketchy salute, explaining he could not offer his sword, since the Under-Captain had it. A few paces away, shading her eyes, not missing anything, a young woman stood, with a weary girl of about five leaning against her, the daughter Luzhan had spoken of.

Dolvid grasped the man's hand warmly. "Yaënsilat is not with you?"

"He is dead." Luzhan no longer needed to disguise bad news with a fixed grin, but despite fatigue and sorrow a crushing weight had been lifted from the man's shoulders.

"I had heard so, but did not know whether to believe it. A great pity." Seconds were hourlong from the effort of keeping his eyes on the men in front of him, while all the time the presence of Kamin-Tarú was burning at his left. He held up a hand to postpone further talk.

"In absolute law, you would for the moment be our prisoners, but in fact you are our guests. I shall be glad to hear tales, and shall have questions to ask, when your comfort and refreshment have been seen to. Your swords will be restored to you — " an important point of manhood for these men of Kargul.

"Our thanks, *Asai*," Luzhan said.

"Dolvid — " coming with a quick, light step, Kamin-Tarú kissed his cheek. Orbanak, just behind, was enjoying the scene.

"I have left him." At the Military Commander's Residence, Kamin-Tarú was alone with Bradhinal, Dolvid, and quietly watchful Orbanak. Her hair, damp from the bath, was tied to one side, and she had changed into a dove-grey day-gown. "I shall not return to the West. If I am *kaël'rolayu*, I shall have to be killed, I cannot go back. As you see, I came unarmed."

"I think not," Dolvid, lightly. Kamin-Tarú gave a soft laugh, but she was graver than he had seen her, and that gave her a curious new beauty, a steely quality not seen before.

Bradhinal asked, "No outlawry other than Kamin-Tolagh's was passed in Council, was there?"

"No. Another was proposed by one of the *nimul*." He thought Kamin-Tarú would know or guess which one, her father. "But the *rabhsai* would not allow it to be considered, much less passed." At midsummer, however, it would be tactless to add, the succession in Kargul had been legally revised, in favor of the adoptive Pedh-Sivai.

"Then I am not your prisoner?" wide-eyed.

"The *rabhsai* is aware it is my intent to offer the hospitality of the Colony to any returning from the Farther West, and has not forbidden it."

In this, as with other questions, he did not want to ignore the edicts of Kadon Dinul, as Saidhan had for years over composition of Army of the West. In brutal fact, he did not have the power; Saidhan's equally reluctant defiance had been empowered by the fierce, absolute loyalty of the Army of the West; Bradhinal was a good friend, but Dolvid would not expect, certainly not ask, his support in flouting law and *rabhsai*.

"I should add, neither he nor I could have expected — " a gesture. No matter how drunk with Morulis, Rodlakh would keep a sentimental regard for Kamin-Tarú, first of three remarkable women he had shared beds with.

She correctly read this as an oblique question. "I cannot endure it any longer," simply. "Kargusai has become an empire ruled by blood and fear; my brother has committed acts, proposed others, to shame our lineage."

The puzzle this set was not easy to solve. Many, and Bradhinal with his guarded expression was one, would have said the chief of all such acts was not less than four years old, and was shared equally by Kamin-Tarú. Leaving their incest aside, there was no imagining what Kamin-Tolagh could have done or proposed to go beyond horrors already accomplished at the time of Dolvid's journey to the Abu a half-year ago, when Kamin-Tarú had shown no real signs of disaffection with her brother.

Though no debater, she kept her uncanny ability to follow unspoken arguments; "Before, there was no chance for me to leave him."

That only replaced one riddle with another. A quarrel had evidently enabled her to leave him in the South, and come to the Abu, where, by arrangement with Luzhan, first to dare proclaim his intention of leaving, she was able to join the defectors as they had assembled at daybreak.

"Why did he permit this?"

Orbanak, who had spent four days riding with Kamin-Tarú, wanted to show he had asked questions, too. "He proclaims he is tired of unwilling and half-hearted allegiance."

"He has had that to live with, at least since Yaënsilat declined to make war on women and children, five years or so ago. Why now?" He gestured to Orbanak, let Kamin-Tarú answer.

"That was the reason announced. But since the time of your visit — the time of defeat of our armies in the south, the desertions you heard about, the suicide of Yaënsilat — Tam has been fearful of plots against his life; assassination on one hand, undivided loyalty on the other, have begun to obsess him. He did tell me he would not be outdone in clemency by Rodlakh *Rabhsai*, but everyone was afraid his offer was only a trick to uncover his enemies; Luzhan and the others hardly dared think their departure would be uncontested, till they found themselves in the midst of your troops."

"But you believed his permission was genuine?"

"I was in his confidence. He never lied to me, although some things he kept to himself."

The same, surely, could be said of the sister. Her revulsion over her brother's cruelties was plainly genuine, that she was here, undeniable, but she was withholding some fact that would make everything much clearer. Better than anyone, Kamin-Tolagh knew his sister's impulsiveness, and that he would allow her to be at the Abu, alone and unwatched at the time fixed for the mass departure, was inexplicable, unless he was mysteriously conspiring at her desertion. That, in a farfetched way, could also explain his surprising generosity to the disaffected; all the others could have been allowed to go simply to provide cover for Kamin-Tarú. To what purpose Kamin-Tolagh had arranged his sister's return to the realm was beyond guessing; he would have heard she was no longer heir in Kargul.

Dolvid, still with the impression she must have stolen away, did try her with: "Could he not have anticipated what you would do?"

She put her head on one side, to shock him: "I announced it, weeks ago, and he did nothing to prevent me, though I am certain he did not want me to leave him. He is too proud ever to say so."

Phrased narrowly, undoubted truth, but not quite adequate. "You will forgive us, *Asayu*. There may be — I am afraid there will be, many questions about the intentions of Kamin-Tolagh — things you may not know you know. For the moment — "

"This lady," Orbanak broke in, "has been a week without a bed, or properly cooked food."

"I was about to say, you might wish to to join us for a meal," with a glance to Bradhinal.

"Sholu, my lady wife would enjoy nothing better. Our food will, I hope, be adequate; we seldom have gatherings of such distinction, here at world's edge."

Kamin Tarú inclined her head gratefully. Turning back to Dolvid she said, "I'll answer as freely as I can the questions you may have."

Again, phrasing was careful, but irrespective of Orbanak's incipient resolve to defend the lady against all base insinuations, Dolvid did not have the stomach for close, suspicious interrogation. He acknowledged Kamin-Tarú, though she may have broken with her brother, was entitled to retain lingering loyalties; there were conditions between person and person he was not justified in ransacking, even out of concern for the welfare of the realm. Worse, he was near felicitating himself on his own irresponsible softness; as he had told Aëlu, he was not really fit to be a *Bôdhrai*.

"Will Rodlakh receive me? I shall write a letter, asking his pardon, but I cannot go to Kadon Dinul without his word."

"He will pardon you, if any pardon is needed," Orbanak said, a forecast based either on his brother's continued admiration, or confidence in his own advocacy.

"In the meantime — " surrendering to unreality, "you may, if you wish, stay at the Great House in Kamsilat."

"That would please me, *Asai*," emphasizing the new honorific, proud she had kept up with events. "It will be good to meet with Aëlu again — oh, and I have wanted to see your children."

Before, Kamin-Tarú had from time to time been obliged to feign a high earnestness alien to her nature, but now it was her old blithe self she had to labor to recall.

Chiefly from Luzhan, but with supportive detail from others of the Kargul' officers, they heard about Kamin-Tolagh's feverish efforts to make good the losses of the Zelu Bablakhi catastrophe, preparations for a war, not of open battle, but of raid and ambush and punishing defense. In the tribal country settlements were being made siege-ready, with foodstuffs stockpiled, ditches dug, higher and stronger fences raised. There had been a shortage of swords and knives, but no lack of bows, and thousands of arrows had been made; Kamin-Tolagh openly allowed the best of his tribal squadrons were no match for *péfrapravádal*, but boasted he could fill wild places with raiding parties hard to hunt down — in short, force the long, costly and bitter struggle Dolvid, with Shumat, most feared. Unless tribes could be pried away from their allegiance to Kamin-Tolagh, such a war, as Shumat gloomily assessed, could be won only by destroying villages and crops, taking hostages, employing a ruthless brutality alien to the loftier aspirations of Rodlakh's realm.

Again perplexing all this intelligence, down to numbers and quality of fighting men, was so readily forthcoming: Dolvid would have expected Kamin-Tolagh to extract a promise of continued silence from defectors as the price of their freedom. Not a promise they could be held to, but absence of the attempt suggested — what? If they remained secretly loyal to Kamin-Tolagh, and were conveying misinformation, what damage could be done to the realm by giving a dozen men admission to the Colony? if they were ever permitted to return to Kargul, Tovakh could be relied on to make sure they had no new chance to undermine the loyalty of his provincial cavalry, and till that time they would be kept, he decided, at Banakit and not allowed to wander.

But in point of fact, he believed their disaffection was genuine; otherwise he would have to concoct a convoluted scheme which included Luzhan's surreptitious approach during his visit to the Abu, the clandestine meeting with and suicide of Yaënsilat, what had certainly felt like a genuine pursuit across Landegh, and finally Kamin-Tarú's appearance, all with the object of giving news which at worst could be no more than mildly misleading.

Her sorrowing mood, lifted in favor of polite kin-talk while she dined at the table of Bradhinal, a distant cousin in several complicated ways, returned when she was once again alone with Dolvid and Orbanak. Any duties the *Valrabh'* owed the Army of the West had been silently shelved.

"He is genuinely hurt," deliberately seeking to modify the earlier, one-sided view of her brother, "that Rodlakh *Rabhsai* has ignored his friendly overtures, of which he had high hopes. I am not saying that excuses some of the things he has done."

"Does Kamin-Tolagh intend to make war on Rodlakh's realm?" The question, Dolvid had abruptly decided, could only be asked, not nibbled at.

She was careful again. "He has spoken of it, at times, as something he might not be able to avoid. At present, everything is going to make up the losses we had. He has barely enough men to keep order in the lands we have."

That accorded with the reports of Luzhan and the others, of preparations as entirely defensive, although from garrison to invading force was no great step, for one who had ships of the

Hrin at his disposal. But Kamin-Tarú's sudden, unselfconscious use of *we* was interesting.

A point Orbanak very likely missed, although having, in a remote sense, rescued her from Landegh, he was taking what could justly be called a proprietary interest, and was eagerly solicitous when, starting to speak about a river called the Hflen, she was suddenly weeping. Twelve when he first met Kamin-Tarú after another desperate journey, he had instantly fallen in love with her unaffected mixture of motherly and kittenish. The difference in their ages remained, but was hardly the same, Orbanak now a young man and a soldier whose major conquests had not been on the field of battle, one who knew that after comforting came shared satisfaction. Men, Dolvid reflected, by no means exempting Dolvid, become hopeless hypocrites when betrayed (as always) by appetite: in his sincerest attempts to console a young woman he had never been able to ignore potential rewards.

From tears, Kamin-Tarú was soothed, her wine-cup refilled, and it became more and more apparent that after days and nights on Landegh, in close proximity but of necessity apart, the bodies of Orbanak and Kamin-Tarú were not going to let another night go to waste. After innumerable unplanned mutual anticipations of posture, their glances and light touchings were flowing into purpose. Inwardly combining a large shrug with a faint sigh, Dolvid had the housekeeper fetched, and quietly decreed the two be given adjacent bedrooms.

All wrong; Kamin-Tarú ought to be treated as dangerous, not let loose alone with the *rabhsai*'s brother. Dolvid did not think Orbanak would come to harm worse than contracting the perilous desire to be her only bedfriend, and in any case was not prepared to summon the squadron or so of cavalry it would take to keep them apart.

He tried to convince himself he regretted dilution of his old intimacy with Kamin-Tarú mainly because it served the realm for him to be in her confidence. Calm, standing to yawn and stretch, she announced her readiness for bed, and bestowed a brief kiss on Dolvid. He smiled and bowed, wondering whether he could count silently to one hundred before Orbanak drained his cup and was also overtaken by weariness. His mood was somewhat sourer than wry, approving his understanding while deploring its results: he was nowhere near old enough to play the affable uncle, bestowing bawdy blessings on young couplers.

Yet when riding with Kamin-Tarú on the long journey to Kamsilat, he let Orbanak bring his squadron, and stay at the Great House for a few days so he could perform the escort duty when Dolvid went to the Mainland. His service with the Army of the West would, in any case, soon be ended. He intended to take up his authority as titular *Nim'* of the Paowan, normally, with the *rabhsai* controlling most of the appointments, and no provincial cavalry of its own to captain, a mere ceremonial post, but more than that now, in Rodlakh's intermittent state of abstraction. Orbanak was now just the age when his brother had blossomed into sudden confidence and authority; curious the same woman may have played a part.

The day after their arrival, knowing she would not let liking for Kamin-Tarú affect her judgment, Dolvid wanting Aëlu's thoughts on the mysterious break between Kamin-Tolagh and his sister, laid out the case.

"She became horrified with her brother's crimes; that I can accept; they were too much for Yaënsilat, who was anything but weak. She had made up her mind to try to leave him, and then comes this strangely opportune quarrel, provoked by *his* behavior, just at the time when he has given leave for the disaffected to depart."

"Kamin-Tarú might have made it opportune. If he had a habit of humiliating her in this way, but she had borne it in silence, then it would be her speaking out that made the breach so timely."

Dolvid, dubiously, "She talked about it as an unprecedented insult. And how angry must he be with her, to make no attempt to prevent her going? They first became lovers, if the tales are true, half her lifetime ago. I would much rather not doubt Kamin-Tarú, but I can't make the sums come right."

"My only love!" leaning back to tease him with her exaggerated wonder. "Your boyhood is now over. Orbanak would not question it if she insisted she had left Kamin-Tolagh because he snores, or because she wanted a chance to be Patriarch. What do I think?" She laughed quietly. "Who would put a grain of confidence in a plot requiring Kamin-Tarú to tell lies, and keep telling them? She has all the guile of a six-week puppy."

"Tell that to Taërinat — " the still-unmarried, still-embittered man she had pretended to love, as part of the plan to join her brother in the West.

"You are right, of course," Aëlu, as if sadly. "When it comes to the one man she wants, there is no honor; the most principled woman can take pride in how sly and how ruthless she has become."

"Revulsion and all, she cannot hide she still admires him."

"Oh, we do, you know." She put her hand on his as if to comfort. "Our great failing, the disease of our constancy, as betrayal is the disease of your appetite.

"Not *yours*," she emphasized quickly, though not quickly enough for his conscience. "Men's, Rodlakh's, Kamin-Tolagh's, who was that nephew of Plakhsila's? — Filat Plakhyali. Sebhal's, but neither of his women could cease to love Sebhal when he began to change."

Âna, and herself. With a start, Dolvid recognized for the first time in its breaking he and his wife had always had an unspoken compact not to exchange personal thoughts on the character of her first husband; he had remained a convention, the exemplary captain, the hero basely murdered.

"Having known Sebhal," calmly, "teaches me a great deal about Kamin-Tolagh — and more, you could say, about Kamin-Tarú. Sebhal was at the first brave, honorable, hungry for fame — and impatient. He hated treachery, despised cowardice, and had the knack of making men, as well as women, love him. We can give Sedukh a lot to be proud of in his father, without needing to lie."

Evidently Aëlu, still faintly mysterious after all these years, had allotted more than an hour's thought to this. "As we have," he said.

"As we have. At times, my love, I have wondered which is a better way, to hold up as model a flawless fiction, or to include, by way of warning, the dangers of talent, and bravery, and fame — and impatience. It was slower arriving, but Sebhal might have become a Kamin-Tolagh, had he lived a little longer."

"He died at Burantal trying to get help for an injured man," but as he protested Dolvid could not forget Sebhal had been there because he was planning to assassinate the then-*rabhsai*, then kill the only witness he was unsure of, Dolvid himself.

"Sebhal," she half-agreed, "began with Saidhan and Doleni, Kamin-Tolagh with Tovakh and Petakoi; that is not a small difference. But in those last years, talk of killing anyone who stood in the way came very easily to Sebhal. Championing Rodlakh's cause, loving Rodlakh, in the end his impatience would have been willing to see him killed, for the sake of what he called a just realm. He meant, Sebhal's realm. Once, he confessed to me he wished there was a way to put a mob in the Avenue of Treaties, and bring about the massacre that would provoke a general uprising — he *wished*. It should have sickened me, did sicken me, but — " she showed empty palms. "Sedukh was conceived not long after, and I was not raped."

Nor was she now, though in a rush of compassion and deep admiration, Dolvid took her in his arms, and only the knowledge of a whole night before them, together with a strong common aversion to unfinished business, permitted Aëlu to pick up the thread of her thoughts, made other as they were by the glancing, tremulous anticipation of certain pleasure.

"Eyes, especially," tracing his temple with her fingertips. "The will to power, passion for the rightness of his cause, that terrible certainty that forgives any useful crime — it shows in the eyes. Sebhal had it. Kamin-Tolagh has it."

"Owan-Alladh, whom you knew mainly as *Menadhi*, he had it, the eyes of a holy warrior, and the voice. When I first saw him, as a child, I imagined he could lead me to fulfillment of all my dreams — and all the time he was going to win and subjugate his perfect realm with an army of *jinzal*. We have to judge means, not the ends we imagine in a man's eyes, or hear in his big words."

"If our blood allows us to judge. Those eyes, and that certainty, are much more muddling than wine, my love. For a woman, they can wake something, oh, a great deal realler than dreams. Poor Kamin-Tarú. She will never find anything to replace the excitement of that power."

Since Kamin-Tarú's case was special for another and obvious reason, Dolvid concluded with a faint melancholy Aëlu's words applied at least as much to Aëlu.

Again, she was swift. "Don't mind. Loving your sanity is much better for my self-regard — " and then, with a blithe lasciviousness Kamin-Tarú would have envied, a readying squirm, "Not only your sanity."

As the very young expect but seldom achieve, they found immediate access to an unchecked mutual ardor, an astonishing newness of discovery. With the old-fashioned Others whose initial bedding came after the nuptials the first weeks were called the Knowing, and while Dolvid and Aëlu had from the beginning been happily suited to each other in their matings, he came now after ninety moons to a profounder knowing, a piercingly sweet opening into absolute intimacy, with nothing withheld or defended. Perhaps it began in her talk of Sebhal, with the undertheme of her own imperfection, the novel idea of vulnerability in imperturbable Aëlu, the trust in him implicit in that admission. Or was it the affectionate tact with which she had skirted the issue of him and Âna? Whatever the cause, however weighty long-term consequences, the immediate effect was anything but solemn; they were lighthearted, infantile, incautiously silly together as had never been; they surprised each other as if frivolity had just been invented.

Rodlakh's reassembly for business of the realm was proclaimed in his pressed clothes, his shave, loss of the blurred outlines, readiness to smile. He jocularly accused him of crossing Arnan entirely for a first sight of the new son, to be called Banat, but being already informed by dispatch of the new arrivals in the Colony, came quickly to that subject, listened to Dolvid's account and speculations, and wondered aloud why Kamin-Tarú had not accompanied him.

"She is here, *Rabhsai*," Dolvid confessed. "She thought it appropriate to wait till she was summoned — " only a slight adjustment, omitting reference to Rodlakh's recent unpredictability.

"Summoned? Tú? What nonsense," not quite glancing over his shoulder, as if expecting Âna to appear.

Tovakh, he remarked, was expected shortly to pass through Kadon Dinul once again. He had gone north for a brief visit with his old friend the *Nim'* of Dramal, but with a bad grace, Vinilat, after proclaiming himself fit for their autumn hunting, having for the third successive year cancelled at short notice. He kept hoping for his broken and rebroken leg to be fully recovered, but in his seventieth year, time was not running in his favor.

"Then Petakoi would be on the Island, as usual," Dolvid said. Circumstances could hardly be more propitious for Kamin-Tarú's hopes of reinstatement in her family and province.

Of meeting between father and daughter, he heard an account, conjecturally improved, a month later. A great deal at Kadon Dinul needed attention, and with the Colony's affairs in reasonable order, and no war imminent, he decided to stay through winter. Bringing the children, Aëlu came to join him, and they dined one evening with Rhunilat and his wife — or with Tellis and her husband, as many would now insist. Against the staid backdrop of Rhunilat, Tellis flashed brighter than ever; her second book *The Bronze Residence* — a title to make Dolvid cringe in advance, at the thought of available revelations — was at the fair-copying stage, and she was readier, as an established figure, to display her sometimes trenchant wit.

"She has lost none of her skill, Kargul's repentant daughter. When she came to the Residence for the meeting with her father, she was all humility, in the plainest of white gowns, and not a bead of embellishment."

The encounter, in the Karguli Suite, was a private one, but Tellis had interrogated a serving-maid who was inconspicuously present.

"Tovakh was standing in the middle of the room, with a face of thunder. Kamin-Tarú came up to him, and put in his hand a small whip, like the one — " with a darting glance at Dolvid, Tellis changed what she was about to say to: " — such as I am certain you would never use on your children."

Rhunilat said, "A timely beating never did me any harm," a disputable proposition, but he was defending his own methods, not commenting on Kamin-Tarú, who was a grown woman of — Dolvid worked it out — very near twenty-five.

"Kamin-Tarú without a word, sank to her knees in front of her father, eyes downcast, bowing to his wrath. '*Just like the Burantal marionettes at Pledging time*,' my spy said."

"Tú, I suspect," Aëlu, with a smile, "is fond of offering submission where she knows it cannot be accepted."

"But has greatest effect. Her father, you would guess, threw the whip aside, and turned his back on her. She rose, followed, put a hand on his shoulder, and as he turned to her, threw her arms about his neck. `And that was when,' my serving-girl says, `you could tell he was her father, madam. Weeping he was, that growly old man.'"

"Weeping, *Tovakh*?"

"Let us allow the serving-girl has heard too many romances read, but she swore there were real tears, on both sides. Kamin-Tarú will manage very well at Inilun Barabhi, if Petakoi does not kill her."

"My dear," Rhunilat objected.

"The Prince of the Paowan is left alone once again — " going from one impropriety to a worse one. "He has no luck with his choices. First — "

"Do you hear from your brother?" Dolvid's interjection was worth a surprised glance from Aëlu, but the harshness was calculated as a warning to Tellis, who had been about to cross into forbidden territory; Orbanak's disappointments brought in Morulis, and Morulis the *rabhsai*.

"Arvat is at Owan Sai," a slight wince acknowledging implied rebuke. "You heard they had another daughter?" Since Elamirr's fall had been ascribed to other causes, Arvat's implication in the Market Gate forgery was still unrevealed, but he had been dismissed from his service at Kamsilat, and soon returned to the Mainland.

The brief answer Tellis first gave was perhaps in consideration of Rhunilat's extreme dislike of her brother, yet the actual subject was her likeliest reason for this dinner, as emerged when she had a few minutes alone with Dolvid, and asked if anything could be done for Arvat.

"He cannot be employed again by either of the Residences."

"That I have heard from my husband, though no one can tell me what Arvat's crimes were." Family feeling was sharpened here by professional pique; Tellis lived for unearthing hidden reasons.

"Listen, *Bôdhr'asai*," with the aggression of long familiarity. "I know Arvat was doing everything but wipe Elamirr's nose, and I do not believe you and other high ones, except perhaps the *rabhsai*, thought wife-beating the worst of Elamirr's offences. If you tell me my brother *betrayed his trust*, I would say that was mostly your fault, for giving him any, having known him so long. But he is still my brother."

"And always, for me, Arvus's son," as if in excuse for all the chances he had given Arvat.

"You do not judge men as you do horses, by their parents. Look at Lambarr."

"If I had not known your father, Arvat might now face far worse than reduced circumstances at Owan Sai. He can keep accounts for some of the ship-owners. Your father, when he ran the Treasury, kept one horse, and one servant."

"Two servants, till you stole the cheaper one, and taught her about writing."

"That's not true — " exasperated by the demands of this nostalgia, and with, unimaginably, a sudden fellow-feeling for Tovakh, abandoned to the rapacity of Kamin-Tarú's submission. "When I first met you, you were fourteen, and already had half Bronal's lyrics by heart. Look, I am going to initiate a quarterly grant for the encouragement of writing, and I do not want to hear where the money goes after it is paid to you. But it must be understood my concern for literature ceases at the first hint Arvat is meddling in politics, or — "

"Yes, *Asai*, yes," ruefully. "Race."

Her Owani husband, who had proudly been showing Aëlu his new indoor winter garden, returned, hymning the clarity of Island glass. Dolvid was wondering about the reference by Tellis to *other high ones*; he was sure she had speculated, uncertain of how much she could know, about him and the *rabhsayu*.

Not, at this period, that there was much to be known. When Rodlakh neglected his shaving, or failed to appear at all, there was a realm to be governed, and at his best the *rabhsai* currently had limited patience for long discussion. He did not emulate his father's affable way of putting off decisions, but preferred to be presented with a proposal fully argued, needing only a yes or no. Âna and Dolvid, often as not joined by Orimat, the Bronze Residence scribe who had exposed Elamirr's dealings with the forger, now Dolvid's assistant, read, devised, disputed long hours together, frequently consulting with Fornival, Sett, or Âna's brother Konir, occasionally with the elusive Shumat, his well-organized surrogate, Kizhunai, or a saddened Orbanak. Âna, additionally, was preoccupied with the new baby, and Dolvid too had family concerns. In truth, he was fascinated by how a marriage anyone, any time, would have called exceptionally successful (though sustained disproportionately by Aëlu's calm stability) had turned to a much odder state, less fixed, with a potential for hurt as well as hilarity, an Aëlu the more extraordinary for having abruptly become less so — less exempt, that was, from the cost of existing, her serenity an assiduous construction rather than a painless gift. Absurdly, he wanted to make up for not having deduced that from the first, but Âna's attuned perception was there to label improbability.

At the Residence, they had worked on into evening. Rodlakh was resting, a description understood as meaning he was with Morulis, and Dolvid, marvelling as often at the economy of words their understanding enabled, unaware of any difference in himself, said something about sending a note to reassure Aëlu, if they were going to continue much longer.

"She must be accustomed to your absences by now."

"Accustomed," lightly. "Not necessarily indifferent."

Âna lowered her chin an instant, then looked up with a smile he did not remember. "It can't be true," with a brief, edgy laugh, also new to him. "You have fallen in love with your wife. Who would believe it?"

A denial heard as false would have been no antidote for the tears that soon came, nor Âna's annoyance with herself over the tears; persistent gentleness was better, the mutual reassurance of unchanged signals. After a time, as they had before, they found a private place and were as good and loving together as ever. Âna asked quiet pardon for, but could not unsay, her words — her accusation. He, her neglect by Rodlakh always in mind, could neither defend against what seemed to be bewildering truth, nor get rid of a guilt that was rationally preposterous. Nothing he had ever told Âna was made untrue, but to say nothing was changed was stupid, if only because she saw him differently. He wished he could do something to prevent that from altering, souring, her past, and therefore poisoning the future.

Sooner than predicted either by the sentimental or the cynical, Tovakh gave notice he would ask the Council to restore his daughter to the Karguli succession, and the light remark by Tellis, *if Petakoi does not kill her*, darkened in Dolvid's mind; Pedh-Sivai's adoption was evidently not to be rescinded, but his place in line behind Kamin-Tarú would be a receding one if she should marry and begin producing offspring; from imminent triumph, Petakoi's long dream of capturing Kargul for the best blood of the Island was abruptly back where it started.

Her hatred would only deepen for a Kamin-Tarú as successful rival in her own best sport, manipulating Tovakh. In addition, she now must know Kamin-Tarú could at any time expose her complicity in the old plot to install the True *Rabhsai* with the help of a *jinzai* army. Absence of any scruples was amply established, as was Petakoi's resourcefulness. Poison was the danger that came first to mind, as characteristic of any space containing that mother and daughter, and the only known safeguard for Kamin-Tarú — he hoped she had acquired others — was that her sudden death would be so satisfactory for Petakoi in so many ways, she would immediately be suspected.

Then came a rumor rapidly confirmed; Petakoi was back on the Island indefinitely, after only weeks at Inilun Barabhi, where Tovakh, no doubt in part to anticipate and forestall uglier speculations, was undisguisedly sharing his bed with a woman young enough, as Tellis wickedly put it, to be anyone but his daughter.

The Patriarch, ga-Dozhusai-Arbhali, normally tendered written notice days in advance of His desire for a meeting, giving a speculative urgency to His note one mid-morning, asking the *Bôdhrai* if He could see him that day at the Bronze Residence — ideal neutral ground, being joint-property of *rabhsayum* and *Mankh'*.

Power, or more germanely, success, agreed with Dozhusai, who had gained some girth along with a great deal of public stature, and was like the happier, robuster brother of the man who had signed a Second Treaty imposed rather than negotiated. Sick at the irrefutable evidence the *Atarlum*, His beloved *Atarlum*, had been guilty of all the deaths in the Jinzai War, He might have thought He would be last Patriarch, raised only to preside over dissolution. An unpromising candidate for widespread popularity, with His piping voice and countrified features, He had shown great skill staying in the saddle of a horse running free, the mysterious general adoption of Zhôl, and even if His successor, still decades in the future, came from the reactionary wing of the *Atarlum*, there was no chance their teachings could ever go back to the narrowly exclusive creed they once promoted, no way to untranslate an invocation. Dozhusai's niche in history was a secure one.

Notably, for this meeting He was without His usual recording scribe. "Our daughter, Petakoi," He began after brief pleasantries, "has now applied to Us for permanent sanctuary on the Island."

"She is an Islander," a trifle mystified, wondering if he should not have had Fornival with him, if legal hairs were about to be split. Over the Island, where the *rabhsai* appointed no magistrates, collected no taxes, maintained no garrisons, the Patriarch, as He knew best, was all-but sovereign, entirely responsible for keeping order. He was still required to surrender to *Rabhsai*'s Law any person accused of a crime committed outside the Island, who had tried to take refuge there. An oddity was that a serious offender extradited to be tried on the Mainland might well be returned to Kamanta as a prisoner — in effect, as forced labor, since the *Atarlum* made use of the *rabhsai*'s convicts in its monopoly industries, harvesting and curing of *raminat*, glassmaking including the secret process by which *ôdul* were made, and, most gruelling of all, splitting and salting-down of eels for smoking.

"True," the Patriarch agreed, and waited. A trick out of the *Mankh'*, as if to say *think it through*, and Dolvid was jerked back almost thirty years, mind working furiously so he could prove he was a clever boy.

"Petakoi," he ventured, "is undoubtedly guilty of grave crimes against the realm. But, Enlightenment, they are part of the same crimes which the *rabhsai*, in the agreement that led to the Second Treaty, undertook not to make public, so long as certain conditions were met."

"An agreement, and a treaty, on Our side scrupulously observed."

He could not be blamed for that small hit against Rodlakh's illegal attempt to restrict the comings and goings of His *atarlal*.

"Petakoi *Asayu*, with her rank, could face trial only in Council. Since the *rabhsai* would be her accuser, Your Enlightenment would be presiding."

"Assuming she retains her rank, *Bôdhrai*. You should know, there is talk of a divorce. While Our granting her everlasting sanctuary could mistakenly be seen as an attempt to put the lady out of the *rabhsai*'s reach, her first concern is safety from Tovakh baKargul, who is now, and for the first time, aware of those crimes We have referred to."

And furious. Dolvid bowed invisibly in the direction of Kamin-Tarú; instead of trying to use her knowledge of the *jinzai*-breeding episode by holding the secret over Petakoi's head, she had simply and intelligently informed her father. Tovakh would have had no difficulty believing; it was too much in Petakoi's pattern, and would have explained many small past mysteries for him.

The news did not make Kamin-Tarú's succession any surer. If there was to be a divorce, Tovakh could marry again, and a new son would instantly become Heir, unless the contrary were formally stipulated, unlikely in that warrior province, with its line of cavalry-captain overlords.

"*G'Asalladhâo*, it is not the rank of Petakoi *Asayu* that has kept her from justice. My opinion is, if the lady behaves herself, the *rabhsai* has no reason to proceed against her, but as Your Enlightenment must see, I cannot give a guarantee."

With this hedged answer the Patriarch appeared quite satisfied, and Dolvid decided he had been rather a slow-witted pupil, after all. Dozhusai had not been seeking an assurance; His object had been merely to inform, to dispel in advance any idea he was shielding Petakoi from the realm's law. Why He had particular interest in protecting the truest ally of His unloved predecessor remained an enigma.

They went on to discuss the ever-hovering subject, Kamin-Tolagh, and Dolvid heard himself being not-quite accused of impropriety in his dealings with at-Dhanurai, a thing he had sedulously avoided. Last spring at Banakit, knowing better than to try turning an *atarlai* into a spy for *rabhsayum*, unable to entirely ignore the opportunity, he had asked his old *Mankh'* acquaintance if he would report instead *to the Patriarch* anything he saw or heard while in Kamin-Tolagh's domains to indicate his intentions, or foreshadow a danger to Rodlakh's realm; it would then be *g'Asalladh's* decision whether to pass on his observations. At-Dhanurai, mapmaking part of his task shortened by his being able to copy from the excellent maps of Kamin-Tolagh's man, Dubovai, was evidently now back at the *Mankh'*.

"First," the Patriarch said, with rare astringency, "any *atarlai*, while there in the West, is under guidance of Our proxy, at-Iruvakh, who is subject to Kamin-Tolagh's laws. Second, neither there nor anywhere does an *atarlai* owe any duty to the military needs of the realm. Third, Our friendly relations with Kamin-Tolagh could be irreparably harmed by Our dealing in such information."

"I ask your pardon, *g'Asalladhâo*. The unprecedented division of Your authority, giving Kamin-Tolagh the right to permit or forbid, a power Rodlakh *Rabhsai* does not possess, is Your Enlightenment's own business. Mine is security of the realm. If a time should come when Kamin-Tolagh is strong enough to succeed with an attack on this realm — "

"Not very likely, is it, *Asai*?"

He toyed with a roster of improbabilities, beginning with this man's rise to the Patriarchate, ending with Tovakh divorcing Petakoi. "If," instead, "he conquered all the Hrin, and taught them how to fight, if we relaxed our vigilance, and were distracted by other troubles, it is remotely possible Kamin-Tolagh could come to rule both in the West and at Kadon Dinul. I think he would want to renegotiate the Second Treaty."

Dozhusai was thoughtful. "We trust he would not attempt to rule over Sons and Daughters of Yoëlladhu as he has over the unenlightened of the West."

"He would permit a *Mankh'* still holding `Children of Yoëlladhu' means only one race."

This Dozhusai began to dispute, launching into an offended account of how, recently, Kamin-Tolagh, far from espousing old pieties, had cynically favored the side of Hrin superstition in a religious dispute over fields consecrated to *ga-Yalum*.

"Your Enlightenment' would say, a purely political decision, based on local conditions. Here, he could never hope to prevail without the support of those who, you must pardon me, retain the word *betrayal* when speaking of Your Enlightenment's success in winning new adherents — who hold the *Mankh'* should still be the home of racial purity and Owani domination."

"Not, *Bôdhrai*, ever only that," rebuking him. "We have always had a place for men and women of true devotion."

"Under your predecessor, a very subordinate place. With Kamin-Tolagh *Rabhsai* at the Residence, Owan-Alladh might reconsider his retirement." This nightmare vision was adequately offensive, and Dolvid did not give the knife an unnecessary twist by observing such a restoration would be welcomed by Dozhusai's new dependant, Petakoi.

The point was won, and the Patriarch backed away from His censure enough to convey some of at-Dhanurai's observations: he had seen and heard nothing, either at the Abu, or in the Hrin lands, to suggest preparation for an early invasion of the old realm. Kamin-Tolagh was indeed trying to teach the Hrin to fight, but appeared to have in mind a militia to keep order rather than a battle-force. Reportedly because of a shortage of big horses, there was a great emphasis on bows, and arrows were being stockpiled everywhere. When asked if they were true mounted archers, Dozhusai answered they had horses, and failed to grasp the distinction Dolvid was making, between those who fought from the saddle, and those rode to battle, but could shoot only when standing on the ground.

In either case, as Shumat later soberly noted, a host of bowmen could mean higher casualties in any war; inferior cavalry might retreat from an oncoming charge, or fail in their own, without killing a single one of their vanquishers. Lightly-armed archers on foot could be easily routed by determined cavalry, but the worst of them would get off a couple of arrows before they fled.

The Patriarch had ended the meeting in an unexpected puzzle. Talk of Kamin-Tolagh's pragmatic attitude to religion led Him into a general consideration of faith, not Dolvid's best subject.

"A teacher of mine, at-Oradhai — you remember him, too; he lived to a great age. He said, the hardest enemy was indifference; a rival creed or a passion against all faith were signs of kindling that could be lighted by truth, but a nature that neither believes, nor cares what others believe, is like sodden wood where no fire can take.

"With the *rabhsai*," having convinced Dolvid the implied subject was himself, "We are gratified to observe signs of a more active interest in beliefs he has surely done nothing to discourage." To clarify this altogether baffling assertion, He handed over a small book, a copy of which He said Rodlakh had asked for, Dozhusai's own brief, unassuming volume of reflections, *Thirteen Steps on Zhôl's Path*. Thanking Him, promising it would be delivered today, unable to connect the request with any Rodlakh he knew, Dolvid could only guess Morulis must have expressed an interest.

"Curse it, Dol," Shumat erupted, causing the young officer brought with him as secretary to cringe and drop his pen. "If you tell me one more time about keeping the southern garrisons strong, I swear I'll resign and keep pigs in Odis Combe. I've had to send twenty fresh squadrons to Narn, and they won't be enough if the raiding begins again come spring. A band of robbers doing as they please up in the Angle, and Hinn keeps promising he'll hunt them down, if he can just have a hundred added cavalry, and then just a hundred more. We loaned two entire regiments to the Army of the West when you were afraid the defections were the spark for war, and now Bradhinal is dragging his feet about releasing them, when you've got good men who could be in the saddle fooling about with pikes at Banakit, my dazzling son leading the way.

"*Asai, Bôdhrai,* sir," imposing control. "The garrison at Thenimala has been doubled since you began saying, watch the south. I have had four squadrons keeping vigil over Finú since you became convinced Kamin-Tolagh was going to snatch her and wave her as his banner. The cavalry-post at the border is up to strength, and there are good *pefral* yawning at stations in the Ní-Tilagh, in case news needs to come north in a hurry. What can we do beyond that? With all that coastline, we can't guarantee against his landing, but if he does land, we'll beat him. With cavalry," a subsidiary sarcasm for the Colony's companies of pikes, which Dolvid should never have imagined could be kept secret from his friend.

Less fierce after Dolvid made some sort of apology for plaguing him on this point, Shumat demanded to be told what was the worst that could happen in the tremendously unlikely event forces in the south were unable to defeat an invasion within days. "Let's say, for the sake of spoiling our sleep, he can overrun Ninkufu before we can collect our main forces. What is his next step? He is still on the wrong side of Ní-Tilagh, another Landegh where he's concerned."

"Not quite, perhaps." Though barren and forbidding, the waste that lay between Ninkufu and the southern borders of the realm proper was less so than Landegh, not altogether waterless. Nor was the sun so fierce, the ground so broken; similar in extent to the western plateau, the undulating brown of the Ní-Tilagh was three dreary but unchallenging days for a very moderate rider.

"Right. Easier terrain for our cavalry, and you can't think those happy tribal armies of his, where deserters are tortured to death, are going to stand up to real *péfrapravádal*. Just north of the border, there's the fortress at Kir, could he take that? I wish he would come; we would not have him to worry about any longer, and I could have a day's peace from you."

"Get some sleep," Dolvid recommended with a grin. The idea of Kamin-Tolagh seizing southern Ninkufu, including the port of Thenimala, then going over to defense while gradually building up more formidable forces, had already been scorned by Shumat, and Dolvid was unable to speak his real, irrational requirement, that Kamin-Tolagh, if he came, must be defeated before Rodlakh could act on the predictable decision this was a personal fight. Even when very old friends, irascible Captains-General could not be asked to defend against visions.

Connection between Kamin-Tolagh and renewed Heartland talk of the great injustice suffered by Finú was no surmise. Khalú's dull brother, Ghuradh, given the warning note his sister had entrusted to Dolvid, had become an informant as to Lavsila's communications, and had quickly remarked on the change of direction, from assertion Kamin-Tolagh on his merits would be a better ruler than the present one, to advocacy of Finú's cause on the grounds of legitimacy. He was also first to note the shift had occurred soon after news had trickled back to the Heartland of Kamin-Tolagh's decision in the case involving the grotesque Hrin cult of the Swan — as if Lavsila conceded the difficulty of representing such a master as true champion of the Old Belief.

A Ghuradh newly eager to display his cynicism was not necessarily a convert, and it was likely the man, echoing Lavsila himself, wanted to keep a foot in each camp. He was no doubt continuing equally to blandish the Empire of Kargusai.

Yet since the fall of Elamirr, methodical review and revision of certain of the tax-laws which, as that rancorous soul intended, had unduly penalized the Families, the old complaints against Rodlakh's reign were nothing worse than a traditional ritual: the influence of the Heartland elect, if no longer dominant, showed no sign of being smashed, and for men and women who characterized the taxation policies of the past eight years as *confiscatory*, their lives remained notably comfortable, luxury-trades flourishing, the summer villas by Shelum still in repair. Though they were obliged to keep wider lands in cultivation, and to share more equitably with their tenant farmers, their great estates were intact, with ample swathes of recreational acreage remaining.

As with the subject responsible for Shumat's near-tantrum, Dolvid received a further, gentler indication he was repeating himself too often, when Aëlu, as another spring came, asked him why he did not make these excellent points to the landowners themselves. Returning from a brief visit to the Colony, he found she had invited several of the leading Heartlanders to a dinner at the house south of the Avenue, adding Rhunilat to the list because Tellis would enliven the evening. Astonished when no one declined, he was made aware for the first time he could now be esteemed as a trophy for snobbery when Aëlu, amused, said, "Come? Of course they are going to come. Wealthy as they may be, how often do you think they ever dine with a *nimu*?"

Not counting huge feasts at the Residence (and leaving aside Zhival with his connections by blood), seldom, probably, but Dolvid protested, "I am the favorite renegade. When it was proposed, most of them must have called my elevation to *nimum* a scandal."

"You will never understand, will you, my love. Rank is rank. These same people, or their parents, used to vilify Saidhan, and boast about it for a month if he nodded to them at a Pledging."

On the eve of the gathering, whose object the *rabhsai* had warmly endorsed, and the *rabhsayu* greeted with ambiguous words of wonder, Dolvid, at the Old Bronze Residence, was handed a much-folded sheet of paper by Orimat. "These have been appearing everywhere."

Noting first the good color and uniform thinness of the page, he read:

> *Our proper* Rabhsayu *has been deprived of her birthright!*
> *Only restoration to her rightful place can end the tyrannies of the usurper House Arbhai-Navu!*
> *United to the House Gabh'Owan by ties of blood, faith and tradition, the Families of the Realm call for justice!*

"Well," with enjoyment that puzzled his assistant. "What do you make of this?"

"Lavsila again?"

A shake of the head. "I am reminded of another document you helped track to its source. Do you happen to know if Elamirr is still in Burantal?"

"No, he's not. He's at Nambalus, working for an importer there."

Dolvid once again felt the page between thumb and forefinger. "One whose imports include Colony paper?"

"He certainly deals in Colony goods — the business that used to belong to the *bôdh'loiki* for Commerce."

"When Sett joined the *rabhsayum*, Shardirr bought him out. He regularly brings paper from Kamsilat." Hardly a proven case, since everyone who could afford it used the excellent Colony paper. Not in the Farther West, but that alone did not prove a text originating with Lavsila had not been recopied. According to Orimat, several identical copies were circulating; this had been left on a table in the hostelry near East Gate.

He was doubly puzzled by Dolvid's idea. "Why would Elamirr write something like this, *Bôdhrai*? How can we be sure it's not Lavsila's work? It is talking about Lady Finú, isn't it?"

"Trying to." Industrious, able, almost embarrassingly devoted, Orimat was no scholar, still struggling to master the Script of Shâl, uncertain with the Owanilú however written.

"This," with confidence, "was never composed in this form by Lavsila, nor by any of his Heartland friends. It calls Finú

`Rabhsayu.' The Lady Âna is our *rabhsayu*, wife to our *rabhsai*. Finú, if she had a sound claim, would reign in her own right, as *rabhsaëyu*. A mistake no educated Owani could make."

Orimat's other question, why? was echoed by Âna, alone today, *rabhsai* having gone to Bathrâd for a ceremony renewing the charter of the Dyers' Guild, not wrecked, as it had predicted, by admission of Others to its ranks.

"Elamirr must want to prove he was right, the realm is in danger, deprived of his vigilance against Owani scheming. You must bear in mind his dismissal, officially, was for a reason judged trivial by his — forgive me."

"No, no, it's true. If I told my father it was for wife-beating, it would be the same as telling him he was exiled for breaking wind; he would wink and smile, as if to say, I understand, you can't tell me the real story. But Elamirr must know."

"He sees his opinions as wisdom, not hatred." Perhaps the hardest lesson of all to keep in mind, that sincerity could exist behind repugnant views, even those that coincided with a fierce ambitiousness. "After a year, he must be surer than ever he was forced out by a conspiracy, yours and mine, and that he can return in triumph as the one true prophet, when my policies are discredited."

"Your dinner is tomorrow? I can hear Elamirr's opinion on that gathering. We let him down too lightly," momentarily forgetting they'd had their own self-serving reasons. "He could be exiled to the Island, just for the Market Gate Letter, with Arvat's letters, and Arvat's testimony, and the man Altorri could be brought back to give evidence."

"No." trying to make his explanation tactful. "For the *rabhsai* to proceed against Elamirr in present circumstances would be seen as spite, not justice."

"Oh, *present circumstances*." She made a sour face. "Your much admired wife, sir, is now the *rabhsai*'s favorite toy. We could have him killed."

"Elamirr?" A fatuous question.

"I thought of it once before, when you were nearly ousted, and he was bribing servants here to say what he wanted them to see. Men on my father's lands could ride to Nambalus by night, and be back in the morning, with nothing noticed."

"Or," he wryly countered, more frightened by her dispassion than he could allow, "we could send a couple of squadrons from the Household."

"You think I am not serious?"

"I don't see how you can be." But he did; the seductive lure of safety, of eternal freedom from this thoroughly superfluous distraction.

After long seconds, Âna said, "Neither do I. Why do you have to be such good men? — Rodlakh, too, when he is himself. I am not allowed to hate anyone."

"Would you want to hate me?"

"No, Aëlu, but I can't do that, either."

"You have no need — " but he was cursing time, that let nothing stay unmarked.

Unprecedented, and not to be repeated under Dolvid's auspices, a conclave of the Old Blood, with only Tellis to sully racial purity, she sanctioned by her husband's kinships and connections long before her celebrity as author.

Standing in the transverse hall, with its newly-laid floor of warm rust-colored kilned tile, its carefully restored false ceiling of intricate stone lacework, Dolvid, chilled by a sudden fear associated with the document championing Finú, first spoke to Tellis, asking as casually as he could about her brother.

"He is well," and, low-voiced, "grateful." Free of his most urgent financial anxieties, Arvat was planning a new venture, to begin at Pledging time, when he intended to offer the considerable experience of law he had acquired in all his Great House years to those who had a case to bring in any of the special courts sitting at that time, where he would actually appear and plead for them. If successful, he would turn it into a year-round occupation.

"For payment, you mean?" Not unusual for those having suits to seek help from relatives or allies with greater knowledge of law, and not unheard-of for the advisor to receive a share in any judgment won, but for someone to make his learning available for hire without regard to personal sympathies or the merits of the case was new.   But obviously Arvat had not renewed his alliance with Elamirr.

"I can find nothing to make it unlawful."

"There cannot be laws against what has never been contemplated." Arvat's covert pension, however, would have to be stopped: if he were to fail in a case against the *rabhsayum* for, say, recovery of taxes, it might be charged he had been bribed to lose. That thought, the teeming opportunities for profit on both sides, anticipated need for a whole volume of new law to regulate what could swiftly become a numerous profession, and a voracious one; Dolvid made a note to speak about this with Fornival, who would frown and shake his head despondently, but fail to conceal his relish at the prospect of hammering out an entire new code to be submitted — with endless explanation and clarification — to a captive Council. Suddenly, no less than his sister with her books, Arvat, in his way, was arguably a figure for history. In the meantime, Dolvid did not add, his clients had better count their change.

Linaëyu greeted him effusively and the tilt of her face mandated a kiss smothered in the scent of violets; once pardonably vain of her birch-slender body, she was now distressingly plump, and her latter taste for ornate jewelry was approaching the outlandish; she jingled as she moved, and her hands were armored in rings and bangles. The thick-lipped son, Ghuradh, was in attendance, pretty, unmemorable wife as always in the background. Linaëyu's husband, Khelagh, wealthiest of all Heartland magnates, was past eighty now, corpulent and slow-moving, breathing in the gasps of a beached fish, and by necessity speaking in short, measured phrases; management of his vast estates was now entirely in his son's large and ever-clumsy, but for these purposes, presumably adequate, hands.

Yet the father, before they went in for dinner, anticipated and to an extent disarmed Dolvid, by producing and flourishing a copy of what would be called the *Rabhsayu* Document, identical to the one in Dolvid's possession.

"What of this, *Asai*," he wheezed. "Is this not treason?"

For the second time so soon, he wished he had included Fornival in this gathering, to supply a truly learned answer. "What it attempts to suggest, sir," he did his best, "appears to come near treason. If anyone were to act illegally on its counsel, the author of the document could be charged with suborning treason, or so I believe.   But he might defend himself successfully by claiming it was only a children's game, or a page copied from one of the romances."

His cheerful offhandedness brought him back on equal terms of unpreparedness with Khelagh.   Prômsilakh, another big landowner and merchant, sidled between women to add his voice: "This is not the first of these, *Asai*. They slander our loyalty."

He sounded authentically aggrieved, but Prômsilakh, though known for his devout adherence to old belief, had generally been an advocate of compromise, when the rest of his circle were threatening defiance of some new measure. On the other hand, if Elamirr's notorious Kin-Law had been adopted, he would have been among first to suffer, with a younger son in the Farther West (to whom, in addition, he was rumored last year to have sent a large sum in gold, for investment in land looted from the Hrin).

"Who," innocently, "do you think is meant by `our proper *Rabhsayu*?"

"*Rabhsaëyu*," Khelagh growled. "We have illiterates putting words in our mouths."

"Finú of Ninkufu, of course," his son supplied. "Another of these pages demanded support for her, *from all those who value purity of blood*."

"Purity of foolishness," the father puffed, using up all his breath, while Dolvid tried to think when he had ever heard the Families disrespectful of Great Family. Oh, Faëdhal had once called Vinilat of Ân an ignorant lout, not to his burly face.

"I remember — " wryly.

"No question, *Asai*, Finú *Asayu* is of good descent," Prômsilakh allowed, so grudgingly a stranger could easily assume these of all people were those to whom bloodlines meant the least.

Dolvid put a halt to the unexpected chorus by telling them this touched on the reasons why he had held this assembly. "Let it wait now, till we have enjoyed our dinner. Old Town forcemeat is a favorite of yours, I remember — " this for Khelagh, whose eyes gleamed.

Recognizing, during the meal, that the desire of at least two of the landowners to dissociate themselves from the sentiments of the *Rabhsayu* Document was help not hindrance to his purpose, Dolvid, when all but fruit had been cleared away, and what decidedly ought to be sincere compliments were being paid Aëlu, shamelessly used the authority of his new rank to turn after-dinner talk into a lecture on wealth and responsibility, observing that in a period of unprecedented prosperity, the Heartlanders' gratitude to *rabhsayum* and to the *rabhsai* whose pacific and moderate reign had made it possible, had in general taken the form of endless carping, resistance to new laws, and, after seventy years of Arbhai-Navu rule, continued nonsense about an imminent resumption of the Gabh'Owani line.

Ghuradh, waving his father's copy of the *Rabhsayu* Document, won a chorus of assent with: "*Asai*, we resent somebody trying to make out this declaration came from any of us."

Dolvid held up a hand. "There must be a reason why *somebody* thought it might be believed he was speaking for the Families of the Heartland. I myself have heard discreeter versions of the same opinions for many years now. When a handful of your restive children went to join Kamin-Tolagh's lunatic venture, there were pages like these, proclaiming they had gone to seek *freedom from the oppressions of Rodlakh's realm*, and I have yet to hear anyone of the Families disown that slander."

The elderly, widowed Zhival, Khelagh's normal ally, inveterate enemy of what he called *mongrelism*, stared down on this point, returned to the earlier one, challenging any roseate view of the commonweal. "These may be good times, *Asai*, for those who have just won lives of ease, deserved or otherwise. Peace, we all agree, is a blessing, but for us, it has been a time of foodstuffs sold at fixed prices, of land kept by law in wheat where another crop would show better profit, high taxes and higher wages to pay — "

"We do not need to give embarrassing details, Zhival, but I could prove with the tax-rolls the Heartland's twelve largest estates — " *nine of them were represented in this room* — "are wealthier, in absolute terms, notwithstanding a couple of recent leaner years, under conditions now remedied, than eight years ago. In the same period, true, many more ordinary people have made their way out of dire need, but is wealth to be prized for itself, or only by contrast with someone else's poverty?"

Beginning to enjoy this, he pointed out to Zhival, along with Ghuradh a leading horsebreeder, that hundreds who had never imagined riding on anything grander than a plowhorse now kept a saddle-animal. Kheval, who had largest share of the shuzi trade, he reminded of how many could now afford garments and other things of that costly fabric, Prômsilakh, as a large investor in fine woods, of the enormous growth in the furniture trade, and so around the table, being specific about how each of them profited from the widespread increase in numbers able to afford what once were luxuries of the few.

He knew his reluctance to enforce rank was notorious, but *nimum* was *nimun*, and the acerbic or sarcastic responses he saw come into the ring of faces flickered and quickly went out. But Linaëyu, on the edge of drunk, said, "Well and good, *Asai*, but there are men who will not rest till we are reduced to powerless penury, and you cannot deny it."

"No one now in office — " the reference to their loathed Elamirr was certainly not lost. "Those who begin to acquire something of their own soon discard the burning desire to deprive others."

He had not stilled the hubbub of assent Linaëyu had earned; with shattering frankness and a loud-jangling gesture, she did that herself. "And, since you ask the question, Dolvidh, I for one will admit, yes, it is good to have things I know others do not and cannot possess; naturally that is part of enjoying our wealth. Well, isn't it?" she challenged the table, but had no immediate takers.

"To take pleasure in what only the wealthy can have," Tellis quietly suggested, "we could do more to encourage our painters and our poets, musicians, sculptors, as we do the goldsmiths and weavers who merely adorn our bodies. Then the historian would say, Rodlakh *Rabhsai* gave his era peace, but the Families of the Heartland made it into a new Blossoming Age."

Unlike the disciplined Tellis of her writing, she would have spoiled the splendid simplicity of this with the example of a deserving young poet from Kanzan Tâl, but Khelagh growled, "I would settle for a new age of respect. For tradition, for position, for rank." He struck angrily at the *Rabhsayu* Document held by his son.

"Agreed," Dolvid said.   "Beginning, as it must, with undivided respect for *rabhsayum*."

The sole tangible prize for the evening, as he told Rodlakh and Âna next day, was made extraordinary by its source; a select committee of the leading landowners were devising an Address of Loyal Gratitude for delivery at Pledging Time.

"Another Loyal Address; I am all blushes," with wearied humor.   Such ceremonies, with formal speeches and ornate scrolls, were not uncommon; the Elders of Burantal, the Sovereign City of Dônshei and the Stonecutters of Ân, for example, would be proffering their devotion at midsummer.

"From the Families, *Rabhsai*, a minor landmark."

Rodlakh kept his faint smile. "I do not suppose they will be any happier, next time we charge one with underpaying his taxes. You did not ask them for a public disavowal of the rights of Finú?"

"I discouraged it, when Ghuradh made the suggestion. I told him it would be gratuitously ungentle to advertise the plain inadequacies of a claimant no one takes seriously."

"No one but Lavsila," Âna said.

"Nothing real," he conceded, when Âna, alone, challenged him as to the significance of the proposed Loyal Address. "I was thinking of peace. When Kamin-Tolagh hears about it, he may at last recognize the true extent and depth of his support here."

"You said once, he can never be content to stay there in the West."

"There might be a day when he can come back a penitent, like his sister."

"He is tiring of Morulis," Âna, abstractedly, obviously not meaning Kamin-Tolagh. Perhaps the thought of contrition, offered or accepted, provided the link.

39.

A month past the anniversary of his sister's departure from the Abu, Kamin-Tolagh blooded his new armies by sending them, spearheaded by experienced squadrons, against the *onhritha* of Svedion. Having low esteem for the fighting potential of that cavalry so easily cowed two years ago, with more men of his own than had been needed to defeat Iolfrant in days, he did not doubt the outcome. There were great advantages to making war on an immediate neighbor: for once, he could if needed bring up reinforcements, men fed and rested, not wearied by a long journey, and the same could be said for their mounts; expended arrows and broken lances could readily be resupplied, without burdening the fighting force with baggage.

Not wanting another war ended with a polite agreement, he did not inform his supposed allies — of which, indeed, Svedion was nominally one — and orders were to destroy the enemy horse; the common foot-soldiers, useful in the future as laborers, could be spared, together, for the same reason, with any of the ships' companies where they posed no danger, but surrender by the others would not be accepted; he wished this pitiless campaign to provide a warning to the remaining *hrithuod*, whose bland pretence of friendship was a constant insult to his acumen. The cowing of possible future enemies might well, in the end, save lives.

The shocking news of the Loyal Address by the Heartland magnates had come to him weeks earlier, when he was at Larghamit for Zhôl's Day. Lavsila, not willing to admit failure, was undecided whether to treat it as a joke, or a cunning feint by the Heartlanders, to put Rodlakh off his guard. Pranúdhanai, at Kafai Zhaëli for the ceremonies, swore he had heard nothing about it from his father, one of the presenters, while Iruvakh said it was not the sort of news *g'Asalladh'* favored him with.

This frustration, inability to know with certainty whether he was being lied to, was, far beyond what he had anticipated, a part of missing Tú, her candor, up to the time melancholy had put a barrier between them. He had never seen to what an extent intimacy was interwoven with this question of trust, nor what a necessary anchor that was; there had been a time when, if his men followed him, as they always had, if they obeyed his orders, laughed at his jokes, relished tales of his prowess with women, that was enough to assure him of unquestioning loyalty. Now he needed, the Empire needed, surer signs of wholeheartedness: he understood and made use of the fact that men, and women too, would act in their own interest, whether seeking pleasure, profit, power, or avoiding discomfort, pain, and death; no mystery there. But for him there were other and higher aims; he wanted glory, nobility, a place in epic tales, and companions who could share those goals.

The climb, he understood, and his sister could understand, was not a succession of impressive gestures; when he taught Kambanal the sometimes shabby, frequently callous devices by which rule was maintained and advanced, it was not to rebuke the younger man's idealism, but on the contrary to make him aware there was no birth without pain and fear and blotches of blood, to make him prize all the more the grandeur of the vision. But Kambanal was an exception, as, at the opposite end, was Freighanai, who had no need of dreams, the faithful man who knew his duty, whose only question was how an object was to be accomplished, leaving policy and conscience to his master. But with the bulk of the Kargul' men, purging last year of the half-hearted had not given him the unmixed devotion he desired, the feeling of shared purpose and the making of history.

Most of all, he was weary of the Hrin. A start had been made on raising new troops among them, and use of lash and exemplary executions greatly reduced the difference between the ordinary Hrin and the other tribes as raw material for his armies. But those he went to for information, the remaining priest-goldsmiths and others of Iolfrant's following, whose submission to a new master had been offered, not demanded, ships' masters of any *onhritha*, were with few exceptions bland, ingratiating and elusive, with the strange lack of any need to make their tales consistent, either with each other or in themselves: the same informant could report the exiled Iolfrant was now desperately short of money, and minutes later that if he still had secret adherents in the Hrin lands, it could only be through constant payment of immense bribes.

He unexpectedly missed the only two of their race who, out of their undiluted selfishness, had occasionally been truly useful to him, Dvasslo and Oyestri, the thin young rat and fat old rat, as Freighanai called them. Guaflidn, Oyestri's replacement as Kambanal's guide to Hrin custom and lore, a minor metalsmith and sometime trader, was younger than his predecessor, less personally repellent, capable of genuine jokes in two acquired languages, but with him as with so many, there was always that guarded pause before an answer came, as if trying to decide what would please his questioner.

Yet largely through his reports Kamin-Tolagh was able to make war on Svedion, whose assistance to his ally-in-exile, Iolfrant, had become intolerable. There had been persistent rumors of Iolfrant's ships making use of Svedion's harbors, and no one could confirm or disprove whether they were sailing and trading as Svedion's; Guaflidn's confident report Iolfrant himself had been seen in full day on the quayside at Tvaidath was enough to to give the excuse for the war Kamin-Tolagh needed to test and harden his rebuilt forces.

He would not risk reliance on subordinates as with the Zelu Bablakhi campaign, still not convinced his personal presence there might not have averted catastrophe: though he did not lead, and never drew a blade, he rode with the main body, able to direct those who sought battle. He found an adversary so unprepared he was actually obliged to pause in his advance, and wait overnight while Svedion collected his army. In forcing this enemy to fight on to the death, Kamin-Tolagh suffered losses, especially to newer squadrons, but to a great extent good casualties, since against an enemy so far from equal those killed werc seldom the best men, but the least disciplined, the inept, those who flinched, and three squadrons so weeded out could be recombined into two better ones. He was encouraged, also, by the success of his newer mounted archers, some four hundred from west of Flamûrai, not with the joyful ferocity of his Hill Froghul, but deadly by any other standard; for the first time in any of his wars, more enemy were disabled by arrows than by blades or lances. On the afternoon of the third day, following a comprehensive and crushing victory in his most determinedly brutal campaign, Svedion a prisoner, Kamin-Tolagh attained the deep, cliff-sheltered harbor of Tvaidath, and wondered if, after all, it would be better to conquer all the Hrin, before invading the old realm With that in mind, he had been doing all he could to build his expeditionary army, and keep it intact, and the decision to postpone any attempt on Kadon Dinul did not much alter the need for that force, whose main purpose from the start had been to ensure he could fight a way to his province. But numbers available were to a large extent determined by the demands of security and order within the Empire, and the swiftness and ease of victory over Svedion set new sums to be balanced. While completing the conquest of the entire Hrinani would cost him casualties, and require added men for ordinary peacekeeping, it would at the same time virtually eliminate the danger he feared most, a sudden treacherous assault from an alliance of the remaining *onhrid*. Kamin-Tolagh's prolonged absence could be the ideal opportunity for such an attack, which might come from any side, or from two or more simultaneously, and guarding against it meant leaving numbers of his best fighting-squadrons in the vicinity of Hyolenstr, where Kambanal could swiftly bring them together.

Nestos was much strongest of the *hrithuod* left in power, but his northward border with Kamin-Tolagh's conquests was indefensible, low and gradual hills which could be crossed at many points. A victory as sudden and complete as here could bring the other minor *hrithuod* to their knees; any losses sustained could be made good in a few months, and next spring at the soonest was when he expected Kamin-Tarú to act.

The palace of Svedion was a skimped lesser version of Iolfrant's where Kambanal now held court, though with the addition of a round central tower with a diminishing spiral stair reaching to a place where a large brass gong was hung. In the echoing central hall of the palace, where, till he had chairs and a table brought, the only seat was a comfortless marble bench on a round stepped dais, directly beneath the tower, its menacing gong high overhead, reflections were interrupted by arrival of a message-rider from Hyolenstr. bringing a letter forwarded by Pivrekhan. Addressed to him in the careful hand of his cyder-making relative in central Ninkufu, the third such passed on to

Kamin-Tolagh, folded inside, as before, were the pages of a letter from Pivrekhan's younger sister, the seamstress at Inilun Barabhi.

It contained, in her breathless, gossipy style, news of unimportant people she and her uncle knew, a complaint about unseasonable cold and wet which, so soon after Halving, had left snow visible on tops of the foothills not many miles away. Connected with that, she surmised, an event for which her fine-sewing would have been in demand, a Great House feast, was cancelled or indefinitely postponed, due to illness of the *Nim'* Tovakh, who had taken to his bed with fever, chills and what the girl called a naughty tummy. He was not believed to be in any danger, though the illness, after getting better, had come back worse. It seemed touching, at least to a seamstress, that Lady Kamin-Tarú had put off her own affairs so as to be at her father's bedside.

This was too soon, sooner than their plans, sooner than full readiness for the expedition. Reading and rereading the symptoms listed in the letter, Kamin-Tolagh could not doubt the poisoning of his father had begun, and had to suppose Kamin-Tarú had acted now to take advantage of some unexpected opening — or, more likely, to prevent something — a marriage, perhaps? No word of an imminent divorce from Petakoi, but if they continued to live apart, Tovakh could accomplish that by simple declaration. Laëntivu, the new bed-partner, warily named in a previous letter, though not much older than Kamin-Tarú, was widow of an officer killed at Dônshei in '42, leaving an infant son, who must now be nine or so; was it not possible the old fool, sotted with gratification after all those years of Petakoi, meant to marry the woman, legally adopt the son, once again displacing Kamin-Tarú from the succession?

Whatever the truth about that guess, facts were unchanged; though the letter had made good time on its long journey, the events it reported were now a month in the past, and if Kamin-Tarú kept to the plan, Tovakh's death would occur within the next fortnight. By that time Kamin-Tolagh's expedition must be at sea, if not already landed in Ninkufu.

He was going to claim the cavalry of Kargul; those were the terms in which he now thought of the invasion; the dash for Kadon Dinul spearheaded by the provincial cavalry, as outlined for his sister, was plainly, for the moment, out of the question.

The more so since the Loyal Address, and Lavsila's obvious discomfiture over an inability to waken any enthusiasm for deposing Rodlakh in favor of Finú; slackening of support for Kamin-Tolagh himself he had continued to blame largely on the unfortunate resolution of the Swan Shrine affair, and the signal it sent to all true Children of Yoëlladhu.

Kamin-Tolagh had been puzzled by Petakoi's reported retreat to the Island, another piece of news about which Iruvakh had no added detail, even though she was said to be in the Patriarch's care; the only explanation was that she must have quarreled with Tovakh over reinstatement of their daughter, obviously accomplished, and Kamin-Tarú's task was actually easier now, with only their father between her and her inheritance. That, once Tovakh's death was accepted as natural, was perfectly lawful, and as *nimu* she could name her brother as captain of her cavalry, defying *rabhsayum* to say otherwise; Rodlakh would surely not want to risk bitter fighting and heavy losses to invade and subdue Kargul. He would try instead to make it into an outlaw province, and to strangle it slowly, but Kamin-Tolagh thought he could count on support, open or covert, of the Great Families, who, though they had acquiesced in his outlawry, would probably assert the right of a lawful *nimu* to name whom she chose to captain her provincial cavalry, and see dangers to themselves in the *rabhsai*'s hostility. With the main breeding-stock for *pefral* outside the *rabhsai*'s control, he could rapidly strengthen both his own cavalry and that of his allies, and there would come a time when the cause of Finú and legitimacy could be revived, backed by enough lances to make it succeed. By that time, too, he should be able to count on a far larger army drawn from his empire.

As Protector, he would expect little trouble controlling Finú, a soft and silly fifty. Her sister Radaghi, however, more formidable though just as crazy, would have to be put out of the way; ten years younger, there was a danger of her remarrying and bearing a child, the Heir, for those who made legitimacy their war-cry in championing Finú. That danger forestalled, the death of Finú, which might reasonably come soon to one so notoriously prone to absent-minded accidents, would allow Kamin-Tolagh to make into law what would already be established fact, his undisputed sway over both realm and western empire.

Much of this, he reflected, was not unlike what might have been achieved years ago, by Tovakh if he had not let Petakoi take charge, by Petakoi if she had not betrayed her husband. Kamin-Tolagh decided when he came to power he would have Petakoi brought back from the Island and tried for complicity in the death of all those killed in the Jinzai War, as Rodlakh should have, years ago. Nor would his *rabhsayum*, that of Finú, have any Arbhai-Navu squeamishness about imposing capital punishment.

The one indispensable element remained his presence at Inilun Barabhi within days of Tovakh's death; despite Petakoi's present exile he could foresee a strong Island-inspired attempt to prevent his sister from consolidating her power, and while he counted on Kamin-Tarú to know and assemble her friends and allies, a warrior would be needed to take charge of loyal elements, and lead them in swift and ruthless action against Petakoi's hirelings.

Most of the ships needed, stocked with supplies, were already at Guodvestr, and if he could find crews, those captured, or left masterless, here at Tvaidath, would make up any deficiency. He sent the message-rider for a lettered soldier to take dictation, one of the Hill Froghul' guards to fetch senior Kargul' officers, and was soon in the midst of orders and discussions. Before the letter came, pondering alternatives, he had come near regretting he and his sister were chained to a plan impossible to modify, and Tovakh's sickness was the cliff-edge, a step there was no going back from. Now, all other considerations swept off the table, everything focused on the one object of getting his invasion force embarked, he was almost blithe, reminded he was in his core a man made to act, not brood, at his best with a clear objective and no room for second thoughts.

Curiously, though he chivvied and threatened, offered rewards to those who made haste and whippings for those who failed to, his own part was largely waiting, once he admitted his presence at waterside in Guodvestr did nothing to quicken the pace of loading supplies, and that the count of men and horses to be assigned to each craft was best left to Pivrekhan, who tottered riskily up and down stone quays, determined to prove he was still useful. For headquarters at the port Kamin-Tolagh took over a hostelry near the harbor — wholly characteristic of the Hrin, their few such establishments were found only in port cities; inland, where the rich did not need, and poor could not afford them, there were nothing but squalid drink-shops where laborers could gather for thin beer and pallid fellowship.

Preparations now in hand, Kambanal rode over from Hyolenstr with his news. Nestos, the *hrithust* Kamin-Tolagh had been at the point of assailing, had already sent a message of congratulation for timely victory over the treacherous Svedion, making an offer for the best of vessels now left without crews. The *Hridveyuth* had also arrived, desiring talk with Kamin-Tolagh.

"My impression is, he is less happy about the defeat of Svedion, concerned about him as a prisoner; he offered himself in exchange for Svedion's freedom."

"Oh, yes. We release a man no one cares about, and bring about an uprising in exchange. Politics is not the *Hridveyuth's* business. We shall try Svedion for abetting our enemy, and hang him — any Hrin should be glad of a quick death."

"Well, if he has to die," was Kambanal's amendment.

Chiefly, Kamin-Tolagh was waiting for needed men to return from Larghamit. Tau-Suaka had been there in the north, in tribal country, with Hunghi-of-the-Whip and two dozen of their men, driving the drills of newly raised levies. When first assigned to that duty, Tau-Suaka had come as close as he dared to disputing the order, observing with suppressed resentment his true task was guarding of his lord. But his lord had to make some attempt to fill the gap left by the defection of Luzhan, and if he could not hope to find another officer with Luzhan's immense patience, his odd harmony with tribal recruits, the only available substitute was the purposeful ferocity with which Tau-Suaka had turned his kinsmen from wild raiders into disciplined, still fearsome fighters. His deputy, Tando had become acting captain of the personal guard, with no detectable loss in vigilance.

Freighanai had also been summoned, and whether he would be included in the expedition was debatable. For the first time, Kamin-Tolagh's formations would be confronted by real cavalry; the port of Thenimala and its hinterland had a Warden's Force less than first-rate, but could call on a standing garrison of

General Cavalry, and unless Rodlakh and Shumat were complete idiots, that must have been considerably strengthened since Kamin-Tolagh gained control of Hrin shipping. Against true *péfrapravádal*, the toughest and most experienced of tribal formations would still need big odds, and to make those numbers count called for as many of the best field officers as Kamin-Tolagh could take. Freighanai would be invaluable, but against that was the continued need to defend the Empire. Already decided, Kambanal would be left behind; his soldierly skills were of equal value in any place, but to take him would be to waste his abilities as an administrator, not to say his standing with the Hrin. The north, true, had remained relatively quiet; unlikely the Army of the West would see an invasion of Ninkufu as opportunity for striking at the Abu, the tribes of the Froghushei had accustomed themselves to the yoke of an empire which continued to improve most daily lives, and even west of Flamûrai major incursions of years past had dwindled to occasional raiding and banditry. In the end, Freighanai's own assessment of the military situation there would determine whether he was to be part of the expedition.

Lavsila would have no option; he was coming; after years assuring Kamin-Tolagh of growing support within the old realm he could not be permitted to stay in comfort at Larghamit while others went to test that thesis. If he had a use, it was for his pen, and Kamin-Tolagh could foresee the need for numbers of carefully-worded communications, to provincial overlords courting their support, the *rabhsai* — in reality, to the realm at large — explaining and justifying seizure of power in Kargul. A request had gone to Larghamit for Lavsila to come south at once, but the orders sent sealed for Freighanai had instructed him to be sure the *sranim'* accompanied him. He would no doubt protest his absence would leave the north without his guidance, but law in the tribal lands was administered by headmen and enforced when necessary by soldiery; as for Larghamit and the Abu, Kamin-Tolagh, setting his teeth, resolved to ask one of the Heartlanders to act as a kind of warden and city elder in one. Not the loud-voiced, assertive Pranúdhanai, whose pretensions would be resented by the soldiers' families, but the former poet and present shopowner, Tavrotosai, who had a reputation for good judgment, and whose family had for generations provided magistrates for the Abfekh region of the Heartland.

Reaching this rather unexpected decision, he allowed a tight smile for the care he was taking over an empire which could hardly hope to survive if he failed in his mainland venture, but which, with all the talents of Kargul and the realm to draw on, would with his success move unimaginably beyond the stopgap strategies of the past eight years. He must keep his gaze to the fore, not distractingly back over his shoulder.

The *Hridveyuth* said, "Time, my Lord, to test which wind is to blow the leaves." He had come striding into Guodvestr, and Kamin-Tolagh had told his guard to admit the man, before the handful of gaping onlookers grew to a crowd.

"How do you know this?" While resolutely unimpressed by the *Hridveyuth* as an inspirer of religious faith, Kambanal had allowed his insights were sometimes amazingly accurate, and Kamin-Tolagh had chided his credulity; the man made lucky guesses, and inflated the results of keen observation to sound as utterances from dark spirits.

He gestured. "These preparations are for things beyond a trading voyage. Lords who go to battle must not be misled by contempt."

He decided to be good-natured. "Whose?"

"Theirs. The *Hrithust* Iolfrant scorned your armies, which he said were made from twig-house people of the north."

"I have anything but contempt for those we are going to battle with. They have more *pefral*." He could be flippant, with his bows proved in battle.

"Not all places, Lord, are to be reached on a horse's back, even a *pefrai*'s. Those who stand still may end by going farther."

"Riddles to make serving-maids gape." Irritation was immediate.

An easy laugh. "Awe is to belief what jealousy is to love, sign of weakness. I do not wish to make anyone gape; I speak as plainly as I can."

"Then tell me your purpose. If you desire to make the Hrin people one, why would you plead for the life of Svedion? His overthrow makes one *onhritha* where there were two, puts an end, also, to the *dveyust-ranga-hrindan*; now all Hrin can believe as one."

"A man with a pack of hunting-dogs that are always fighting, could cure it by killing all but one. But then he would no longer have the pack. The Hrin are one people, and their differences are Hrin, also."

"If they came to see themselves as one, who would be their overlord, *hrithust* of *hrithuod*?" A wasted question; this man was too wily to admit personal ambition.

"One who would seek what it is said the *rabhsai* of your birthland seeks when he is raised to power, guidance of truth."

"With you as its interpreter?"

"Lord, I do not interpret. I only speak what comes to me."

For the final night before embarkation, having returned to Hyolenstr and to the house by the river, Kamin-Tolagh decided he would cross the small bridge over the canal, and sleep alone where he and Kamin-Tarú had spent their happiest times — and where, since her departure, he had enjoyed a procession of young tribal women, less various in retrospect than they individually appeared, but serving their function, his diversion.

He had dined with a Kambanal soberly aware he would be real ruler of the Empire till Kamin-Tolagh returned, a taciturn Freighanai impatient to be started now all preparations were complete, Niburai with many too many questions, and Lavsila, who, running out of excellent but unacceptable reasons why he should deny himself a part in an expedition he yearned to be with, had discovered as many arguments for postponing departure.

"I would feel happier, Lord, with some word from one of my informants as to the landowners' exact purpose with their Loyal Address; it would be best to concert our ideas with theirs. In a few months, maybe — your armies, too, will be stronger."

"No matter what time we chose, there would be some part not perfectly prepared — " recognizing to an extent Lavsila spoke for all; clearly everyone had been puzzled by his abrupt urgency.

"It has always been my plan," he improvised, "to begin as soon as the troops had been tested in battle. Between our Heartlanders and Iruvakh's *atarlal*, Kadon Dinul has timely word of everything we do. To keep this to myself was the only certain way to be ashore ahead of the news of our coming."

Freighanai and Niburai left early, riding for Guodvestr so they could be on the quays at first light, overseeing embarkation and loading of last supplies. Lavsila sat a while with Kamin-Tolagh and Kambanal, drinking a pink Hrin wine, then asked leave so he could write to Khalú, left at Larghamit. Till now he must have led her to expect he would be able to excuse himself from the expedition, and be back in a few days.

Kambanal's conclusions about this venture were an enigma. A man of large natural curiosity, there were infinite questions he might have asked, about its purpose, tactics, duration, chances of success, the true reasons for its abrupt urgency. He chose: "The expedition, Lord. Is it possible, pardon me, you will be reunited with your lady sister?"

Curiosity, flavored with soldierish sentimentality, odder in that Kambanal could hardly approve generally of brothers and sisters as lovers.

"Why do you ask?"

The younger man kept his head down. "Anyone can see Kamin-Tarú *Asayu* has been missed here." Now his eyes came up, and whether he knew it or not, this was an offer of actual friendship — one Kamin-Tolagh might be able to accept, at some future time, with his place so high and secure it could not be assailed or diminished in revealing true feelings, hopes, fears, to a close circle of intimates.

Over whom, after all, he would hold unchallenged the power of life and death. He said, "Many things are to change, that I know."

From the sideboard, he took an elaborately ornamented scabbard, and partially drew the finely chased sword for Kambanal to admire.

"This blade, over seventy years ago, in the hands of Rodlakh's grandfather, Saidhan, killed my great-uncle Tobhsila. That enabled Banak, other grandfather of Rodlakh, to seize the powers of *rabhsai*."

"How did the sword come to you, then?"

"In a mood of gratitude for my part in the Jinzai War, a mood that soon waned, Saidhan handed me this sword."

"So to say, he wished you could be *rabhsai*, over his grandson?"

A quick grin. "Hardly. A token, he said, between his house and mine, the end of old enmity, a pledge of peace, honor, fair dealing." He slid the blade home.

"And so I became Captain of Household to the usurper's grandson, and was lied to, excluded from his inmost counsel, sent to the West fed with earnest untruths, my triumphs here ignored or condemned. I am, as you know, an outlaw, just as Tobhsila was proclaimed to be."

Kambanal said nothing, rapt, not having heard him in this dynastic mood, whose force surprised Kamin-Tolagh himself.

"You have seen this at my side, never bared. I would not draw this blade against *jinzal*, against the half-tamed of the Froghushei, nor overtamed Hrin, but I have kept it sharp. Tomorrow, it goes home with me. Perhaps there it can find a heart worthy of its history."

40.

Quite reasonably, Dolvid thought, it could be asked why he, the *Bôdhrai* whose place, when not in the Colony, was at Kadon Dinul, a *nimu*, moreover, entitled to have the hard work done for him, was riding, road-weary and damp, with a small, silent escort, down the last slope to the outskirts of Kanzan Tâl, in the afternoon of a cheerless late-autumn day.

Shumat could have given a forceful answer, *interfering!* — and an unflattering reason, *nerves!* — but Shumat was a long way from here, far in the north, and his sortie from Kadon Dinul was contributory to Dolvid's, each of them pursuing a preoccupation; disturbed by ominous news, upset more by scarcity of news from the distant Northeast, where in summer the sea-raiders were thought to have established a less ephemeral foothold on the coast, Shumat had finally badgered Rodlakh into permitting him to take reinforcements there in person. There was some justice in his pointed comment, that Narn, no less than Ninkufu, was an important part of the realm, and territory actually invaded by unnamed corsairs was at least as worthy of his attention as parts conjecturally threatened by a Kamin-Tolagh baKargul, yet there was a difference; no one had suggested or could dream any raider of the Northeast had power to strike at Kadon Dinul, or attempt to depose the *rabhsai*; Narn was in fact farther from the capital than Kamin-Tolagh at the Abu that used to be Lunu Jinzalladhiyu, and the immense northern journey would increasingly be hampered by snows as winter came. For that same reason, Shumat, who had left before Halving, having spent, as promised, no longer than it took to assess danger and initiate a cure, had already begun the return journey, before he could be trapped by weather.

His absence had been, in another sense, Dolvid's opportunity for a brief tour of southward garrisons to assess their readiness; Shumat would have seen through the flimsy excuse he had used, urgent need for a conference with *Nim'* Laënakh at Nivu Din about a point of law, and there would have been another storm over an obsession Dolvid could fully explain only by shamefaced reference to his recurrent nightmare, Rodlakh and Kamin-Tolagh reliving the tale of Saidhan and Tobhsila, but with an outcome not known.

More peaceably, then, before leaving, he had been able to confer with Kizhunai, Captain-Counsellor for Armies, and what he heard was not altogether reassuring. Thenimala itself was up to its increased strength, and so was the fortress city of Kir, where auxiliary bows could readily be levied, but reinforcements for three cavalry stations between those widely-separated points had been delayed, most recently when Shumat was collecting every available man for his expedition to the Northeast.

Kizhunai, with the elaborate tolerance always encountered when questioning professionals on military matters, insisted the provincial cavalry of Nîv, together with the royal garrison at Kanzan Tâl, would, as the Captain said, make it a long march north for any enemy; even the Household were nearer the southern border here than Thenimala was.

"I do not doubt any invader could be defeated before he saw the Heartland, but we have to consider the damage he could inflict on peaceable people — look what no more than two dozen were able to do over in the Lunu Tezh'. We have no considerable forces up in the north of Ninkufu?"

A shake of the head. "A couple of squadrons; there is nothing much to guard, there. That post is really a way-station with fresh mounts for message-riders, and a beer place for travellers across Ní-Tilagh."

If you did not count civil war, not for some eight or nine centuries had the Old Realm east of Arnan been invaded, and Dolvid must be to Kizhunai a timorous nuisance, inventing improbable perils to compensate for lack of real work. Yet when, tactfully, he mentioned he would look in on some of the southward garrisons on his journey to Nivu Din, Kizhunai said only it could do no harm to keep them on their toes.

The cursed *nimum* again; he was now too eminent to be resisted head-on, and like any lord would be humored to his face, only ridiculed in his absence. Yet with Kizhunai he had formerly and for years been on terms of a mutual respect he had thought genuine.

"Your son, Captain, is still unwed?" Badh-Kizhai Kizhunati had attained a small, unwitting place in the annals by being the one to take Morulis, or be taken by her, to the summer-house where they had been surprised by her husband, the occasion of the beating that brought about Elamirr's fall.

Kizhunai nodded, and was all at once confiding. "In my day, *Bôdhr'asai*, we used to say, sport for pleasure, take a wife for estate and to get children, and never speak vows with the candle standing straight, if you see what I mean."

"I have heard of such things."

"No matter what foolery we got up to, we had the sense to price jewels that might be our own, not hunger for a ruby ring off a *rabhsai*'s finger."

Kizhunai had a touch of songmaker concealed under his immaculate military tunic; dark bloom of a Navuki ruby was instantly evocative of Morulis. Agony, no doubt, for Badh-Kizhai, these persistent yearnings were good news for Dolvid; there was a possible solution for Rodlakh's dilemma.

When bidding good road, the *rabhsai* had come near yielding to Dolvid's sudden suggestion they ride together, as in past times now measurelessly distant, a chance to reestablish some of the old intimacy, hint he was making too much of the entanglement with Morulis. But after wistful thought, Rodlakh had shaken his head, saying he had too many commitments at Kadon Dinul. "Commitments," he repeated.

Kanzan Tâl, smugly nestled behind its famous Golden Walls, liked to call itself the city of chance meetings. Meeting place, certainly, of roads; the Royal Way, broad and well-kept, swooped down into the faint dell of the main city, mounting on the far side to continue its long march south, from southwest met by another good road which, not many miles beyond, sent branches on either side of the great Kôbh river, serving respectively the Lower Paowan and northern shores of Kargul. Yet another way, most used by farming folk, least by travellers, climbed more steeply from Kanzan Tâl's eastward side, winding away into distant reaches of the province, to lanes and tracks that would lead to empty Asekh, to the hills of the Upper Dakbân, an entire unknown world.

All the realm rests at Kanzan Tâl, its hospitable inhabitants proclaimed, if an overstatement, a beneficial one, to the extent that pride had made its hostelries eagerly competitive, one with another, boasting collectively any food, any wine, any pleasure of the known world could be enjoyed here.

The captain of garrison, Mattin, must by now be accustomed to use of the Military Commander's residence as another of Kanzan Tâl's hostelries, this one for the high, the rich and the titled; practically the only house of consequence here, hence an overnight resting-place for provincial overlords, their wives and retinues, on journeys to and from Kadon Dinul. Influential Heartlanders, with villas on nearby Shelum-shore, also spent the occasional night. The house, with its wide courtyard, extensive stables and roomy wings, imposingly made of the same tawny stone that gave the Golden Walls their name, dated from times when military commander was also magistrate and administrator for the region, normally connected by blood to the Great Families. Mattin, a good, somewhat colorless acting-captain, his responsibilities limited to the garrison, occupied the great house like a caretaker.

Lean and long-faced, his surprise was barely perceptible when he understood he was not expected to make his usual discreet withdrawal, that one of his elevated guests actually wanted to confer with him. He and Dolvid had first met at the Battle of Dônshei, when Mattin, then a *kímukan*, leader of those General Cavalry who refused to follow Bolan against the banner of their *rabhsai*, had been as defiantly unrepentant as any good soldier whose conscience forces him to the unthinkable act of mutiny. Still unmarried, he was of an age with Shumat — also Dolvid's age, although now, entering the mid-forties, was when the longer normal lifespan of the Owani began to tell; not for a dozen years would Dolvid expect to show these thickenings and thinnings, signs of middle life.

Once he began to forget he was addressing the *Nim'* of Nowhere (as Dolvid wryly styled himself) what Mattin had to tell was agreeably unexpected; his slightly under-strength squadrons maintained at battle-readiness by means of exercises which must seem pointless to men at the safe heart of a peaceful realm. Better, Mattin, through constant revision, kept current the muster-rolls of bowmen and other auxiliaries available at need, confidently asserting that given twelve hours he could have four thousand bows, all with assigned positions behind the Golden Walls. He took Dolvid to see his impressive store of arrows, kept from weather in what had been a feed-barn near the stables, enough to give each archer a bundle of two dozen to add to those already in his possession.

Asked about men he could quickly send to a distant battlefield, he was less positive; he had already given up two squadrons in a northward shift that freed men from Dônshei Bridge for Shumat's campaign, and was, with every captain in the whole history of armies, dubious about the wisdom of contributing any more. Told, rather, it would be a question of putting this command in such order that he could personally lead a battle force, Mattin had no further reservations, and asserted he could have three-quarters of his regulars moving with saddle-supplies within hours.

This was over an early dinner. After, Dolvid, left alone, was recording his observations, thinking about a letter to Aëlu, when a servant sent by Mattin announced another visitor had arrived. Returning to the main hall, he found himself being embraced and warmly kissed by Kamin-Tarú, who at last light had ridden in from the south.

Though swathed in a shapeless riding-cloak, and with a indefinable air of distress or anxiety, she appeared, was there a word? *grander* than he remembered her: perhaps with the dignity of a landowner. After the rupture in his marriage, Tovakh had bestowed on his daughter large parts of the lands that had been Petakoi's. These included the lodge with its lands above Peframi Gorge, which this summer, for unmarried men of family, had become a truer place of pilgrimage than the nearby, spurious Tomb of *Kirova-Kindhri* had ever been. Vinodhai of Dramal had gone there, and so had his adoptive cousin, the younger, more personable Tansilakh of Nîv. The inextinguishable Island candidate, Pedh-Sivai, had attempted to regain in marriage what he had once thought his by adoption, and afterwards, again thwarted, joined Petakoi on Kamanta. Even the former unwilling decoy, Taërinat, had visited Kamin-Tarú, and whether or not she adopted the same technique of contrition as had succeeded with her father, she sent him away still a bachelor, but, so was said, with his rancor all dissolved. Only Orbanak failed to make the journey, remaining at Kadon Dinul, proud but not unconsoled; he appeared to alternate between two girls of the Families, without suffering much pain.

"This is lucky," she said. "You, above anyone, I was hoping to see." In the smaller dining-hall, she had the slightest edged look for the solicitous Mattin, who, catching a hint he had seen before, made sure food and hot drinks would be brought, fire adequately stoked, before performing his well-rehearsed disappearance.

Impatient to speak, Kamin-Tarú had difficulty beginning, and when she did, the question was an odd one: "If my brother were to be defeated in a war against the realm, what would happen to him?"

Dolvid had often wondered. "Kamin-Tolagh," tentatively, "is always in the forefront of any battle."

"Anyone who makes war might be killed. You do not have to speak to me as a child."

"If he were wounded and captured," acknowledging the rebuke, "I say, wounded, because I cannot imagine he would let himself be taken while he could fight — "

"Would Rodlakh have to put him to death?"

A difficult question, *have to* the core; Rodlakh had followed — or restored — the tradition of the House Arbhai-Navu by opposing death as a remedy for crime, but a captive traitor, capable of bringing death to thousands, was different from an ordinary lawbreaker, and Kamin-Tarú's tormented face meant this was no hypothetical case. "I do not see how he could ever be freed. What word could he give for his future behavior? He was among first to swear personal allegiance, and took another vow as Captain of the Household — is there an oath he has not broken?"

"He would never endure captivity. He would take his own life."

She was anguished enough for it to be accomplished fact. "He has yet to make open war on the realm," Dolvid reminded her.

"How has he become what he is? Tam was not like this, filled with death and the infliction of pain. He was too proud to be other than honorable."

All this she had said before, when first she left him, and Dolvid was mystified why it needed saying again, as if she had to persuade herself.

Calming, she shook hair away from her face. "He is coming."

"Here?"

"To invade us. I am sure of it."

"When?"

"Now, in days; he may already be at sea. My father, you know, was ill, but he is better now."

"I passed him on the road, near Bathrâd." Riding with a squadron of his provincials, a half-squadron of General Cavalry ceremonially accompanying, on his way, he said, to give Vinilat another chance to cancel their autumn hunting. That sardonicism aside, he was more cordial than Dolvid ever recalled; if he had ever known it was Dolvid who wounded him at Dônshei in '42, he no longer bore any grudge, sitting easy in the saddle to gossip for a while. Tovakh's sly remark about bed-hunting together with the *rabhsai* instead, a jocular reference to both Morulis and his own young widow, would surely have been made only to a brother-*nim'*, but his speaking at all of his Laëntivu in terms of lechery made less likely he contemplated making her his wife.

"I hope Vinilat is indisposed. My father thinks he is still a boy, to ride all day in a cold rain, then take his meal and sit in talk while his clothes dry on him. That's how he became sick in the first place."

"Not that he is old," hastily, as if Dolvid would be offended by that assessment of a man twenty years his senior.

How all this bore on the question of imminent invasion by Kamin-Tolagh was still obscure, and Kamin-Tarú was struggling to supply the connection. Picking up her cup with the warm *raminat*, Dolvid led her to fireside, and when she was seated, gently prompted her. After a deep breath, she began talking in a flat voice to the fire, and soon the hairs on his neck started to prickle, as she told all about a fantastic plan of Kamin-Tolagh's, whereby she was to have poisoned both her parents. No longer puzzling, what she had said last year, coming off Landegh, that her brother had *proposed acts to shame our lineage*. Not to say, obliterate it.

"You pretended to fall in with this?" Here, at last, was the hidden reason Kamin-Tolagh had not prevented his sister's departure.

"I never said I would not do it, and he took that for consent. It was the only way I could see to leave him. I could not stay with him, as he had become. To believe I would agree to such a scheme is proof enough of his madness."

Dolvid, helped by Aëlu, understood what Tú did not and could not say: revolted as she was by her brother's atrocities, she had still needed his unwitting help in almost pushing her away.

"My intention was to do nothing. His skin-bag of poisons, with a large stone added, I drowned in the middle of Arnan. I thought Tam would wait, and wait, and at last see I was not going to carry out his murders. Then he could get on with his empire in the West, and I could live my own life; there must be many brothers and sisters who go their own ways — "

"Indeed — " amused and oddly touched by the need for this assertion.

"When my father was ill just past Halving, I gave it very little thought; he came back to health; I had business on my own lands, and there is no great friendship between me and the wonderful widow, who is, take my word Dolvid, no Aëlu, and her son is a barracks-bred lout. How — " She checked herself.

She had been back at Inilun last week, for her father's departure or in a vain attempt to prevent it, and then, just three days ago, had called in Pivrekhan's small sister, to do some fine-sewing on a gown.

"And," Dolvid prompted firmly, convinced she was about to give details about the alterations she had wanted.

"We talked of my father going to hunt, and she said it was marvellous, really, when he had just been so poorly, and it is not the same when you get past a certain age, as she said when she was writing to her uncle in Ninkufu." Kamin-Tarú regarded Dolvid, waiting for the ripe plum to fall.

He had it, Tú having described in detail the action of the two poisons. "That was to be Kamin-Tolagh's signal. Her letter will have been forwarded to him in the West."

"I was supposed to spend a month-and-a-half poisoning my father," and now she could sound for a moment derisive. "To give Kamin-Tolagh time for his invasion. He had said, the first few days after my succession would be his moment."

A three-part plan, seizure of Finú and securing the provincial cavalry, both to serve the main object, a march on Kadon Dinul to depose the *rabhsai*. But beyond the landing in the south, she knew nothing about the larger strategy, not hard to guess; a northward thrust with his main forces, and then Kamin-Tolagh, with fast-moving troops, would make a dash for his home province. He would wish to reach Inilun Barabhi to claim what he supposed would be the vacant *nimum*, and no doubt hope to gain support, on his way, of the provincial garrisons. With Rodlakh's best forces drawn well to the south, into Nîv or even the Ní-Tilagh, to defend against the invading army, cavalry of Kargul under Kamin-Tolagh would race north and hope to take a surprised and under-defended Kadon Dinul. Alternatively, he would strike at Kadon Dinul across Arnan, transporting the provincial cavalry by ship from one of Kargul's ports; but the first alternative, hoping to trap large royal armies between his main force and Kanzan Tâl, was much the likeliest. If Tovakh had indeed abruptly died, Dolvid was far from certain the plan would not have succeeded in purely military terms: fallacy crept in with the idea that by taking Kadon Dinul, Kamin-Tolagh could supplant Rodlakh and his house, when it would be only beginning of a war he would inevitably lose. But as Dolvid deduced and Kamin-Tarú confirmed, Lavsila had constantly exaggerated support Kamin-Tolagh could expect to receive in the Heartland.

"Now, without the cavalry of Kargul," Tú said, or asked, "he cannot hope to accomplish this."

"Nor, pardon me, could he with it." Dolvid had a strong sympathy for Kamin-Tarú's dilemma. Not everything she had done had been heroic, or even creditable, and she blamed herself for cowardice in hoping passively the plan would die, rather than making clear to her brother, after she reached Inilun Barabhi, that she was no longer his ally. Her first and natural thought on realizing how he would take the description of his father's illness was to find a way to tell him it was a mistake, prevent his setting sail. Seeing she was already too late for that, she had set out for Kadon Dinul, not clear in her mind how much she was going to reveal, but with the notion that if Kamin-Tolagh arrived in a realm fully prepared to resist him, if he could then learn Tovakh was alive and in good health, he might withdraw. "He has not become foolish. He will not fight where the odds are hopeless." Alternatively, he might be made to surrender, the reason for her initial questions of Dolvid.

"But if he is kept locked up, and takes his own life, I still have killed him." She was very near tears. Dolvid tried to give comforting, but his mind was racing away to dispatches that must be written, for fast-messengers to take on overnight rides, and calling a servant he asked for a quick and accurate scribe to be brought.

Kamin-Tarú smiled waterily. "The Hrin would say, our *tveyusta* is to meet so, on the road, by chance. There is no one else I could have told so much. After all that has happened, I still want my brother to live."

"If he is captured, and any guarantee could be found for his conduct, I would actively connive at his escape, if he would return to his West, and keep the peace."

"But he kills men there," unintentionally rebuking Dolvid's clemency. "I can't think of anyone he has not spoken of killing, when the time comes — oh, not me, never me. I am to sit next to him, and applaud as he invents new ways to make death interesting. That was in my mind when I left Inilun Barabhi; he cannot win, but if he did win, pure Owani as our blood is, his rule would be worse than any tainted Arbhai-Navu. A thousand times worse, and he would want me at his side, relishing all our splendor." She shuddered, and again Dolvid was reminded of Aëlu, with her prediction from experience: *Poor Kamin-Tarú. She will never find anything to replace the excitement of that power.*

Yet deliberately to lighten the mood while he waited for his scribe, he asked abruptly, "Do you mean to marry Orbanak?"

The old Tú came back, yet for an instant nearer discomposure than he had seen her, outside a bed. "Not just yet," becoming smug.

"If I am permitted, let me say it does very well." He was not solely thinking such a union would virtually will Kargul to become a true part of the realm, with the *rabhsai*'s loyal brother, considering his wife's impatience for state affairs, effective heir.

"They will say he is too young for me."

"Whoever you choose," with the gallantry she so readily aroused, "men will urge good reasons against it." In purely practical terms, the difference would be all to the good, thirty years on, when Orbanak's physical age would have caught and passed hers, the unmixed Owaniyu. "Orbanak is in some things older than most men will ever be; he is not afraid to show his gentler side."

A side which would surely prevail with Kamin-Tarú; as often in recent years, Dolvid wondered whether, for most people, any idea of morality was innate, or whether the boundaries of the permissible were entirely defined by their alliances and associations, the ethics of a chosen time and place — as also by how much power they possessed to act upon whims, tantrums, purely selfish desires.   At Drin Navuna, Kamin-Tarú had recounted, with no trace of remorse, in fact with some pride, how, when playing out the estrangement from her brother, she had the five tribal serving-girls whipped, so to make her anger more convincing. By the standards of Kamin-Tolagh's domains, a very minor cruelty, but one hardly to be tolerated, or even imagined, in Orbanak's sphere — although, like Rodlakh, like Dolvid himself, he might reluctantly keep prescribed pain as answer to the most atrocious crimes.

Unwillingly, and with a shudder, he remembered beloved Âna coolly suggesting they could have Elamirr murdered, and that, till turned into a joke, had been quite real. If by a sequence of events far from inconceivable, Sebhal had become *rabhsai* and divorced Aëlu to marry Âna, perhaps she would have become Sebhal's equal for harsh and arbitrary solutions — what Aëlu called impatience.

One thing of value Tú had brought back from the West; she was more patient now, content to sit sipping her drink while Dolvid put in motion the machinery of the realm, no longer fidgeting or sighing, as she once had when attention strayed from her. Mattin came, and said he could find as many as four fast-messengers accustomed to night riding, and let himself be bid up to five when Dolvid was struck by a new thought. Kamin-Tolagh was said to be going heavily to archers, and massed bows were a problem for which the best and most inventive cavalry captains never hit on any better solution than improved body-armor, and braver cavalrymen, to keep going forward with men and mounts dying around them. But Kamin-Tolagh would have to do the attacking here, and to stand against him Dolvid wanted the companies of pikes from Banakit. To fill invaluable ships with infantry at this crucial time was a decision to infuriate Shumat as much as it would delight his son.

To reach Shumat, somewhere in the north, the first message written was already on its way. At best estimate, Kamin-Tolagh could be ashore as soon as eight days from now, and Shumat, when last heard from, was at Sebira, at least that far from here for a fast rider. But that news was not less than a week old, and if he had marched without pause, he should by now be nearing Dônshei, if not already beyond there, in which case there was time for him to bring his forces south before Kamin-Tolagh could cross the Ní-Tilagh.

The other commanders, to whom, south and north, messages were going, to be endorsed and sent on, would say it did not matter; with or without Shumat's presence, Kamin-Tolagh had no chance of reaching the realm proper. After years, literally, of sounding his warnings about Ninkufu, Dolvid had to resist an urge to warn the captains not to concentrate too much to the south. An advantage of rank was that he had no need to authenticate how he knew invasion was coming; *information has reached me* was more explanation than a good soldier had right to expect, though for Shumat he had given a little added detail.

The *rabhsai* had to be told, and with this message greater care was required; taking the pen himself rather than dictating to the scribe, Dolvid felt the loom of all old forebodings. Rodlakh's first thought would be to lead troops in person, and he had to be told his presence on the battlefield would merely confer on Kamin-Tolagh the ability to wound the realm beyond his actual powers, and to do so even in defeat. A brief note for Âna was to enlist her in the same cause, and there was another for Orbanak, hoping he would use his persuasions. In this case there was double purpose, since keeping his exalted brother away from fighting would necessarily do the same for himself.

"If there is to be word for Orbanak," Kamin-Tarú warned from fireside, just as he was writing the name. "He is not aware yet of his intent to make me his wife." She was smiling conspiratorially.

"When he learns," with a laugh, "he will, I predict, be more than delighted."

Going back to his message for the Colony, he thought of an improvement. He said to Kamin-Tarú, "I am bringing troops from Kamsilat. It would save time and weariness if they could be landed at Zelkova, and marched through the eastern region of your province. Will permission be waived?"

"Permission is granted. I grant it. And I'll go to Zelkova, if you would wish, to be sure there is no procedural delay." Other kinds of authority came with ownership of lands.

"What are your plans?" she asked, when the last message had been sent, and Mattin instructed, "Your own."

He had none. After furious activity, he was not urgently needed anywhere, though in the morning he would ride on southward to confirm he had made things begin to move.

"I must have a bath," she said, standing. "You remember those Vrobanil baths, east of Kadon Dinul?"

"I could hardly forget." He wondered if she also remembered at that time they had been going to ask her brother's help against *jinzal*.

She was laughing. "When I discovered they belonged to her father, I asked Khalú whether you had enjoyed them. Well, have you?"

This was her old style of open provocation, to lighten his heart; a broad grin was his only answer.

She made herself mockingly demure. "But I was about to say, if you are done for now, would you wish to come to my bed? For the sake of old acquaintance?"

For the sake, also, Dolvid guessed, of not being alone with the reproaching ghosts. He rose and bowed. "Nothing could give me greater pleasure."

Memory said, no mere figure of speech, but while eyes and touch agreed she was more desirable than ever, and she was not diminished in either enthusiasm or accomplishment, he was below his best, back of his mind churning with troop movements, counting days, with Kamin-Tolagh and Rodlakh coming closer together. Not disconcerted, she did not pretend not to notice, and told him to be patient; for a while they simply lay side by side, and she began to talk about a young man or boy of the tribes, named Chamya, whose death at her brother's hands was, above any other, the act that caused her to leave him.

"This was not hatred — he was proud of Chamya, as his own invention, and killed him for *policy*. He built a house for us, there, in the Man-mani village, where they call him a god," an almost whispered aside. "As if I could be happy in that place."

She told an entire story like one recounting a dream, making clear, but with none of her customary playfulness on the subject, that she had bedded the youth, and enjoyed doing so. When she came again to Chamya's death: "Such a waste. My brother said the same, but he could teach other men of the Man-mani to speak the Owanilú, or to manage a *pefrai*, to carry a lance like one of our princelings. The real pity is, Chamya was the only man of his tribe to learn how to be with a woman. They can make children, those men, but they need to be taught how to love."

By intent, an implied comparison here, warmly stimulating to Dolvid. More and more, as life lengthened, he was able to surrender to what he once would have called sentimentality, and discover his best pure sport was at the heart of aroused affection. Not to be summoned at will, and he doubted there was anything about it in any of the reputedly comprehensive manuals of variegated ecstasy, but when, as now, all at once present, inciting beyond all comparison, renewing itself through the gratitude fulfillment created. Their *tveyusta*, if that was the word, his and Tú's, was to create simplest and most accomplished joy together at times when the future of the realm trembled in precarious balance.

41.

Violating established wise procedure, Kamin-Tolagh sailed in a ship which also contained Freighanai, Niburai and Lavsila, as well as Tau-Suaka. This, he reasoned, was not an army whose mission, under a deputy, could survive death of its commander; if he drowned, the invasion was over before it began; who else died with him was of no military consequence.

Besides, there were strategies to settle; the landing, from so many ships, was bound to be disorderly, most of his attention and that of his officers going to sorting the troops and matching them to their mounts; no time for plans to be calmly discussed, particularly if they were interrupted or awaited by defenders.

One hundred and fourteen vessels of every size had set sail. To attempt holding together such a mixed fleet would have been difficult, by night dangerous, yet landing in force was necessary, in case they were resisted. The dilemma had been resolved in talk with Hrin mariners who, when the weather was rough, never attempted the rock-sown approaches to Thenimala, but waited out the storm at anchor among a small group of islands to the southwest of Ninkufu, known to them as Antan Dezhuni, of which the largest, Dezhun Raiba, in the shape of a crescent moon, was itself a vast protected harbor. Allowed to divide into many smaller flotillas, the entire fleet would reassemble there, and hope for calm seas and steady breezes to keep them together for the final stage.

The main landing would be made not at or near Thenimala, but far north of there, on the narrow neck of the Ninkufu Peninsula, dry, empty country at the fringes of the Ní-Tilagh, and a whole day nearer his real goal.

"Is this wise?" Lavsila, perhaps with comfortable sleeping-quarters in mind. "Quite aside from the prestige of capturing a city, the port, in your hands, would be a great asset."

"At Thenimala," with labored patience, "they keep a watch seaward. We would have to fight our way ashore, and maybe fight in the streets. As you have seen at Larghamit, these ships do very well without wharves, and can be beached anywhere. The port can be taken at our leisure, when we have cut its lifeline to the realm."

If that, he did not say, was within their present capacities. That there was not going to be any immediate attempt on Kadon Dinul, that all other original objectives of the invasion were now thoroughly subordinate to a singleminded determination to reach his home province in time to claim its cavalry, none of this been revealed to anyone, though Freighanai would have to be told, after the landing. But Niburai, who, with nearly a third of the whole force, was to reach Kred' Ludhai and secure the persons of Finú and her sister Radaghi, Niburai with his nurtured taste for heroic achievement, would fight better not knowing his action now was nothing but a diversion to draw defenders too far to the south, and keep them occupied while Kamin-Tolagh advanced northward.

At the island anchorage was a two-day delay. One slower-moving cluster of about thirty vessels was overdue, and Kamin-Tolagh was reluctant to proceed, since the missing ships, with many spare mounts, also held over one hundred of the mounted bows which were to be the striking force to atone for any deficiency in his cavalry.

On the second night, sleep not coming, he emerged from the partitioned deck-house into bright moonlight, a night cool but calm, the host of ships, tethered in ranks, riding easily on the slow swell.

"Lord — " Tau-Suaka, out of shadow, addressed him. "Lord, after this victory, I shall wish to be married."

"You have a wife." The woman he had shepherded out of the Great Fire, now mother to his four offspring.

"Lord, we are nothing now."

"That is your business, not mine."

"Yes, Lord." Tau-Suaka exhaled noisily through his teeth. "Lord, I now desire a woman of the Man-mani."

In the old raiding days, he would simply have taken her, killing husband, father, or brothers as necessary. Perhaps the woman, in the past, had been one of Kamin-Tolagh's, and Tau-Suaka wanted to be sure of giving no offense.

"Do I know this woman?"

"You know her well, Lord, the mother from the head-man's hut, Osré-dnë."

Taken altogether by surprise, Kamin-Tolagh did not immediately answer. The Man-mani valley was where Tau-Suaka had been training tribal levies, but that he and the woman had so much as a language in common was news. Since Chamya's death, the Man-mani had remained without a head-man, and Osré-dnë had been chief arbiter of their disputes. But a changed tribe, prosperity, military service, intermarriage with other tribes loosening the grip of their traditions; Kamin-Tolagh had heard the Man-mani youths now regarded rope-catching as only a game, holding that to be trained as a soldier was the true sign of manhood.

The match was unthinkable. As his personal guard, and to strengthen their devotion, all the Hill Froghul had been encouraged to regard themselves as apart from common men: at Hyolenstr he had lodged them in one of the lesser palaces, and given them servants for their off-duty hours; their decorated blue-and-silver tunics were, or so they believed, envy of an empire, and their captain must consider himself almost equal in standing to Kambanal. That did no harm so long as Kamin-Tolagh remained unquestioned master. But clearly out of the question for his bodyguard to be commanded by a man whose wife had no doubt Kamin-Tolagh had deliberately killed her only son.

"You would hardly ever see Osré-dnë, if you wish to remain as you are when I rule at Kadon Dinul."

"Lord — " there was unplanned reproach in the man's voice. "Osré-dnë has said she wishes to be where the lord's business takes me. Osré-dnë would then serve his needs in all places, as she did at the Man-mani place — " like a shrewd shopkeeper finding added reasons to praise his wares.

With startling incongruity, he saw Tau-Suaka was making the same mistake Tovakh had in marrying Petakoi, hoping to add the woman's wisdom to his sinew, when in reality he would be lending her cunning his killing strength. What Osré-dnë dreamt as a future was outside imagining — Lavsila, long ago, had suggested, to rule over all the tribes of northern Froghushei. She would have to be killed, but in such a way Tau-Suaka could never suspect it was Kamin-Tolagh's doing.

"This is no time for such a decision," he told the man. "After victory, we shall reward the faithful, give the unfaithful their just payment, too. The richest prizes I have given before will be as sand and stone." He wondered if there was not a young beauty of the realm to entice Tau-Suaka away from his present sinister choice. If they were really about to take Kadon Dinul, he might have let him have this Morulis, who must be desirable indeed, to distract Rodlakh, with Âna waiting at home.

Near dawn, the missing vessels came gliding to anchorage, having strayed off course to the southward. Only war mattered now. It was, as near as he could calculate from the inexact details in the letter from Pivrekhan's sister, forty days since Tovakh had first fallen ill.

In a slowly narrowing firth, as they hunted for a broad stretch of gently sloping shore, no sign of movement could be seen. To prevent so large a fleet being observed, they had stayed well off-shore as long as they could, creeping northward under driving clouds and occasional swirls of rain, but the sky was blue now and the sun high. A day and a half ago, at sunrise, Niburai's contingent had begun their disembarkation well to the south of here, the same shelving shore where the vessels had beached when he came to fetch Kamin-Tarú. Jostling of ships, curses from Hrin sailors, high whinny from a horse reluctant to step from deck into sandy shallows, but the landing was otherwise uneventful, if observed by hostile eyes, without immediate consequence. Niburai was beginning to assemble squadrons on the treeless rise beyond the sands when the main fleet resumed its northward sail; by now, marching inland for Kred' Ludhai, he had probably found an enemy to fight. Few of the troops with him were of the best, but if Niburai's feats in the forest war had been overblown, he had nevertheless displayed there a certain dogged resistance to adversity. Having secured Finú and Radaghi, it would be logical for him to escape northward with his prize, with the object of rejoining the main force, but Kamin-Tolagh had given him the incompatible task of delaying, if possible defeating the squadrons which were expected to move up from the Thenimala garrison — to act, that was, as a distant rearguard for the main army, while also keeping watch to his own northward. Niburai might be puzzled by these orders, but on past performance he would fight, even when, as was not unlikely, he was hemmed in from both sides. If he could purchase Kamin-Tolagh's advance two days freedom from pursuit in strength, allowing the best fighters to concentrate on attack, he would have served his purpose. Again on the example of the Zelu Bablakhi campaign, Niburai might break out of encirclement, or Kamin-Tolagh, once having the cavalry of Kargul at his command, send a force to relieve and rescue any remnant.

All these harsh calculations assumed his invasion, including seizure of Finú, if not immediately expected, had been generally anticipated by Rodlakh and his advisors. Hrin traders had long ago reported an obvious increase in the Thenimala garrison, and Kamin-Tolagh expected Shumat to do as he would, given the resources of the realm; place a strong force in the vicinity of Finú's home at Kred' Ludhai, and enough troops at Thenimala to be able to send reinforcements without leaving the port defenseless.

By late afternoon, the last-landed were being sorted into their proper squadrons on grassy downs above the pebbled shore, littered for most of a mile with the beached Hrin vessels, and he began to wonder if he had given his adversaries too much credit for forethought. Some of Tau-Suaka's men, first to disembark, placed as a watch on the most commanding nearby eminence, had nothing to report, though the main south-north road, which swung well to the west before crossing into the emptiness of Ní-Tilagh, could not be too distant.

Freighanai, though repeatedly instructed on the voyage, wanted to be clear beyond question about the rules for starting a fight. "Well," on being told once again that the enemy must be forced to offer the first blow, "but, *Asai*, we can't put ourselves in their jaws, you know, let them surround us, or take up all the high ground, while we're being peaceable and all that. I mean, these won't be Hrin we can just huff at and blow away."

A reassuring grin. "I doubt there is to be much parleying. I hope for surprise here and now, but in general we have long been expected, and the formations the *rabhsai* sends will not be to greet us."

"Not like back in forty-one, is it, *Asai*."

He knew what was meant. Then, they had gone north to Kadon Dinul with provincial cavalry by leave of Rodlakh's elder brother, the *Rabhsai* Ban-Sila, or at his request, to help maintain order, and if their riding had not been all flowers and kisses, nor ended with the cordialest of welcomes from their new colleagues of General Cavalry or Household, it remained a happy episode, a return of Kargul to an honored place in the realm, after a half-century of exclusion.

Yet not as different as Freighanai thought: not he nor any of the troops had been told that for Kamin-Tolagh's family that ride was merely part of the plot to overthrow Ban-Sila — as Kamin-Tolagh himself had not known that within that long-cherished Karguli scheme simmered Petakoi's own plans to betray her adopted house, and supplant Ban-Sila with a *rabhsai* nurtured by the *Mankh'* and empowered by *jinzal*.

A question yet to be properly posed was how well the tribal squadrons would perform against real cavalry, whether at any odds they would stand up to the discipline of true *péfrapravádal*. Not necessarily win; the test was for them to maintain formation, give the mounted archers a chance; if they broke and fled, the enemy would soon be on the bowmen, who had no counter for lances and swords at close quarters.

He had, by late afternoon, an answer of sorts, when the advance guard, mainly seeking a sheltered spot to make camp, rounded a low hill and came unexpectedly on an elbow of main road, the Royal Way. Almost at once they were challenged, then engaged, by General Cavalry, a four-squadron detachment on its way south. Without time for a reconnaissance, they would have routed the six squadrons they could see, but for his moving up swiftly with far greater numbers, including additional mounted bows brought in from the flank positions. Overmatched, the royal squadrons did well to disengage, fully half saving themselves by retreat to the southward, Kamin-Tolagh's advance having blocked the way they had come.

At effective odds of six-to-one, then, his mixed force could defeat regulars, yet he was less delighted with the small victory than he made appear, perceiving his standards had eroded away in the West, where his fights had been against feeble foes. Remaining men of Kargul now seldom rode and never drilled in formation, and with the tribes, where rudimentary horsemanship sometimes had to be laboriously taught, he and his officers had gradually come to be satisfied when a simple drill came nearly right: not till he watched the General Cavalry squadrons wheel successively into the initial fight, or observed how, outmatched, they retained discipline to prevent rout, allowing so many to escape, did he recognize the width of the gulf between first-class cavalry and his own.

Still he had won, with small losses, and though the retreating enemy might recover enough to add to Niburai's troubles, no word as yet was racing north to where the big garrisons were. Not far in that direction must be the tiny border hamlet — it had no name Kamin-Tolagh knew — with a minor cavalry post his forces should be able to envelop and subdue, and beyond there, a clear run across the Ní-Tilagh.

"Well, *Asai*," Freighanai reminded. "But we're not going to slip past the fortress at Kir without a challenge."

"If we were going there." Known, like a less-storied Drin Navuna, as a frontier fortress, Kir did not in fact mark the boundary of the realm. That was reached some half-day to the southward, at a small river, the Rufeni, and just across Rufeni Fords, the road was intercepted from the west by a lesser way Kamin-Tolagh — and Freighanai — had ridden before. Mounting up into what remained of the Forest of Nîv, through sparsely-peopled foothills, it eventually descended in long loops to the southern corner of the Kovilanu, easternmost region of their province. From there was an easy ride down the course of the Nanakh to the port of Zelkova, or, staying high on the skirts of Kargan baDulfu, westward to the seat at Inilun Barabhi.

Freighanai said, "Won't the Fords be defended?"

"You have seen the place. The shallows there are no barrier, and there are no walls or ramparts." Nothing but a small clump of dwellings where the two ways met.

"Hard to hold with less than an army," Freighanai agreed.

"If we can outrun word of our coming, at most we'll encounter a squadron or two there. Once we brush them aside and reach the forest road, we cannot be taken in flank, and in the narrow places Tau-Suaka's bows can discourage any pursuit."

That idea baffled Freighanai, whose assumption was the Fords, once taken, would be held in strength, till the powerful detachment under Niburai could catch up.

"If it is feasible. But our vanguard must not lose any time."

"Coming down on the other side, *Asai* — " Textbook military wisdom; strung out as they would be, on a road without space to deploy, they would be at their most vulnerable. News they were on the march, as Freighanai noted, would be carried north by fast-messenger, and arrive in the Kovilanu long before they could.

"But the troops that meet us will be Kargul'," triumphantly. "We will be reinforced, not resisted."

With Freighanai still showing skepticism, he added quite casually, "There has been sickness at Inilun Barabhi. Several there have come down with it, but my father worst of all. He may be near death."

Lavsila, who had just ridden forward, was near enough to hear. "I have had no news of any sickness," but the suspicion was all for the reliability of Kamin-Tolagh's source.

"I heard it from a Hrin trader, just before we sailed. Tovakh may be too ill to take the field against us. Without him there to bully them, the cavalry will do as they have before; join us."

Freighanai nodded. "Men there I've bent elbows with, I don't doubt. Defenders at the Fords, *Asai*, they would be General Cavalry again?"

"So I would suppose — " then he saw what was being asked. "The *rabhsai* would never trust Laënakh's provincials not to join our cause — as they well may, after we have Kargul."

"His brother of Ân, and Vinilat, too," Lavsila added. "The *rabhsai* had a hard enough time getting your outlawry through the Council."

Not exactly how he had told the tale before, but it did not matter. "The common cause of the Great Families has been allowed to doze off under our soporific Rodlakh." He liked the sound of that. "We have come to waken it."

That night, as he tried for a couple of hours of sleep, it came to him as remarkable so much had not been said in that talk. They had been only an hour or so beyond the start of brief clash, the first time troops of the Empire had assailed and deliberately killed men of the realm, for all of them a step into territory from which there was no return. No expression of regret, no claim of being misled, no repentance could bring them back; the only safety now was in victory.

Yet the forces to be sent against them, men who had grown up in familiar places, Bathrâd, Dônshei, Lower Paowan, were discussed in exactly the same tone of dispassionate assessment as when speaking of Hrin soldiery or nomadic invaders of the Kufshei: the leaders of Empire had been trained by the demands of continual warfare to judge purely in terms of military necessity, with no room for squeamishness.

Not much after, there was a brisk skirmish at the tiny frontier settlement, where only a half-squadron had been left, most given no time to mount. Kamin-Tolagh had sent the Hill Froghul bows in a wide circle to waylay the northward road, and their arrows brought down all who tried to escape that way when the fight was plainly hopeless. Useful supplies and half a hundred *pefral* fell into Kamin-Tolagh's hands, and the spring and cisterns there were used to water all the mounts, fill bottles and skins for the crossing of Ní-Tilagh.

Here too they took their first prisoners, eleven of them, most wounded, and here was one difference needing no explanation for any of the men of Kargul, impossible to overemphasize in instructing the tribal troops; this was to be a war fought by civilized rules, where capitulation was accepted, and captive wounded given aid. These were both bewildered and surly, gazing in disbelief at the host of small, strange men who had engulfed them, bitter and angry with the more recognizable cavalrymen from Kargul. Questioned, the highest surviving rank, a senior file-leader, imparted little; he insisted "the captains" had been informed Kamin-Tolagh was coming, and in trying to reconcile that claim with the apparent unpreparedness of this outpost, inadvertently revealed strong formations had passed through on their way south. Neither officer nor any of his men could say where news of the forthcoming invasion had come from, and no one had heard anything at all about Tovakh baKargul or his health.

With early light slanting in through the windows of the commander's quarters where he had lain down, he began to believe the prisoner must simply be boasting, saving his pride; there had not been time for Kadon Dinul to know he had set sail;

if one of Iruvakh's *atarlal* spending a night at the Abu had somehow discovered the contents of Kamin-Tolagh's message to Freighanai, and had improbably been prepared for an immediate departure, riding as well as a strong cavalryman he could not have achieved Drin Navuna before the fleet sailed. With fast-messengers and the necessary ship for the passage of Arnan all working ideally, the soonest for the news to reach Kadon Dinul would have been the day before yesterday, and Kadon Dinul was not less than six days and nights from here by fast-messenger.

Having splashed water on his face, he went outside, where the overnight camp was stirring into life for a punctual start to a long day's march. An early patrol, Hill Froghul under Hunghi-of-the-Whip, appeared over the brow of the first drab ridge, coming at a dusty canter, to report sighting of fresh enemy forces, some six to eight squadrons, having evidently continued their march overnight, or resumed it before dawn after brief rest. Some squadrons, the man said, were uniformed as those that had been fought here, but others had shinier breastplates, and lighter tunics faced with dark orange, the same color as the border of their plain white banner.

"*Household*!" Freighanai, in disbelief, having emerged still chewing whatever his breakfast had been. "What are Household doing down here?" — but Hunghi, urgently requestioned, stuck to his description. Not having seen Household soldiers before, he could hardly have made it all up.

Incredible; superbly-trained troops, Household were used in war as need arose beyond resources of the other cavalries, but their primary place was with the person of the *rabhsai*, and unless Rodlakh had chosen this moment for a sojourn in the South — and he would hardly have made overnight rides to do so — the only explanation was that not merely a rumor but absolute certainty of imminent invasion had come to Kadon Dinul more than a week ago. As Freighanai and his officers hastened the packing up and mounting of troops, Kamin-Tolagh once again counted days, and still could see no way it could be done.

He had a sudden fear Kamin-Tarú had been accused in the death of his father, and forced to confess the whole scheme: in that case her succession to *nimum* was already void, and his dash to Inilun Barabhi as doomed as it was useless. Otherwise — and at last he saw a shipowning spy among the Hrin at Guodvestr, overhearing talk, deducing Kamin-Tolagh's intentions from earliest preparations, as the *Hridveyuth* easily had, could have sailed ten days earlier than the fleet, and with no delay in the Dezhuni Islands, been at Thenimala as much as two weeks ago. From that point, impossibility whittled down to feverish haste, but if the spy were in Dolvid's pay, set to watch for this one event, there would be no delay of disbelief in his story, only immediate action.

At some indefinite future time, he would relish discovering the identity of that spy, to give him a death commensurate with his crimes. For the present, there was no better place for dealing with the new enemy than here, at the very fringe of Ní-Tilagh, where slight growths of bushes and stunted trees provided cover for ambushing bows. More troops were out of sight behind structures of the hamlet, and a hundred of Tau-Suaka's best sent to lurk behind a low, lightly wooded ridge over on the left, observers concealed at the crest.

One point was clear; Shumat, if he was in tactical command, had believed the landing would be farther south; as reported, the approaching detachment, squarely on the road in fours, was riding as a strategic reserve, hastening towards a distant fight, not men who suspected an enemy was near.

He spurred forward, passing between squadrons to take his place at the head of his main formations of cavalry, mounted bows visible on either flank, beginning their gradual advance athwart the road, alert for first sight of banner and breastplates as they would appear at the head of the long, gradual slope in front. He did not quicken the pace, and would be content to intimidate this company into withdrawal, so as to keep his forces intact; even Household could not hope to triumph at these odds.

Seven squadrons, three of them Household. Seeing the mass of opposing army, they halted their march, and quietly reformed on a front of four squadrons in eights, going to their places as if at some ceremony, the two banners, Rodlakh's and General Cavalry centered at front. Between, their commander was rather short in the saddle, but broad-shouldered; for the first time Kamin-Tolagh was facing in battle a man whose name and reputation he knew, his supposed subordinate in the Lunu Jinzalladhiyu expedition eight years ago, Dorrmas.

42.

"I have ridden this far," Rodlakh said. "What could be sillier than to go jogging back without definite news? You are the one who said there was no danger here."

"No danger from the enemy." There were indeed few places safer than the thick-walled fortress of Kir, and instead of lamenting his failure to prevent the *rabhsai* from leaving Kadon Dinul, Dolvid ought to count it as victory to have persuaded him to go no farther south in his quest for fresh and reliable news. But Rodlakh remained in danger from himself, his conviction he should be in the field, leading troops in person.

"This is, at its heart, my quarrel."

"It is not your quarrel," losing patience at fifteenth repetition. "Your realm, yes, and you have soldiers just as you have carpenters. This is their task." Unfortunately, continued absence of the master-carpenter, Shumat, gave Rodlakh's arguments some leverage.

"I have often thought, princes, not people, make wars. They should be settled in single-combat between the instigators."

As if a dank draft had wandered into the room, Dolvid felt a chill contract his shoulders. "Hardly fair to Kamin-Tolagh," thrusting away nightmare with light irony. "If he were winner, the realm would not make him its ruler, and he would have the same war to fight and lose."

"A good bargain, then," half-smiling. "If he is killed, lives are saved, and if I am, it is no worse than before. Orbanak would rule, with your guidance, and Âna's, till Lambakh is of age. Did I mention Faëdhal has decided to unmake his retirement? He asked if he could return to teach the children, Lambakh in particular. A rebuke for me, I am afraid, but I could not be more pleased."

"I thought Tellis was tutoring the children in language."

"She was excused, when she began work on her new book."

"I saw Faëdhal last month. He said nothing to me."

"This happened after you left for the south. He came to consult a volume in the Residence library, and while there heard young Lambakh speaking — mangling, I am informed Faëdhal says — a few words of the Owanilú. He decided on the spot he is not too tired, after all, to give lessons. It is going to be good to have him fussing about as before."

Indeed, but Dolvid, while delighted, was not deflected. "*Rabhsai*, I rejoice your children will be able to read Nilradh's epic in the original, but they will be more grateful to have a living father."

A swordsman saluting an opponent's skilled sequence, Rodlakh nodded acknowledgement of an argument that had no answer.

"You know," tone becoming hushed and confidential, "*this* has been great help to me in troubled times, a true friend." From somewhere he produced the small volume sent him by the Patriarch, *Thirteen Steps on Zhôl's Path*. Astonished, a little disappointed that one who had never needed belief outside himself was contracting religion, Dolvid remained detached enough to see benefits, wary enough not to overlook dangers. The cult of Zhôl had become the other great unifier of the realm, and what Rodlakh had come to for its own sake, a calculating ruler would long ago have ostentatiously affected, to make it a tool of his power. As a leader among believers, Rodlakh. already popular, could become irresistibly beloved.

Yet past fusions of *rabhsayum* and religion, if sometimes beginning in sincerity, had too often ended in oppression; for those in power a perilously easy step from *I draw comfort from my faith* to *everyone should*, and from there to proclaimed orthodoxy as basis for advancement, a test of absolute worth.

"I am glad," handing back the little book. "It is good you found help — pleasant also, to live in a time when anyone is free to choose his own path, or none, if that is his nature."

Heavyhanded. Rodlakh laughed and called him 'patriarch of *facts*,' but briefly his eyes had shown the hurt of one who, having come upon the sole right answer, cannot wait for others to share it. Dolvid resolved he would find a way to write into law what he had called *pleasant*, and have it enacted, soon, before the once-oppressed airily ceased to see any need for it.

Without a word said to Rodlakh, so as not to risk the charge he was ignoring his own advice, Dolvid rode down to Rufeni Fords in company of an old acquaintance, with whom he had shared some heartening exploits, both in the remote Northeast, and on soil of the Heartland, Kennar, who commanded the Kir garrison, an effective leader of cavalry. With them went just two squadrons, and Kennar remarked they were one-third of all regulars available, not counting house-guests, by which he meant the Household troops of Rodlakh's personal guard, and a couple of provincial squadrons sent down from Nivu Din by Laënakh.

By the time Dolvid, eight days ago, had first arrived in Kir, bulk of the troops, augmented by fresh arrivals from the north, had already gone hastening to meet the expected invasion. Just hours behind, Dorrmas had ridden in, at head of a mixed force of Household and General Cavalry. He brought no good news; so early in the season there had been heavy snows over much of Dramal, and Shumat was presumed to be immobilized at Dônshei, with a large part of the General Cavalry. No doubt they would dig their way south till they could reach and cross the Paowan, but this setback had crippled an effort to prevent the *rabhsai* quitting Kadon Dinul; he argued the squadrons of Household protecting him would be more widely useful if he came south.

Dorrmas had left next morning, receiving with distant tolerance the warning the fighting might not be so deep into Ninkufu as was being generally assumed; all senior officers were unshakable in their conviction Kamin-Tolagh had to capture Thenimala and collect Finú before marching on Kadon Dinul. As Dorrmas patiently explained, that there might be no march on Kadon Dinul was neither here nor there, if the invader was destroyed before he could reach the Ní-Tilagh. That same evening Rodlakh was in Kir, and Dolvid's labors to keep him there had begun: the *rabhsai*'s somewhat forced imitation of a boyish zest for battle was less worrisome than his unknowing adoption as an argument Dolvid's haunting fear, that he was destined to be Kamin-Tolagh's personal adversary.

Next, news from Shumat, a scrawled two pages from Dônshei Bridge. Freed from snow himself, he still had troops to assemble, but here at last, if belatedly, was support for Dolvid's warnings; he was strong against sending too many troops across Ní-Tilagh. Kamin-Tolagh, he wrote, was the one with the need to gamble; he must come north to have any hope of victory, and knew the realm would triumph in a protracted war. Just possible to detect was Shumat's conviction inhabitants of Ninkufu, mainly Owanil, would suffer little abuse at Kamin-Tolagh's hands.

Two blank days had followed, and then at last a message from the south, endorsed by several intervening hands. The commander at Thenimala reported a ship just docked had observed a flotilla numbering thirty to forty of the twin-hulled Hrin vessels, riding low in the water as if heavily laden, just off the Dezhuni Isles. He had sent out craft to find and ascertain the intentions of this fleet, but the sighting, when this news came to Kir, was a week past, and the following three days were filled with nothing more nourishing than speculation. No purpose but invasion was imaginable for so large a fleet to be assembled, but if the count was accurate and complete, Kamin-Tolagh's force, with supplies and mounts, could hardly be above twelve hundred, a thousand-and-a-half at the outside. The most insane optimism could not hope to overthrow Rodlakh's *rabhsayum* using so few; with recent reinforcement, the realm by now had about as many regular troops within the confines of Ninkufu.

Kennar was willing at least to entertain membership in the Thenimala faction, those who held Kamin-Tolagh must attempt to seize the port, and defend it, while his control of shipping enabled him to build up strength at leisure. Dolvid shook his head. "As Shumat says, he is aware the realm can muster greater forces than he can ever bring; two weeks from now the Army of the West could be here." Below, the road opened on the fords, a broad crossing, a break in the screen of trees which elsewhere marked this side of the river's curving course. Immediately to their right was the opening to the narrow road, not much beyond a track, which climbed into the heart of what had once been the magnificent Forest of Nîv, now mainly close-set, spindly growth, concealing many stumps of the great oaks and beeches they replaced, a scattered few still rising, here and there, aged, defiant warriors waist-deep in a wheatfield. The rest had been consumed, first in the building of Kir and Nivu Din, later mainly for fuel, and it had taken a royal decree, near the end of Lambarr's reign, to prevent complete denuding of these hills.

"That road, much more than Thenimala," with a gesture, "is what he must have." Kamin-Tarú's revelations, now shared fully only with Rodlakh, gave them the advantage of knowing how central the Karguli cavalry was to the plans of Kamin-Tolagh, who quite possibly still believed his father was dead or near death.

Kennar grunted. "He's going to have to beat a lot of good fighters to get here."

True enough, but it had been defense of this place, the fords, Dolvid had thought about when he sent for the companies of pikes — and down that same small road word of their approach would come.

In the hamlet short of the ford there was a small hostelry, but it was full, with soldiers sleeping five or six to a room, and Dolvid declined to turn any of them out, exercising authority instead at one of the dwellings, where the elderly householder surrendered one of his three cluttered rooms on learning from Kennar that his guest was of an importance beyond simple description.

By first light, all strategies were superseded; a slightly wounded, wholly exhausted Household man appeared out of the Ní-Tilagh, with a tale of defeat. Near the Ninkufu border, his squadron and the others under Dorrmas had encountered head-on a great host of cavalry and mounted bows. Despite scant time to adopt battle-formation, the seven squadrons had met and actually checked five times their number, small, not unskilled men on horses inferior only to *pefral* for a fight. Then Dorrmas's flanks had been assailed by hard-riding, deadly bowmen, and again on his right by fresh lances, emerging from concealment. Seeing his fight hopeless, unable to regain the road, he had retreated to the eastward with all he could save, the enemy following with their bows, but not pressing their pursuit beyond a few miles. The main enemy resumed their march to the north.

All this was in the hastily-written dispatch, where Dorrmas also made time for a first professional assessment of Kamin-

Tolagh's armies. The lances he judged formidable solely in their numbers, no match for *péfrapravádal*, but the mounted bows were excellent riders, dangerous marksmen, deficient only in their darts, which, while tipped with some sort of steel or iron, rebounded, even at close range, from helms and breastplates, unlike those of the Frontier archers, which would punch through any armor. Nevertheless, enemy arrows could and did pierce faces and necks, shoulders, arms and thighs, and had brought down many *pefral*; Dorrmas had lost half his men, but would attempt to edge past the enemy to rejoin defenders at Kir. He had also sent riders southward, circling wide to avoid enemy scouts, in hope of rapidly recalling the forces sent there; obviously Kamin-Tolagh must have made his landing in their rear.

Though he had ridden hard, the messenger here could barely be a day ahead of the enemy host, and in that open stretch of Ní-Tilagh there was nothing to delay Kamin-Tolagh, not a single defender, not a scout. Observing Dorrmas evidently expected the next effective defense to be mounted at Kir, Kennar proposed a withdrawal to what was, after all, his post. In part because he and Dolvid had survived other desperate times together, he made no open objection to an order the fords were to be held, or must at least exact a toll for passage, but his face was critical.

They were cheered by the unheralded arrival of Mattin, bringing a last pair of squadrons down from distant Kanzan Tâl, and contributing the thought that if the fords were forced, it would still be feasible to retreat in good order on Kir. With the same rank, it would have been logical for Mattin to relieve Kennar so he could return to his command, but Kennar had all at once accepted the argument Kir did not come into the calculation, and politely proposed Mattin return there instead, to ask for every available man to be sent. A happy arrangement; Kennar was the more experienced field officer, or at least had a longer habit of being on the winning side, and now pointed out that except where the road spread into the crossing, the riverbanks were an abrupt drop; with bowmen in the cover of the trees along the near side, it would be difficult to outflank defenders.

Still, compared with tales of enemy numbers, they seemed very thin, as men assembled through the afternoon, not five hundred all told, more than a third of them levied bows who would fight on foot. Having had his crisis of doubt, Kennar now declined to be gloomy: a trader settling on a satisfactory bargain, he remarked that while weight of numbers might carry the fords, cost to the enemy would more than justify this defense.

It had remained dreary, becoming warm as a day strayed from its place in late summer, but with not a glimpse of sun. As the confusing brown dusk of Ní-Tilagh gathered, dull sky becoming one with dull rolling hills, a scout rode in to report distant, steady advance of a dense mass of horsemen, spreading inkily on both sides of the southward road. At almost the same time. a single rider emerged from the opening to the forest track, drew up cautiously at sight of cavalry, then resumed his approach with a gesture between a wave of greeting and sketchy salute, Shudarr, mount, breeches and even his face blotched with mud. The pikes were at most three hours behind, and would arrive tonight.

43.

"I say they mean to wear us down gradually, *Asai*, coming at us a few squadrons at a time."

Kamin-Tolagh stared, before recognizing Freighanai was making one of his rare jokes. "It is going to take them a while," belatedly grinning. In three engagements against regular formations, his men had routed a dozen squadrons, with their own losses one hundred and forty killed and disabled. The only shadow on his high spirits came from away eastward, where the defeated Dorrmas was holding a body of men together, keeping pace with the northward march. Challenged by mounted bows, they repeatedly faded out of range; he could have headed them off and encircled them only at the cost of unacceptable delay, but Dorrmas would already have found a way to send messengers speeding ahead, so the next enemy encountered would not be a minor detachment, taken unprepared.

Lavsila, who had his own technique for fading from sight when fighting appeared imminent, kept his place next to Kamin-Tolagh at safer times. "If, as I now gather," with the reproachful sanctimony of an advisor not supplied with adequate facts, "our main purpose is to reach Kargul, I wonder we do not parley before fighting."

"About what?"

"You have no designs on the realm, and do not come as an invader. We should be permitted to pass, on a peaceful errand."

"A peaceful errand?" swinging half-around in the saddle, inviting Lavsila to view his army through the eyes of a defender. "As is, we have encountered nothing to parley with. Why should we lose time with words, so long as we are not seriously opposed? Any delay merely gives them time to assemble their forces."

"Men live by words, most of them lies. They are told they are defending their homes, fighting for their *rabhsai* — they may lose their ardor, hearing you have no designs on either. Besides, there will be a future time, when you have wider aims, and it will help if you can say `*I came in peace, but war was forced upon me.*'"

Perhaps those already inclined to support him might cheerfully swallow the idea he had landed some thousands of alien troops to further a peaceful purpose, but none of this was worth considering so long as his advance continued without check.

"Just one last fence — " and he treated Lavsila and Freighanai to a strategic review: "Ahead of us, they are forewarned by now, but the bulk of the forces Rodlakh had ready have plainly gone south, and those left back here will see Kir as best place to stand, as indeed it would be, if we were going there. Once across Rufeni Fords, we have won our way to Kargul. At the fords, there will not be anything that cannot easily be swept aside. If anything is to be gained by talking there," he allowed, "we shall talk."

"I would like to find out more about Kargul. Should we be going to Inilun, if they have an epidemic there?" Lavsila used the Owanilú *konúrai*, a plague, but there was no sign of the mockery first suspected. Neither he nor Freighanai had seen any need to pretend he might be anxious over his father's condition.

A slight fidget was sign of saddle-sores, but Lavsila, as in the past, showed surprising endurance for long days in the saddle, and had not complained. "The longer I consider it, the shrewder the Heartlanders seem, with that Loyal Address of theirs. When time comes, you will not lack for friends."

He was fighting hard for his usefulness, but Kamin-Tolagh said nothing. The country was beginning to change, running into long brown ridges, troughs between with sporadic vegetation. They had passed a favored overnight resting place two hours ago, and could reach the fords near nightfall, but would halt short of there, and cross in the morning; he did not want to go stumbling up the narrow forest road by darkness, and knew of no convenient place to camp this side of the summit. The need was for speed, not headlong haste; the forces of the *rabhsai* hurrying south would be kept occupied by Niburai, and even if his detachment had been annihilated by now, any considerable enemy to his rear could scarcely be less than three or four days away. The remnant with Dorrmas was still keeping pace, occasionally visible when the two forces were on crests of parallel ridges, too few to be worse than an annoyance.

Most troubling was the question of Kargul, of which he still had no news. A captured Household man, going beyond their former prisoner, had been sure Tovakh was alive, and had passed through Kadon Dinul within the past three weeks, but under close questioning admitted this was only an impression he had, not based on an actual sighting.

Alive? Had Kamin-Tarú, then, lost her nerve after she began the poisoning, or had she been detected and forestalled? If Tovakh, after all, had recovered, the cavalry of Kargul was still his to command.

Was it possible, alternatively, the death had occurred, but Rodlakh had by some means conspired to keep it secret? There was a near-example for this, about a century ago, when the deaths by drowning of the *Rabhsai* Dromladh and his son were concealed from the public for nearly a month. But that had been so as to aid the peaceable accession, in a factional realm recovering from civil war, of Dromladh's elder sister; Rodlakh had no such motive in the present case, and how, from a place so distant as Kadon Dinul, could he prevent the news from getting out of Inilun Barabhi?

Petakoi might. She would have the nerve and the means, if she came back suddenly from Kamanta, and Petakoi had a motive; with her Island cronies she could move to block the proclaiming of Kamin-Tarú, hiding Tovakh's death till she was sure of the cavalry — assured, that was, they would accept Pedh-Sivai as the new *nim'*.

Either of the two likelier explanations meant his sister was now in great danger, if not already dead; it was the clutch of a cold fist beneath his breastbone, yet he declined to believe her death could occur without his feeling it, instantly, no matter where he was, as an abrupt absence from his life; absurd as to say he could lose his right arm and not notice.

Nor would he ever let thoughts of worst imaginable case weaken his resolve: on that first expedition when by stern persistence they had found their way to Zelu Bablakhi, he had often been certain the *rabhsai*, in his absence, would launch an attack on the Abu, destroying what Kamin-Tolagh sought to enrich. To let those thoughts deflect him would have guaranteed failure, and here, as then, he could only go forward.

And still with the thought of success. Though Tovakh was said to have reorganized the provincial cavalry, he could hardly have weeded out all admiration and support for Kamin-Tolagh, who cherished memories of his previous homecomings, when soldiers sent to oppose or arrest him had given a hero's welcome. If Petakoi had contrived to have Pedh-Sivai installed, Kamin-Tolagh would wrest the soldiery away from him, as he would from his father, though they might draw the line at causing Tovakh's deposing.

Well, if he was alive, he could remain so, and keep his *nimum*, if he would acquiesce in Kamin-Tolagh's right to be in the province, to defend its eastward borders, swell his armies, mount them on *pefral* bred in Kargul. When time came for reckoning with Rodlakh, the cavalry of Kargul would be tempered edge of Kamin-Tolagh's weapon, and for none of this was Tovakh's death an absolute necessity.

Morning arrived dankly, mist clinging to the ground. With the great camp of his army rousing, he rode ahead with Freighanai and Tau-Suaka, to start of the long, gradual downslope to the fords. Except for outcroppings of dun rock, island clumps of bramble, and a few wizened trees among struggling grasses, it was clear and open space, the road where it came to the river losing itself in a fanning of worn tracks. On farther side of Rufeni the landscape abruptly began to darken with stragglers from the mounting forest, hills behind black under colorless morning light. From rising ground leftward of the road the slope to the river was steeper, and there the opposing bank rose abruptly, while upstream to the eastward the long ridges and furrows tapered down to where the river ran in a deep slot of its own making; here and there, an individual, leading his horse, could find a place for scrambling across, but fords were the only feasible crossing for a large body of men, certainly with the far bank defended.

As now, bringing him halfway to surprise. Dawn scouts had crept close, and returned to report small numbers of troops there, but he had expected them to stay only for a token challenge, before falling back on impregnable Kir.

Perhaps defenders were holding their position just long enough for the shadowing remnant under Dorrmas to bid for safety; over to the right horsemen could now be discerned, picking their way down from a crest, and Kamin-Tolagh made his opening move, sending forward bows supported by cavalry, to a position where they could cut off any dash by Dorrmas for the fords, yet readily be reinforced against a sortie from the other side of the river.

Troops were awake there, taking up positions, and while hard to make an exact count, or estimate their quality, there could not be above a few hundred. The main body of their cavalry, assembled where the main road climbed again, was less than Dorrmas had begun with when routed three days ago.

Tau-Suaka, granted permission to go forward on his small horse to within two hundred paces of the ford, came cantering back with a contemptuous assessment.

"Bowmen, dismounted, hiding behind trees, Lord. For horse, they have about six squadrons, Lord, and in front of them — " he spat on the ground — "some foot forming up, three deep, I think. Their weapon is — the thing like a heavy lance."

"Pikes," Freighanai said. "Levies."

"Aye, some timid *kímukan* or under-captain," Kamin-Tolagh guessed. "He does not know which he fears most, yielding the fords without the look of a fight, or risking his precious cavalry, so he has found farmers to do the dying, while his squadrons swirl about, and soon decide it is time for a retreat." Shumat, obviously, was not here, and Dorrmas in no position to direct the defense; no experienced cavalry-officer would plant a slight screen of infantry in the path of such weight of mounted forces as Kamin-Tolagh possessed. Near-criminal, bad as the Hrin trying to halt horse with their human walls of slave-infantry, yet sound enough if the tactical object was to preserve regular cavalry for another battle.

Swiftly-arranged battle-order divided the army in three, smallest, including the lightly-wounded, guarding baggage, spare mounts and prisoners. In the first section, sixteen squadrons would be led by Freighanai, supported by bows, whose chief task would be to duel with and silence lurking enemy archers. Kamin-Tolagh held higher ground for a general view of events, and in theory had direct command of a reserve twelve squadrons strong, though apart from keeping an eye on Dorrmas over to the right, the only orders he expected to issue would be to resume the forward march when the fords were cleared.

Start of Freighanai's slow-gathering advance was a stirring sight, Siv'loi Banner floating on a freshening breeze, gliding forest of lances, helms shining in cold dawn light just now tinged with the arriving sun, purposeful nod of horses. They were on a front of thirty-two lances, four squadrons across riding in eights, backed by the same formation three times repeated, and they quickened their pace on the faint downslope, becoming a force of incalculable menace,

The opposing infantry had started a crossing of the river, barely visible in the depression, under the trees. Expecting them to retire so as to take advantage of the counter-slope where road resumed on the far side, he was mystified to see their advance continue, emerging from the fords and moving up to where the ground was almost level.

There were about four hundred, with their tall oblong shields and curiously staggered pikes so different from any foot he had ever encountered, he wondered whether, like himself, the *rabhsai*, or even the province of Nîv, could now be hiring foreign mercenaries. But they were also the best-trained infantry he had seen, movements into formation crisp and precise like well-drilled *péfrapravádal*, as, directed by a couple of mounted officers, they placed themselves in two dense rectangles, suicidally in the way of the coming charge.

Gaining speed, ranks still good, it struck, and Kamin-Tolagh could no longer see defenders, only dense-packed, rearing, plunging cavalry. But something, suddenly, was wrong; following squadrons were riding into the backs of comrades, and at the center the charge was checked. For a moment, a space opened, and he watched as a newly arrived squadron, quickly followed by another, charged into the infantry, impossibly whole, apparently untouched. It vividly recalled the shielded harbor at Zelkova, in spring, when a combination of high tides and wind out of the northwest could bring giant waves rolling across the breadth of Kôbh Estuary, glittering masses of water nothing could resist, smashing into and inundating the great stone sea-mole, so that its destruction seemed certain. Then the mole would, as it were, shake its shoulders free, with shattered water streaming off in whorls and useless fists of foam, not merely undemolished, but unperturbed.

So with this new infantry, which did not break, or as much as step back, but with its jabbing points held off and felled horses and men. The following squadrons were thrown into confusion, trying to press on against a solid but seething mass, part trying to wheel away, others halted, many still trying to go forward. Pressure forced some, unwilling, into the narrow lane between companies of pikes, and as the horse wrapped around them, they changed effortlessly into squarer formation, acting like a single creatures of multiple legs and half as many deadly spines, rather than collections of individual soldiers.

Crowding was densest yards short of the defensive front, and as the attack recoiled, there was a remarkable sight, infantry advancing against and driving back horse. If the pikemen had suffered losses, they had seamlessly closed gaps, and maintained their shield-wall, straight and firm as if held on a rigid frame. In the horsemen hesitating to their immediate front, the unmistakable, head-turning signs of panic began to appear, and wheeling quickly to his trumpeter, Kamin-Tolagh had him sound rapidly three times recall for the cavalry, at the same time moving his unengaged formations forward and right, so as not to leave the mounted bows uncovered to a small but ready reserve of enemy cavalry, those not already moving up to the flanks of their infantry.

The duel of archers going on at the same time was, by extension, a struggle for the flanks, especially upstream to Kamin-Tolagh's right, where a strong defending contingent of archers exchanged arrows with Tau-Suaka's bows. Kamin-Tolagh's forces had superior bowmen, those of the realm much better position, protected by trees, and able to move freely along the farther bank. Without those bows, Kamin-Tolagh could sweep about the infantry, and ride swiftly for the fords along the riverbank, but at the same time to allow the realm's cavalry a free run at the mounted bows would enable them next to wheel and fall on the flank of the muddled mass of disengaging attackers. Kamin-Tolagh sat alert in the saddle, waiting for the counter to advance too far, so he could circle for the fords untroubled by bows, but someone in command for the *rabhsai* was prudent enough to recognize the danger, and the pikemen first halted, and with threat receding, actually began to retire, making their move in short, overlapping spurts so half the pikes were always pointed at the main foe.

Freighanai came cantering. "We'll have to soften them with bows, *Asai*," meaning the infantry. An obvious resort, but its speaking had a disproportionate effect on Kamin-Tolagh's outlook: he had erred in underrating the extraordinary infantry, but was still in full control of greatly superior forces; instead of scrambling to save this first attack from failure, it was not too late to begin the battle again, lesson learnt.

The ground where the enemy infantry slowly withdrew was choked with the wreckage of men and horses. One wounded half-*pefrai* rolled over on its back with a high shriek, and a lane opened in the wall of shields so the officer could ride swiftly to dismount, and finish the writhing horse with a decisive thrust to the throat.

"Shudarr Shumats-son," Freighanai said. "The young bastard waved a greeting to me."

"We are not going to break any more cavalry against them."

"Aye, but all the same, *Asai*, they'd never stand up to real *péfrapravádal*."

Scanning the field for Tau-Suaka, Kamin-Tolagh did not answer. Yet to be tested, but already he more than half believed they would, that enough infantry, trained and armed as these, could change warfare for all future time. This was only a handful, and would be beaten by numbers, but considering the cost of breeding and keeping horses, a thousand such foot could be raised cheaper than eight squadrons of *péfrapravádal*, and five thousand of this quality might scour any field.

Freighanai, angry with the enemy, had a wound on his left forearm, and was ravenous for revenge. So was Kamin-Tolagh, whose anger was for himself; he had the bows, and should have used them in his main assault; the cavalryman's confidence had betrayed him into assuming lances alone would break the enemy. *Lords who go to battle must not be misled by contempt*, the *Hridveyuth* had said that, and also, *not all places are to be reached on a horse's back*; what had been at the time typical mystification now came back as plain and accurate forecast. Nonsense, however; as Kamin-Tolagh had remarked another time, rebuking Kambanal's credulity, the man made so many portentous utterances, one or two were bound in some fashion to come true.

Getting one step behind, he was using all his energies today trying to catch up. If he had thought the defenses worthy of any subtleties, he might have begun with feint of a cavalry charge, pulling it aside at the last moment, to give a clear field to mounted bows. Now, as with greater care he set a new order of attack, the infantry had withdrawn to near where he had first expected them to take their stand, in the actual fords, forming their line along the long, gravelly bank at midstream. Still vulnerable to arrows, their new site meant his mounted bows would have to come in range of enemy archers, numerous and effective, despite Tau-Suaka's early boast that his men would nail them to their trees. It was as if Kamin-Tolagh's intentions were being read, and the question of why they had not taken up this position from the start suggested the uncomfortable idea they had *known* he would take them for easy game, and had been put out there precisely to tempt an assault by cavalry alone, which they *knew* they could withstand.

Again, his foresight failed; before he put the lead squadrons in motion, from far over on the right, in no formation, a long skein of horsemen went galloping along the nearer riverbank, the forgotten men under Dorrmas, racing for the fords, which they reached unchallenged; not only relative safety for them, but reinforcement for the defenses; one of the men of Kargul, Sonadhil, gave the count as one hundred and twenty, nearly two-and-a-half additional squadrons.

Though more fully planned, next phase of battle deteriorated into even more of a brawl, Kamin-Tolagh loth to break off and regroup within reach of his objective. The considerable royal forces there must be at Kir had surely been sent for, and would be here before day's end, or early tomorrow, latest.

It began with demonstration of another well-rehearsed trick by the companies of pikes; when squadrons of mounted bows advanced, the men at midstream went down on one knee, board shields going up in virtual unison, forming what was crazily like a roof made of huge tiles, volleys of arrows raining down to thud harmlessly into the wood. At closer range, the bows could do damage, but only at the cost of casualties from opposing archery, and when Kamin-Tolagh pulled his bowmen aside, the fresh cavalry assault he launched was again halted by immovable pikes, thrown back by a short counter-charge of barely six squadrons of lances.

One detachment of these, Dorrmas at its head, seized the opportunity to swing to its left and sweep along the bank, bearing down on mounted bows, still duelling across the water. Kamin-Tolagh was near enough to lead a flank-attack against those, at last finding work for his own sword-arm, meeting muscular cavalrymen of the realm with furious joy and all his old skill: the inadequate enemy force was quickly in disarray, survivors scurrying for safety. Freighanai, meanwhile was farther upstream where the broken riverbank was less formidable, and soon leading what troops he was able to collect into the river. Pikemen came doubling along the opposite bank, and while here they no longer could adopt tidy formation, they had compensating advantages; slowed by knee-deep water, horses had to scramble up a steep, loose-packed, shifting rise, riders unable to wield their lances against iron-tipped pikes that stabbed from above. Only a small wedge of horsemen, led by Freighanai, gained a footing on the opposite bank, a minor success Kamin-Tolagh could not collect the men to follow up; most of his cavalry were now backing away from battle, and by the time he bawled and browbeat enough for an attempt at the stream, Freighanai's tiny contingent had been enveloped by Household and General Cavalry.

There were confused and scattered clashes at and near the blandly inviting fords, and to Kamin-Tolagh, without time to consider the fate of Freighanai, it remained unacceptable that passage could be denied him by so few, as if he might yet hit on the missing trick to make his numbers count as they should.

With the morning gone, a soft rain began, and fighting subsided of its own accord. He was not assailed, even by bows, as he waved his men, formations gone, back to where rest and a meal could be had. At a cost of what must be nine hundred lives, though many more were wounded, he appeared to have won the right to move unchallenged on the wrong side of the river.

His mind ran on other times, other fights; the Lunu Tezh' Gate, the hill-road down to the final bridge and the plain of Kamsilat, and storming in at the gate there; the first victory over the Hill Froghul, followed by the cowing of Sranadatta's brood, the the Man-man hailing him as No-Sra-Lal-Hin; submission of the Hrin after Yaënsilat emerged from disgrace to turn that brawl, and then the greater Battle of Hyolenstr, perhaps his masterpiece, when it was as if he commanded for both sides.

And a dozen lesser fights, always victorious; only deputing the fighting to others had he ever seen defeat, and even now, surely, his presence must be a guarantee of eventual triumph. He willed it so.

Lavsila sat on the ground, back to a boulder, eating cheese. "Is it too late for a parley?"

"We can still sweep them away. In the Jinzai War, we had to change tactics, but we won." Not altogether a reliable parallel, and he found his thoughts going to Freighanai's long-cherished idea of using siege-artillery in the open field. Near Guodvestr, they had actually experimented with a more mobile *zhin'pefrai*, but after being wound up and successfully discharged twice, third shot brought the machine to its knees, large, canvas-wound Hrin wheels breaking free from the strain. Lavsila's recommendations for strengthening the frame were still to be realized, project languishing for want of a solution to the larger problem, finding a ready supply of missiles when urgently needed. Still, a few good-sized boulders sent arching would soon have made those neat formations of foot break and scatter for cover. Freighanai, a practical, professional soldier with no heroic aspirations, must be alive as a prisoner, to be exchanged-for when that time came. Kamin-Tolagh had no captive to match him in rank, but would cheerfully give all his lesser game to have the man back.

Tau-Suaka, despite loss of nearly half his men, had an appetite for further battle, and wanted to reopen the exchange with enemy bows, picking off men momentarily exposed, killing the leopard with a thousand fleabites. He was promised further fighting, but first given the part of shepherd to the army, taking men on a wide circuit to sweep up and bring back stragglers. Some diminished squadrons had simply dismounted and sat down where they were, while other small knots of men were continuing to drift unobtrusively away.

At the same time Kamin-Tolagh permitted those tribal soldiers who wanted it to search for wounded comrades on the field. No truce had been signalled or proposed, but the enemy never emerged to impede them, and venturing within easy bowshot of the river they were not molested at their task, which with some extended to laying out dead in rows, collecting weapons and small articles of value.

Among those men when they rode back, among the strays rounded up by Tau-Suaka, he scanned varied faces, the rounded heads and wide mouths from east of the hills in the Froghushei, keener look of the Man-mani, dark, coarse features from west of the Gulf, a scattering of chinless Hrin, all made into one family by a kind of sullen listlessness under the faint but unceasing rain. They had never had any idea of what they were fighting for, but few soldiers ever had, and were dragged reluctantly into history by leaders of vision; by far the larger part of all lives were lived out and caused nothing to happen in the world. Even in death, which would have come to them sometime if they had never heard of him, he had given them a purpose beyond any of their dull imaginings, but he could see he was not going to rally them to another attack this day; all his strength of will would be needed to keep his army from quietly melting away; so suddenly he had come to that. To hold them together, he still had Tau-Suaka, fearsomely loyal, and Hunghi-of-the-Whip was unhurt.

Quiet rain fell, but away west there was a near-parting of clouds, and a sun, redder than it should be while still so high, gave an eery copper glow to hands and faces.
"Blood and tears," Lavsila said.

Just short of Rufeni Fords, Dolvid was breakfasting on lamb-bones heated at a roadside camp-fire, when Shumat, weary, rode in at the head of six weary squadrons.
"Look at you, *Asai*," dismounting. "*Bôdhrai* to the realm."
"Well met — " using a piece of rag, not over-clean, to wipe grease from mouth and bristly chin. Near him and across the road, officers had sprung to their feet, Dorrmas dropping and

Kennar trying to conceal chunks of meat. Shudarr, a short distance away, also stood, bandage around his head covering but not denying an arrow-wounded ear, which he wore with a becoming show of modesty.

"Captain," Dorrmas gave the salute as senior officer present, "the fords have been held."

"As, against all expectation, I see."

"Mainly by infantry, Captain," Shudarr was unable not to say.

Shumat gave him a cold stare. "Squadron-leader, is it your place to speak without permission, when these captains are here?"

"No, Captain."

Shumat nodded, and then to Dolvid's huge satisfaction he stepped forward to seize his son in a mighty hug, saying, "Kindness of Zhôl, it is good to see you safe." He must have heard, from Mattin at Kir, of Shudarr's presence in a defending force not expected to survive.

"As the squadron-leader says," Kennar put in, as father and son stepped back to regard each other, "pikes, not least the company he commands, did most of the work here."

"And our enemy now?"

Dorrmas gestured where the smokes of Kamin-Tolagh's encampment were rising in the clear air of a dry but chilly morning.

"No retreat? He will not pass this way now. Almost another thousand cavalry I left to rest at Kir will be here in hours."

"If he has thought about retreat," Dolvid said, "he has left it too late." Only an hour before, a messenger on foot had come in from the south, having left his mount tethered to bushes somewhere, so he could work his way quietly past Kamin-Tolagh's army before full light. He brought a dispatch from another army on the march. There had been hard fighting in Ninkufu, near Kred' Ludhai, against invaders led by a Captain Niburai, remembered as the paraded hero of the Zelu Bablakhi fiasco. Outnumbered and surrounded, he not only capitulated, but volunteered the information his squadrons were a fraction of the force landed, most of which had gone north. Replaced defensively by men from the Thenimala garrison, the large contingent of General Cavalry was now returning, and those men were by now on Ní-Tilagh, not thirty hours away.

Dolvid, whose biggest part in the battle for the fords had been to convince Kennar companies of pikes could truly perform as Shudarr swore they could, noted the realm was continuing to survive vast miscalculations, not least, the importance to Kamin-Tolagh of Finú. That had turned out a distraction as little worth serious thought as the vague lady herself.

"Foot? Against cavalry?" Shumat was toying, but his glance at the equipment of the pikemen, taking their ease by the fords, was shrewdly assessing, and Dolvid knew they could have a serious talk before long about the future of royal forces. Legal limits on the armed strength of each province had always been enforced, imperfectly in the case of Kargul, through the *rabhsai's* control of needed *pefral*, but anywhere that bred men could have infantry.

Shudarr would have wanted to give full elucidation of pike tactics, but his father, patting his shoulder, murmured, "Later, later. I'm pleased you fought well.

"And you — " turning on Dolvid accusingly. "I made sure you were dead, as you soon will be. Passing through Kir at dead of night, I couldn't speak with Rodlakh *Rabhsai*, but they say he's wild enough to see you hanged." Rubbing his hands together over the fire, he asked, "Is any of that scorched meat left? It smelt good to me when I was still two miles away."

Kamin-Tolagh woke from vivid dreams of a river that ran red with blood. blossoms of pink foam spinning on its surface; fully wakened, not a dream but a recollection. He cherished a curious feeling there would be word Freighanai, having fought his way free, was back with the army, but when a sparse breakfast was interrupted by Drusilakh, the young officer held captive a time in the Colony, his news was less good. He was bleeding profusely from a fresh wound at front of his thigh, inflicted by a man of the tribes. What was left of two squadrons badly mauled in yesterday's fighting had made up their minds to end their service, and Drusilakh had been stabbed and ridden down trying to stop them.

As troops were mustered, there was a brooding, watchful mood, to suggest many would be ready to join the deserters, once certain Kamin-Tolagh could no longer recapture and punish them. He could not, for any foreseeable time; the Hill Froghul, only available avengers, though they might preserve illusion of his control, were only enough to protect his person.

Scouts came back and reported the fords were reinforced with fresh cavalry. The inexpert eye of Lavsila, surveying assembled squadrons, could judge their mood. "The time has come," softly, "for talk."

Siv'loi Banner carried crosswise in sign of truce, accompanied only by Lavsila and a dozen of the bodyguard, he rode to the fords. Gravelly shoals at midstream where the pikemen had taken up their second stand was where he met with his enemies, represented, to his astonishment, by Shumat and the even less explicable Dolvid, flanked by Household men. Lining the stream, watchful men leaned on their bows.

"Well met," jauntily.

"To me, it is very ill met," Dolvid replied. "What do you wish to say?"

Lavsila, prepared, spoke. "Surely the question, *Asai*, is not why we are parleying, but why we fought."

"Tell me your reasons. Ours is, that an outlaw has come at the head of a bandit army. We shall cease to fight when our soil is free of invaders."

Kamin-Tolagh put a hand across to silence Lavsila. The position was impossible; to answer the insult to his troops by calling it the army of the sovereign Empire of Kargusai would concede this was an invasion.

"No need to wrangle over names. Truth is, I have no quarrel, either with this realm, or with its *rabhsai*."

"No quarrel!" Shumat burst out derisively. His features were beginning to thicken in the way of his father's race, but he looked fit as ever. "Some brave men have died for nothing, then."

"Is your son safe?" Someone had seen him struck by an arrow.

Shumat was stubborn, but Dolvid said, "Yes, he is safe, and savoring his first victory."

"Freighanai is your prisoner?"

"He is dead," with apparently genuine regret. "He fought bravely, too bravely, in a bad cause."

"The cause is only that I seek to return to my province."

"With an escort in the thousands?" Shumat demanded.

Lavsila said, "The Lord Kamin-Tolagh came amply protected, because there are too many men jealous of his success, who want to see him brought low. What happened on this ground confirms the wisdom of his precaution."

Shumat gave a snort, but Dolvid was iron. "In any event, Kargul is not your own province. You have renounced it by your actions; your outlawry was proclaimed in full Council."

"These things, as you know, *Bôdhrai*, can change very swiftly. Proper that I return, now succession in my province is in doubt."

"If there were a question of the succession in Kargul, it would not be settled in this way. There is none. Kamin-Tarú *Asayu* is the undoubted heir, but not likely soon to succeed, with the *Nim'* Tovakh in robust health."

He met Kamin-Tolagh's eyes full on, and plainly he knew more than he should, equally, he was speaking the truth.

Lavsila did his best. "Word came to the West of his grave illness."

"Some weeks ago, Tovakh *Asai* did suffer a transient indisposition. He is fully recovered. Indeed, he has gone to his autumn hunting with *Nim'* Vinilat."

"I would seem to have been misled," fighting for composure, experiencing the terrible scope of his failure, its annihilating implications.

"If that were not so," Dolvid scolded on, "if you were Kargul's heir in good standing, with a reason to be here, you could not be permitted to come at the head of a foreign army, killing men of the realm doing their lawful duty. If there were to be a reconsideration of your outlawry — which, I must say, is now extremely unlikely — it could only be after you had downed arms, and submitted to the will of the *rabhsai*."

He forced a laugh. "I called for this parley hoping to save lives in a dispute that has no meaning. I am not defeated; I have yet to employ my full strength. Whether your *rabhsai* gives his leave or not, I shall pass."

Shumat was laconic. "You couldn't pass yesterday. Today, you are weaker, while we're stronger. Look at it: you're where you can't be reinforced, while we can draw on all the strength of the realm — all." A near-gesture went with this, and Kamin-Tolagh followed its direction, to see, beyond the nearest foot-soldiers where the road began its climb, a formation of lances in fours, clad in the familiar long tunics with light-blue facings of Kargul.

"Who commands these — ?" but Kamin-Tolagh was stopped by a slight parting of the sentinel pikemen. Through the gap threaded the crab-faced Talfoyan, earliest of all senior officers to defect from the Empire, wearing his reward from Tovakh in the form of an under-captain's insignia. He was making way for Kamin-Tarú. For Kamin-Tarú.

Clad for travel, including an overmantle of oiled shuzi, its hood hiding most of her lustrous hair. Head down, she prodded her mount into the stream, coming soberly towards the midstream conference. Shumat sat quite still, but Dolvid, turning and leaning over in the saddle, put out a hand in slight token of restraint, and murmured words that sounded most like, "*There was no need,* Asayu."

Certainly, she looked up at him with a sad smile, and said, "Yes. Yes there is."

"I see you make use of any weapon," Kamin-Tolagh taunted Dolvid, but though his anger was real, accusation was absurd; his sister was no sort of hostage or coerced captive.

"Tú," urgently. "What happened?"

She would not yet look in his face. "Nothing happened. It never could."

At a guess, Dolvid was the only hearer with any clue what this meant. Lavsila was wearing the face of wise rumination always his answer to being left out, while Shumat was patently baffled.

"If I had known we had no plan," wryly reproaching, "I would not be here now. You might have told me."

"I couldn't tell you."

"Are we not the halves of a single mind?"

"Once."

"Once is enough, if it is for all time."

Now her chin came up, and it pained him that her expression was anger rather than regret. "I failed to oppose you because it gave me the chance to leave you, and all the death, the talk of death."

"To rule an empire — " but that was not what he needed to expound. Bewildered, he said, "You know I could never harm you."

"How could I know? I used to have a brother who could not have killed Chamya."

Chamya? As sometimes in the distant past, the workings of his sister's mind left Kamin-Tolagh utterly baffled. "Did I want to kill him? You remember how I liked him." The texture of that time came back to him, and all at once he was irritated; she was accusing him, when it was her own actions that had made that death a necessity.

"Not just Chamya. There was Yaënsilat, those Laughing Owl men — you spoke about killing Osré-dnë, killing Oyestri, Kambanal — a dozen others."

The last was a quick substitution, not lost on Lavsila.

"If you were tired of me, or the West became unbearable, you could have said so. Beyond anything, I wanted you to stay with me, but not to make you unhappy."

"But it is true," as she turned her head away.

Dolvid said, "You must see your fight has no object now but to spend lives. Niburai has surrendered in the south, and the army that defeated him will soon be on your back."

"End it, Tam," his sister pleaded. Of course she was sincere; having brought him to a place where he could be killed, she wanted to save her repute, by being the agent of the *rabhsai*'s illusory clemency.

"If, to save lives, I disarmed myself," he asked only her, "do you imagine Rodlakh would dare to let me live?"

"If we could find guarantees — " Dolvid began.

"I was speaking to my sister, *Bôdhrai*. Pardon me, I want to hear what she believes, not what you assert — " a perfunctory apology, but acceptable to Dolvid, who also stopped Shumat from taking offense for him.

Tú was shrunk into herself, forearms against body as she held her reins. "It has to end. I did not want you to come. It's all a mistake."

"A mistake," bitterly, "is when you do up a button wrong. This — " He had no adequate conclusion.

"End it. This is too much dying. Stop it; Rodlakh, I know, will be generous."

Shumat's mouth opened at that, but he did not speak. That word, *generous*, was intolerably galling to Kamin-Tolagh, its glow of condescension, more so for how it irretrievably aligned his sister with the enemy, its implied comparison, as if he had been lacking in magnanimity.

"The *rabhsai*," cold-voiced but trembling with fury, "is lucky to be able to call on such devotion. I shall not tax his generosity." He started to swing his horse around.

Dolvid tried to call him back, and Lavsila, too, wanted the debate to continue.

"In my view," he began unctuously, "an accommodation may yet be — "

"Come. We are finished here," from ten paces. His sister had already turned away, and even his bitter anger for her kept desire at its center.

"I only wish to make my personal position plain."

Gaining the bank, Kamin-Tolagh turned again. Lavsila had not moved, but was ignored by the others, Shumat already mounting opposite shore, Dolvid leaning protectively from his saddle to lead away Kamin-Tarú.

Before riding to parley, Kamin-Tolagh had instructed two of Tau-Suaka's archers to watch Lavsila for any sign of treachery, and now he signed to them to be ready.

"*Bôdhr'asai*," Lavsila called.

"You are to come, now," Kamin-Tolagh said, clear warning in his voice.

Lavsila instead started his horse forward. "I have never — " he was saying, but Kamin-Tolagh nodded to the pair of archers. Arrows struck Lavsila, neck and mid-back, and it was as if he leapt from the saddle.

On the farther bank, bows came up at the ready, and Kamin-Tolagh raised a pacificatory hand. "A domestic matter," he called out to Shumat. Lavsila had rolled over once in the water, and died an equal distance from either bank.

Chiefly to keep the troops occupied, he formed up for battle once again. As he would have predicted, the squadrons whose sullen faces and grudging adoption of formation showed them closest to rebellion were those with a high proportion of Laughing Owl, always most troublesome of valley tribes, not counting the eradicated Hwenala. After the desertions, after the attempt at his murder on Landegh, when the Hwenala assassin had come from the midst of a largely Laughing Owl squadron, he should have been harsher with the tribe, spread enough terror to make them understand they could have the same end as the marsh-people; their neighboring Jai and Anga-Jai, the few impoverished Chon-la, would have been glad to share out Laughing Owl pasturelands.

The Man-mani, with whom he remained Noh-Sra-Lal-Hin, were at the other extreme, ready for his orders, wondering why he had not yet shattered his enemies. Five years ago, before the *Atarlum* came, he should have tried, with Iruvakh's help, to make himself a god among all the tribes — and yet he had done more than enough as man, as goldgiver, to claim their devotion. Before his coming to the West, not one in a hundred had handled a coin more precious than bronze, most owned the set of clothes on their backs, household goods of any kind had been rare, and they all lived in terror of Hill Froghul' raids. According to Iruvakh, however, the leading cause of death then was being born, with childbearing next, except in years when crops completely failed, and starvation became chief killer. A commonplace that subjects owed their lives to their lord, but in his domains, plain truth, and yet he had needed whips and steel to enforce obedience; they were like unruly children who understood nothing but fear. For a prince over a docile people, to make gestures of lordly generosity as if living in the romances was easy, but Rodlakh had never had to wonder whether the effect of leniency would be loss of his realm.

He did not attempt new attack on the fords, but reopened duelling with the enemy's bowmen, taking a couple of the steadier squadrons in provocative foray near the riverbank, in hopes Shumat would be goaded into a sortie. While another repulse might shatter Kamin-Tolagh's main army altogether, drawn up in a semblance of readiness for battle their numbers were still impressive, and they would surely fight to defend themselves. There were fresh losses to arrows on either side, but with cavalry ready at the edge of the river, Shumat showed no sign of taking the offensive. If what had been said about armies to the south was true, he was militarily correct; he had no need to attack. Time had never run in Kamin-Tolagh's favor, and with the army dispirited, food getting short, it was Shumat's best ally.

Circling away from the fords after his warlike demonstrations, he was intercepted by Sonadhil, one of the most senior of officers left to him, and like all the men of Kargul obviously bewildered by today's tactics.

"Lord," he called out, "I have seen the *rabhsai.*"

"The *Bôdhrai,* you mean," but Sonadhil had been among men of Kargul seconded to the Household, and would not make that mistake.

It must be true; one of the Household squadrons assembled on the road was showing the white banner with Rodlakh's Beech-Tree emblem, displayed only when he was present.

Before he could decide what difference it made, Kamin-Tolagh was welcomed back to the camp of the army by a little delegation of Kargul' officers, Drusilakh, leg bandaged from the wound given by his own tribal troops, Nuvakh, Sonadhil, again their spokesman.

"Your pardon, Lord," cautiously, but with a new cutting edge beneath respect. "Men are wondering if there is to be a new plan."

A fair question, and he did not brusquely send them back to their duties, though not yet ready to take them into his confidence. Kamin-Tarú had convinced him, as nothing else could, that to go forward, if feasible, would be futile, yet there was no direction for retreat. Slipping away by night to westward, a course passing to the south of the Kargan baDulfu would in theory lead to the Farther West, but that journey, largely through unknown, roadless and waterless lands, was over twice the width of Landegh.

"Shumat is a good soldier, but cautious, and he has lost battles before — it was not his boldness that brought us victory against the *jinzal.* Rather than accept casualties, he now hopes to watch us defeat ourselves."

In fact, as these men or any could see for themselves, there was only one whose death or capture meant anything to the realm, and that, not over-caution, was why Shumat was in no hurry; he saw no reason to spend lives killing men who, without Kamin-Tolagh, were negligible.

Sonadhil tried again. "No one, Lord, says we shouldn't fight, if we have an objective."

"Be patient. True, we were robbed of an ally I counted on, surprise. There was treachery." Speaking this, he knew it must be so: the preparedness he had encountered, and tried to blame on an imagined, fleet-winged Hrin spy, was more simply explained: Kamin-Tarú. She had never intended to carry out their scheme, and the letter telling of Tovakh's sickness was bait in a trap. One certain to catch him, because he could never doubt his sister; entrusting the poisoning to anyone else, no matter how devoted, he would have wanted confirmation before embarking an army. Altogether different now to recall how, so she could come to him in the West, she had made Taërinat think she loved him, and kept up the deception for months.

"I would accept offer of a truce, one that acknowledges we are undefeated. But we must stand together, hold the men together, show our nerve has not failed." The empire still stood; Kambanal controlled the docile Hrin, patrols were setting out from Larghamit and Gronu Kizh'klaëdhiyu, coins with his likeness were passing from hand to hand in the Froghushei. If he could make his way back to the West, even at the cost of abandoning these men, setback could be overcome, fresh armies raised, and he would set about conquering the remaining Hrin, before another bout with Rodlakh.

Southward scouts came back mid-afternoon to report steady approach of a mass of cavalry, twenty squadrons at least, in three divisions, roughly equal numbers advancing on the line of the road, and a half-mile to either side. Recent news, evidently, had reached them; their order of march, each division on a front of eights, outriders to the fore, indicated readiness for battle.

Highest ground available was westward of the road, above where camp had been made, and as he began gathering his squadrons there, Tau-Suaka called out, and pointed to the fords, where a knot of riders was emerging, both Household and General Cavalry, banner held in sign of truce. When he rode down to meet them, the leaders were an under-captain not familiar to him, named Kennar, and Dorrmas, not much changed.

"The *rabhsai*," Dorrmas, with obvious relish, "commands me to say: You are now where you can neither advance nor retreat, and enveloped by superior forces. Rodlakh *Deghi* calls on you to lay down arms, to avoid unneeded slaughter."

Kamin-Tolagh smiled condescendingly. "Wonderful, Acting-Captain, that the *rabhsai* can be so sure of what we can or cannot do. What if we decline?"

The question surprised Dorrmas. "Then we attack, with our full strength."

"I think, Acting-Captain, you may find we are more costly to slaughter than infants and pregnant women."

"And you, that in battle the *rabhsai*'s soldiers are not as merciful as the *rabhsai*." Years leading the Household had taken off some of the rough edges, but Kamin-Tolagh's thrust hit flesh, and Dorrmas had darkened in color.

"Unusual for captains so certain of easy victory to plead for a laying-down of weapons. No army undefeated in the field can be required to disarm. To gratify the *rabhsai* and his tender heart, I would agree to a truce, and the unmolested withdrawal of my forces."

"I am not empowered to negotiate — " and like a well-learned lesson he had waited to recite: "While the *rabhsai* is inclined to let men not of this realm depart unharmed, an absolute condition of your surrender is that you remain his prisoner."

"Did you imagine I would negotiate with you, Acting-Captain? Tell the *rabhsai* that in one hour I shall ride to the fords, under *madh'loi*, where he and I can discuss the sparing of lives. Only with the *rabhsai* in person am I willing to make any agreement, and if he declines to meet with me, I shall take that as his answer, and prepare to fight to the last man, against whatever forces the realm can muster."

Dorrmas appeared suspicious of some trick or treachery mere delivery of the message would assist. The other officer spoke close to his ear, and Dorrmas nodded. "Very well, we'll give the *rabhsai* your message, though I think and hope he will refuse to meet you. If this meeting does take place — " adopting an attitude of muted menace — "Let me say, there will be a hundred bows at the ready, and no one had better see the glint of any weapon, if you want to reach the fords alive."

"I shall be wearing my sword," disdainfully. He had been wonderfully exhilarated by his control of this exchange.

44.

"No, no, no," Dolvid said. This was not the same as with Kamin-Tarú, a need that had to be deferred to. Tú had arrived at Rufeni Fords escorted by Talfoyan, ostensibly to offer, on her own authority, twelve squadrons of provincial cavalry waiting only for permission to cross into Nîv, but though she had said and meant she had no desire to be face to face with her brother, that was a farewell of sorts the past had demanded, and a painful one to witness.

A spasm of terror for Dolvid when Rodlakh rode in, as if the confrontation always feared had possessed from the first a will of its own, a contriving mind to guide it through all hindrances, ignoring any improbability so as to achieve itself. And now came the message brought back by Dorrmas.

Shumat quickly aligned with Dolvid. "Kamin-Tolagh is in a hopeless position. You have nothing to gain from talk; *Deghi*, he wants to name a price for what's already yours."

Seated by Rodlakh, Kamin-Tarú appealed to the three men standing. "If I could speak with him again, I might make him give up."

Unlikely, Dolvid thought, from how the former meeting had ended, but he could not blame her for doing all she could to keep her brother from a death bound to haunt her, not only because of what they had been to each other. As Dolvid had told her three times, Kamin-Tolagh's folly had brought him here, not anything she had done or neglected, but she would not forgive herself so easily.

They were in the shabby room where he had been sleeping. The tough old owner, who eked out a wayside living doing minor repairs to harness and brewing a murky ale, also, to judge by the smell an easterly breeze wafted from the rear, collected horse-droppings to sell as manure; the past few days must have brought him a harvest without precedent. After letting out his room grudgingly, he had grown increasingly gratified at use of his house as an informal headquarters; he had a married daughter and numerous grandchildren living near Kir, and his button eyes gleamed in anticipation of stories he would have to tell, that legendary day when his bigroom at one time contained the Captains of Household and of All Armies, the daughter to Kargul, the *Bôdhrai*, and, if you'd believe him, Rodlakh *Rabhsai*, in person. By demanding a bed for the night, Dolvid was afraid he had become midwife to a bore.

Rodlakh spoke thoughtfully. "No, I had better talk with him, if it can bring him nearer to admitting hopelessness. There are things only I can say, after all."

"*Deghi*," Shumat said. "Can't they be said as well after we have him captured?"

"He says he will surrender only to me in person — " glancing to Dorrmas for confirmation that was correct.

Dolvid objected, "I have not heard that Kamin-Tolagh said he would surrender to anyone."

"A truce, then, and withdrawal of his armies," Dorrmas allowed. "If he won't negotiate, *Deghi*, let us crush him. With the new forces from the south, it shouldn't take an hour." A bloody hour, Dolvid thought. He had been angered yesterday by that pointless sortie, unnecessarily costing nearly twenty Household lives; the man stumbled in some way whenever he commanded troops in the field. He could be replaced at the head of the Household without dishonor, by restoring his title, otherwise held only by the fabled Kheval, Royal Master of Weapons. As Kheval's had been, the swordsmanship of Dorrmas was unequalled; only his judgment flawed.

"With loss of how many lives?" Rodlakh asked.

Dorrmas shrugged out an obscure monosyllable.

"What is left to him? As you say, he cannot withstand us, and must know it. But pride prevents him from relinquishing his sword, unless he can offer it to me."

"That would be his way," Kamin-Tarú tearfully agreed.

"Should we coddle his pride," Shumat asked. "After all he has cost us?"

"If it saves some dying, the added price is small." Rodlakh had been saddened to hear of the losses defending the fords and before; no count had come for the fighting in the south, but reports were of a fierce and bitter battle. He had been scarcely less shocked by the heavier enemy casualties, unable to watch bodies of men and horses being hauled out of the river.

"I am against this meeting," Dolvid, impotently, as miserable as anyone. Had there ever been less elation among leaders of a realm on the brink of resounding victory?

The Siv'loi Banner flapped bravely ahead of four squadrons still resembling men willing to fight, and ahead of them, Kamin-Tolagh with a small personal escort, Tau-Suaka broodingly in charge. He had asked if this new talk meant Lord Kamin-Tolagh was to be taken without a fight.

A grin. "Such an act would be beyond the *rabhsai's* imagining."

"Then what is to be gained, Lord?"

"Our chance to change everything."

Misunderstanding, Tau-Suaka had hunted in his bulged leather bag of belongings, and found a small knife, blade slender as spear-grass, and started to fit in his sleeve a cuplike scabbard where it would rest point out. So armed, he boasted, he could kill at twenty paces with a sudden gesture, and he was disappointed when told to leave it behind.

From the edge of the river could be seen nothing but watchful soldiers of the realm. He reached the place where Lavsila had died, and at his instruction the standard-bearer planted the banner with a quick thrust into the stony shoal.

He sat like a statue. On this campaign he had brought two swords, and for the first time was wearing the finer weapon given by Saidhan, the blade, still celibate in Kamin-Tolagh's possession, that had killed Tobhsila, seventy years ago.

Tau-Suaka fidgeted. "Is the *rabhsai* to come here, Lord?"

As he spoke, pikemen drew aside to allow passage to four riders, one a young Household man with the Beech-Tree standard. The others were Rodlakh flanked by Dolvid and Shumat.

The *rabhsai* halted at a distance about the length of his mount, and folded his arms. Kamin-Tolagh gave no kind of salute; Rodlakh, he thought, looked scarcely older, but a little below his best, pallid, as if too much indoors.

"*Rabhsai*. You have used your soldiers well."

Shumat was the one to respond. "Your army will not say the same of you. Niburai, if you meet again, won't be so complimentary."

"He knew his purpose. With all my men, he knows I never ask anyone to do what I would not dare myself." He would continue this purposeful taunting of Rodlakh, whose silence was unreadable.

And stretched on, as Dolvid produced and read a prepared statement. "*Your military position now being untenable*," he began, "*the* rabhsai *will accept your surrender, on the following terms: your followers will submit to disarming, and be treated as prisoners-of-war. Those of origin other than this realm, dependent on their good behavior, are to be permitted, so far as can be arranged assisted, to return to their homelands. Those who have taken oaths as soldiers of Kargul are to be subject to the law of their* nimu, *except the* rabhsai *gives his personal pledge to intercede with the* Nim' Tovakh *for remission of all penalty beyond dismissal from his service.*

"*As for your own person —* " glancing up from the page, and Kamin-Tolagh waved genially for him to go on.

"*While you are* kaël'rolai *under the laws of the realm to which your oath was given, and therefore condemned by your simple presence, the* rabhsai *does not seek your death. After surrendering your sword to the* rabhsai, *you are to be treated with all due honor, as a prisoner of highest rank. At some future time, the* rabhsai *may consider your release, if guarantees can be found for your good conduct.*"

Three times slowly, Kamin-Tolagh clapped hands together in sardonic applause. "So," he said, "I am to become Emperor of the Marionettes, hung up in a cupboard at Burantal, taken out at Pledgings, and when some drunk on the Avenue shouts `Freedom for Kamin-Tolagh,' a whole realm trembles. I am dizzied by all this clemency.

"And yet, *Rabhsai*," softly, "your desire to spare lives condemns an empire. Without me, there is no empire in the West; those lands will fall into anarchy and war, with widespread starvation to go with murder and rape."

"The *rabhsai*," quickly, before Rodlakh could answer, "cannot be accountable for your failure to provide for orderly succession."

Orderly succession! Kamin-Tolagh only just held back a laugh of derision at the picture of tame ceremony, there where nothing held back chaos, except his will.

Rodlakh spoke at last. "I do not want anyone to starve. But you must admit, this realm has scarcely benefitted from existence of what you call your empire, which began in defiance of my express command. We have had insult, threats, attempts to subvert the loyalty of my subjects, incursions and injuries within our borders, and now a full invasion, with many deaths. Do you expect me to mourn the passing of all this?"

"Are you done?" Kamin-Tolagh asked Dolvid, who had not put away the page of terms. "Let me point out, I am not a prisoner, my army is undefeated, though I understand your wish to impose defeat by words, at no further cost to yourselves. My men are not laying down their arms, my officers are not going to be surrendered to Tovakh's vengeance, and I am not to be a prisoner. I shall never be a prisoner," he emphasized. "Do you know nothing about me, *Rabhsai*?"

"The *rabhsai* knows you are beaten," Shumat said.

"The *rabhsai* knows war takes unexpected turns. There is a price for avoiding its uncertainties. I would agree to a truce, and to marching my men, with their weapons but escorted as you see fit, to Thenimala, to await shipping, or, properly supplied, to their homes by way of the Colony and Drin Navuna."

"What about yourself?" Rodlakh said.

"I remain at their head."

"This is nonsense," Shumat protested. "You are defeated in a war of your own making, and now you want everything to go back to where it was before."

"My coming here was an honest mistake. My sister must have told you that."

"This is, as Shumat says, nonsense," Rodlakh, still even-voiced. "You are asking me to ratify your sovereignty, as a reward for attacking me."

"I was less slow to acknowledge yours — " Kamin-Tolagh admired his own shrewdness. "Without my allegiance, and the blood of Kargul, you would not have come to where you can sit in judgment over my acts."

"My title was lawful," but with a trace of pain at Kamin-Tolagh's reminder.

"When Dolvid first came to me those years ago, asking for an end to civil war, I misunderstood what he was seeking, and said it could be decided between Rodlakh and myself, lance to lance, sword to sword. Let me say that again, *rabhsai*; we can settle this in single fight. Your wish is to save lives, and one added death can accomplish that. If mine, you have your peace, without the embarrassment of a captive you can never dare let go; if yours, the terms as I propose become effective."

Rodlakh looked up keenly, but Dolvid's response almost elbowed him aside: "This is a question for *Rabhsai*'s Law, not his lance. The future of realms cannot be decided by the chances of single fight."

"It happened before. The *rabhsai*'s house was established so. Why not single fight? if the future of realms can be changed by the scrawled gossip of a seamstress — " but he was not completely certain anyone here would understand that allusion.

"What does the *rabhsai* say? His grandfather claimed *rabhsayum* for his triumph, but all I want is safe-conduct back to lands I have made my own."

"I'll fight you on those terms," Shumat said. "With the *rabhsai*'s leave."

"For myself, I would be honored." Any smile was at the absurdity of the offer, not at Shumat, nor his prowess. "But mine is now a simpler world, where deputies would not be understood, only chieftain against chieftain. Great Banak did not fight Tobhsila, but only because he was not there."

"We — no need — " Dolvid uncharacteristically stumbled, and began again: "We need not be slaves to history. It is a different world; fitness to rule is proved by good laws and just decisions, not with a sword." He was speaking mainly to, or at, Rodlakh, and was nearer showing panic than Kamin-Tolagh could have imagined; the man had appeared fearless on his visit to the Abu, and had demonstrated a frustrating cool-headedness in the subsequent pursuit across Landegh.

"But the *rabhsai*, I think, has a personal grudge, and is unwilling to see more men die, settling his quarrel — " becoming surer that Rodlakh, not having instantly rejected his challenge, was going to fight him.

"If I decline this?"

"Then, *Deghi*, we shall both have fewer subjects going home to their wives and children. Your captains tell me we have no hope; we'll fight without it."

"What weapons?" The quiet question brought wordless interjections from both Dolvid and Shumat.

"Those of the *péfrapravádai* — " lance, sword and a parry-blade.

"Under the ancient rules, but waiving the wounding clause."

"To the death, in short."

Shumat, Rodlakh having shown small interest in his objections, tried another way. "This is a fight," he told Kamin-Tolagh, "you can't win. Do you believe we'd let you go free, if you won?"

"You are Rodlakh's men. No one has said the *rabhsai* is not a man of his word; to go back on his solemn undertaking would be a shabby way to honor his memory."

For the first time, Rodlakh came near returning his calculated mockery. "I am not yet a topic for memory alone. But I shall not be remembered to history as a snake who could still bite when dead. We shall prepare a written statement of the agreement. The document should afford me amusement, years from now."

"There is to be no such fight," Dolvid said.

"Oh, yes," Rodlakh contradicted. "The only proper ending."

"It is not needed, *Deghi* — " but he was obviously handicapped by the awkwardness of public dispute with the *rabhsai*.

"When?" Rodlakh asked.

"Now, if you wish." Nothing was reasonable in Rodlakh's decision to fight; if he could win, which he could not, it would still be a foolish choice; any delay, with calm time for reconsideration, together with a massive effort from his advisors to change his mind, might lose Kamin-Tolagh this last chance to save the Empire.

"The light is poor," Shumat said. Daylong sun had vanished behind a wall of westward cloud.

"At first light, then."

"Here, by the fords? You will wish to spend a last night with your troops."

"And you, *Rabhsai*, will no doubt wish to instruct your squadrons in the field not to take any offensive action against us."

The serenity of Rodlakh's assent was hard to fathom; barring outlandish accident, he would die in the morning. In well over eight years since the Jinzai War he could hardly have handled a lance except ceremonially; he had been skilled, but it was an art needing constant practice. Could he be tired of life? But he had an accomplished wife, children, an ardent bed-friend, a realm. Âna as a widow, a diversion to be deferred, though no conceit but simple calculation no thresh she'd had with the inexpert Rodlakh could have effaced memory of her pleasures with him. With nothing further owed to Kamin-Tarú, he might think of marrying and making an heir, though it remained true that Rodlakh's brood would have to be disposed of, not in malice, for the sake of safety.

"Till tomorrow, then," he told Rodlakh, and had a pleasant nod for each of the grim-faced companions.

Rodlakh had been writing. "All the advantages are on my side. Not really a fair fight. Kamin-Tolagh and his mount have both been either at sea or in the field for weeks."

This new blithe mood was worse than the impassive determination it had succeeded. Dolvid had come from a serious discussion with Shumat on the possibility of forcibly restraining Rodlakh, invoking the doctrine of incompetence to rule: they could call his state a fit of madness, restoring him to his rank after Kamin-Tolagh was safely disposed of. They were, however, only two votes in Council, where they would have practically no chance of winning retrospective approval; nor would they be forgiven by a *rabhsai* declared back in his right mind.

"True," cheerfully, "disuse can be worse than weariness, but I have ridden a course with lance from time to time, and do not think I have lost much of my skill. So they tell me."

So they, young soldiers hoping for promotion, told the *rabhsai*. The practice course was in the Residence grounds, and

Dolvid had witnessed a canter by Rodlakh there, a year or so back. Horse had been managed well, the rider had missed no targets — none of which had meaning for an actual bout; as he knew from his own swordfighting, fundamental ability did not rust, but the capacity for tiny adjustments, quicker than thought, for a particular adversary, the amazingly small difference between victory and defeat.

"At the time of the war," not boasting, merely assessing, "I was, I believe, the better lance, though there was not much in it."

"Since the Jinzai War," Dolvid lectured, "you have shown yourself the better ruler by far. The realm has no shortage of lances." In any other question, he, in Âna's absence, would have best chance of changing Rodlakh's mind, but here his old prophetic dream was a handicap, robbing his voice of conviction when he tried to insist there was to be no duel.

"Oh, the realm could survive my loss better than yours," simply. "Or Âna's. You can add this to your bundle." He sealed and handed over a letter for Orbanak. There was already one for his wife, and a witnessed codicil to his testament, all to be opened only if Rodlakh failed to survive.

"I have told Orbanak, you must remain *Bôdhrai*, not that it needs saying; he is your greatest admirer." With Rodlakh's son still a child, the succession, because of an incomplete mingling of two traditions, was not quite a settled thing, but Orbanak would be no less than Protector, and generally expected to step aside when Lambakh reached eighteen.

Rodlakh stood, to place his hands on Dolvid's shoulders. "With the aid of Zhôl, I do not expect to lose. But I know you would give Orbanak all the help and loyalty you have shown me. Âna, too, with the children, will be grateful for your friendship. As for — " but he swallowed that, and substituted, "But I shall win, by Zhôl's grace."

For an instant his eyes had held unhappy bafflement, as when he had refused to so much as discuss reconciliation with Kamin-Tolagh, the muddle he suffered when choice between right and wrong was not a clear one. This time, it could only be Morulis, and Âna's instincts must be right; in a fog of gratification Rodlakh had vowed the girl more than should ever be vowed by a man who, in the end, would always choose wife and children. But absurd to suppose he was courting death because he regretted his words, because he could not tell a girl, not especially fascinating, unearthly beauty allowed-for, that he had made a mistake when he talked about eternity, and had now worn out his interest.

"As for Morulis," Dolvid supplied. Rodlakh's start confirmed the guess.

"That is not mentioned," but lightly.

"Then for this one time, let me claim privilege of long acquaintance and shared dangers to say, Morulis has every reason, now and no matter what, to be grateful for your favor, and if you were to round out the benefits you have brought her with the gift of some land, her considerable attractions would be yet-more irresistible. Any number of Heartlanders, once she was free, would beg for her hand if it had nothing in it. Badh-Kizhai, Kizhunai's son, to name only one."

"But she — "

"Was not indifferent to Badh-Kizhai, before she was invited to a post she could hardly decline, even if she had not been altogether dazzled by her quick change of fortune. She is from a family filled with good sense."

Rodlakh, after indecision whether to be annoyed or to ask for further detail, nearly grinned. "Is this the way it is managed?"

"Through intermediaries, the custom was, before your father made royal adventures unfashionable. Unless you want to, you need not see the lady face to face. You are *rabhsai*."

For a long moment Rodlakh contemplated nothing in particular, till a distaste for the process was overruled by relief at its result. "I thank you."

"If you want to thank me, call off the fight."

"You know that cannot be."

The *rabhsai* breakfasted on bread and a glass of wine, and having armed went out where his mount was waiting. While he was waking, attempts to alter his determination to fight were incessant, and when he slept the plots to achieve the same result all ended where the need to protect him began; he was the *rabhsai*.

Dorrmas lay in wait. "*Deghi*, respectfully, I wish to claim the right to ride against Kamin-Tolagh, who has insulted me personally." To Dolvid's ear, it sounded over-rehearsed; Shumat must have coached him.

"My wrong takes precedence, Captain. If he wins, you may then challenge him; he has no rank we recognize, and the Ní-Tilagh is outside the realm."

Dorrmas became awkward. "Not because I had any thought of his winning, *Deghi*... "

"How would you wager?"

"He's good," at once the professional. "Good, but he can be careless; he hasn't often fought anybody near his equal, you see, and these past few years he's been out among hackers and prodders. I recall, he sometimes carried his lance a little wide. If it was my fight, I would go for the lance, first pass, and see if he could be disarmed."

Rodlakh pushed out his lower lip. "Should I want that? With swords, he is probably my better."

"Well — you highborn, pardon me, always do, but there's nothing in the Rules of Honorable Combat to say you have to throw away your lance, *Deghi*, just because he's lost his."

"So long as the disarming is fair," Shumat, missing not a syllable. "Within the rules, he will use every advantage."

Dolvid chimed in: "His own sister calls him a killer. No gallantries." Killing Kamin-Tolagh before the fight could begin was one of desperate expedients discussed with Shumat, and now he was ashamed of a wisp of hope Dorrmas would be the one to do it. Dishonorable, treacherous, an act of unthinkable baseness, but Rodlakh would survive. He would also be furious, and between that and his need to disown the act, might in this one instance approve of execution for the murderer — but Dorrmas with his blood up had sometimes been oblivious to consequences; while Dolvid could never put the thought in that impetuous mind, self-disgust would not make the idea go away. But he still kept looking up the road, in the other more admissible hope that, after so many unlikely arrivals, Âna would come, and with a few words shake Rodlakh's unneeded resolve.

Mounted, Rodlakh tugged on his gauntlets.

"Do not rely on justice," Dolvid warned. "Being in the right is not enough; Rheduban killed Sebhal."

"Yes, yes, yes." He tested his sword was free in its scabbard, and with an open hand asked for his lance.

"I have thought through what I am about. Where could you make a better bargain? If I win, as I mean to, we are rid of him; if not, we are rid of him; after this mauling he will be in no hurry to try the realm again. I often find my life wearisome," he added, not much above a whisper.

"Not wearisome." pushing aside sententious words about the duty to endure tedium. "More perplexing than you would prefer."

"Perhaps. Well, wish me good fortune."

"Zhôl watch you," grasping the proffered left hand, pieties emerging to rescue the inadequacy of reason. "Hrafi guide your skill."

Morning for Kamin-Tolagh was a slow, ritual dance, watched rather than taken part in. Breakfasting on cheese, he noted there was no one to talk to; Kambanal was far away, the rest killed, or lost to him. The companionship of Tau-Suaka was that of a faithful dog who had learnt a few devoted words. Lavsila — Lavsila was a fool, who had brought his own death. Presumably, Khaëlu would find a new mate; she had never been happy with this, or any of her husbands.

With nothing said, the river had till now served as a line of truce, and he was momentarily annoyed to see soldiers of the realm spreading from the fords, to take their stand on his side of the stream. However, with armies from the south already camped to the rear of Kamin-Tolagh, there was no military gain in this advance; on the contrary, the men were more vulnerable with their backs to the water. They must want to view the duel.

Dawn mist was being dispersed by a fresh breeze from the southeast, and in pale sunlight pennons planted to mark the starting-places, five hundred paces apart, fluttered brightly. Leaving much of his sullen army on high ground, Kamin-Tolagh moved some squadrons down to face riverward, ignoring the enemy behind; as he told Sonadhil, there was only one man with fighting left to do.

His other companions as he rode out were Tau-Suaka, and a man with the Siv'loi Banner, and when Rodlakh appeared he was again flanked by Dolvid and Shumat, with his standard borne by as lofty a rank as Dorrmas.

In silence, a grim-faced Dolvid proffered two pages containing the agreed terms, one to be signed and returned. The tense faces of Rodlakh's soldier companions made Kamin-Tolagh increasingly confident he would win.

The two principals, accompanied now by only their first deputies, Sonadhil and Shumat, rode shoulder to shoulder, as was customary, to the stake marking midpoint between pennons. So far, eyes had not met, but when they halted Kamin-Tolagh thrust out his gloved hand.

"I bear you no malice, *Rabhsai*."

"Nor I you." Helmed, Rodlakh half-turned to face him, but did not take his hand. "No more than I would a pestilence."

Too proud to show anger, Kamin-Tolagh made a gesture Rodlakh must respond to, drawing sword and saluting him. The *rabhsai* did the same, but chief object was that he see and recognize the blade Kamin-Tolagh was displaying, the one to slay Tobhsila baKargul. But he had been lucky enough to die in a deep-grassed mountain-valley of his home province, not a forsaken place, officially nowhere.

Deputies withdrew, and as he jogged back to the starting place, unslinging his lance, he felt perfectly prepared, taut yet calm like the favorite chestnut *pefrai* under him; his long-weapon was light and living to the hand.

Halted, he raised it in sign of readiness. After a moment, the distant Rodlakh did the same, then dipped his point. His rather blunt-headed roan was a little skittish, but soon settled into its trot. For once, as he started forward, Kamin-Tolagh detached the helm from his saddle-bow, and one-handed placed it on his head; he guessed the *rabhsai*'s extensive circle of expert advisors would have dwelt on his habit of fighting bare-headed.

The splendid *pefrai* was a continuation of himself, the two great horses consuming space between them, as they moved to the canter. Rodlakh's point, up and across, gave away early that he wanted to pass right; not for any particular advantage, but to toy a little, Kamin-Tolagh edged his beast left, and left again, and just when he had influenced Rodlakh to change his mind and cross with his point, swung hard right instead, flicking the *rabhsai*'s shoulder-guard with the tip of his lance. A sound, a knowing sigh, came from many watchers; Rodlakh had been unable to bring his lance back in time.

Circling wide about the opposite starting-pennon, a laugh in his throat, Kamin-Tolagh settled to his second run. Closing with a determined Rodlakh, perhaps remembering his last serious bout with lances had been with Chamya, he was surprised by a deep resentment, of Rodlakh, as of Shumat and Dolvid, all men who had fathered sons. Kamin-Tarú, not noted among spectators, would marry now, bear children, a distracting thought. He was close to Rodlakh, who made a feint at his shoulder, pulling wide, and instead banging down hard on his lance. A shout sounded from riverward, a groan from his own men; in jarred astonishment Kamin-Tolagh saw lance falling behind, beyond reach of his lunge to regain it.

Wheeling instantly, he drew sword, and pressed after Rodlakh, not to let him open a space for a good run, lance to sword. He would accept the advantage; this was deadly business, not courtly dance with snouted weapons. The disarming was obviously planned.

Unable to make space he wanted, Rodlakh tried a sudden, shorter run, surprising Kamin-Tolagh, who needed all his horsemanship to avoid being taken on the left. Cool and clear-headed, he waited for the second lunge, leaning to let point slide past his elbow, sweeping back for a cut at his adversary's wrist, but striking instead thick part of the lance-haft. Glad to keep his seat, he ducked away, and there came a second, louder groan. When he could turn, he saw Rodlakh had dropped lance, and was shaking out the stung fingers on his right hand.

Instead of crowding in, mastered by his love of style he halted, and with an ironic salute allowed Rodlakh to collect himself, and draw his sword. The *rabhsai*'s great chance had been lance against blade, but advantage now had swung back: Kamin-Tolagh believed himself fitter, in better practice, while the light, strong blade he had was very much to his taste. In battle, a heavy cavalry sword might be better for beating down a crude defense, but between skilled opponents wearing body-armor, it was most often thrusting point that found flesh. Also, he would tire slower, if the fight was prolonged.

He closed with Rodlakh, no bad horseman himself. Their opening exchange was muscle rather than art, a clanging double series of forehand and backhand slashes, Rodlakh evidently feeling his best chance was to keep his man off-balance. He went for head and neck, and Kamin-Tolagh was waiting for it when the low backhander came, turning it off his thigh, grinning as he did so, and coming back at once with some flickering point-work that had Rodlakh defending, and hauling his horse aside.

Feeling well within himself, he let Rodlakh come at him again, and yet again; the *rabhsai's* lack of regular practice would soon be felt in the sword-arm, turning it to lead. Kamin-Tolagh laughed at another failed sequence, and Rodlakh, exasperated, lunged wild, wounding the neck of his opponent's *pefrai*.

Not specifically forbidden under the rules, an attack on the mount was despised far beyond many acts that were. Rodlakh, backing to defend against the counter, observed blood on the horse's neck, and grimaced.

Kamin-Tolagh might have been angry, but imposed control. "An accident, *Rabhsai*," lowering his point.

Settling into the saddle, Rodlakh for the first time displayed a token courtesy. "Do you wish to remount yourself? If you are short of animals, use one of ours."

He laughed, but not mockingly. "I am to fight for my life, on the back of a beast I do not know?" He would fight on, but it was painful to see the *pefrai* bleed. The cut was deep, but the animal appeared to feel nothing. "I would be willing to see us both dismounted."

Rodlakh considered it, then nodded.

While Kamin-Tolagh cantered to where Sonadhil stood, and dismounting told him how to care for the wounded *pefrai*, Rodlakh rode away in the opposite direction, to leave his mount with Dorrmas. Having also discarded their helms, they now paced for center of the fighting space, and Kamin-Tolagh was aware that like a wall creeping behind him, spectators were drawing closer. A part of his advantage was gone; not for years had he crossed blades with a swordsman of the first rank, while Rodlakh's practice, no matter how infrequent, would have been with Dorrmas, a master.

Both now additionally drew their daggers, used mainly for parrying. After a touch of blades, Kamin-Tolagh sprang to the attack, but Rodlakh's defense was deft, and he used his feet well, not easily hurried out of balance, keeping his counters short and quick. The fighting lost its crudely muscular side, and became a spectacle for young soldiers to watch with profit, two well-trained swordsmen in full manhood, matched for height and reach, both fluent and inventive. Needing skill to stay alive, Kamin-Tolagh could at the same time admire; they were making a bout that would be talked of while there were swords left in the world.

For fully five minutes, neither gave the other any respite. In a fight for his life, the *rabhsai* did not scorn to attack legs, while Kamin-Tolagh kept his threat flickering chiefly at face and throat.

A turning, close-quarters movement, where swords rang and slithered in strange music, and if watchers gave voice, Kamin-Tolagh did not hear; his world was their nimble feet and breath working hard in nostrils, magical knowledge of where the next thrust would come.

In a momentary separation, Rodlakh tried to gulp in air, and Kamin-Tolagh stepped back to lean on his sword, smiling. Rodlakh looked wildly in his face, and seeing a momentary ebbing of grimness, Kamin-Tolagh thought and nearly said, *smile then, curse you*. As he almost did, but then gathered himself, bringing up his point.

"Let us finish this."

Back and forth, weaving, the fight went. "I have built citics, *rabhsai*," teasingly, "what have you made?" The only reply was a new rush, not easily fought off.

"I have planted the desert. What have you grown?"

"I have lived in peace," the last word underlined by a sweeping mow at Kamin-Tolagh's legs.

"Peace is for the old and dead. Does peace teach this?" He unleashed a dazzling sequence, point again and again in face, at throat, his middle. At last, somewhat awkwardly, Rodlakh ducked away, Kamin-Tolagh letting him disengage.

A hooting cry, that must come from Tau-Suaka, a warning, and Kamin-Tolagh caught what was meant; he was in the dangerous state of savoring his artistry, enjoying the bout too much to end it.

When they closed again, Rodlakh sensed his new purposcfulness, concentrating on defense.

"I have pleased your *rabhsayu* in ways — " taunts, too, had a newly cutting edge, but breath and moisture were becoming scarcer, and Kamin-Tolagh did not finish the thought; no further words were exchanged as fight went back and forth again. The faint throb at his shoulder was to be welcomed; it must be much worse for Rodlakh with his heavier blade, and his feet were beginning to drag a little.

At the moment of that assessment, Rodlakh stumbled slightly going back, and as his guard wavered, was wounded inside the right elbow.

He rallied furiously, using dagger to cover and leaping forward, while droplets of bright blood spattered the ground. The sheer desperation of it had Kamin-Tolagh defending hard, but as he went back he saw the sudden wobble of the *rabhsai*'s point. Slipping a tired thrust, warding a jab from the dagger, he let Rodlakh's body slam against his, and saw pain in the face, heard the labored breathing.

"You could yield," though that option had been waived. If the rule were in effect, Rodlakh's wound would not be enough to oblige Kamin-Tolagh to give quarter.

The *rabhsai*'s eyes held what was either contempt for the offer, or defiance of pain. Kamin-Tolagh thrust him back, and with that body, all responsibility for its end. Against slowed blade, he made his final, deliberate advance, repeatedly stabbing at the face. Rodlakh parried five, six, times, pain in his eyes growing. His point drooped.

A long, strange moment. Nothing was needed but a thrust to the throat. In Kamin-Tolagh's mind were too many thoughts, that Rodlakh's death meant nothing, that for him there was no place left but the West, a West without Chamya, Freighanai, Lavsila. Without Kamin-Tarú, for whom it was made.

In the same tiny division of time, beat of a bee's wings, the *rabhsai*'s face had almost time to form a frown, and Kamin-Tolagh thought of Kamsilat, where Rodlakh, with a kind of insane bravery, had plunged among *jinzal* to save his life, and where they had stood together, shoulder to shoulder, using their swords with a power and a skill never surpassed.

"Oh, curse it," he muttered. He could not; he made a futile gesture with dagger hand, lowering his point. This could be settled, he wanted to say, by other means.

Exhausted, bleeding, weakened, teetering back from a last brink, Rodlakh never read Kamin-Tolagh's intent, seeing only inexplicable loss of resolution. With a grunt of effort, the *rabhsai* stumbled in to plant, left-handed, his dagger above the other breastplate.

Disbelieving, Kamin-Tolagh watched the slender blade slide in, and felt hot pain. Rodlakh tugged the weapon free, and stabbed again, now to side of the neck.

He saw astonishment; Kamin-Tolagh's sword dropped from his hand, which went up to paw at protruding haft of the dagger. Lurching slowly back, he tried to speak, and where small rocks jutted, fell. He half sat up, rolled over in much blood, coughed, and died.

There was, perhaps, a shout from the *rabhsayanil*. Going to where the weapon had fallen, Rodlakh stooped to pick it up, the sword once Saidhan's, its chased blade gleaming in weak sun. With a quick, nearly blind move, he laid the sword next to Kamin-Tolagh, now still.

Âna said, "Shumat allowed *it could have gone either way*, and a man willing to say that much could have said more. Rodlakh told me Kamin-Tolagh's nerve failed at the last. Is that what you believe?"

"Let it be." That terrible and tremendous duel had acquired a rapid fame outside its principals or circumstances, and Dolvid was questioned about it everywhere, as if there was (or could be) a mystery about an event so public, played out in clear light with a thousand witnesses, outcome broadcast from Narn to Drin Navuna within days.

Inadequate, no, inaccurate, to speak of a failure of nerve, and Dolvid had seen Rodlakh weep when first he alleged it, but there was to be no legend of Kamin-Tolagh. Given scales for balancing all the acts of their lives, Rodlakh's would dip decisively on the side of benefit, Kamin-Tolagh's come banging down on the side of harm, and yet Dolvid, and surely he was not unique, had not misread the gesture in which he had declined the kill. Rodlakh, clinging to life by fingernails, could be forgiven, but Kamin-Tolagh, beyond eradication, had displayed in his end a quality his adversary aspired to and at that most testing time failed to find. A tiny moment, and not one to be judged by standards of calm and leisured choice, but anyone could be compassionate, generous and right given an hour; unfairly or not, it in was such irretrievable blinks of an eye that lives were ruthlessly evaluated.

"What would you have done if Rodlakh — if it had ended differently?"

As always, he knew exactly where she had gone. "All I could, but I do not say I could have left my family."

She nodded. "In his care for all our futures, the *rabhsai* seems not to have considered that without him, I would not be *rabhsayu*. I would have been nothing at all."

"Mother to the Heir."

She brushed that aside. "As for me, if there were no Rodlakh, I would want to come to you, if it meant never seeing my children again."

"Except you would despise a man who could abandon all I have at Kamsilat." He had just come from there.

"As you say," sadly, then with sudden fierceness, "No. Aëlu is everything I am not, everything admirable, but I hate her for having you."

"You do not." And once said she had tried and failed.

"You don't know me."

"Who knows you better?"

"Give me the task Kamin-Tarú had so as to be with the man she wanted, and see whether I decline it."

Dolvid grinned, though she believed she was entirely in earnest. "Like her, you would stop loving him when he became the man who could propose such a plan." Not exactly what had happened; that would have been much easier for Kamin-Tarú.

"Well," dubiously, "if you know me so well, you use it only to make your flattery more convincing. No wonder women have loved you." She made it sound a deficiency.

Long-postponed decision they would no longer bed together was by common consent, but she had been the one to speak it; with Morulis abruptly betrothed to Badh-Kizhai, Rodlakh was taking his father as model for marital attentiveness. That was now, but as Âna herself had once observed, *rabhsayum* sat awkwardly with self-denial, and she might have a future Morulis or two to endure, now Rodlakh had acquired the important technique of disengagement. For Dolvid, if there was to be no more than talk, ever, these times alone with Âna would remain a treasured necessity; there was no marvel sweeter then this sure alliance of temperament, and he was going to maintain, notwithstanding her gruff displays, their indestructible affection.

As so often, he encountered Faëdhal in the library, a reminder of past time, and it would be foolish to say more; his return to tutoring had slighted his many minor ailments, not cured them. The old scholar was placid now, remoter, and at times made no response to greetings or queries, not through deafness or any weakening of wits, but in a spell of self-sufficiency no longer to be broken by social obligation.

Today, he was alert to others, and like everyone eager to discuss Kamin-Tolagh.

"His death, as I hear, was anything but that of a coward. A point which may be of some small consolation to, ah, those who must remember him — as, indeed, for all of us who had such great hopes of him, great hopes."

"And even great memories," thinking of the tremendous ride to Kamsilat.

"Indeed, indeed. Yet, correct me, Dolvidhai, that courage by which we mean carelessness about death is to my mind a virtue that can be too highly prized — no virtue at all, unless found together with some of the gentler ones, as with Banak-rai — or, may I say, our present *rabhsai*. Did Kamin-Tolagh ever weep?"

"If so, he did it as a child does, because his toy is broken."

Yes, yes, but not enough; riding down a darkening Avenue for his house, empty except for servants and guards, Dolvid was mystified and exasperated by the sorrow he continued to feel. Hard, quite naturally, to say farewell to Kamin-Tolagh as a problem, subject of so much thought and strategy, assessments of his strength and guesses at his intentions, but with that allowed for, there was still what ought to be a shameful sadness, as at passing of a unique glory, regret not driven away by the orderly recapitulation and fresh deploring of all the terrible crimes and cruelties, the logical supposition there must be others as bad or worse not known.

It connected with the success of pikes at Rufeni Fords. As their foster-father, Dolvid was proud of how they had performed, of their steadfast courage and drilled effectiveness, yet in the triumph was a dour efficiency new to war, marching in a different age, to which individual dash and daring of the *péfrapravádai* would be at best marginal — Kamin-Tolagh at Lunu Tezh' Gate, lengths ahead of his men, riding against massed *jinzal*, and laughing as he did. That had happened, as had the proud courtesy with which he had given the shaken Rodlakh time to recover and rearm after losing his lance, but if there had been occasional splendors, their gleam should surely be dimmed by all the spatters of innocent blood.

Were we all in our yearnings criminal monsters? or was it that the self-obsessed child who wanted the world arranged for his gratification and convenience, not caring who suffered to make it so, was only layered-over and suppressed by the experience of life, surviving in the heart to recognize, furtively exult in a Kamin-Tolagh, with his lordly and childlike contempt for rules, his unconcern over the pain and death he caused? He had been wicked to transcend the terms of his own cynical view of history, a book written by the winners, where only crimes of the defeated were recorded; virtue triumphed in his death. Yet his scale had not been small, and the sensation of loss, however reprehensible, could not be pretended-away, a sentimental nostalgia for that callous striving after glory which lifts a heart far beyond small, grey, licit gains for wisdom and compassion.

End of the Sixth Part

*EPILOGUE**

The death of Kamin-Tolagh at once divided the Empire into distinct parts. South, the occupied Hrin lands, for a time also included the trading-station at Zelu Bablakhi, with intermittent control over the distant port of Larghamit. Kamin-Tolagh's successor at Hyolenstr was Kambanal, who sustained his rule with largely native troops. After two years, those formerly of the realm remaining petitioned *Rabhsai* Rodlakh to extend amnesty. At that time, the Hrin lands were in turmoil, following assassination of a popular religious leader, the *Hridveyuth*, and Kambanal was at last forced to take refuge with his followers in the fortified port of Hyolenstr.

Blockaded there by land and sea, on the point of unconditional capitulation, the Heartlanders and men of Kargul were saved from probable massacre by intervention of Hvrayos, hitherto least powerful of provincial overlords, but now emerging as a conciliator in the complex religious and social struggles of the Hrin. A warm admirer of our heritage, who had become friendly with Kambanal, Hvrayos with his intercession enabled the Heartlanders, who faced no charges in the *rabhsayum* of Rodlakh, to return to their homes by way of Thenimala. The men of Kargul were given refuge with Hvrayos till word came they too would be permitted to return, on the same terms as their predecessors from the northern empire. Among them was Dubovai, who, despite injuries sustained in war, has since been able to pursue his craft, and is of course the well-known Dubovai Mapmaker, whose skill has contributed to this and several other volumes.

This repatriation ended any alien claim to Hrin territory, but was the beginning of our present much closer relationship with that people, following their eventual unification under Hvrayos, now first *Hridyust*, a title closely equivalent to our *rabhsai* (though possessing, also, some religious significance). Kambanal, with rank of *bôdh'loiki*, titular Advisor to the *Rabhsai* for the Farther West, with special reference to the Hrin, has occasionally visited Hvrayos in his seat at Hyolenstr, as have others of the realm, including this writer in Kambanal's informative company.

[*] *Extracted from* **The Empire of Kargusai: A Brief History** *of Dolvid Vidukhati, published at Kadon Dinul in the Year 15 Rodlakh (2957).*

For the most part, defeated armies of Kamin-Tolagh were returned to their homes in the Farther West in a crossing of Landegh, under escort. The comparative handful of Kargul' cavalrymen remaining at the Abu (formerly Lunu Jinzalladhiyu), having had word of the invasion's failure, made no attempt at further war, and most, together with the women (many now widows) and other dependents were granted conditional amnesty by the *rabhsai*; former soldiers of Kargul were for a time resident near Banakit in the Colony, most returning to their first homes when their *nimu*, Tovakh, made clear they would not be regarded as deserters.

With them on the journey back across Landegh came numbers of the expatriot Heartlanders, notably Khalú, widow to Lavsila, who has since become wife to Vinodhai, the Heir in Dramal. At the Abu, meanwhile, a generous quantity of grain and milled flour, the gift of Rodlakh *Rabhsai* to help the tribes through this difficult period, was quickly plundered and the spoils fought over by rival bands of tribal soldiery (troops of the realm having been instructed to use weapons only in their own defense), an accurate forecast for the fate of the Northern Empire.

Withdrawal of the garrison at Gronu Kizh'klaëdhiyu was a factor in the rapid disintegration west of Flamûrai, while in northern Froghushei, Tau-Suaka declared himself chosen successor to Kamin-Tolagh, and after marrying Osré-dnë, claimed overlordship of the valley tribes, with Man-mani hegemony to be enforced by the bows of the remnant Hill Froghul (whose losses at Rufeni Fords had been heavy) and the whip of Hunghi. Doubtful of his capacity to defend the Abu, which was too distant to be useful to his control of the tribes, Tau-Suaka soon abandoned the place, after stripping away everything valuable that could be carried off. His headquarters became the Man-mani village, and he lived in the splendid but incomplete house on the hill, which Kamin-Tolagh had built for himself with Kamin-Tarú, but never occupied.

On both sides of the dividing range, the tribes resented rise of the Man-mani, traditionally regarded as an alien tribe, but loathed the rule of Tau-Suaka, whose arbitrary cruelties surpassed those of his predecessor, and who condemned many to starvation by claiming heavy tributes in grain and livestock. Nor was there much love between the confederate ruling groups, the Man-mani resenting the arrogance of the Hill Froghul, which for them now included their own Osré-dnë.

Unaccustomed glory was their eventual ruin. In his fourth year of rule, Tau-Suaka, south of Banakit, met and routed invaders from west of Flamûrai, which, like his forces, included vestiges of squadrons from Kamin-Tolagh's armies, and celebrated victory with a sodden three-day feast at the hilltop residence, an unusually wet winter having contributed to brewing of unprecedented quantities of beer. With vigilance relaxed, a force including practically the entire active manhood of the Laughing Owl, Chon'la, Jai and Anga-jai tribes, making use of what had once been best ally of the Hill Froghul, the hillside brush, now dense as before, lay silent siege to the village, and in the hours past midnight when most of the feasters were in drunken sleep, swarmed across the undefended fences, and butchered their oppressors. Practically all the Hill Froghul and many leading Man-mani were victims; Tau-Suaka and his wife were among earliest to die, but care was taken to capture Hunghi-of-the-Whip alive, presumably to suffer the same agonizing death he had so often inflicted.

Most of this latter information about the Northern Empire was supplied by possibly the last of all our people to return, Iruvakh. All others of the *Atarlum* had long preceded him, but Iruvakh, fearing loss of the revenues of empire, and neglect of the skills he had taught, would lead to widespread hunger, ignored the Patriarch's order that he return to the *Mankh'*, and, in effect, for the second time repudiated his oaths as an *atarlai*. For a while he was able, as before, to travel the tribal country, but following the massacre at the Man-mani village, when the liberated tribes at once began warring among themselves, he abandoned the struggle, and made his way alone across Landegh.

Upon his return, he gave generously of his time and recollection to the compilation of this history, before going to his original home at Irbat, where he has recently succeeded his father, the late Iriban, as Hereditary Warden.

He recounted that Man-mani had long been grazing their goats on the flanks of the green mound with its white stone to mark the grave of Siv'loi, which, however, they had begun to identify as the spot where Noh-Sra-Lal-Hin was destined to return. With survival of the Man-mani as a tribe in precarious doubt, it seems likely even the legend will be lost.

THE END

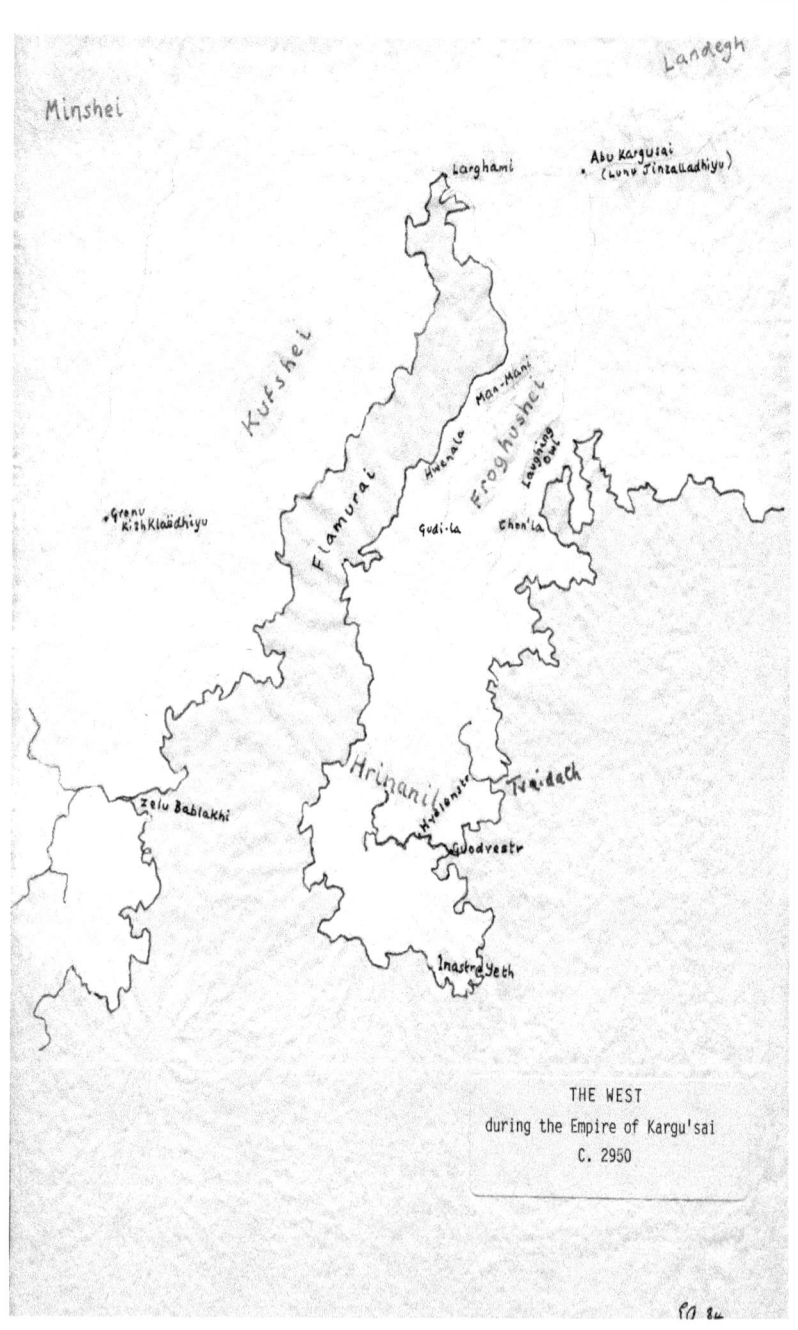

THE WEST
during the Empire of Kargu'sai
C. 2950

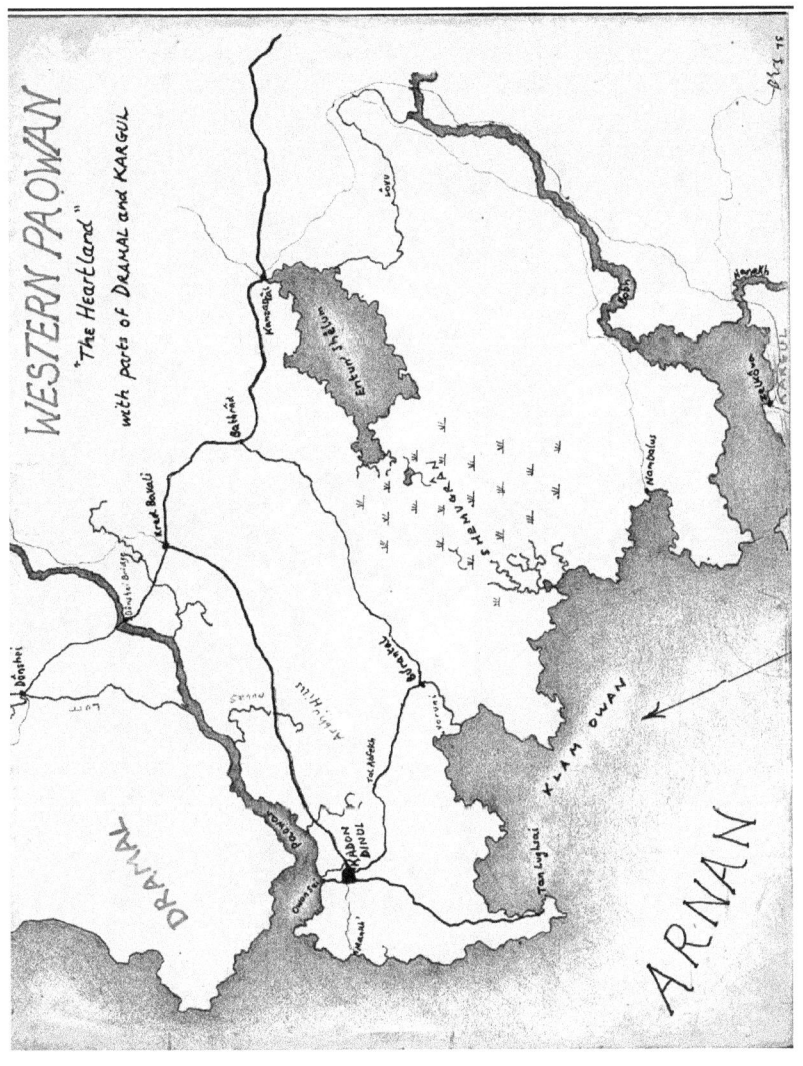

Kamin-Tolagh   Edwin Ahearn

Genealogy
Rabhsayum: Owen Navu

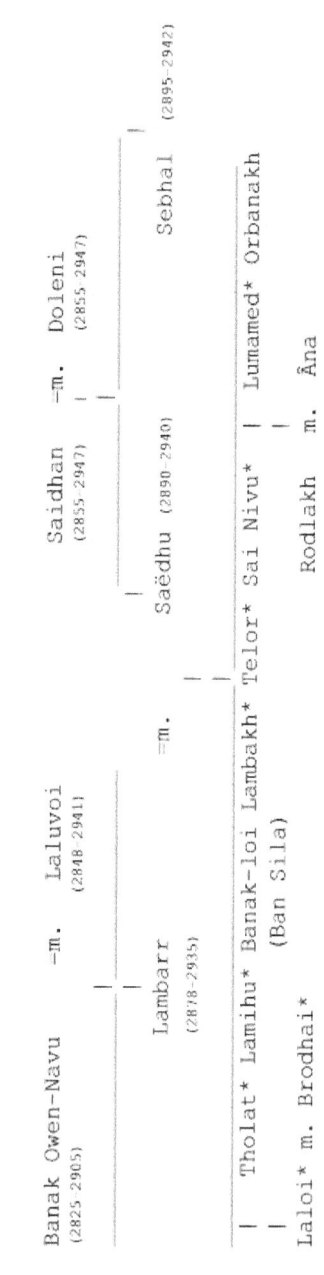

Kargúl

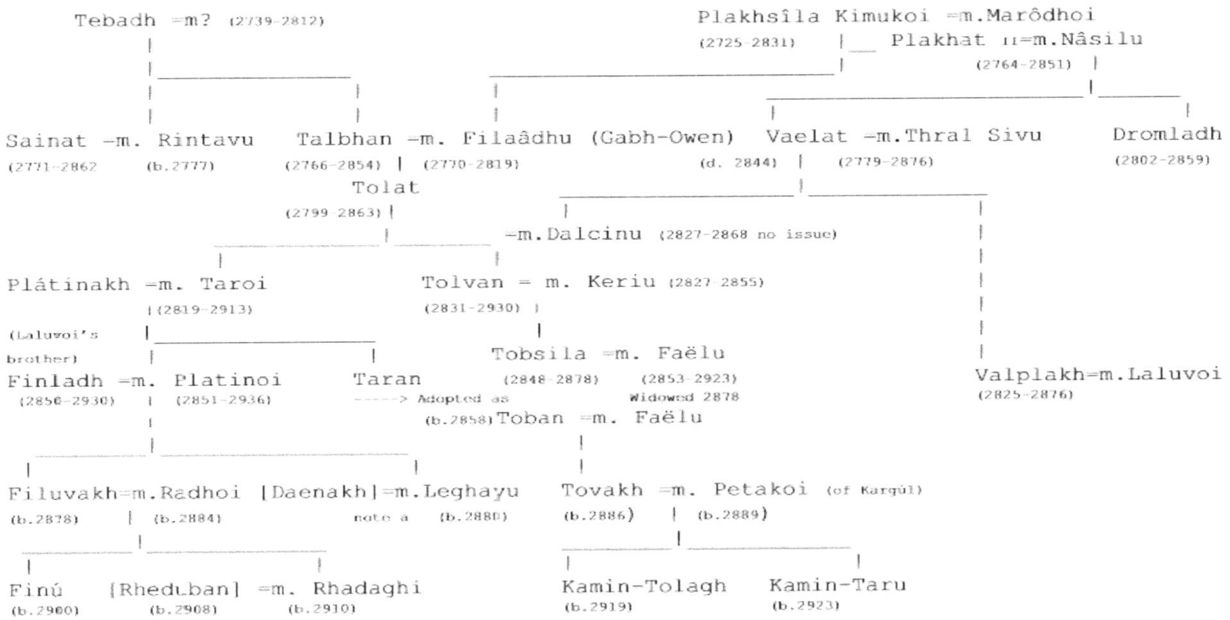

Tebadh =m? (2749-2812)

Plakhsíla Kimukoi =m.Marôdhoi (2725-2831)
Plakhat II=m.Násílu (2764-2851)
Dromladh (2802-2859)

Sainat =m. Rintavu (2771-2862) (b.2777)
Talbhan =m. Filaádhu (Gabh-Owen) (2766-2854) (2770-2819)
Tolat (2799-2863)
Vaelat =m.Thral Sivu (d. 2844) (2779-2876)
=m.Dalcinu (2827-2868 no issue)
Valplakh=m.Laluvoi (2825-2876)

Plátínakh =m. Taroi (2819-2913)
(Laluvoi's brother)
Tolvan = m. Keriu (2831-2910) (2827-2855)
Tobsíla =m. Faëlu (2848-2878) Widowed 2878

Finladh =m. Platínoi (2856-2930) (2851-2936)
Taran (2848-2878) ----> Adopted as Toban =m. Faëlu (b.2858)
Tovakh =m. Petakoi (of Kargúl) (b.2886) (b.2889)
Kamin-Taru (b.2923)

Filuvakh=m.Radhoi |Daenakh|=m.Leghayu (b.2878) (b.2884) note a (b.2886)
Kamin-Tolagh (b.2919)

Finú |Rhediban| =m. Rhadaghi (b.2900) (b.2908) (b.2910)

(a) Brodhal, son of Leghayu and Daenakh m. Laloi bi Atbhi Navu, 2932; both killed at Tan Luqsal in 2935. Brahdial, their second son (b. 2910), led the Cavalry of Ân under the command of Bolan Bakir, Yuvakh Din 2928.

Telnauv ("The Colony")

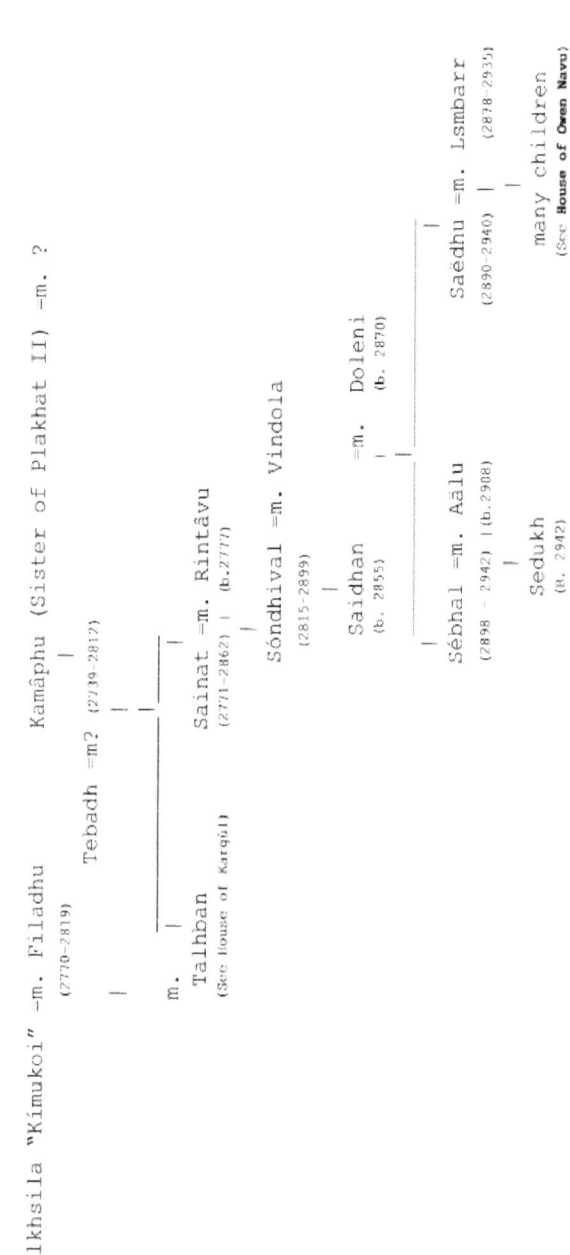

Outline History

[Among the various races of Arbhal only the Owanil possess a continuous written record, however self-serving, from earliest times. Their method of reckoning dates was generally adopted after the Return, and is used here.]

Early Period

Time is held by the Owanil to begin with the *Descent of Yoëlladhu*, which also places the birthplace of their history as in north central Kamanta, where Yoëlladhu's Watch-Rock, a free-standing natural pinnacle, may still be seen. About the four centuries following this legendary event very little is known, except that the Owanil gradually gained control of the Mainland shores to the east of the Island.

477 Traditional date for founding of the Paowanu *Mankh'*, shrine, temple and Patriarchal seat, near the fortress of Drin Kaëdhu (future site of Kadon Dinul), proclaiming the permanence of Owani settlement on the Mainland. There had been (and still exists, though in much-rebuilt form) an earlier *Mankh'* (known as the `First' or `True' *Mankh'*) on the Island.

c.600 Owani hegemony over most of the area now making up the western Paowan, Dramal, Kargul and northern ("Old") Nîv. War-captains struggle for increased power: to this time the Patriarchs had been rulers as well as religious leaders.

c.800 Yuvakh, known as *the Martyr*, killed in wars between His patriarchal forces and religious dissenters, joined by rebellious soldiers. Empire of Owan now includes southern ("New") Nîv, western Aëni, and the Paowan beyond the Angle.

868: Hruval, Yuvakh's grandson, with large armies led by his brother, makes war on the *Aëni Confederation*, an alliance of various peoples of the Northeast with those Owanil rejecting patriarchal authority. Victorious, Hruval becomes both Patriarch and ruler, *Nímurai* (880), but is the last to combine both functions.

[*Greatest of all epics of Owan, the* Frela'olurai Yuvakhatilai — *though composed many lifetimes after the events — gives the entire story of the bitter struggle against what became the Aëni* Confederation, *from the* Martyrdom of Yuvakh, *who "Great as was his suffering, died defiant, the primacy of the Fourfold One still laughed into the faces of his foes...", to the* Conciliation of Yubhsilai, *Hruval's Captain (and younger brother), who "Turned at last away from vengefulness, and spared his imprisoned enemy, chief of all enemies, moved by the noble courage and the beauty of his Petitioner — " Noirúlu, daughter of the captive chieftain, who afterwards became Yubhsilai's wife. Their son, Yuvsilâo, renouncing all civil power and eventually becoming Patriarch, accomplished the final separation of His office from that of the secular ruler.*]

c.1000 All the territories east of Arnan comprising the present realm (and including the now-deserted province of Ásekh) are under Owani control by this date. In the southeast war begins with the Empire of Vrobhan.

First Empire

(Age of the Shâl')

[*The two terms are used interchangeably, although strictly speaking the Empire was not proclaimed till the reign of Shâl IV. There were twenty-one rulers in the period, of which fifteen were named, or adopted the name, Shâl. Dates in parentheses, (), are of birth and death, in brackets, {}, years reigned.*]

1165 Accession of Shaëlai. Renewed war with Vrobhan, at first to recover lost territories.
1172 Overthrow and destruction of Vrobhan Empire. Shaëlai, later styled **Shâl I** {r.1165-1198}, brings many captive Vrobanil nobles and artisans to his capital, Undaëni Shei (Dônshei).
1302 Rhuval II {r.1292-1327} moves capital to Kaghedonu' Dinul. During his reign the armies of Owan establish footholds on the forested shore west of Arnan, especially at the mouth of the Navu River, and fight with the untamed forest tribes.

1328 Accession of **Shâl IV** {r.1328-1407}, founder of the Western Empire, first ruler to style himself (from 1347) *Nímuraibáki* ("Emperor"). Crushing victories over confederations of western tribes, especially by his Captain, **Larghai** (?1335-1430). The frontier in the Northeast is also extended in war with Gabhanil.

[*Though they later adopted the name for themselves,* Gabhanil *is of Owani origin, used to describe a hunting and trapping people (Owanilú* gaëbhu, pelt, hide) *or related group of peoples, probably coming from across the Eastern Ocean, but already established in the Northeast by c.800. Recovering from their* *defeat by Hruval in the ninth century, they had pushed westward, and under the great warrior-chieftain, **Pir Perus** (fl. 1350-80) were able to resist and even reverse the Owani advance.*]

c.1380 Final defeat and death of Pir Perus, Mutilations at Luskran Bay. Empire of Owan resumes expansion to Eastern Ocean.

1384 Shâl IV brings about the deposing of the Patriarch Kamanasalladh' II, and the installation of a Patriarch more to his liking, thus laying claim to supreme authority, even over the *Mankh'*, a question not to be settled for many centuries.

1494 With the submission of Tufani the Empire (including "protected" territories of the Farther West) attains its greatest extent. The lands of the Vrobanil have become a waste, but the Empire stretches from beyond Flamûrai in the West to the Eastern Ocean at Naënai Aëlva (now Narn).

1500 Traditional central year for *Shud'rai baSibadhum*, the so-called Blossoming Age (c.1420-1580) when Owanil arts, architecture, song, dance and decorative crafts are all held to have attained their highest perfection.

1550 Yuval III {r.1502-1550}, on his deathbed, fixes the westward boundary of the Empire at the head of the Great Gulf, Flamûrai.

[Yuval, 110 at his death, had long been alarmed that the resources of the Empire were being drained by the vast length of its frontiers, and the constant need for increased armies to defend it. It is probable the effects of a long-term change in climate, with diminished rainfall throughout the West, were beginning to be felt, with consequent widespread hunger and unrest. At about this time also, jinzal, *first recorded c.1475, began to appear in increased numbers.]*

1604 Shâl VIII {r.1584-1639}, unable to defend Yuval's Frontier, abandons much of Tufani, now arid and unproductive, and establishes the new frontier along the western edge of Landegh, constructing extensive walls and forts.

1703 The Frontier of Shâl VIII, overrun at many points by nomadic raiders and by *jinzal*, collapses. During this reign, that of Shâl IX {1702-1717}, most territories west of Arnan are lost.

[*The final six rulers of the First Empire, all named Shâl, presided over a rapid decay. Because of scant rainfall the great western plateau of Landegh was no longer capable of supporting the armies needed to defend it. Later, the drying of Shemufegh' Rai, the Great Salt Marsh, permitted enemies for the first time (c.1725) to enter the Old Realm, passing north of Arnan.*]

1728 On the Island the great mathematician-astronomer Patriarch, Owan-Alladh IV *Kirova-Kindhri* (`Star-Conqueror') begins construction of **ga-Tembúrai**, the Great Hive of Mysteries, adjacent to Yoëlladhu's Watch-Rock. Not completed till 1815, the edifice incorporates in its proportions and dimensions many astronomic observations and mathematical laws.

1750 Shâl XIII killed near the present site of Irbat, while leading his army against tribal invaders.

1771 Accession of **Shâl XV**, known as *Ifradhi* (`the Last'). During this reign control over the remaining lands east of Arnan becomes intermittent, and communication with the remaining enclaves of Owani resistance is uncertain. About 1800 the Patriarch Owan-Alladh VI offers Shâl XV refuge on the Island, if he agrees to acknowledge supreme patriarchal authority. The invitation is renewed at intervals during the confused decade that follows.

1809 Shâl *Ifradh'*, defeated in battle near Shelum, makes a difficult retreat to the Arnan shore, and with what remains of the aristocracy and the army embarks for the Island.

The Night of Owan

(1809-2477)

[This period is named as in the only continuous record, although Owani history for these almost seven centuries is confined almost entirely to the minor events of the Island. Shâl XV left no direct heir, and after his death (1815) the line was regarded as extinct. After some early raids on its shores the Island was largely left alone, and, with no need for a great captain, could be and was ruled by a long succession of patriarchs, mainly concerned with preserving Owani tradition, regarding the outside world as having lapsed into disorder and darkness. It wasn't until late in this period, when the stability of the Island realm began to be troubled by internal dissent and by invasions, threatened and (in more than one case) actual, that new leaders outside the Atarlum *began to emerge.*
On the Mainland minor pockets of Owani rule persisted in the southern enclave of Ninkufu, in western Kargul, and for a time at the fortified city now called Dônshei. With the disappearance of the armies of Owan from the Northeast the Gabhanil at intervals resumed the westward extension of their power, much of the time under clan chieftains, who chose a supreme leader only in extreme circumstances. They possessed their own runic alphabet, but the few accounts descending from before 2000, concerned mainly with individual deeds and isolated struggles, do not lend themselves to the construction of a coherent, detailed history. By 2000, however, it is clear Gabhanil settlements were established in Dramal, trading and sometimes warring with many petty local warlords and self-styled kings. More often than not the Gabhanil formed alliances with the remnant Owanil, whose learning they admired, and upon whom in return they exerted considerable influence, especially in weaponry and methods of warmaking.

In speech, the Gabhanil were always notably ready to borrow and adapt, and as they became more dominant a form of their language, altered by contact with the Owanilú, became general east of Arnan, spoken even by the Owanil of the Mainland, with whom the Old Tongue became a ceremonial and religious language. Intermarriage between Owani and Gabhani became common, though discouraged by the Island Mankh', *which, by c.2240, had renewed communications with pacified regions of the Mainland, and reasserted its claim to primacy, at least in religious questions, with the Mainland Owanil. Patriarchal insistence on Owani preeminence caused friction with the Gabhanil chieftains, but there were Owanil among the following of the Gabhani* **Pir Kallikuk** *when he entered Kadon Dinul in 2430, and began its rebuilding.*]

2430-2477 Traditional (Owani) dates for the *Wars of Cleansing*, though the process of reordering the lands once included in the Old Realm had been carried on by the Gabhanil for most of the two preceding centuries.

[*While it was under the captaincy of Pir Kallikuk that the critical battles were fought and won, the* Mankh' *histories place great stress on the advice and assistance he received from leading Owanil of the Island. Nevertheless it is likely that the new realm which emerged would have been dominated by the Gabhanil, but for the coming of* Konúrai, *the Great Plague, which decimated the ranks of the Gabhanil nobility. All peoples suffered from this terrible illness, but the Owanil seem to have been the least susceptible, and were also helped by the* ramidul, *priests of the Healing Order, who were sent from the Island.*]

2464 Pir Kallikuk goes to the Island to plead with the Patriarch, Kamanasalladh VI {P. 2460-2495} that He order the *ramidul* to minister to the sick irrespective of race or belief.

[*According to the* Mankh' *account, it was during this visit Kallikuk caught a glimpse of the young* **Plakhat**, *and recognized the future ruler of a restored realm. The truth seems to be that Plakhat, tracing a tortuous descent from Shâl XII, had already* _been chosen by the Patriarch, who made reestablishment of an Owani aristocracy His price for healing. This hard bargain was at first rejected by Pir._]

2472 Alarmed by renewed ravages of _Konúrai_, Pir Kallikuk returns to the Island, and opens negotiations for a restoration of the Owanil which will at the same time preserve Gabhanil rights.

2476 Having provisionally approved Plakhat's elevation to the monarchy (with safeguards for his own people), Pir Kallikuk himself succumbs to illness. Treaty of the Wind Caves divides power between Plakhat and the _Mankh'_, without reference to the Gabhanil.

The Return

[_The surname_ Gabh'Owan _chosen by Plakhat at the founding of his House was seen as a good omen by those of Other Race, since it appeared to combine the names of both major races. Those who feared the racial and religious exclusivity of the_ Atarlum _were further encouraged by Plakhat's abrupt rejection of patriarchal tutelage. As Pir Kallikuk's lieutenant in the final campaigns of the Wars of Cleansing he had an army behind him, and once sure of widespread support from the Owani aristocracy he proclaimed the powers of the_ Mankh' _were to be strictly limited and defined as quite separate from those of the secular ruler (whose title was now to be_ Rabhsai). _Though war for a time seemed probable, Kamanasalladh recognized He could not find sufficient support and the rival leaders met in southern Dramal, where they negotiated the famous Treaty._]

2476 Treaty of the Wind Caves grants or reaffirms many patriarchal prerogatives, while virtually depriving the _Atarlum_ of any sovereign power, except over the Island;

the Patriarch's armed forces to be limited to a small bodyguard (the *Adanum Plakh'*).

2477 The Return. Installation and investiture of **Plakhat Gabh'Owan** at Kadon Dinul {r.2477-2514}. With the remnant Gabhani leadership in disarray he moves swiftly to reestablish the Island aristocracy, and to place those of the so-called Old Blood in positions of power and authority; all provincial overlords, most high-ranking army officers, and all but a very few magistrates, tax-assessors and other local officials.

2480-85 Promulgation of the doctrine of *Preference*, denying high rank to all those without required knowledge of Owani language, customs, history and belief. While the *manal* (schools) of the *Atarlum* are said to be open to all, their prerequisites for entry virtually exclude all but the children of established Owanil families. Increasingly from this time the Gabhani-Mixed majority were ruled by a numerically far inferior Owani aristocracy, and denied entry into many of the skilled crafts.

[*Thus, in the first decade of his reign Plakhat I established the basis for the bitter resentments and often brutal struggles of the next four-and-a-half centuries. It was later observed that while the* Gabh' *element in the surname of the ruling house was the same as that found in* Gabhani, *it also relates to* gâvu, *"shield," and it was as the Shield of Owan that Plakhat and most of his successors ruled.*]

Gabh'Owan House

(successors to Plakhat I)

Kamsila, son of Plakhat {r.2514-2567}. Became *rabhsai* when his father, at the age of 70, abdicated. Continued most of Plakhat's policies, but chiefly remembered for reestablishing a foothold on the western shore of Arnan (popularly attributed to his insatiable appetite for the oysters of the Navu estuary). Flattered as a new *Nim'raibaki* (Emperor), Kamsila never made use of the title, perhaps fearing ridicule, when the "Colony" was measured in acres rather than miles. The port city of *Kamsilat* preserves his name.

Kanavakh, his (younger) son {r.2567-2576}. The elder son of Kamsila was Plakhan *Rhaëli* ("The Lost"), of the celebrated Bride-Quest and subsequent disappearance. Kanavakh thus became Heir, and in his brief but terrible reign amply earned his cognomen, *Vakh'biSegh* ("Bloody"). His many cruelties helped establish (or renew) the legend of the True *Rabhsai* (here thought of as his vanished brother) who would return out of the West to cure the ills of the realm.
His forced abdication was brought about by a conspiracy among the provincial overlords, the army, and the Kadon Dinul Families, concurred in (and perhaps fostered by) the Patriarch Owan-Alladh XV, who agreed to invest Kanavakh's only son.

Plakhval {r.2577-2652}, son of Kanavakh, whose long reign is remembered chiefly for its hopeful beginning, when nearly one hundred prisoners condemned to a variety of lingering deaths by his father were set free. The rule was without large events, but patriarchal influence was at its height, and the complete victory of Preference drove the Others deeper into poverty and despair.

Kamzhinu {r.2652-2667}, the first *rabhsaëyu* (woman reigning in her own right), elder daughter of Plakhval, who outlived his only son. She abdicated at 75, and was succeeded by her nephew, son to her younger sister, Kamnâvu

Plakhat II {r.2667-?2732}. His dates are misleading. Due to unpopular measures and his weak character this reign was plagued by factionalism and attempts to depose him, in favor either of his aunt and predecessor, Kamzhinu (who lived to 2689), or of one of his sisters, especially Kamâbhu, married to the *Nim'* of Kargul. After his second flight from Kadon Dinul (2698) Plakhat II lived mainly in Ninkufu, and is known as *Arnaël* ("The Exile").

Plakhan, his son, recaptured Kadon Dinul from Kargul' usurpers for the Gabh'Owan lineage in 2707, but while he was acting for his father his own supporters prevented the Exile's return; Plakhan was thus *rabhsai* in everything but title from about 2708, but declined to adopt the style till after his father's death; the official dates for his reign are therefore: 2732-2737. He died young (51), especially for an Owani.

Plakhsila, his son, succeeded (under a *Moradhilum*, or Protectorship) just short of his twelfth birthday. Once of age he emerged as one of the most powerful, popular and effective rulers. He attained the age of 106, and his reign {2737-2831} falls only six years short of living up to his sobriquet, *Kímukoi* ("Century").
Plakhsila believed the underlying cause for the unrest of the past eighty years was to be found in the undue influence of the *Mankh'*, and the system of Preference. This was all-but abolished, and a series of "agreements" and "understandings" arrived-at with the *Mankh'*, more strictly defining the limits of patriarchal power, were in fact largely Plakhsila's dictates.
He also undertook to rebuild Kadon Dinul, clearing much of the plague-ridden Old Town, laying out the Avenue of

Treaties, and constructing the New Residence. The so-called Bronze Residence which had served his seven Gabh'Owan predecessors was small for its function, and had the added disadvantage of standing (as it still does) outside the city walls. Plakhsila occupied the New Residence from 2800, though work on it continued for many more years.

The reign was notable for widespread prosperity. The quarrelsome province of Kargul was curbed, unrest quelled on the northeastern borders, and the westward frontier of the Colony advanced to the old First Empire fortress of Drin Navuna, which now began to be rebuilt. While his will was seldom challenged, Plakhsila habitually went through the motions of submitting his proposals to the nominally sovereign Council of Thirteen, provincial overlords and other high officials, a process which, paradoxically, reconfirmed and strengthened the powers of that body in succeeding reigns. Though sometimes accused of excessive vanity Plakhsila remained generally admired, and firmly in control till his peaceful death.

Plakhat III {r.2831-51}, son of Plakhsila, was sixty-seven at his accession, and is known as *Plakhat `Afoi'* ("The Old"). He was always in poor health, and during his twenty years of reign the Patriarch Owan-Alladh XVIII won concessions restoring some of the privileges lost in Plakhsila's reign. Plakhat abdicated in favor of his son.

Dromladh {2851-2859} was fifty at accession, still with his lifelong interest in the building of ships. He is credited with the idea for the slender, swift, oar-driven rammer, and with many innovations in methods of construction, hence the irrepressible but erroneous belief that the ship in which he and the Heir were both lost in a sudden squall on Arnan was of his own design. His cognomen, *Prafu* ("Ship") thus has somewhat sinister connotations.

Thral-Sivu {r.2859-2876}, Dromladh's elder sister, was a widow of 60 at her sudden accession, and might have declined the rule, except for the feeble physical and intellectual qualities of her son, Valplakh, who now became Heir. During her reign the ambitions of Kargul were reawakened, and their growing military strength openly displayed for the first time; she was fortunate in possessing a captain as resourceful as Banak (b.2825), who demonstrated outstanding courage and leadership on the western frontier, and in the three civil wars in which Kargul, with the covert but generally suspected support of elements within the *Mankh'*, tried to seize supreme power.

[*The marriage (2861) between Dalsinu, Thral-Sivu's daughter, and Tolvan baKargul was part of the attempt to heal this rift, but Dalsinu died suddenly in 2868 without issue. The Heir, though widely regarded as half-witted, was more fortunate in his choice;* **Laluvoi** *(b.2848), married to him at 17, was already a young woman of remarkable intellect, charm and force, and a celebrated beauty. Though descended from ancient Owani blood, she was soon loved and admired by all the races, to whom she showed impartial favor. Childless through more than ten years of marriage, she conceived in early 2876, and decided she would bear the child in the milder climate of her native Ninkufu. That journey, accompanied by her husband and his mother, the* rabhsaëyu, *ended in the* **Disaster of the Ní-Tilagh** *(2876), amply described elsewhere, and the extinction of the Gabh'Owan line.*]

Valplakh {2876} appears to have died somewhat later than his mother,
thus becoming, for a few hours, the twelfth, and (discounting the unnamed male child born prematurely to Laluvoi at Kir) shortest-reigned and last of his House.

The War of the Widowed
The Arbhai-Navu Rulers

*[After the Disaster the initial prize for the warring factions was
the unborn Heir, but when it was learned a child (as was for
many years believed) had been stillborn, the conflict became one
between the two survivors of marriage to the children of Thral-
Sivu, Tolvan baKargul and Laluvoi, championed by Banak. It
was a brutal and bitter war, but the young captain, **Saidhan**
(b.2855), Banak's apprentice, whose swift actions after the
Disaster had, by ensuring Laluvoi's safety, begun the war, also
ended it with his famous killing of Tobhsila baKargul in single-
combat. By then (2878) Banak and Laluvoi were man and wife,
with an infant son.]*

Banak and **Laluvoi** {2878-2904} are the only recorded
joint-rulers, Laluvoi both *rabhsayu* and *rabhsaëyu*, and
Banak was the first *rabhsai* with admixed heritage (his
paternal grandfather, Rodelam, was of Mixed descent).
Although Banak was inevitably accused by many Owanil
of favoring those of Other race, the policies of this joint
reign were in fact a resumption of the evenhanded course
set by Plakhsila *Kímukoi*.   Unsuccessful in their
proclaimed object of ending all conflict among the races,
Banak and Laluvoi took great strides in making both
justice and high office available to all the people.
Banak's health began to fail around 2900, and he and
Laluvoi decided on joint-abdication in favor of their son
when he reached 25.

Lambarr {r.2904-2935} was betrothed to and soon
married Saëdhu, the daughter of Banak's lieutenant and
great friend, Saidhan (who, in 2894 had become first
Nim', hereditary overlord, of the Colony). Lambarr, a
well-loved rather than powerful or decisive figure, is
chiefly notable for the mildness of his reign, and his
devotion to the *rabhsayu*. She bore nine children in the

first fifteen years of their marriage, and eleven (or ?twelve) in all.

[*The realm was fortunate in continuing to benefit from the prestige and wise guidance of Laluvoi, widowed in 2906, who lived on to great age, with little diminution of her powers. Details of the latter reign of Lambarr can be found elsewhere; he, together with the Heir and five others of his offspring were lost in the* **Tan Lughsai Fire** *(2935), and he was thus unexpectedly succeeded by his second son.*]

Ban-Sila {r.2935-2942} was originally named after his grandfather, Banak, but in his youth became universally known as *Banak-loi* ("Little Banak," by contrast with *Banak-rai*, Great Banak). Being short in stature he decided at his accession to rid himself of the slighting suffix by changing his name. It was remarkable that he chose a new name in Owani form, but an accurate harbinger for a reign which the *Mankh'*-educated Ban-Sila devoted to the restoration of Owani supremacy, notwithstanding the Mixed element in his own paternal heritage.

[*The results of the policies pursued by Ban-Sila, and his eventual assassination, are dealt with at length elsewhere. He was succeeded by his younger brother.*]

Rodlakh (b.2922) came to power after victory in the **Great *Jinzai* War** (2942). Upon investiture he married Âna Konats-daughter, of common birth, but with uncommon gifts of intellect and character; their children (to 2950) were sons Lambakh (2943) and Banat (2948), and daughter Seluvoi (2945). Rodlakh began his reign by forcing the abdication of the hostile Patriarch, Owan-Alladh XX {P.2936-2942}, replaced by the more conciliatory Dozhusai-Arbhali, signatary to the new Treaty between *Mankh'* and Residence. Other than a number of measures (such as land-reform, and opening of the Guilds to other than Owani membership) aimed at making prosperity more general, chief event of the early reign was the defection of Kamin-Tolagh, and rise of his so-called Empire in the Farther West, described in detail elsewhere; Kamin-Tolagh's attempted invasion of the realm in 2950 was quickly defeated, and Rodlakh himself killed Kamin-Tolagh in single fight by Rufeni Fords (2950).

abu (n.f.)   home
adana (n.m.)   brother
adanum (n.m)   brotherhood
-adh   (n. suff.m.)   "son of" (*cf* at, ati)
aëbhu [O.O] (n.f)   home;
    used of Arbhal = homeland: *Arbhu* Hills
aëlu [O.O] (n.f.)   = *êlu*
aëlva [O.O.](n.m.)   = *elva*
aënoi (adj.)   far, distant
aën'modha (n.m.)   ("distant vision") enlightenment
afoi   (n.n.)   (the) old
afonu   (n.f.)   bridge, causeway: *Drin b'Afon*
ak   one
akaëkhai (n.m.)   market-place
akan (n.n.)   (the) one
akhadu (n.f.)   beginning, origin
akhi (n.m)   fire
akshi   (conj.)   which
alladha (n.m.)   father
amakh   eleven
amit (adv)   also, equally
amshu (conj.)   when
anib'anuli   (n.n.) (male) homosexual
anta (n.m,)   island: *Kamanta, Antal Iruvalin*
aradh (v.i,)   go
aragh   (imper.)   go!
arnaël (n.n.)   exile, (*cap.*) = *Plakhat II* [see Appendix b]
arnan (n.f.)   sea
asai   sir, lord
asaloi, as'loi (n.m.)   lordling
asikha,-u (adj.)   empty
asayu   madam, lady
asumu (n.f.)   well: *Eshaël Asumun*
-at, ati (n.suff.m.)   son (of)
atarlai, -layu (n.)   priest
atarlum (n.m.)   priesthood
avai (n.m.)   hedge
ayu (n.,n.suff.f)   daughter (of) (cf *layu*)

ba, **b'** (prep)	of, from
Baëdhrai (O.O.)	Minister [see Glossary]
Baëdhral	[see Glossary]
balaki (prep.)	among(st)
bavu (n.f.)	wax
bedhai (n.m.)	finger (also a measure, 1/4 *rodukhu*)
bekufi (n.m.)	middle-finger
betufi (n.m.)	index-finger
betuloi (n.m.)	little finger (also about 7/32 of a *rodukhu*)
bi (prep.)	
bikh	
bina (adv.)	through, by means of
blakhi (n.m.)	gold (the metal only, see *plakh-*): *Zelu Bablakhi*
bledhu (n.f.)	waterfall, cataract; (pl.) -*l*, rapids
blen, **bleni**	seven
botadh (v.t.)	advise, counsel
botadhai (n.m.)	advice
bôdh'loiki (n.n.)	lesser counsellor
bôdh'loikim	(the rank of)
bôdhrai (n.m.)	(chief) advisor, counsellor
bôdhrayu (n.f.)	feminine of *bôdhrai*
bradhi (n.m.)	iron
bronai (n.m.)	oak: *Talbronu*
brôdhai (n.m.)	smith
butradh (v.t/i)	meet
daëni (n.m.)	cliff, rock-face: *Daëni Tâl*
daënighai (n.m.)	eagle
dakradhi, **-iyu** (n)	killer
danamadh (v.t.)	please, gratify
dankegu (n.f.)	reminder, memento
danu (n.f.)	wall
dashimagh (v.t/i)	question
dashimu (n.f.)	question
dazhai (n.m.)	fear, dread; *gá-dazhai* awe
dazhidh (v.t/i)	fear
dazhu (adj.)	forbidden
degh'asai	(an honorific) "high lord"

degha,-u (adj.) — high
deghi — (an honorific) "high one"
dhanakai (n.m.) — craftsman, "master"
dhanayol (n.n.) — craft, skill
dhanadh (v.t.) — make, design
dhanai (n.m.) — mason, architect
dhosai (n.m.) — sprig, shoot (of a plant)
dhozhu (n.f.) — spring (season)
dinu (n.f.) — settlement, dwelling: *Nivu Din*
dodhi (n.f.) — leaf
dolinu (n.f.) — peach-tree
dolu (n.f.) — peach
donu, **don** (n.f.) — town, inhabited place: *Kadon Dinul, Dônshei*
dranu (n.f.) — sorrow
drashimu (n.f.) — plea, petition
drinu, **drin** (n.f.) — fortress: *Drin Navuna*
drin'loi (n.n.) — fort, blockhouse
dromai (n.m.) — sword
dubhai, -u (adj.) — blue
dulfu (n.f.) — sky

ebadh (v.i.) — run
edhradh (v.t/i) — grow
ef- (pref.) — (fractional prefix, equiv. of Eng. suffix *-th*, Fr. *-ème*, &c; see also *if-*)
efradhi (n.m.) — one-quarter, also a coin ("fourthing")
eftak (n.m.) — one-half
elodhai (n.f.) — moonlight
elu (n.f.) — moon
elva (n.m.) — port: *El'tuf*
embi (adv.) — also
enshi? — why?
entunu (n.f.) — lake: *Entun Shelum*
ênu (n.f.) — skin
erâdhu (n.f.) — garden
ev- — = *ef-*
fega -u (adj.) — salty, caustic
fegha (n.m.) — salt: *Shemufegh Rai*
fekha (n.m.) — sand: *Tâl Abfekh*

fêlu (n.f.)   lily
filso (n.f.)   strait(s)
finadh (v.i,)   flow
finna (n.m.)   tide
flamu (n.f.)   gulf: *Flamûrai*
foi (adj., m/f)   old
frei (adj., m/f)   dry
freladh (v.t/i)   tell, say
frela'olurai (n.f.)   epic tale
frelu (n.f.)   speech, language

ga (prefix)   holy, consecrated
g'Asalladh'   title of Patriarch, "Blessed Father"
g'Asalladhum (n.m.)   the Patriarchate,
                            Patriarchy [see Glossary]
gaëbhu (n.f.)   hide, pelt: *Gabhani*
ganradh (v.i.)   die, die out
gatadh (v.t.)   bless
gâvu (n.f.)   shield
'ghai   (interj.)   [orig. obscure]
gominu (n.f.)   poplar
gradhu (n.f.)   tar, pitch: *Grâdhasumi*
grâna, -u (adj.)   dark: *Shemugrân*; *Luskran*
grônu (n.f.)   pass, gap
grumu (n.f.)   fence
gruva (n.m.)   pike

hr- (OO) see **rh-**

ido   with
if-   (ordinal prefix, like, e.g., English -*th*,
                            French -*ième* suffix)
ifaka,-u (adj.)   first
ifra, -u (adj.)   last
ihu (n.f.)   air, breath
ikhadh (v. t/i)   breathe
imbhai (n.m.)   tree
inanadh (v. t/i)   obey
inilu (n.f.)   pine tree: *Inilun Barabhi*
izhadh (v. t/i)   speak

jinza'dazhai (n.m.) paralyzing terror inspired by *jinzal*
Jinzalú   the (non-existent) speech of *jinzal*;
                               hence, nonsense,   babble.
jinzayu (n.f.)   the (non-existent) *jinzai* female.
jinzayum (n.m.)   the attributes of a *jinzai*

kaël'rolai (n.m.)   an exile illicitly returned
kaëlai (n.m.)   return
Kaëlurai (n.m.)   The Return of 2477, see Appendix (B)
kafa (n.m.)   hill
kafan (n.m.)   ridge, line of hills, hill country: *Kafan
Burantali*
-kai (suff.m.)   proud, fine (fem. *-koi*)
kambu (n.f.)   house, dwelling
kana   (n.m.)   (head of) hair
karga   (n.m.)   mountain: *Kargul*
kargan (n.m.)   mountain range: *Kargan baDulfu*
kâlinu (n.f.)   apple-tree
ke- (pref.)   (indicates   repetition: "again", or
reciprocity,"back".)
kebaghai (n.m.)   dye
kebaghi (n. m/f)   dyer
kedadh (v.t.)   recall, bring to mind
keghu (n.f.)   memory
kelaradh (v.i.)   return
kema,-u (adj.)   proud
kemoradh (v.t.)   guard
ke'naëmpo   "and my pleasure,"
                             a courteous response to greeting.
kezhu (n.f.)   (often pl.) record, history
khaëlu [O.O] (n.f.)   (= *kholu*)
khedsinu (n.f.)   daffodil, narcissus
khemai (n.m.)   pride
khôdai (n.m.)   apple
kholu (n.f.)   apple-blossom
ki
kidolai (n.m.)   trumpet, bell of flower
kímukan (n.m.)   "centurion", officer commanding *kímuko*
kímukanum (n.m.)   the above rank
kímuko (n.m.)   one hundred, one hundred cavalry
                             (paired squadrons)

kímukoi (n.n.)   century, (*cap.*) = *Plakhsila*
                           [see Appendix b]
kinaëni (adj.)   beyond
kinama -u (adj.)   deep
kindradh (v.t/i)   win, conquer
kindrai (n.m.)   victory
kindhri (n.n.)   victor, conqueror
kirova (n.m.)   star
kirovanai (n.m.)   constellation
kizhai, -u (adj.)   silver, silvery
kizu (n.f.)   silver
kladi (n.m.)   spear
klamu, klam (n.f.)   bay
koëlu (n.f.)   law
-koi (suff.fem)   (see -kai)
kolukezhai (n.m.)   invocation
konu (n.f.)   sickness
konurai (n.f.)   plague, epidemic
kradhu (n.f.)   death
krana -u (adj.)   black
kred' (n.m.)   encampment
kudha (n.m.)   day, sunrise to sunset
kudhanoi (n.m.)   "well-omened day"
kudukh (n.f.)   dayride (distance)
kufa (n.m.)   south: *Ninkufu, Kufshei, bekufi*

la (prep.)   in, at
laëdhai -u (adj.)   near
laëdhi (adj., adv.)   almost
laghi   (adv.)   inside
lakha -u (adj.)   genuine, true
lalai (n.n.)   gentleness
lamai (n.m.)   year
laradh (v.i.)   come
layu (n.f.)   daughter
leghi (n.n.)   truth
legha -u (adj.)   true, clear, transparent
lekha -u (adj.)   pure
loda -u (adj.)   close
loi (adj.,m/f)   small, little
loika (n.m.)   (a) little

lughu (n.f.)   soil, earth: *Tan Lughsai*
lukhu (n.f.)   (the) earth
lunu (n.f.)   valley
lusi (n.m.)   fish
lûva -u (adj.)   bright
luzhadh (v.i.)   fish

madh'loi (n.f.)   truce
maëdhi (n.m.)   (the) wise
maëdhai -dhu (adj.) wise, learned
Maëdhrai (n.m.)   (Lord) Protector (of the realm)
maënadh (v.t/i)   learn, discover
mai (n.n.)   "presence"
mâlu (n.f.)   peace
manadai (n.m.)   learning
Manadilum (n.m.)   Teaching Order (of the Atarlum)
manai (n.m.)   school
manidu (n.n.)   teacher, *atarlai* of the *Manadilum*
mankhai (n.m.)   temple, shrine; *Mankh'*
margú (n.f.)   hostelry
midhu (n.f.)   table: *Lunu Midhi*
minu (n.f.)   territory, region
modha (n.m.)   vision, insight
modhum (n.m.)   eyesight
monagh (v.t/i)   glance, skim
moradilum (n.m.)   protectorship
moragh (v.i/t)   watch, look, guard
mômai (n.m.)   wit, good sense
muradh (v.t/i)   look, watch
muk   ten
mukoi (n.n.)   decade
mûnu (n.f.)   glance
mûru (n.f.)   look, gaze

na (prep.)   for
Naëdhi (n.m.)   Head of *Nôdhilum*; see Glossary
naëmpo (interj.)   "my pleasure"
naëna -u (adj.)   outer: *Narn*
nanna -u (adj.)   low
namaki (adj. m/f)   happier
nampagh (v.t.)   please, gratify

nampai (n.m.)   contentment
navu (n.f.)   west: *Drin Navuna*
nedhu (n.f.)   end, goal
ní (pron. m/f)   (indicates "that place") *Ní-Tilagh*
nibhu (n.f.)   wood, stand of trees: *Nîv*
niburai (n.f.)   forest
nidaëni (adv.)   hence, away
nim'raibakim (n.m.) "greater realm", empire
nimu (n.m.)   provincial overlord, "earl"
nímurai (n.m.)   "great lord," former title for rulers
nímu-, **nim'raibaki** (n.m.)   "greater lord,"
                              ruler of the Empire
ninu (n.f.)   province
nizhu (n.f.)   grass
nôdhu (n.f.)   pleasure
nôd'adanai (n.m.)   [*nôdhu + adanai*; see glossary]
nôd'yanu (n.f.)   [*nôdhu + yanu*; see glossary]
nôd'yanum   [see glossary]
-noi (suffix, m/f)   fortunate, happy
nuri (n.m.)   smile
nuridh (v.i.)   smile

ôbavai (n.m.)   candle
odhoi (n.f.)   flame
ofrat (n.m.)   end, result
oladh (v.t/i)   be
oladhun (n.f.)   existence
olu'rai (n.f.)   epic, epic poetry, poem
olútalai (n.m.)   a stringed instrument
om   yes
orabhai (n.m.)   alliance
ôbhai -u   (adj.) light (i.e., not dark)
ôdu (n.f.)   light-globe
ôlu (n.f.)   song
ôthu (n.f.)   light (of an *ôdu*)

paghai (n.m.)   state of mind
pai (n.m.)   mood
papavi (n.m.)   third-finger
pava (n.m.)   east: *Pavani*
pedinu (n.f.)   willow-tree

pefrai (n.m.)   warhorse
péfrapravádai (n.m.)   cavalryman
pevraloi (n.m.)   colt
pevruloi (n.f.)   filly
piva (n.m.)   field
plakha -u (adj.)   gold(en)
plakhi (n.m.)   a gold coin (of Arbhal)
prafadh (v.t/i)   ride, be buoyant
prafu (n.f.)   ship (*cap.*) = Dromladh, see Glossary
prânu (n.f.)   cart, wagon
pribhu (n.f.)   peat
prôma -u (adj.)   grey
prova (n.m.)   ash-tree
prufu (n,f.)   ride, journey

rabh- (pref.)   all
rabhsaëyu (n.f.)   (female) ruler
rabhsai[1]   (male) ruler
rabhsayani (n,m/f)   loyalist
rabhsayu (n.f.)   consort of *rabhsai*
rabhsayum (n.m.)   monarchy, administration
radhai -u (adj.)   whole, square
radhi   four
radhizan -u (adj.)   fourfold
radhum (n.m.)   wholeness
rafai -u (adj.)   safe, protected
raf'yalu (n.,f.)   [see Glossary]
rai, -rai (adj.m/f)   great
raibaki (adj. m/f)   greater, extended
rakhi (n.n.)   oath
rakhu (n.f.)   word, expression; *rekh'rakhu* mot juste
raku (n.f.)   truth
ramadh (v.t)   heal
ramidh (v.t/i)   renew
raminat (n.n.)   [see Glossary]
ramminai (n.m.)   (indigenous tree, source of *raminat*)
ranaghai (n.m.)   wretch, rascal
ranidukh (n.n.)   renewal, daybreak
rashudhai (n.m.)   eternity
rekha -u (adj.)   white
rekhi (adj. m/f)   true

rhafa (n.m.)	safety
rholai -u (adj.)	lost
rhuva (n.m.)	thumb
ridho (n.n.)	number
rodukh(u) (n.f.)	hand, handspan
rok'olu (n.f.)	lyric poem
rubha -u (adj.)	brown: *Dramuru*
rubhinu (n.f.)	chestnut
rughoi (interj.)	enough!
rumu (n.f.)	autumn
ruvinai (n.m.)	chestnut-tree: *Rufeni*
sai (adj. m/f)	new: *Tan Lughsai*
seghu (n.f.)	blood: *Ásekh*
sekhai -u (adj.)	bloodstained
sepa (n.m.)	stream, brook: *Rekhsepa*
shan'loi (n.f.)	lane, alley
shanu (n.f.)	trail, track
shavu (n.f.)	wind: *Kreshavu*
shei (adj. m/f)	free: *Dônshei*
shemu (n.f.)	marsh: *Shemugrân*
shi-, -shi	(interrogative affix)
shibani?	whence?
shilai?	who?
shilat	whom
shilavi?	how many, much?
shilní?	where?
shilshu?	when?
sholum (n.m.)	beauty
shôla -u (adj.)	lovely, handsome, beautiful
shudai (n.m.)	time
shud'rai (n.m.)	age, era
Shuda'sai (n.m.)	Midsummer [see Glossary]
shufloi (n.m.)	stream
shufa (n.m.)	river
shumu (n.f.)	water
sibadh (v.i.)	bloom, blossom
sibh'loi (n.f.)	flowerlet
sibhnu (n.f.)	standard, banner
siladhi (n.m.)	champion, standard-bearer
sivu (n.f.)	flower

sobadh (v.i.)   flee, run away
sumu (n.f.)   spring (freshet)

tabru (n.f.)   thatch
taëladhi (n. m/f) ambassador, emissary
taëvu (n.f.)   copper
tagha (n.m.)   (cut, quarried) stone
tak   two
tamak   twelve
támakan   file-leader (junior officer)
támako (n.m.)   file (of cavalry)
tanu (n.f.)   cape, headland
taruna (n.m.)   linden tree
tâl (n.m.)   village: *Burantal*, *Kanzan Tâl*, *Tâl Abfekh*
teghi (n.m.)   peak, summit
tembu (n.f.)   hive; *Tembúrai*, see Glossary
temu (n.f.)   bee
temuvoi (n.f.)   queen-bee
tezha -u (adj.)   hidden, secret: *Lunu Tezh'*
têdhu (n.f.)   secret, hidden thing
theruna (n.m.)   locust-tree
thraëlu (n.f.)   wild rose
thrama (n.m.)   heath: *Dramal*
tïlagha -u (adj.) between: *ní-Tilagh*
tobhai (n.m.)   a bronze coin
toghai (n.m.)   carpenter
toladh (v.t.)   send
toladhi (n.m.)   sender
tolvu (n.f.)   bronze (metal)
tosa -u (adj.)   green
tovrelunai (n.m.) copper-beech
tôvai -u (adj.)   bronze-color, bronzed: *Tovakh*, *tobhai*
trakha (n.m.)   stone, rock
trosinai (n.m.)   scabbard
tufa (n.m.)   north: *El'tuf*, *Tufani*, *betufi*
tulfai (n.m.)   frost
tulvu (n.f.)   snow

ubh-, **uv-** (pref.) light- or bright-colored
utalai (n.m.)   bow
uzhu (n.f.)   tale, legend, epic

uzh'freladhai (n.m.)   epic poet, historian

vaëdha (n.m.)   honey
vaëlai -lu [O.O] (n.m/f)   = *vâlai, volu*
vakha -u (adj.)   red
valrabh' (n.m.f.)   heir (to *rabhsayum*)
van'naëdhu (n.f.)   "outwoman", exogamously obtained
wife
vanu (n.f.)   woman, wife
vâlai (n.m.)   heir, inheritor
vekh   eight
vi   without, lacking
volu (n.f.)   heiress
vôl- (prefix)   deputy, proxy

wana -u (adj.)   shallow
wônu (n.f.)   ford, shallows

yaëladh (v.t.)   give
yali (n.f.)   gift
yalum (n.m.)   dedication
yanu (n.f.)   sister

zhanu (n.f.)   road, way
zhavu (n.f.)   gale

---

[1] *rabhsai*: *rabhu* (n.) "whole, all" + *sai* (adj.) "new."

The word has a complex derivation: the original title for supreme ruler was *nimurai*, from *nimu*, "overlord" (orig. from *ní*, "place," which gives *ninai*, "province, little realm," and *nimu*, its ruler) + *rai*, "great." This, with elision of the *u* and addition of the suffix *baki*, "more, greater," became *nim'raibaki*, roughly "emperor." At the end of the Night, the Island Owanil, who had continued to acknowledge a *nimurai* for their lessened domains, wanting to distinguish between this diminished rule and their renewed claim to dominion over what had formerly been their land of Owan, conferred on Plakhat Gabh-Owan the unwieldy designation *nimúrabhusai*, including the elements "whole" and "new," above. Dropping of the *nimu* prefix, which by itself now referred to one of the six merely provincial overlords, and once more eliding the enclosed *u*, gave *rabhsai*.

Note that a peculiarity of the Owanilú is the existence of a number of "neuter," or hermaphrodite adjectives; although when used as part of a compound noun, *sai* can take the feminine form, *sayu*, (as in *rabhsayu*), the adjective *sai*, "new," is both masculine and feminine, and the same is true for *foi*, "old," *frei*, "dry." *shei*, "free," *rai*, "great," *loi*, "little," and some other common adjectives.

www.ingramcontent.com/pod-product-compliance
Lightning Source LLC
Chambersburg PA
CBHW071149250626
47159CB00001B/31